PRAISE FOR *THE DARK WORLD*

"S.C. Parris weaves a beautiful story within a world that will leave you breathless. *The Dark World* is a refreshingly new take on the Vampire and Lycan war that has slathered the dark fantasy realm since *Underworld*, and will take the entire community by storm. Xavier Delacroix could very well be the new Lestat."
– Kindra Sowder, author of *The Executioner Trilogy*

"S.C. Parris may be a young writer, but in *The Dark World* series, she reaches for something remarkable: a vision of horror firmly rooted in the great gothic tradition of vampire literature, but completely original. *The Dark World*, populated by mixed monstrosities, magically gifted humans and the descendants of Count Dracula himself, will be instantly recognizable to lovers of vampire tales but accessible to those new to the genre. Some great story-telling here, with something for everybody. S.C. Parris is a talent to watch."
– Jamie Mason, author of *The Book of Ashes*

"With intricate characters just as delicious as those from Game of Thrones, you truly can't help but become invested in the sequel and thirst for more!"
– A.Giacomi, author of *The Zombie Girl Saga*

N

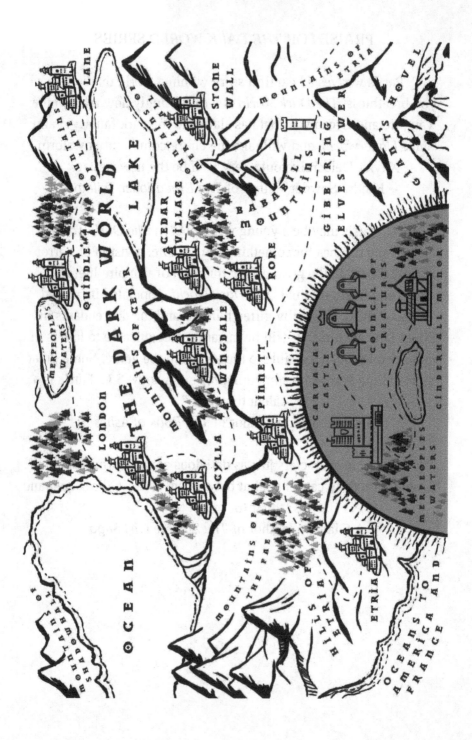

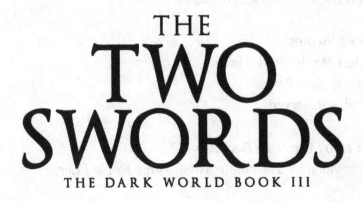

THE
TWO
SWORDS

THE DARK WORLD BOOK III

S.C. PARRIS

A PERMUTED PRESS BOOK

ISBN: 978-1-68261-083-1
ISBN (eBook): 978-1-68261-084-8

The Two Swords
The Dark World Book Three
© 2016 by S.C. Parris
All Rights Reserved

Cover art by Christian Bentulan
Map provided by The Noble Artist, Jamie Noble Frier

PERMUTED
PRESS

Permuted Press, LLC
permutedpress.com

Published in the United States of America

Dedication

To those that have always been by my side
even though I'm incredibly difficult.

Thank you.

Also by by S.C. Parris

"A Night of Frivolity" short story

The Dark World Book One
The Immortal's Guide Book Two

Coming soon: The Phoenixes of the Nest

Chapter One

THE ORDER OF THE DRAGON

The sky swirled with cold wind, the clouds dispersing as it blew, sending the trees to pitch and roll against their brothers, scattering bare branches along the wet ground.

A deep silence pressed against the trees, for the land had not been touched in the month that had passed since the Great Vampire's death. Dark Creatures, even the bravest, did not deem it wise to venture to these woods, for the strange air that had plagued the Dark World, and indeed the world of humans, had thickened considerably, seemingly the worst at this spot.

The place where Dracula had died.

Arminius the Elf stared through the trees, staring grimly at the dark splatters of blood that littered the wet grass. *No one has bothered*, he thought, *to clean up the mess they have made. But I suppose it is our mess now.*

The withering bodies he passed with every few steps were now stiff and frozen. Some had their hands out as though to protect themselves. Others looked as though they were resolved to get a spell out before death.

All of it, horrible, the Elf thought, stepping gingerly over their corpses, remembering lightning leaving the fingertips of the most skilled Enchanters, those same Creatures falling to their deaths...

He had gotten to the large tree just before the clearing when he felt the wind grow cold, and he sighed, knowing that he had arrived, as usual, just in time.

He did not wait for the wind to disperse. "You're late, Nicholai."

The tall, silver-haired Vampire appeared in the next second, his face stern, the smile he wore boyish as he placed a gloved hand over his dead heart and bowed towards the Elf.

"You are always early," Nicholai said, straightening. The white gloved hand fell to his side, and he stared at the Elf, his blue eyes narrowing in the light of the sun. "You grow restless."

Arminius tightened his grip on the long white cane in his left hand, sure to keep the malice out of his voice: "I grow scared. We cannot sit on our hands and continue to wait for the king to rise to his duty."

The Vampire appraised him, removing the white gloves from his hands. "It is not our place to intervene." The Vampire held no gold ring on any finger. "Evert said—"

"I know what the Creature said, Nicholai," he snapped, remembering the tall Creature bending low to place the glowing necklace over his head. "I know the oath we took—I was the first, after all. I just do not understand how these other Creatures operate—that old *Vampure*, most of all. To test Xavier Delacroix like that—"

"You assessed the Vampire was ready after you met with him."

"I did—left to Dracula's constraints—the *Vampure* was, indeed, ready. He had full belief that Dracula was truly not at fault—even when I made it clear the *Vampure* had caused discord among other Creatures in the Dark World." Arminius hissed. "He was the loyal lap dog."

"Loyal as he may be, you are right that he has not risen to his duty." Nicholai stepped aside and waved a hand, gesturing for them to walk further.

Arminius obliged, stepping with his cane beside the Vampire, their destination unclear. "What can be done about it?"

The Vampire stepped over the corpse of a Satyr. Its horns had been ripped off its head, the pool of dried blood blackening the grass. "As gifted in persuasion as I am," Nicholai said, "I doubt my...gifts would ease the new king into his true role."

"So we are stuck, waiting for a *Vampure* that places the minimal duties of his newfound royalty above that of the entire Dark World?"

Nicholai's blue eyes darkened as he lifted the sword from its sheath at his waist. "It appears that way," he said, the low growl leaving his throat.

Arminius narrowed his own black eyes, lifting the cane straight out before himself, the dread in the air thickening, swirling.

It was not long at all before three Creatures appeared, their gold-lined robes shining in the sparse sunlight that passed through the trees above their heads.

Ready, Vampure? Arminius asked the Vampire with his mind, never lowering the tip of his cane from the three Creatures.

One of them raised a long-nailed hand, a whisper of a spell shaking the air in turn, but Nicholai was quicker, moving past the ripple of air, slashing the Elite Creature across his robed chest sending his spell to disperse in the wind.

The red of the medallion blared beneath Arminius's white robes as he uttered the spell, catching the splash of blood that left the Creature's chest: It solidified into a dagger, swirling in the air, moving straight for another Creature's eye beneath its low hood.

The pain-filled screams rent the air, the last Elite disappearing in a haze of terrible dread before Nicholai could turn his glowing sword on him. The wave of dread reached Nicholai, Arminius saw, the red medallion beneath the Vampire's cloak letting out a brief burst of red light, and then the sword fell out of the Vampire's hands.

"Nicholai!" Arminius cried, hobbling over to him, kicking aside an Elite Creature's boot with his good leg. "Nicholai, what's wrong?"

Closer now, he could see the Vampire was clutching his chest, a hand squeezing the protrusion as though trying to separate it from its place beneath his clothes. The Vampire's eyes were completely black, a low snarl leaving his lips in clear anger.

Arminius could barely ask what had happened when the Vampire eyed him, his wavy silver hair shaking around his sharp face.

"The way is blocked. The way is for naught. The Vampire is mine, Elf. His truth—is mine!"

And he slumped forward, his hand falling from its place along his chest, the medallion letting out a feeble glow before it dimmed completely. Arminius let a low whisper leave his throat as he knelt at the Vampire's side, holding the cane upright to balance himself.

With a quick hand, he rolled the Vampire over, alarmed to see the eyes were now closed, a curse of fear leaving his lips. *What on Earth was this? How could her Creatures, her energy, do this? The medallions were meant to be beacons, meant to be impenetrable against all that stood in the way of the Goblet...*

So what-what was this?

He could barely move a hand to lift the medallion from beneath the Vampire's traveling cloak, when the voice entered his ears:

"Hello, old friend."

Arminius turned, rising to his injured foot, his breath leaving his throat in surprise as he eyed the tall Vampire, the long silver hair resting freely behind his back. His violet eyes were content as he surveyed them, the robes he wore quite unlike anything Arminius had ever seen.

They were black, but they were not tattered like the other Creatures' were. These robes were lined with dark red silk, the same red used to adorn his chest, for it was there the metal remained, forming a sort of dark armor that seemed to emerge from the Vampire's skin itself.

He took a simple step forward, black boots pressing into the earth with a grace the Elf could only admire, and he said, "Do not worry about the Vampire, Arminius. He will rise, shortly."

His grip on the cane tightened as he stared at the Vampire before him, so calm, so focused... And that's when he noticed it: The armor atop the Vampire's chest, shimmering in the sparse sunlight, the deep red of its color drawing the eye. Arminius inhaled, his mind spinning with bewilderment. *Dragon skin? Why-why on Earth would she need Dragon skin for her Creatures?* For he knew that most impenetrable skin would make magnificent armor, all Creatures knew it, but none ever dared disgrace a Dragon in such a manner, dead or alive...

"Stare at your leisure, my old friend," Victor Vonderheide said, something of a smile tearing his face in two. "Yes, it is Dragon I wear, and yes, I have killed the Dragon to wear it. What is more important, surely, is that you and your...friends get one thing clear."

Arminius asked, "And what is that, Victor?"

The Vampire folded his arms across his impressive chest and stared at the Elf. "You cannot touch her empire, for it grows with every passing day, every passing hour." He stared past the Elf to where Carvaca's castle remained. "We are prepared to kill your king if ever he decides to arrive here. Oh yes," he said, eyeing the Elf's surprise, "we know you intend to bring the Vampire here—we know he has more business with this...Ancient Creature."

Victor waved a hand. "We have learned the ways of your... toys, Arminius, and we are growing stronger in stopping their goals. Dracula should have thought better about his tools."

Arminius stared, unable to believe what he heard. *They were able to stop the medallions? Able to stop the power it afforded the Creatures that wore it? How?* "What...do you want, Victor?"

"We want you to stop your incessant goals. We have the castle surrounded—if you don't stop, if you bring Xavier Delacroix here, we will kill that Ancient Creature. As we understand it, he is needed."

"You can't be—"

"Serious?" Victor snarled, his careless demeanor dispersing. "I am very serious, Elf. And so is Eleanor. Surrender Xavier Delacroix to Eleanor Black or continue with that Vampire's foolish plan and see it all end—either in that Ancient Creature's death or your own."

The red medallion pulsed once, the ground behind him beginning to shift. And without turning to look, Arminius knew Nicholai was beginning to rise from his forced slumber.

"You will see our graves before you see Xavier Delacroix again, Victor," Nicholai shouted.

Victor let out a vicious laugh, before stepping away from them, and behind himself, Arminius knew Nicholai was beginning to rise to his feet: he felt the ground behind him grow heavy, heard the rustle of wind...

Arminius saw fear upon Victor's face then.

Scared of Nicholai? Arminius thought, watching closely the Vampire's gaze: it never left Nicholai, indeed, even as the Vampire fully rose to his feet, a hand moving instinctively to the medallion swaying freely atop his cloak. It glowed profusely, bathing the Vampire's face in its glare.

It was true Nicholai Noble was a most celebrated Vampire in the Dark World for his many battles against Lycans, Etrian Elves, rogue Enchanters, and even, though it were only one time, a Dragon, but to have the great Victor Vonderheide step away because the Creature was now awake? It made no sense.

Wasn't he, Victor, a most powerful Vampire, and hadn't he undergone the transformation all Eleanor's Creatures underwent?

Arminius stared at the Vampire, taking in his focused gaze, his cold air...yes, the Vampire was still just that, although the Elites

6

were known to hold each form perfectly, making it quite difficult for anyone that wasn't an Elite to know the difference.

"Nicholai, are you all right?" he asked the Vampire that now stood, prepared to strike Victor, the light upon him a clash of low blue and bright red.

"Perfect," Nicholai snarled, beginning to step towards Victor.

Arminius watched him take but two steps before he was on the ground again. The medallion let out yet another feeble pulse and then the light died, the Vampire appearing to lose his balance as he fell sideways, landing roughly atop a dead Elite Creature, smearing blood upon his cloak. He did not move.

"Nicholai!" Arminius yelled, confusion marring his senses. He heard Victor say something that sounded like, "Interesting...it lasts," before he was getting to his knee, a steadying hand placed on the Vampire's arm. Nicholai still did not move.

Anger filled him in a harsh wave as the medallion flashed where Nicholai's no longer did: Its dim glow was feeble, but at least it was there. *We can figure out the rest later, surely, all that matters,* Arminius thought, *is that we get to safety.*

"Victor! What did your kind do to him? To his medallion?!" he yelled.

The Vampire was still laughing as he responded, "Think of it as payback for what Dracula's bitch did to her men. We are learning your secrets, Arminius. Soon you won't have a thing to hide behind. Dracula is dead—"

"He still lives!" he roared, mad was he with the energy coursing through him, the endless shouts filling his mind the more Victor spoke: *"Protect the Dragon! Protect the Dragon!"*

And with the look on Victor's face, Arminius knew he had struck a chord with the sanctimonious Vampire. *There was, at last, something the damned Creatures did not know!*

"What do you mean, Elf?" There was a tremor in that voice that gave away his fear.

"I mean what I say!" he yelled, never removing his hand from the unconscious Nicholai. "Dracula still lives, but not in the form you have grown accustomed to. The *Vampure* still lives in the hearts of those that carry out his goal! We—the Knights of the Order—still live! Xavier Dela—"

The snarl was vicious as it left his lips in a hurry. "That Vampire is nothing but a liar—just like Dracula, you broken Elf!"

"That *Vampure*," Arminius countered, "*is* Dracula—the *new* Dracula—chosen by the Phoenixes to lead the Dark World anew!"

Victor said nothing for quite some time. Then, his voice devoid of all emotion, he said, "He was chosen...by the Phoenixes of the Nest to take Dracula's place?"

Arminius squeezed Nicholai's arm. He felt the energy surge within him, the red light making it terribly difficult to see the Vampire clearly, the voice inside his head a terrible roar. And he knew what he would say next, the consequences be damned:

"He was chosen by the Phoenixes of the Nest as the new Dracula. He takes that title, the Creature that held it previously all but forgotten."

"What do you—"

"*Dracula* is nothing but a name—a title for the one that takes the torch up for the betterment of the World. A name given to the Creature that swears to drink from the Goblet of Existence. The savior; our hero: The Dragon."

There was a palpable silence between them. Arminius could see the utter confusion that filled Victor's violet eyes: they seemed glassy, as though he were prepared to cry. *But how ridiculous that would be—*

"If what you say is true, Arminius," Victor said, shaking his head as though to rid himself of unbecoming thoughts, "then where *is* your savior? Why is he not here—why is not fulfilling his duty in seeing this Ancient Creature that he must?"

"He is busy cleaning up the mess you Creatures created, Victor."

"Hmm. Then he will be busy for quite a time."

Arminius said nothing. He knew what he'd told the Vampire would remain in his mind, perhaps clouding his thoughts, driving him away from Eleanor in search of a truth not readily known.

He knew that he should not have told the Creature about the truth of Dracula's name, the burden that the Creature who bore the title held, for he had not even told Xavier, himself, yet. And how could he, when to request an audience with the Vampire proved to be close to impossible?

He released his grip on Nicholai's arm, knowing that they would need to change how things transpired from here—they needed the rest of the Order together—the threat that was Eleanor Black's Creatures was all-important now.

Victor gave him a disconcerted sniff before disappearing in a burst of cold wind.

There were no flecks of dread, however miniscule, on that breeze: *Victor had not turned. But what did that mean for the Order? For Eleanor?*

With a furious sigh, Arminus rolled Nicholai over onto his back, and stared at the closed eyes of the Vampire. *Still alive.* That was just one small silver lining in the darkened blade that was his duty.

✳

The dancing flames in the large grate offered a cozy light across the brown desk, the black chair beyond it empty. And the Vampire that stood against his desk stared at the long-eared Creature before him who had been prattling on about his freedom and other things Xavier Delacroix was, truthfully, not listening to in the least.

His mind was gone on thoughts most dismal, as it had been since the Vampire City was destroyed by the hands of Eleanor Black that miserable night. He could barely return to his mourning for the Vampire before an Elf, Vampire, or some other Creature entered his office (against his greater wishes), to speak to him about the state of the dwindling Dark World.

It was not enough that Xavier was putting all of his energy, and indeed the energy of all remaining Vampires who had survived, on reestablishing connections between the various towns and cities, and most importantly, between the Vampire City and those on the surface. For there was not any way to communicate back and forth what those on the surface were doing, nor was there a way to do so with those who, bravely, remained underground.

The Clearance Committee Building had been ransacked that dark night, and the only remaining Committee members that survived were the annoying Civil Certance, and Richard Yore. They took up the helm in place of the other two dead members, but it was not easy work. There were tales that droves of Vampires and other annoying Creatures arrived at the Clearance Committee building's newly built doors seeking answers—for everyone had heard of the attack on the Vampire City, Lane, Quiddle, and Cedar Village.

Everyone wanted answers—but most importantly, everyone wanted a glimpse of him in this vaulted office.

He knew they watched him as best they could desiring to see what he would do with his new title, and he also knew, as he crossed one leg in front of the other, leaning back against the desk, that it would never stop.

Xavier folded his arms across his chest and the Elf closed his mouth abruptly, having just realized he had not been listened to this whole time.

"Do I bore your Grace?" Swile hissed, his thin lips curling in disdain.

"Bore me?" Xavier repeated, thinking still on the sight of Victor just beside her atop the steps to Dracula's mansion, the clear betrayal in his eyes, the anger... He blinked, staring upon the sanctimonious Elf whose large ears protruded from behind his curtain of blonde hair. "No, not at all. I just find it curious how you gained entry into my office, indeed, my city." And he let the amused smile disappear from his face—it would never truly be his city.

The Elf's nostrils flared, and it was as though he could not find the words to retort with. "Your security is not as rigid as you *Vampures* would have we Creatures believe! There are ways to get into this godforsaken city." He waved the tightly bound scroll he held in a long-fingered hand. "Now, see to it that our Request for Freedom is at *last* honored. Dracula is dead. There is no need to continue this unnecessary—"

"It is quite necessary, Swile," Xavier said. "I have read Dracula's files on the reason he ordered you Elves to banishment. The trick you pulled—the slaughter ensued. I daresay, Dracula had every reason to order you to fight alongside us. And you will do just that."

Swile's red eyes widened in indignation. The scroll fell out of his hand, as it shook violently now, and Xavier half thought the Creature to strike him, when Swile spat, "You are no different than the previous king! No different than the murderous bastard! He must have trained you to utter perfection—how you mirror his words to me in this very room that month before! Is there some script, some paper he offered to you t-to tell me these things whenever I arrive?!"

"Hardly," Xavier snarled, the Elf stepping away from him. "You are just so maddening; it appears there are only a few things that can be said to you without tearing your head off." And he smiled coldly at the affronted gaze he was now given. "You truly did lose your freedom when you attacked us—you Etrian Elves and your skills. It will do us well in battle against the Elite Creatures."

"I daresay!" Swile screamed, eyes bulging in their sockets. "We cannot fight th-those Cr-Creatures!"

"Yes," Xavier said, watching the terror that gripped the tall Elf, "they are worse than mere Lycans, aren't they? But you will fight them alongside my growing Army. So you Elves won't be completely helpless."

"Bu-but it's preposterous! We do not deserve this kind of treatment—we do not deserve to be treated like slaves—at you *Vampures'* beck and call! Ostracized! Outcast! Far from where our fruit grows! This isn't—it's not fair!"

And Xavier remembered, all at once, the very day the Elf said the same words to Dracula in this very room. Irony would have curled his lips, but he chose to focus on the Elf's previous words, not liking how daft the Creature had to be to not see the death his kind had caused.

"Do not *speak* of fairness to me, you simpering idiot! Your kind attacked the home of the King of All Creatures! What did you think would happen?! You would be patted on the arse and sent on your merry way? You sent good Vampires to their permanent deaths! You destroyed the Armies—leaving us defenseless against Eleanor Black's Creatures when they came to attack! The destruction outside these walls is your fault! If we had more Vampires, if we had more men, we would not have to start from zero to rebuild before she attacks again!

"That is why you will fight alongside us, you damned Elf. That is why you will remain at our side until we need you. You will *never*, truly, get your freedom—your kind does not deserve it. Not in the least."

There was a terse silence throughout the room, the crackling of the fire in the grate the only thing that could be heard besides Swile's shallow breathing. And then, when Xavier thought the Creature had nothing else to say, the Elf spoke:

"If it were not for that damned *Vampure*, we would not even be in this predicament. I question the order of the Vampire City when detractors—betrayers—are allowed to exist. Nay, work alongside those he betrayed."

There was a quietness to his voice that Xavier found unsettling. "Who are you talking about, Swile?"

He looked mad, unhinged, as though his mind was full to the brim with dark thoughts. He kept his unusual red eyes on Xavier, and he rubbed his hands together as though he was about to say something he certainly shouldn't have.

"I speak," the Elf hissed, "of the dark one. The *Vampure* Dracula allowed into his ranks after the...attack on your beloved city."

Xavier removed himself from the desk and stood up straighter, staring daggers at the Elf. "Damion Nicodemeus?"

Swile nodded, the gleam in his eye one of desperation and it dawned on Xavier that the Creature may have very well thought he'd see his request for freedom granted if he imparted this little story. "That *Vampure* came to Alinneis a four years ago, seeking to form some plan with him. The Great Alinneis turned him away, of course—we wouldn't dream of doing business with a *Vampure*," and he paused briefly, his gaze uncertain, as though he rethought what he'd just said. "Nevertheless, the Creature was determined to seek an audience with us. He visited us in the Etrian Hills...and he told us of his story to take down the Vampire City: we Elves would get a new home, and he would rule alongside Alinneis after Dracula had been felled."

Xavier raised an eyebrow. Damion had truly lost his mind to promise such loose hopes to the Etrian Elves. "You surely didn't believe him?" He remembered Dragor Descant's accusations against the dark Vampire.

He bowed his head in what seemed to be shame, his hands pressed together at his chest as though seeking forgiveness. "I questioned the sanity of a *Vampure* that spoke so easily of taking down another *Vampure*—but Alinneis's eyes sparked with his greed. He thought with a *Vampure* at our side, the attack would be easier." He then opened his eyes. "Alinneis was a fool." And it sounded as though the Elf regretted having to say the words. "He should have *known* the *Vampure* was not...pure—less pure than you *Vampures* normally are. But being blinded by greed is a strong fog. I'm not sure I, myself, would have been able to see past the *Vampure's* claim if I were in Alinneis's shoes. Nevertheless, we went along with the plan. Damion took us to a secret tunnel he claimed he had forged for this very plan that would give us easy entrance into Dracula's mansion. I see now that it, perhaps, had always been there."

Xavier's dead heart pulsed once in alarm, and he moved to Swile immediately, placing a careful hand on the Elf's shoulder, staring him in his alarmed red eyes. "What tunnel is this? Where is it?"

The Elf pointed a long finger to the back of the room, where a green curtain hung against a wall and Xavier narrowed his eyes, anger rising. *Betrayer, indeed.*

Before he could ask Swile anything more, three terse raps hit the door. With a quick intake of air, Xavier smelled the cold blood of Nathanial Vivery, and removed his hand from Swile's shoulder, never tearing his gaze from the green curtain. "Come in," he said.

The door opened and Xavier heard the quick footsteps as the Vampire approached.

Xavier turned to Swile, who had taken to staring at Nathanial as though he were the most beautiful thing he'd seen yet, and said, "I'm afraid this will have to wait. You can stay in the lounge if you so please."

The Elf's red eyes did not turn to eye him. Instead, he looked down at the floor, and Xavier knew the Elf had no intention on staying.

"I'm afraid I've overstayed my welcome, your Grace. I shall... take my leave." He stepped past Nathanial, and disappeared through the open door.

Xavier waved a hand and it closed, mind still on thoughts of Damion, how desperate the Vampire was for power. He only turned his attention to Nathanial when the Vampire stepped forward, and for the first time, Xavier noticed the tightly bound scroll he held in a fist, his long red robes swaying as he moved.

He said nothing as the golden-eyed Vampire undid the red ribbon, the scroll unfurling in his hand, and by the faint light of the torch, the concentrated light of the fire within the grate, Xavier read the words:

Help. Elite. Nicholai injured.

There was nothing else.

He eyed Nathanial in bewilderment. "Nicholai?"

Nathanial threw the parchment into the fire where it puckered and curled immediately upon being touched by the flames. He watched it burn before he eyed Xavier and said, "I'm not sure. However, it's the way the letter was received."

"How do you mean?"

The golden eyes appeared to flash in the light of the torch near the door as he said, "Other Creatures have reported receiving the same letter, your Grace."

He stared, feeling his blood surge in his veins, hearing the faint voice of the dead Vampire in the back of his mind... "What Creatures, Nathanial?"

The Vampire eyed him. "Aurora Borealis was the first to arrive here, your Grace. Aleister Delacroix, Peroneous Doe, and Dragor Descant arrived shortly after her."

Indeed. For he knew his journey was not truly over, he knew reaching the book at last and venturing through it, hearing of Dracula's plans, would not be the end. "Let me guess," he said, moving for the sword that leaned against the wall beside his desk, "they all bear a medallion."

Nathanial said nothing, and when Xavier turned to face him, sword in hand, he was surprised to find he was now alone. The Ascalon pulsed in his grip, pulling his attention, and he stared down at it, remembering when he'd used it to kill Elite Creatures... How it had not been touched in the four weeks that had passed since then...

He lifted the sheath from the floor, and placed the Ascalon atop his desk. He then settled the worn leather strap around his waist, his right hand pulsing with an urgency to hold the sword again.

How strange...

The pulsing did not subside when he grasped the Ascalon's handle, his fist squeezing around it, and he could not help but the feel the sword had a mind of its own. Would that be so farfetched?

He placed the glowing red sword within its home at his waist, and eyed the green curtain. It was as if he could see the dark Vampire emerging from behind the cloth, the many Elves at his heels...

Mind gripped on the dark Vampire and his truth, he stepped for the door, hearing the continued words of his predecessor issue faintly in his mind as he passed the fireplace, its flames licking the dark air in his wake:

"With the power I have given you, you alone can do it—must do it."

And as the dark door closed behind him, he had a feeling the Great Vampire's words would be truly put to the test, and quite soon.

※

Aleister Delacroix rose to his feet as the Vampires entered the large hall. All at once, the hurried voices of the Creatures around the partly destroyed table died away, and he let the scroll he'd crumpled and smoothed out for the past hour fall away from his grip onto the bloody floor.

"Xavier," he said, relieved to see the Vampire well.

He looked far better than Aleister remembered, quite impressive against the bloodied walls, the broken bookshelves, for he wore his long black hair down freely behind his back, the dark green blouse buttoned to his collar bones, the black vest atop it simple in its design: black thorns weaved their way through the front of the vest along with the black vines they were attached to. At his legs were black breeches, and always at his feet were his black riding boots.

Aleister eyed the leather grip of the Ascalon protruding out of the sheath, and something of a sigh left his lungs. "Xavier," he repeated, stepping to the Vampire who embraced him in a terse hug. "I'm so glad you're all right."

"Why wouldn't I be?" Xavier asked.

And Aleister realized he had no idea.

He released the hug, stepping back to watch the Vampire, feeling the surge of red light pass through his blood. The medallion at his chest let out a bright pulse of light, burning his skin, and he quickly removed it from beneath his traveling cloak, letting it shine brilliantly against Xavier and Nathanial's eyes.

Both Vampires raised arms to shield the light, and from the table Aurora Borealis said, "Aleister, replace it. It...won't do to have it out in the open. Especially not here."

Aleister turned to watch her, seeing her gaze dart to the two Vampires towards the back of the room behind a tall, long black desk. The blond-haired Vampire with a simpering sneer had his brown eyes placed on the medallion around Aleister's neck, the gray-haired Vampire at his side never tore his blue eyes from Xavier.

He cursed softly, replacing the glowing necklace beneath his traveling cloak, letting it rest against his blouse instead of his skin. It still glowed with its strange heat.

"What's the meaning of this, Aleister?" Xavier asked, having replaced his hand upon the Ascalon, and Aleister could not help but stare at its pulsing handle.

He turned to eye the Vampire. "We received these letters five days ago, your Grace. I was contacted by Aurora, she, by Peroneous. Dragor put two and two together and sent word for all of us to meet. I was in Quiddle, your Grace, when I received the letter—Cedar Village when I received Dragor's letter. We met briefly—the only way we could in such a time—through the mind. When we saw that Arminius and Nicholai Noble were not present, we agreed it would be best to meet here. Something has happened to them, your Grace— and for you to receive a letter as well...we are sure this has something to do with our purpose...your purpose."

Aleister stared at his son as the news settled, watching the green eyes so like his darken with his thoughts, and then, "Elite Creatures attacked them, surely."

"Aye," the dark Enchanter from the table called, "we can deduce that much from our four word messages. Nicholai is injured and we know not where they are. If you ask me, without the battle-worn Vampire, we are far less of a threat than these damnable Creatures that continue to grow in their power."

"Peroneous," Dragor Descant warned, blue eyes wide.

As the Enchanter scoffed, Aurora said, "He is right, Dragor. With Nicholai injured, our defenses as a unit are all but void. My magic can barely withstand the Elite Creatures' energies the more I use it. They do grow stronger."

"I'm sorry," Xavier said, "what *are* you all talking about?"

Aleister watched the three Creatures stare at each other, the golden-eyed Vampire's eyes on Xavier alone. When no one would speak, Aleister turned to his son and said, "These...are the Creatures who hold medallions. I believe you knew about them from the book."

His brow furrowed. "Something of it."

"Well," Aleister said, waving a scarred hand towards the table, "these are them."

Xavier stared, a hand leaving the Ascalon's handle to graze his chin. "I thought you were going to get them after we arrived back here, Aleister."

"I was busy," he said, mind rapt on the number of Elite Creatures he'd faced once he'd left the destroyed Vampire City—it was as though they were waiting in the bushes for any Creatures that survived. Shaking his head, he turned to the others. "I imagine we all were. Whatever the reasons, we're here now. We can move forward."

Aurora Borealis stared at her own scroll. "We should have moved the moment you and the king arrived in the Vampire City." She looked up at him with contempt. "Why did it take so long, Aleister, to even tell him who we really are? Three weeks to drum up the courage?"

Anger flared in his dead heart. "I was up to my neck in Elite Creatures, as were any of you! And those three Elite Creatures we accosted gave us a great deal of information on Eleanor and her plans!"

"Did they?" Aurora mocked, rising to her feet, causing the legs of the chair to scrape against the blood-splattered floor. "And what did they tell you? That she would only grow stronger in the coming weeks? They would use Victor Vonderheide, sending him all about the Dark World, rattling more Enchanters? Or perhaps they let slip through your Division's myriad torture tactics that no magic could bloody well touch them?!"

"Excuse me!" a sniveling voice sounded from further down the hall. They all turned to eye the two Vampires at the long desk to the back of the room, and Aleister let out a frustrated growl as the blond-haired Vampire dislodged himself from his chair. He stepped around the long desk, down the three steps, and strode towards them, his golden robes shimmering in the sparse torchlight that lined the walls.

"I do implore you Creatures to keep your voices down! We can't have our guests alarmed at your most *exciting* conversation."

Aleister stared around before turning his glare back at the annoying Vampire. "We're the only ones here, Civil," he snapped. *Time is being wasted—we can't afford to do nothing while Arminius and Nicholai are—*

"And this conversation doesn't concern you, Certance," Dragor said.

The brown-eyed Vampire opened and closed his mouth. "I'll have you know, Captain—" Civil began.

"Former Captain," Dragor said, looking up. He eyed Xavier with a curt nod and something of a smile. "Isn't that right, your Grace?"

Xavier's eyes narrowed. "You *wanted* to be escorted out of the City? You wanted to leave?"

He tilted his head forward, waving two fingers through the air. "I didn't want it, your Grace, but the former king knew I had been... bequeathed a beacon. He knew my time at his side was at an end."

"So Damion, the Etrian Elves—"

"Oh, definitely something we did not foresee. But useful, nonetheless," Dragor said. "I never did trust that slimy Vampire. Even when he was a soldier in the Armies, he always rubbed me the wrong way, eyeing my position. I was surprised he had the gall to convince the bloody Elves to go along with it."

Xavier shifted his footing. "But you came to me—asked me to see the Vampire taken out of the Order, was that—"

"No, not at all. I truly *wanted* the Vampire out of the Order. Indeed, the former king agreed it would be the best time to bring it up. Damion's...treachery. Use it to shed light on the damned Vampire, to get me out of City."

"So you attacking him—"

"Planned."

"And you being taken to the Caddenhalls?"

"Admittedly, I was not sure. But it did end up for the best."

"And Damion—why would Dracula induct him into the Order if he knew the Vampire caused the war?"

Dragor's eyes fell upon the parchment. "He had his reasons. He was quite focused on the Caddenhalls. And when Darien...learned what he learned, he had to be discarded. After the war, Dracula moved Damion into the Vampire Order to keep better tabs on him, it seemed."

Aleister shifted his footing, feeling quite uneasy about the heavy gazes now upon Xavier, and he knew what they had to be thinking next.

"And why are all of you," Xavier said at last, "holding medallions? Why doesn't Damion have one, Darien? Each of the Caddenhall Vampires?"

Aleister's sharp gaze found Aurora's and in it was mirrored his alarm. *There needs to be a better way of explaining this*, he thought. But before he or Aurora could utter a word, Peroneous Doe said it, the current conversation seeming to draw him out of his boredom-induced trance.

"It's quite simple, your Grace. We're the lucky Creatures chosen by the Phoenixes of the Nest to help the king carry out his goals." He spread two dark hands wide in front of him, the open scroll rising before his dark face, and the words appeared one by one, as though burned with a golden flame:

Order of the Dragon

The more Aleister watched, the more the words seemed to glow, burning themselves into the back of his eyelids. He eyed Xavier, who stared at the words as well, an absent hand gripping tight the Ascalon at his waist, which had started to glow a brilliant red.

Before anyone could say a thing, one by one, atop their chests, beneath their clothes, the medallions blared, red and hot, and as each

Creature removed their medallion from within their shirts or robes, the red light grew, bathing them all in its brilliant glow.

They stared at each other. Aleister very much felt his hand was suddenly heavy, as was the rest of his body: all attempts at movement were futile. And then the loud voice boomed within his ears, and he knew the others heard it too, for their gazes through the red light betrayed that much.

"Protect the Dragon!"

Xavier's voice issued first over the roar of the voice in his head: "What on Earth is that?"

And as the brilliant red light dimmed from their faces until only the faint glow of the orange torch light around them illuminated their frames, Aleister asked in disbelief, "You heard it too?"

"Of course I heard it," Xavier said, his eyes wide, roving quickly from Creature to Creature. "Why wouldn't I hear it? What *was* that? I've heard it once before."

Aleister cast one alarmed gaze to Aurora before he looked towards Xavier again. "It was the Call, your Grace. It was the Call of the Phoenixes."

"The Phoenixes?"

Dragor said, "Aleister—I can *feel* it." And Aleister turned to eye him, beginning to feel the immense pull as well. "We need to find him—he is quite possibly our only hope to gathering Arminius, securing Nicholai."

"I know," Aleister whispered, not understanding how it could be done. Aurora seemed to read his mind, for she said next, "We need all the Knights. We've been far too isolated as it stands."

"Arminius knew it," Dragor said, bringing all eyes to him, "he knew it and we ignored him, mostly, going about our own lives, trying to postpone the inevitable. We have to round up the last, and get to Arminius and Nicholai. Not necessarily in that order."

"Who? Who is this last?" Xavier asked. "Aren't you all in this—this Order of the Dragon?"

Aleister stared at him. "We are not all...there is—there is one more of us."

"Who?" Xavier asked, confusion filling his eyes.

Aleister stared in fear at Aurora, Peroneous, and Dragor. With a deep, cold sigh, he turned back to Xavier, knowing the veil would have had to be lifted sooner or later.

He opened his mouth and said the name, watching his son's eyes widen in even greater bewilderment, and perhaps, at least to Aleister, a shadow of the dread he'd been encased in just three weeks before:

"Christopher Black."

Chapter Two

FAMILY TIES

James inhaled the putrid scent of Vampire blood and opened his eyes. *Lillith Crane.* The dark of the room blinded him, and he rose to sit atop the bed, an unsteadiness in his movements causing him to shake. He stared at the wall across from him, the long rows of fangs flashing across his vision. A flair of panic seized his heart, his breathing quickened, but he regained himself, pulling the dark sheets off his legs. Swinging his legs over the bed, he recalled all he knew of the world.

There were not just Vampires, no, there were Dragons, Giants, Mermaids, gifted humans with magical ability called Enchanters, Elves, and Fae, women with a most enchanting air who had the gift of Sight, a rare ability to see into one's future.

He had been plied with something called Unicorn blood (a thick, dark blue liquid that smelled as horrible as it tasted), and bidden to the large bed in the lavish room in Lord Damion's home. He had not seen his aunt in the three lonesome weeks that had passed, and only had the uncomfortable company of a silent Lillith Crane every other day or so when he was to have his drink.

He had noticed something was different about her when he would see her now. It was as though he was tainted, for it was so little she would look at him. But the other night he knew something had changed in *him*.

She had entered to administer the Unicorn blood, but when she opened the door, he was greeted with a horrid scent that sent him rising from the bed with disgust. He stepped from her quickly, the piercing blue eyes shining brightly in his direction.

Her stare was suddenly threatening: he found he could meet it for long. He turned from her, nausea claiming his throat.

"James," she said, her voice shrill and unpleasant in his ears, "what's wrong?"

A hand clutched at his throat and his eyes bulged with every breath he inhaled as he was forced to smell it—her blood—and it was all he could do to remain standing away from her. He had very much wanted to run at her, but what he would do once he reached her he could not know.

She had taken a step, her wide eyes darkening. "*James*, what are you feeling right now?"

At her voice, he growled. And with it he felt something in his chest begin to expand to all reaches of his body, a terrible pain spreading through his veins—

"*James, listen to me. Breathe deeply. Control it. Control what's happening.*"

"St-Stop talking!" he spat, "just stop—I can't—what's happening to m-me?"

He eyed her, her eyes narrowing at his voice, her hands balling into fists at her sides as though she fought to reach forward and...and what? Attack him? He watched her bare her fangs and struggle with a terrible urge...but what it was he could only guess, for he felt his desire to attack her overwhelm him.

She said, "Please, don't move from this room." And she was gone.

At her voice and the abrupt rush of her scent, so thick and unavoidable, he let out a much louder growl. He felt his chest thump, felt his heart beat hard against his ribs, felt his breathing quicken into deep, drawing heaves.

Then it happened.

His arms extended in front of him as though he were a puppet, and he watched in sheer bewilderment as his hands began to grow brown thick fur, his nails extending into sharper, blacker, more formidable-looking claws and they grew to accommodate his now massive paws.

Lillith Crane appeared again, this time with a silver canteen. She eyed his arms with distaste and moved towards him, shoving the opening of the canteen into his mouth and tilting it. The taste had not left his tongue since he'd awoken and to have it pushed down his throat... He retched, blood pouring from his lips, but she had remained, not budging until it was empty.

As soon as it was, she jumped back from him. His hands pressed against the floor as they began to shrink, the long sharp nails beginning to retract and clear, the many vestiges of brown hair receding into his skin, his arms shrinking to their previous state, his mind spinning with pain, pain and terrible confusion.

He forced himself to look up at her, no longer smelling her scent or any scent for that matter; it was as though nothing had happened. But the horrid taste of the blue blood he had been forced to consume lingered on his tongue, making him desire something to wash it away.

She said, "What did you feel, James?"

"What?"

"You are beginning to transform. What did you feel? Inside? Your blood?"

"It was like... I was aware of my blood...and yours."

Her blue eyes shined, though there was still an edge to her expression. She looked as though she was ready for him to rise from the floor and attack her. "And you feel...normal now? You don't desire to kill me? "I felt like killing *you*. It's only natural that you, who have been bitten by a Lycan, would want to kill me of different blood."

His eyes widened. "Why didn't you?"

A small smile formed upon her lips and James found the effect quite unsettling.

"Christian told me Xavier told you of our existence," she said. "We will not lay harm to you until we know just why he did this."

"He...never said—I saw him, on the beach. He was attacking Lord Damion—"

"You saw him?"

"I—yes...Lord Damion's eyes were red... That was how I knew he and Master Xavier were not—never human."

"Perceptive, Addison. We have told the Vampires that came to help when you were attacked that Xavier, himself, told you what we are. A rule that would be broken. Christian figured it best...seeing as how you were bleeding in his courtyard. Though as it is...it may be better that you are dead."

Darien Nicodemeus entered the room, desiring to speak with her. And she had left with him, leaving James to his bewilderment.

Now James stood in his room in Nicodemeus manor and stared out the tall window overlooking the treetops towards the rebuilding of London, doing his best to ignore the heavy scent of Lillith Crane.

He stifled a growl as she knocked on the door, pushing the flare in his heart, the burning anger down into the recesses of whatever control he could muster. But it all went away when he heard the door open and smelled her scent in full, the growl unable to remain hidden as it left his lips and trailed on the air.

✳

Darien stared at Dracula, watching as he placed another paper within a drawer at his side. He said nothing as the Vampire sat quietly. And it was a long time before anything stirred at all, and it was the Vampire to do so.

"I trust you, Darien."

"I thank you, my Grace," he said, not allowing his thoughts to turn to what Eleanor had told him the night before.

"I trust you," Dracula continued, "but I do not trust Eleanor Black."

ere it was. He shifted in his seat. He felt quite exposed, whatever she'd said was for the greater good. He'd had a feeling she planned to take this a bit too far, Dracula's precarious words only pushing his thoughts further into realms of suspicion.

"If there is anything you," Dracula began, "know of her intentions, Darien, I would implore you to tell them to me now. Secrets would not be advisable, as you know."

Darien sat forward in his chair, staring at him, keeping any hint of apprehension out of his black eyes. "Eleanor Black, as far as I know, my Lord, is the consummate warrior." The fire crackled in its grate to his left, casting a sharp shadow over Dracula's right. "She takes quite...strongly to her training."

He moved a hand slowly over his mouth, and it was though Dracula had not believed him, but then he said, "I know she takes 'quite strongly' to her training, Vampire—I'm there when she is! What I need to know from you is what—what are you two whispering over when I leave the room? What are you two sharing with each other through low words?"

He could only stare in disbelief, his dead heart sinking into his stomach with the recognition that the most powerful Vampire in the world knew he held secrets from him. "We whisper nothing—" he began, not knowing what to say.

"You whisper words I cannot catch, Nicodemeus," Dracula said, staring him dead in the eyes. "What words can *you* whisper that *I* cannot catch?!"

"My Lord, if you think I hide anything from you—I tell you now, I don't. I-I cannot! None of us can!" he almost shouted, only catching himself when he saw the wide, bemused brown eyes of the Vampire before him, the seething anger within.

How the hell can he know? We were so bloody careful!

He watched as the Vampire moved around the desk without a word, striding straight towards him, the anger thick in eyes, his furrowed brow. And he flinched as Dracula bent low, white hair falling over his shoulders, a curtain surrounding his handsome, haunted face, the low words reaching him with much more anger than he had ever known the Vampire to hold:

"The only reason I opened my doors to you, Darien Nicodemeus, is because of her word. Her keen interest in you. And I knew it was because of your damned curse that she gained her interest—I wonder if she were able to weasel even that out of you."

When he said nothing, Dracula continued, "Well?"

"I told her nothing of the Caddenhalls, my Lord."

"You didn't..." he whispered, the piercing stare holding him heavy to his chair.

The cold skin grazed his arm and he opened his eyes with a start, the bright light blinding him the moment he did so. He only blinked where he lay for a single moment feeling the warmth of the light against his skin, and then she spoke.

"My Lord?" Minerva Caddenhall said, and he turned slowly, eyeing her.

She leaned against the vacant side of the bed, hand still outstretched, her blonde hair falling over a blue eye.

He sat up at once. "What's happened?"

"It's Alexandria Stone," she said, her voice filled with contempt, he thought, for her part in continuously failing to locate the woman, "I cannot smell her blood."

"This is not news to me, Minerva," he said, relaxing slightly, swinging his legs over the side of the bed, giving her his back. "You have failed to get a read on her blood since London was destroyed." He gazed out the window just beside his bed where over the tops of the trees in the distance, beams of red and brown light flashed in the morning sky. Buildings shot up from the ground as though they had always been there, and he turned away, remembering the smell of death that had filled the air since Eleanor had sent her Dragons and Giants to ruin the city.

He and the Caddenhalls had remained within his home, safe under their many enchantments, surprised when a battle-worn Lillith Crane and James Addison had appeared at their door. They'd let them in and Darien soon found his large home quite full.

But he had not known James had been bitten by a Lycan until he smelled the man's scent.

"I know I have failed you before, Master," Minerva went on near the door, "but I have grown better. I am close to my Age!"

Darien stood and turned. Her blue eyes scanned over his bare chest and he cleared his throat begging her gaze away from his scar. She obeyed, eyeing his face.

"You may be close to your Age, Minerva," he said, "but you have been more than useless to me in locating the woman. What brings this mess on now?"

Her lips opened and closed, trembling with fear. "I-I...my Lord. Her blood escapes me completely. I once thought it to be Eleanor Black's energy but Alexandria's blood—it is as though it does not exist."

He narrowed his eyes. "What?" And he recalled all he knew about the woman. Her blood, how it had filled the air for months, only to be blanketed by Eleanor Black's all-consuming lilac and blood and dread. Never-ending dread. He looked out the window once more, the flashes of light in the sky only second to the sun's glow. *Where is she?*

He cursed himself again for not grabbing her in London those days before it fell. He had been completely enraptured in the three Elite Creatures in Lycan form that had appeared within his woods, something that should have been impossible, but he had long since learned Eleanor had a gift for exceeding expectations.

He did not take his gaze off the buildings that filled the empty sky, just able to make out the heads of the Enchanters that worked hard to restore the city to its former glory. "We stay the course, Minerva," he said, turning to watch her. "Now that Dracula is finally dead, what little protection we've been afforded shall surely begin to dwindle. Check Delacroix manor again—I don't believe Christian would leave it, not if his brother has not emerged from below ground."

She looked as though she wished to protest but her shoulders dropped and she nodded, turning to leave when the tall, old Vampire appeared behind her.

"I beg your pardon, my Lord," Minerva said, stepping around the withering Vampire whose sharp blue eyes would not leave Darien's.

Ewer waved a long-fingered hand and smiled kindly at her before stepping into the room, right up to the bed, and placed a hand on a golden bed post. "With the young one here...there is much excitement in Nicodemeus manor, now."

He stared. With a sigh the door closed. "Indeed," he said, stepping to a dresser and opening it. He began to peruse his clothes while the old voice went on.

"And that...mongrel in your mother's bed. Are you not the least bit at odds with keeping a Lycan here, Master Darien?"

He ran a dark hand over a dark red shirt. "Lillith has told me what happened. If he is to be kept alive because he is Xavier's servant—because Xavier told the man what he is, what we are—who am I to object?"

There was a sigh of exasperation and then silence.

Beside himself, Darien turned.

Ewer Caddenhall was staring at him with a pained expression. "Dracula is dead, my Lord. The magic that keeps you alive—forgive me for saying so—will begin to wither."

"It has already begun," he interjected, recalling the dream. "And Minerva has just told me she can no longer smell Alexandria Stone's blood. I am aware of the predicament we face, Ewer. If we do not find her—if I do not take her blood..."

"Do not think on it," he said, "you cannot."

"But it happens all the same and I would be a fool to deny it!"

There was strained silence and Darien saw Ewer's thin lips purse. "Just...my Lord, let us figure out another way—there must be something Dracula set in place should Minerva fail—"

"There were things, Ewer," he said, snarling, "called Nicholai Noble, after him Eleanor Black, after *her*, Xavier bloody Delacroix! But since none of those brilliant Vampires could fall in line, here we are. And I will do everything I can to aid Xavier on his quest, Caddenhall despite this. Do not question me again."

"I never...of course, Master Darien," Ewer whispered, but Darien could not truly hear him: the pain that had lingered just underneath his skin the moment he'd awoken surged with his anger, and his jaw clenched against it, resisting it. But it was already too late.

The visions swirled within his mind's eye, and he tried to keep at bay the pain which was blinding now. A flicker of horrified recognition swept across Ewer's face.

"I will get Minerva!" he cried, moving to leave the room when Darien swept a dark hand forward, forbidding him leave.

"Tend to me—do it now," he snarled, the pain bringing him to his knees. Jagged breaths left him in painful gasps, and he could feel the air leave his lungs, leave them permanently, and the fear was great now—

The cold hand was pressed to his head, and he felt the fingers clench around his hair, pulling it back, and he knew what would pierce through the pain.

Yes, it was not long at all before the cold blade was brought against his neck, and as his blood gushed forth, the blood on the blade joining his own, he knew the memory to return sharply before he could try and stop it:

"Drink her blood, Darien."

"I—she is human—"

"Do it, or you will die."

And so he moved forward, gathering her arm in his hands, and quickly he bit, the blood filling his mouth with exhilarating speed, and try as he might, he could not catch all—

The gasp left him as he stared up into Ewer's eyes, once again feeling the hard floor beneath his knees, the cold air that surrounded him, and then the Vampire spoke:

"You are running out of time, my Lord."

He said nothing but rose slowly to his feet, not sure what was up or down. As he braced himself on the old wood of the dresser, he saw Ewer's golden robes leave him, towards the tall double doors.

"I will ensure the Lycan is not too much of a burden on Lillith Crane," the old voice said, "and I will ensure Minerva locates the woman, but I fear even she may not be able to save you." And before Darien could yell his displeasure at the statement so boldly uttered, Ewer Caddenhall had opened a door and stepped through it, leaving him to his pain and even darker thoughts.

✳

Damion Nicodemeus lowered himself against the black and green scales as the large Creature settled herself atop the ground, her long claws digging into the earth.

"Thank you, my dear," he said, swinging a leg off her back.

"Thank you for the vacation," Dammath said, her long nose nudging his shoulder. "I trust things were pleasant in my absence."

He scoffed. "Hardly, I could have used you those weeks you were gone."

She unfolded a large wing, sending a terse breeze to press against him, his traveling cloak whirling up. "There was trouble?"

"If I could give you the half of it, I would," he said, when the loud sound issued from beyond the high stone wall.

He turned to eye it.

"Damion?" she said lowly, a puff of black smoke leaving her nostrils beside him.

"All is well," he said uncertainly, waving a hand to keep her behind, while he moved for the large doors set into the wall. "All is well."

He left the large Dragon, stepping across the dirt yard to reach the high doors. Before he could open them, they blew open, the sight of the thick forest coming into view. He watched intently as a few Fairies flew past the first line of trees, their golden lights flittering in their panic.

He stepped forward and stared at the dark leaves atop the high trees. They shook, several falling to the grassy ground, before he emerged, black cloak tattered, long blond hair waving wildly behind his head.

"Yaddley?" Damion called, watching in awe as his blue eyes happened upon him and then the large Dragon at his back.

"Lord Damion," he said, brandishing a black dagger from his waist. There was dried blood on his dirtied shirt, and his hair clung to it. "Lycans tried to breach the woods. They appeared in human

34

form and once they reached the trees..." He fell to his knees before he could finish.

Damion stepped forward, pulling the Vampire up to stand by the shoulder. Once he was on his large feet, Damion said, "Lycans? Where's my brother? Ewer?"

"Inside the manor," Yaddley whispered, "they did not know— I've yet to tell them."

"Well we must!" Damion said, anger coursing through him. *Lycans near my home!*

Yaddley pressed a hand to Damion's chest. "No, Damion—they came for the boy. They knew he was here. Smelled his Lycan blood."

He released the Vampire, confused. "What boy? What are you talking about?"

"Xavier Delacroix's servant. The young man who was bitten. He and Lillith Crane moved for your home when London was destroyed. They have been here for three weeks."

He stared, the heavy breaths of Dammath behind him sending the breeze into his back. "Bloody hell. Three weeks?! Has James turned? Has he taken to the Unicorn blood?"

"He did turn slightly once. He has kept the blood under control since then."

Damion moved past Yaddley towards the door leading into the manor. He did not turn as he said, "Close the doors for Dammath, it would not do to have Lycans, or worse, the Enchanters laying eyes upon her."

"But, my Lord, they will surely return. I cannot hold them off myself."

He stepped through the woods, hearing the various Creatures rustle the grass around him. "You won't," he said, mind burdened with dark thought on Darien and just what the Vampire allowed to enter their home in his absence.

Chapter Three

ALEXANDRIA STONE

She pressed a hand to the fresh sheets, trying to keep her unease at bay.

"Hand the woman her drink, yet?" the girl beside her asked. She was also bent over her wicker basket, patting down the clothes already inside it.

The slight breeze brushed past her, her dark blonde hair brushing past her ears.

"You know it isn't right to wear your hair down like that, pretty as it is," the girl said. "What'll the Master say when he sees it?"

She picked up the basket by its straw handles, setting it on her hip as she rose to stand. "He's already seen it, and he's no qualms to its nature," she said shortly, seeing the girl's cheeks warm with her embarrassment.

And with that she turned, leaving the girl to stare after her, her own cheeks burning with her boldness. While it was true she had seen the incredibly handsome man just an hour before, she had had no real idea what he thought of her unbecoming hair style, for he'd only nodded to her while passing in the hallway.

The quiver of fear in her chest bloomed into full alarm with the thought. She tightened her grip on the basket, stepping slowly towards the looming white doors.

Once she reached them, she balanced the basket on her hip while extending an arm to open the door. A flash of wind pressed against her, blowing her skirts against her bare legs, and the door opened.

His black eyes stared down at her, unreadable in their glare, but he was smiling. He stepped aside without a word, allowing her entrance, and she dropped the hand that was still stretched dimly for the handle, grasping the basket's grip instead.

She curtsied, taking a step into the hall, head bowed, gaze on the floor, when a slight breeze blew past and she heard his voice, so clear, so quick, "Take the drink to her, now."

The gasp left her lips, and she looked up, his gaze locked on hers, and how everything seemed to slow, how nothing else mattered in the world but those cruel, black pools of remarkable indifference—

"Something wrong?" a deep voice asked from somewhere far away.

She blinked, and everything resumed its normalcy, or at least, the wind, and the birds' chirping continued on; he had not changed from his serious stare in the least.

"N-no," she breathed, unable to tear away from the eyes, the smile that still lifted his cheeks, "nothing, nothing, my Lord."

And then she was stepping away, very aware his eyes followed her back. She felt their heat, even as she rounded a doorway and entered a rather cozy sitting room, the high fire burning brightly in its grate spreading great relief over the two red armchairs in the center of the room.

She placed the basket atop a small table behind an equally red couch and allowed her hands to release their steel grip on the basket's handles.

Those eyes, those mad eyes, she thought, clutching her black skirt to still her trembling hands. "No man under God should have such eyes," she whispered.

"How God matters into it," the deep voice sounded from behind her, "I cannot fathom."

She jumped, her heart diving into her stomach, and she turned, an unsteady hand flying to her mouth in her alarm. She eyed the Master of the Manor, Lord Christian Delacroix, his black gaze trained on her as though he did not desire to look anywhere else. His blouse was unbuttoned, she noticed, and how it looked as though he hadn't slept in days: dark circles under his eyes gave him the appearance of a bedraggled man, bidden to the many responsibilities at his back. From the looks of it, she thought, Lord Delacroix had not accomplished any of his responsibilities in quite some time.

"I—my Lord," she began, embarrassment filling her cheeks, "I did not mean—"

"It's quite...all right," he whispered, pushing her into silence. And she watched in bewilderment as he took a slow step forward, hands splayed. "I know my gaze...frightens. Unfortunately, there is nothing I can do about it...well, there is...but..." And she watched as he brought his hands together, the motion too fluid to be real, but the more she stared, the more she saw him press two fingers against a golden ring, and slide it off a finger before placing it within the pocket of his dark breeches.

Before she could say a word, he sighed, his eyes closing as though he desired to dream. They opened before long and another gasp left her lips as she stumbled backwards, for his eyes were now a brilliant red, illuminated further by the orange light of the flames in their place.

"Wh-what?" Her voice was far gone, her senses as well, for what trick of the light was this? She dared to take her eyes off the... man before her for a second, if only to stare around the room, eager to see what mirror, what well placed light made this glow possible.

"I am most sorry," he said, his voice low, almost soft in its call: she suddenly felt as though she desired to sleep.

Blinking rapidly, she took a step away, trying her hardest to keep him in her sights: he moved far too quickly, far too smoothly, his every movement drawing her gaze, only for him to appear closer with every second that passed.

"F-for what, my L-Lord?"

"For this."

And he was just before her with her next blink, his pale chest taking up her vision before she could realize it. A cold hand was placed upon her cheek in the next second, its startling cold numbing her skin where it touched—

"Wh—"

His thumb found her lips, pushing her words down into the recesses of her fear. His red eyes found her brown ones with ease, and she could not look away, would not look away, what horrors he had seen...had, perhaps inflicted upon others... Yes, it was all so clear...

His mouth opened, the two sharp fangs at the front of his mouth sending her gaze there, her terror quite real.

She knew her blood to turn cold, so immensely aware her heart thundered against her chest... And then she stared over his shoulder, his head buried in her neck, and she braced herself, indeed, unable to move, for the pain that would pierce her soul...

Nothing happened.

She remained there, his strong, cold hands wrapped around her arms, keeping her in place, and yet, he did not move, did not flinch, did not...bite, but he merely remained there, her breathing rapid as it pressed against his ear.

And when she thought she would lose her breakfast at last, he released her, something of a horrible sound leaving his throat as he turned from her and stepped towards the door.

"Get the drink from the cellar and meet me in her room," he said, his voice just as commanding, just as deep.

The shiver that ran through her jolted her to the here and now, his long black hair disappearing behind the door's frame as he left her alone with utter bewilderment and the belief that she, somehow, escaped certain death.

※

He stared down at her, his anger clear.

She had stopped him, for the hundredth time. Stopped him from feeding, stopped him from receiving the nourishment he so rightfully needed, *deserved*.

And what was worse, he thought darkly, pacing before the bed in which she lay, eyes closed, she was quite unaware of the frustration she had put him through. When she would rise she would not remember any of it, her red light would retreat, she would look upon him with those eyes so brilliant, that unshakeable gaze most adamant.

And he would find his anger misplaced, he would find the inability to feed from any of the fresh, young maids dim in the gaze that was *hers*.

"I prefer you awake instead of dying, Miss Stone," he said aloud, knowing it the stark truth: She *was* dying.

It had become quite noticeable a week after they had returned to London. She had started to sleep for longer periods of time, the red light blaring, dulling his senses, stilling his desire for blood, until she was mostly asleep, that red light issuing forth from her skin without fail.

She hardly ate, she hardly opened her eyes, and when she did, she was noticeably weak, but her gaze...how it would remain no matter her physical state.

"Goddamnit! Where *is* that bloody girl?!"

He had told her to gather the damned blood almost thirty minutes before. Perhaps he had scared her—he had known it was foolish to try it again, but damn, the need for the sweet liquid of life had almost driven him mad.

The door opened and in she stepped, her gaze never reaching his eyes. She held no silver tray today, but only the jar filled with the thick blue liquid in shaking hands. She said not a word as she stepped towards Alexandria atop the bed, the woman whose head was propped up on many pillows, her eyes closed, the red light still shining.

The young maid stepped up to her, hastily unscrewed the top of the jar, the thick, awful smell of Unicorn Blood filling the room as she did so.

She pressed the opening of the jar to Alexandria Stone's closed lips, gently working to pry them open, the red light pressing against her face, illuminating her terrified expression. Christian stifled a growl of frustration, the truth of his desire unable to reach him here... but it would not be long now, not long at all...

Yes, the thick blue blood slipped past Alexandria's lips, and Christian watched her throat closely as the blood went down; it was not long at all before the red light dimmed until it was no more.

"Thank you for your assistance," he told the maid. He took a simple step towards her, knowing the desire to taste her blood was there, deep inside him, but how it was subdued, still. He appraised her for a few moments, her brown eyes watering in her fear, and then, with a wave of a slightly trembling hand, he dismissed her, turning his back on her as she stepped out of the room, the empty jar of Unicorn Blood tight in her uneven hands.

He had not been able to wipe her mind this time, make her forget this foolish attempt to take her blood for his own. He had had enough energy the many days before he had tried to do so. Now...

He stared at his hand, how it shook with an unsteady tremor.

Two weeks.

It had been two weeks since he had had blood, and that blood he had had to travel to another town to acquire. As the days wore on, Alexandria's...condition keeping him close, he found he did not have the energy to make the trip...and indeed, the coach he had called a time after that first excursion had not gotten him anywhere.

The poor man served as his meal that night, the horses the next few nights.

Now he was starving.

And he let out an aggrieved sigh, for there it was, the smell of her blood. It filled the room and he lowered his hand, staring down at her, willing her to rise, to challenge him, to say—or do—anything that would warrant his hand to slip across her neck, his fangs pressing into the tender vein that held such alluring blood.

Yes, he had thought about that blood, had wanted to know what it tasted like, the smell as intoxicating as it was, and with Xavier at his new helm underground, he had found his...need to keep her safe, to keep her alive, was fading, and fast.

The more days passed that he heard nothing from his brother, the more he was resolved to just end her life. She had to be kept alive, she had to be kept safe, but for what? What real purpose did she hold?

Other than her alarming blood, the...curious vision shared by Aurora Borealis and Nathanial Vivery, Alexandria Stone was not worth the week of protection he had given her.

He could not bite her, could not taste her blood, could not know what her truth was, only that she blared red light every time she slept, only that she stifled his urges, his true urges at every turn.

"Christian?" the soft voice breathed.

He blinked, her brilliant eyes staring right at him, confusion deep within them, confusion, and what seemed to be...relief?

"Who else would it be?" he asked, hearing the bite in his words.

She did not seem to. "I dreamed," she said, a hand grasping his arm as though to steady herself. He stared at her touch as she propped herself higher against the pillows until she sat upright. And with a distasteful grimace, she licked her lips. "That...drink is horrid."

"Yes," he said, staring at her hand on his wrist, able to feel her blood pulse strongly in her grip. He swallowed. "It is." Gently shaking his wrist out of her hand, he sat on the edge of the bed, feeling his desire to drink disperse completely. "What was your dream?"

She stared at him, her gaze never faltering, and he felt, curiously, as though he were being surveyed by a most formidable Creature...

"A Vampire came to me," she said. "I was but a child—my mother was in the other room. This Vampire was...odd—kinder than I've seen... That is, he did not seem to desire to bite me...he merely watched me."

"How odd."

She shifted slightly within the bed, and he could not help but realize she wore nothing but a rather thin chemise, a pale slip beneath it. "It wasn't until I acknowledged him fully—held his gaze—that he said anything at all. It was most odd, Christian."

"Go on."

"He said, 'You are the key against the beasts: the blood-stiller.'"

At this, he sat up straighter, turning atop the bed to eye her. *The blood-stiller?* "What does that mean?"

She watched him, the hint of tiredness dressing her hollowed eyes. "I cannot say, although...his eyes...he looked upon me as though...as though he knew me..."

"Knew you?" And then the thought returned, the many nights she would call out the name of the Vampire he had never seen. "That Vampire, could it not be Dracula?"

Her eyes widened. "I haven't the faintest idea what he looks like—"

"But you have called out his name many a time while you've slept."

"Yes...you've...mentioned my outbursts..." And she sighed deeply, seemingly pressed with troubling thoughts. "Have *you* ever seen Dracula, Christian?"

"Never."

"Then how can you be so sure it's him?"

"Based on your blood...the Lycans' reaction to your blood, blood-stiller seems to be a most appropriate name for...what it is your red light, your blood can do. I do believe Dracula knew the reason behind it—it can only be he that visited you in your dream."

Her tired eyes seemed to shine, and then she leaned forward, her tousled dark brown hair falling over her shoulders. He fought the urge to stand when she grasped his hand: he felt the slight tremor and knew she was scared. "Christian," she said, "the Lycans, I haven't thought of them in weeks—my blood calls them to me, doesn't it?"

"From what we've experienced, it's safe to say so. I have thought about their presence, and I have monitored the grounds nightly. There was never anything out there."

She said nothing and then she released his hand.

He massaged his hand before rising from the bed, her bewilderment filling her gaze as it followed him. The touch. How simple it had been, how full of her desperation to claw, to reach for another that could help.

He was a Vampire most unable to keep the Lycans at bay and she was a human whose blood seemed to call them to her...whose blood seemed to cause such curiosities in all who remained near...

He watched her from the corner of his eye, her fear full on her face as she stared once more at her hands. Her hands so wrapped up in themselves, shaking vigorously, he half-thought she would break her own fingers...

And there it was, the sliver of doubt. Had he been too hard on her? This mysterious woman whose blood filled his mind? This curious creature who knew not what was happening to her any more than he, and had she not assisted where she could? Had she not told him of the vision she had—Lore at the manor waiting for James Addison? Had she not come back for him in those woods when chased by both Elite and Lycan Creatures?

Something like admiration filled him the more he stared. Yes, he was weak, yes, he desired blood, yes he desperately needed to feed, but all of this, though it was because of her, it most certainly was not her fault.

No, Alexandria Stone was not the reason for her own plight. She had been, like Xavier, like himself, born into the madness of the Dark World—born into the mess that was Dracula's creation. For Christian had known, once Aleister had lifted the spell, that he would have suffered the same fate as Alexandria if not turned into a Vampire when he was.

A clearing of a throat pulled him from his thoughts, and he turned to the doorway where a different young maid remained, her hair black in its hold. Her small dark eyes stared at him as though she looked upon something most indecent, and he realized, indeed, that Alexandria was in her night clothes—how wrong of him it was to be here, but he, like her, had hardly cared.

"Er...my Lord," the maid began, in her hands a silver tray upon which remained a folded, yellowed, piece of paper, "this just arrived. There was no name, nor did the footman leave one... I did not want to intrude, but..." And her eyes found Alexandria atop the bed, a blush of red filling her cheeks.

He let one side of his mouth rise with his amusement. He stepped for the girl, nodding once to her. "Thank you," he said, his stare moving to her neck.

She stared before lifting the tray forward, and he stifled the soft sigh that threatened to drift past his lips. *Humans and their fear...* He removed the note and nodded to her, begging her leave. Once she was gone, he closed the door, turning to eye Alexandria.

He peeled the note open, noticing how brittle it felt in his fingers. It was as though it'd been housed in someone's pocket for ages.

The miniscule penmanship showed itself once the note was open wide.

Dear Christian,

It is imperative that we meet. Something has happened to your brother—it is vital we get to the bottom of this matter immediately. We can convene at noon in the Dragon's Cavern.

And bring Alexandria. We cannot risk her being left alone in these terribly dark times.

Your Oldest Confidante,

V. V.

He reread it several times until the words burned into the back of his eyelids.

Something's happened to Xavier? And he was never told? Of course he wouldn't be—only now would someone even think of sending him a letter. But who?

His black eyes perused the sharply penned initials at the bottom of the parchment. *Victor?*

He had seen neither hide nor tail of Victor Vonderheide since it was agreed that Christian would be the one to keep Alexandria in his stead. If it was him and something had, indeed, happened to Xavier, he could not sit idly by.

He looked up at Alexandria. She remained staring upon him as though greatly scared: her eyes were wide, almost filled with tears, but she said not a word. He realized after a moment that she was waiting for him to speak.

"Something has happened to Xavier, Alexandria." He folded the note and placed it in the pocket of his breeches. "Victor wants us to meet him at an inn called *The Dragon's Cavern* at noon."

"What?" she whispered, a hand moving to throw the thick sheets off her bare legs. He could not find the decency to turn away. "Did he say what's happened?"

Christian blinked, clearing his throat, pushing his desire down into the recesses of control. She was off limits, blood and otherwise. "Ah, no," he said, turning his gaze to her eyes. She began to move toward him, her tousled brown hair falling freely over her shoulders, "He didn't say. Only that it's imperative we meet him at this inn. You are well enough for the trip?"

Her lips pursed and he half-thought she were going to say no, for her eyes and their dark circles gave her the look of needing perpetual sleep, but she said, "Yes, I'm fine."

He stared at her. "Alexandria, you look ready to keel over—"

"If I can help your brother in any way—if he's in trouble and he's the only one remaining who knows of me and my blood—we have to help him. We have to find out what he knows."

He opened his mouth, unable to find fault with her words. If Xavier was harmed in any way, there went their only shot to figure out who she really was, what the Vampire that could have been Dracula in her dream meant by naming her "blood-stiller."

She was determined, this he knew. And no amount of coercion or words to the contrary would turn her. "You will need to eat, of course," he said at last, seeing the relief fill her eyes with his response.

"Send in Amelia to help me dress—I will take my breakfast here," she said, and he marveled at the assuredness that seemed to cover her now. But with a quick blink, his eyes resuming their red gaze, he could see the palpable fear that filled her beating, beautiful heart. A shiver of need filled him with the sight and he replaced his black gaze with ease, bowing his leave from her presence.

Her damning, maddening, blood-stilling presence.

Once he reached the long hallway, he turned his thoughts to her importance once more, Victor's letter quite heavy in his pocket.

Xavier, what's happened? And why was no one sent?

He left her, stepping down the hall, turning his thoughts to the number of maids that tended to the house when he realized he had no idea who Amelia was.

✳

Alexandria Stone strode to the large closet where many dresses hung for her. Her fingers skimmed over the soft fabrics, mind stretched on who would harm Xavier Delacroix—Eleanor Black, surely, any number of the curious Elite Creatures they had met on their journey across the Dark World those weeks before...

She recalled the violet-eyed Vampire she had met a month before when taken to a ball. Victor Vonderheide had seemed so kind, so assured, and she'd learned with Christian that he'd taken over for Xavier in his absence. *So why*, she asked herself as she lifted a deep blue day dress from its place, *do I feel so uneasy?*

Yes, she admitted, something was wrong—and it seemed to go far beyond Xavier Delacroix being harmed. She couldn't understand it, but she felt she knew that he was perfectly fine.

"Miss Stone?" a young voice called from the doorway.

Alexandria looked up, eyeing the beautiful young woman who stood there, long blonde hair flowing freely down her back. "Hello, Amelia," she said with a smile, gesturing a hand for the woman to enter. She watched as the maid lifted her skirts and stepped over the threshold of the door, and the closer it was she neared, the more it was Alexandria saw the woman's brown eyes were filled with water. "Oh," she gasped, staring more closely at her, "what's wrong?"

Her hands were shaking when she sat down, and Alexandria moved around the tall golden post and sat beside the girl, placing a careful hand upon her shoulder, gently moving back some of her hair to eye her neck. No holes remained. She breathed a slight sigh of relief, but narrowed her eyes, for something had startled the woman, and if it weren't Christian's...nature, it must've been something else. Perhaps a beast?

Fear rising in her heart with the thought, she squeezed the shoulder of the girl, keeping her eyes trained on her wet face, waiting for her to respond.

She soon did.

"Th-the Master," she gasped through tears.

"What of him, Amelia?"

"He," and she kept her gaze on the wall just before them as though she could not bear to look anywhere else, "he is unlike anyone—the way he cares for you—I fear for your life, Miss Stone." Tears fell in earnest now, unstoppable sobs causing her chest to heave, and without another word, the girl cried loudly, wailing as if she'd lost all that was precious to her in the world.

"My dear," Alexandria began, half-aware Christian would hear and would return, indeed, "please. You mustn't cry. Please—please—tell me what you saw of the Master? You did see him act in such a way that you would fear for my life?"

Her tears slowed, if only for a moment, her brown eyes moving to watch Alexandria, something of defeat lining them. "Every morning he demands I gather that most foul liquid for your consumption, Miss Stone. I travel to the cellar where he keeps the jars—so many of them, Miss Stone—and they're quite heavy. It is all I can do to hold them well enough to carry them up the many stairs. Heaven forbid I ever drop one.

"But it is Master Delacroix, Miss Stone, his stare...the way he looks upon me...the other girls...yourself... I once thought him a strange man, but now...well, I daresay he is no man at all. His eyes—there's nothing in them! And something, he did something to me earlier...or, he tried to, Miss Stone. I don't know what...but he couldn't. He just...he left me standing there."

Alexandria felt something like anger rise in her throat, but how the words would not push past her lips. He tried to bite the maid— take her blood! Surely it wasn't enough that there were a multitude of humans he could choose from, wandering the streets. Surely the Vampire wasn't greedy enough to try to take the blood of his very maids when there were—not that it was better, she admitted—many more humans out there, even criminals who would not mind having their blood drained?

So why, she wondered hotly, would the Vampire try to take the blood of his help?

And she remembered it, then, his hand pressed to her heart, the cold terribly numbing, his gaze never wavering from her own, the uncertainty, the fear that filled her the more he looked at her with the eyes so unseeing... But that was not true, she knew. Those eyes saw everything.

And those eyes had looked upon her with more hate than usual, lately.

But why?

"That's enough, my dear," she said, being drawn out of her revere with a particularly loud sniffle, "Lord Delacroix's eyes are perfectly fine and I'm sure you were just imagining whatever it was you think he tried to do.

"Now," she said, rising from the bed, doing her best to still the fear that filled her heart, doing her best to keep tears from clogging her throat, "please, help me dress. The Master and I must attend to a friend today, and it's very important we get there on time."

Alexandria watched her as Amelia sighed, her eyes hard, and then, all at once, the girl rose from the bed, a smile filling her face.

She wiped stray tears from her cheeks and said, "You are right. I—perhaps I was just imagining it all. Master Delacroix is a bit off-putting but..."

"Am I now?" the deep voice came from the door.

Alexandria looked up to see him standing there, his gaze was held on Amelia steadily.

She saw truth to the girl's words.

He *had* tried to drink her blood.

"I didn't mean—" Amelia began, but Alexandria turned to her and smiled, gesturing her to keep her silence. She obeyed immediately as Alexandria said, "You have to admit, Christian, you do come off a bit far away."

"I'm not sure I'm to be offended or amused," he said dryly, stepping into the room.

The maid let out a small gasp, but she ignored it, for he was just before her within the next second, and those hateful eyes were staring down upon her in full. She felt as though the room had become much smaller, as though time had all but ceased.

"I see you're not yet dressed," Christian offered, though the words were laced with something more. A chill rose up Alexandria's spine.

"I was comforting the girl," she answered, never removing her gaze from Christian's. *Endless black pools of death and thirst,* she thought vaguely, *and I will have the same quite soon...*

"Comforting? Whatever for?"

"She feels a bit ill," Alexandria said, "I gathered she could use the rest, a comforting ear to hear her troubles."

Christian's snarl was slight but it was there.

Of course he knew I was lying, she thought, *but what did it matter? He tried to bite her—perhaps all of the girls—for how long? How many had he succeeded in tasting?*

51

"That is always a comfort," he answered dimly, and his eyes roved to the young girl behind her, and something like anger appeared in his gaze before it was gone. "I hope...you found her words easy to digest, Alexandria." And the mocking implication could not be pushed aside.

Toy with me all you want, she thought angrily, you *won't get your hands on her again.*

Before she could say a word, Amelia ran past, the glimmer of tears flying down her cheeks. The door closed with a slam behind her, her sobs fading down the hall along with the thunder of her slippers against the hard floor.

His hand found her face and the gasp left her lips with her surprise, his fingers tilting her chin upwards, as to give her full view of his face, which was somehow colder, hardened with an anger she just realized had been seething in him for weeks.

And it was directed at her.

"You keep me from my meals, even awake," he said, eyes red.

Her heart began to thunder in her chest, but she found she could not move, and she half wondered if this was what he did to his victims, if this was how he controlled them before he killed them...

Opening her mouth, she moved her tongue, aware she could not feel it in her mouth, but she knew it was there, knew she had to use it, knew she had to keep him from drinking from any more maids...

"I do no such thing," she gasped, "I haven't kept you from the feeding frenzy I'm sure you've indulged in those days I've been gratefully asleep."

"Hardly." His gaze grew colder. He was telling the truth. "I cannot bite, I cannot suck, I cannot drink. The closer I am to you," he ran a thumb across her chin, his gaze thoughtful as though appraising her, "the less my desire consumes me. But I still die."

She wondered what the truth was, if it truly remained behind those blank veils, that angry gaze. "What...do you mean?"

"I cannot take the blood I so desperately need the more your red light blares, and even when it doesn't," he said, eyeing the blue dress atop the bed, "it seems the effect remains the same."

"You cannot feed?"

"I cannot."

"Then how—what have you been doing to—"

"I have been snarling, brooding, trying to recapture my urges, trying to retain the vestige of myself that will allow me to tear into flesh, to be rejuvenated. I can do no such thing."

"While I remain around."

"Yes," he said, the sadness permeating his voice, "while you remain around. I have had to go into other towns to procure my meals, but even that was short-lived, as I soon did not have the energy to make the trips.

"I tried on the maids only this week, but I would have enough energy to wipe their thoughts..." His gaze found hers once more. "Today, it seems I've run out of even that simple power."

Her eyes widened. "You've been starving for weeks and still you stay by my side? Still you would listen to my mad dreams of Lycans and Vampires?"

A wry smile found his lips. "I grew to hate you the more my need grew. You, this thing I could not kill, you this thing I could not taste, you this thing I could not truly *know*. For if I could not know you, Alexandria, know your purpose, I wanted to kill you, and if I could not kill you, I wanted to be far from you, but your dream... Victor's letter...we may get the answers we seek today."

The spark of happiness that had filled her with brief thoughts of his desperately begging her to wake, faded in the words so harshly spoken. She said nothing for a while as the words filled her mind.

"I am but a thing to be researched, figured out, a puzzle for you Vampires," she thought aloud.

He eyed her, and she felt the gaze wasn't meant to scare, but it did just that all the same. "Whatever you are," he said, nodding towards the dress, signaling she prepare, "you are powerful. To destroy a Vampire's urges just by being near, it is a dangerous thing. You could bring the whole of the Vampire World to its knees...if you weren't to die.

"And that is why I stay by your side, even though it appears you may very well be the permanent death of me. My brother's too busy to tend to you, and apparently he's gotten himself in trouble—and after what we discovered about you, the fact that you came back to me in those woods, Alexandria—whatever your blood does to me, to other Vampires, you are powerful. And that power may very well end this reign of Elite Creatures. And I will see it through to the end, regardless of the outcome.

"That is why I stay."

Tears filled her eyes before she could stop them. She saw in his gaze the words that had meant the most to him: *"You came back."*

She said nothing, not daring to tell him that she had believed him better than those Enchanters, that she had one constant in the Dark World since she woke up in it those months before, and it was him.

He nodded as she struggled to find the words to respond with, and he turned from her, moving for the door, his movements much too quick for her to make out that she was all alone a moment later.

Chapter Four

DRACULA'S SECRETS

"I'm sorry," he said once the door closed behind him, "care to repeat yourself father? I must not have heard you correctly." The bitter sting of the words told to him but an hour before not leaving his mind. *It was ridiculous*, he thought hotly, watching the older Vampire avoid his gaze before the brightly burning fire.

It had taken an hour to leave the Clearance Committee Building and get the Vampire alone, for the remaining Members of the Order of the Dragon had wanted to speak more on plans and ideas, on how best to gather Arminius the Elf and Nicholai Noble, and—though he could hardly entertain it as a real idea—Christopher Black.

Xavier Delacroix stared at the Vampire coldly. "Who is he?" he asked, not wanting to hear the answer, the thought of it ridiculous, but it had been there in the way the green eyes had left his own once the name was spoken...

Aleister Delacroix looked up at last, the unease in his gaze palpable. "He is...her brother, Xavier."

"*Brother?*" he repeated, eyes wide.

"Yes," the older Vampire said, as though burdened with yet another secret he did not desire to spill. "Yes, her brother. Eleanor Black's sibling, though we doubt she knows of him. Procured after Eleanor came to him, out of the fear of their mother's heart, or so he let slip to me." The scars on his face then, illuminated gravely by the fire he stood near, made him seem quite small, Xavier thought. The scars no longer the only thing sullying the Vampire's visage—there was so much more to Aleister, to all the Creatures in this Order of the Dragon that Xavier had read about, but to know it was real, given life in the forlorn Vampire before him...

That Dracula could keep his secrets hidden well, yes, but this...

"Why did he take him? What use would he have for—" But his words died in his throat, for Christopher Black must have been yet another thing, a pawn for the Great Vampire to carry out his plan, to find his replacement, for even then, Xavier thought darkly, the Great Vampire had to have known when he would permanently die...

A strange nothingness filled him, and he half-wondered what Eleanor would think had she known she had a brother, and why didn't her mother, Sindell Black tell her anything? He had long resolved the wistful thought of Dracula not desiring to share his secrets freely...

Aleister said, "There is much that must be explained, Xavier, Dracula's...deceptions are numerous—but what is most important now is that the Vampire is acquired. Though our...task has been activated, we are truly not a formidable strength until we are all assembled."

He pushed aside thoughts on family Black to stare clearly at the Vampire. "What strength are you talking about? Those medallions?"

Aleister turned away. He let out one long sigh before he said, "The medallions are imbued with a kind of power—Dracula's blood—his light. It is the light of his soul, what little he could recover while forced to roam Earth as a Creature of the Night. When all Creatures who hold one are pulled together, a working unit, truly, the red light intensifies around each Knight, and we are...as I am to understand it...impenetrable...at least, by previous Dark World standards.

"The medallions were created in a time before Elite Creatures— we do not know what affects her dread would have on the beacons. But if the disappearance of Arminius and Nicholai are any indication, it seems they may not be as all-encompassing as once thought.

"The medallions are pure in Dracula's blood, his light. Eleanor's...power, though taken from the same source, is not. Two things, much like we Vampires and our adversaries, the Lycans, that when placed together can have...disastrous consequences."

Xavier stared. It would make sense for her dread to interfere with the medallions when their power was put in such base terms. After all, it was the blood of the Ancients and the blood of humans that could create either Creature, indeed.

Then what, he thought, *would be the end result of two vastly different powers filling the World?*

Eleanor's dread already encompassed all, if the only thing that would stop it is the gathering of all Knights of this Order, there would be nothing for it but to find this Christopher Black, Arminius, Nicholai, and see what true power this Order of the Dragon holds.

He was immensely curious as to the supposed power of the Creatures chosen, and if they would be imbued with this red light, impenetrable throughout the Dark World like Aleister said...what would it hurt to ensure they were truly all gathered?

Dracula's world was now his, secrets, rules, and all...

"Do you know where Christopher Black is located? Where Dracula had him?" he asked next, staring upon the Vampire that had taken to staring into the orange flames.

"Of course not," he said hoarsely, "I'd only learned of his existence when given a medallion—they truly *are* beacons." And his gaze found Xavier's. "I...received my medallion one dark night, the very night I left Dracula's...graces. A Creature cloaked in darkness arrived at my home, and before I even knew I'd been invaded, the medallion was around my neck and it couldn't be removed... I didn't see the Creature, Xavier, I felt him, knew he was there, but he was... something else entirely."

"What?" Xavier asked.

"I hardly know. Regardless of it all, the medallion," and he clutched a hand to his chest, "would not lift itself from my neck. I've tried everything throughout the years—magic, spells, hexes, curses, weapons, hammers, daggers, spears—nothing would work." And his stare held a haunting desperation.

Xavier stepped for his desk, moving to the drawers most near his chair, and pulled the topmost one out, vaguely remembering the name he'd seen atop one of the parchment folders...

"Xavier?" Aleister's voice sounded over the crackle of the flames, the whispers of Dracula in his head.

He did not respond, even as he located the folder at last and opened it, staring intently on the many papers that remained within it: *"Necklace-bearer,"* he read aloud, *"can never be contacted again."* He looked up to see Aleister staring at the folder, his lips curled into a frown, brow furrowed, eyes black.

"Wh-why would he have that?" Aleister whispered.

Xavier closed the folder. *What was this about?* "Why wouldn't he?" he said carefully, placing the folder on the desk; Aleister's gaze followed it expertly. "He has a file on every Vampire, every Creature. I've read almost all of them—"

"Including mine? You've read mine before?"

"Yes."

His black eyes widened, his lips parting, the words a cold breath prepared to be uttered. But they never came.

Instead, he turned and strode the length of the office, stopping just before the green curtains, Xavier's mind running to if he were to pull it aside and reveal a door, but he did no such thing, instead, he exhaled a deep breath, and turned, saying, "That Vampire hated me. My reluctance to seek out my only sons, to turn them into Vampires, my procrastination on the matter...he would not let up about my *need* to do it.

"When Christian showed up, I silently begged him to leave—and when you found him and forced him to leave—I was relieved. But he returned and I knew...something more was at work, be it fate or destiny, I don't know but—Dracula's voice would not leave my head the more I stared upon him...explained what I was...what I could make him...

"I bit him," he continued slowly, methodically, as though the words, the memory would disappear the more he talked, "I tasted his blood, I drank it greedily though I was not thirsty. And when you arrived," he turned, his stare a strange mixture of resolve and apology, "I feared you would not...agree...you wouldn't...take as easily as Christian..."

Xavier stared.

Aleister continued, "You did—you agreed so readily, and in your eyes I saw what you would become. As you rose from the floor, the coldness of death so complete around you, I knew the moment Dracula laid eyes upon you..."

Xavier saw it clearly, the sight of Christian upon the floor, the Vampire, once so clouded in his memories, now clear, Aleister, staring upon Christian, forlorn...

"He forced you, all of you Creatures, to do what was against your very being," he began, watching the scarred Vampire, "I read the files, I know about you, about Aurora, Dragor, Peroneous—Dracula's...obsession with his plan to have a taste of humanity...

"I know you hate him, father, but what's done is done. If we must move for Christopher Black, for Arminius, Nicholai, then we must."

"I know, Xavier, I know!" he shouted, his voice thunderous, echoing on in Xavier's ears. "I know what must be done—"

"Then why did you not move immediately to gather the others? To tell me what must be done?"

"I told you already, I was busy with Elite Creatures—"

"You were stalling," Xavier snapped, narrowing his eyes at the Vampire before him. He could see it all so clearly: Aleister taking refuge in his newly rebuilt cottage in Cedar Village, not opening the black door, not taking a step outside to eye the darkened sky, the sky that would not shed light, not anymore. "You stalled the more it became clear Eleanor's forces were growing. You all did."

And he stepped to his father, feeling the red light surge within him as he moved. The red light blared through Aleister's cloak and robes, although muffled, its heat could still be felt. He said, "I understand Dracula lied to all of you, I understand he forced many of you to do the unthinkable, but father, we cannot spare anymore time. I've spent three weeks repairing connections between towns, cities, making sure all Vampires, all Creatures, knew the Vampire City was safe once more.

"But that cannot really be true unless we stop her," he said, letting the words he had let sit in the back of his mind leave his lips at last. A hand gripped tight the handle of the sword at his waist. "I must go back to Evert, and the Order of the Dragon is coming with me."

"Xavier—"

"No, father. These are my Creatures now; this is my world. I cannot...sit behind that desk and talk Elves down, not when Arminius is missing, Vampires injured," and the thought surfaced before he could press it down: *I truly understand how he felt.*

The sense of urgency was all around him, the pull of the sword, the red light that would flare whenever he would think on Dracula, hear his voice deep within his mind...

Even as he sat at his desk those three weeks, addressing various Creatures, he felt the desire, no, the very need, to rise and *do* for the Dark World consume him, but he did not move, for he had told himself that if something was truly amiss, his ever-strong father, the Creatures promised to him would rise and tell him what, if anything, was wrong.

He almost laughed at the thought now.

"Round up your Creatures, father," Xavier said, staring past him at the green curtain that lined the wall, wondering, indeed, what more Damion knew about the mansion that he did not. "We are taking back the Dark World, whatever the cost."

※

Arminius lifted his hand from the ground and stared at the faint light of the sun hidden behind the clouds of terrible darkness, dread. He let out a slow sigh, stepping gingerly with his cane along the single street that led straight through the quaint town.

The street lamps flickered between the darkness as he moved quickly past shop and home, never stopping until he reached the large shop whose green sign above the equally dark green doors shone in the orange light.

He pulled open a door and exhaled a huff of tired breath, allowing his lungs to catch up with him. It was with a distasteful thought of getting old, "Bah!" that he knew he would not be able to appear and disappear from places as he pleased for long. His magic was not as strong as it once was...

The medallion beneath his robes let out a pulling heat, and he straightened, wiped sweat from his brow, and pressed forth into the dark shop.

But the old man that sat in the large dark green armchair did not stir even as the Elf moved for the brown wooden door behind the low, long counter to the back of the room. "We must do something about that Vampire, Arminius," he said, his voice low.

Arminius dropped a long-fingered hand from the door's knob to turn and stare at him. He cradled a small blue book in his wrinkled hands, but did not appear to be reading it. It remained closed, unreadable black letters on its cover.

"Has he attempted to leave again, Terry?" Arminius asked.

The old Enchanter nodded his head, his long gray hair swaying as he did so. His small blue eyes gleamed in the darkness as he looked up at the Elf at last. "The door shakes with his attempts. I cast a simple Impenetrable Spell every so often...of course, who knows how long it will last...how long it will be before I cannot do even that."

A flitter of darkness passed across Terry's eyes, then, and Arminius knew he thought on what every magic-enabled Creature feared: the loss of their powers. For it was coming, this Arminius knew, he just didn't know when.

"Your efforts are greatly appreciated, my friend," he said, opening the door, stepping through into darkness. He descended the stairs and whispered, *"Visor Emmolis."*

White balls of light left his fingertips and danced about the large cellar, illuminating the covered chairs, armchairs, desks, tables, and lamps pushed against the four walls. To the center of the room there was one table uncovered, the body of Nicholai Noble atop it.

As a ball of light moved towards the table to shed light over his sharp face, eyes red with hunger, Arminius stepped to him, and placed a single hand over the place the medallion rested against his chest. *"Reparilis Nam Emmolis-Cora."*

All at once he felt his feet leave the floor and he soared higher and higher into a dark red air that he knew was the defunct medallion, and he waited.

His breathing hitched and became sparse the more the energy pressed around him, and he was not sure which he despised the most, Eleanor Black's energy or the Phoenixes'.

Yes, in no time at all there appeared the vision he desired, the vision he had been desperately trying to bring forth into the Vampire's consciousness, for he hoped it would help Nicholai remember what drove him to join the Order of the Dragon...

There he was, a noticeably younger Nicholai Noble, his silver hair slightly shorter than its current neck-length ruffle, seated before Dracula, his brown eyes warm as he looked upon the young Vampire.

"Now, my brilliant Noble," Dracula began, his voice sending the other Vampire to squirm in his chair. This seemed to be a most long-coming announcement. "You have proven yourself brilliantly in the 3rd Army. Lieutenant Trace speaks very highly of you."

"Thank you, your Grace," Nicholai said, his lips parting into a wide smile showing his sharp fangs.

Arminius stifled a shudder at the sight.

Dracula waited but a moment before continuing. "Now, there is something important I need you to do for me. But you must...reach your Age before it can be done. Do you understand, Noble?"

The blue-eyed Vampire's brow furrowed with his confusion, but he said, "I do, your Grace."

"It's fine if you don't, Nicholai," Dracula said, though Arminius could feel the air of something important in Dracula's demeanor the more it was he stared at the young Vampire. Appraising him, judging him, hoping against hope that he had not made a mistake in his choice...

Nicholai must have felt it as well for his smile disappeared and he said, quite sternly, "I do understand, your Grace. Whatever your Grace needs from me will be done to the best of my ability."

Dracula smiled and the red overtook the scene, but before long, and with yet another deep, haggard breath from the Elf, another scene appeared.

The room was dark but the two figures within it were wide awake, staring at each other with equal alarm.

The woman was feral in her fear, her dark brown hair loose as it fell around her shoulders and back, her exquisite blue day dress sitting upon her body, but it seemed, the more Arminius stared, the more he could see the anticipation had been thwarted, a layer of unease replacing it.

"Wh-what are you?" she asked the man who stood on the opposite side of the room.

Nicholai Noble had reached his Age. His hair resembled what it did now, his blue eyes retained their cold, calculating stare, and the sword at his waist looked as though it belonged there. And there was a protrusion beneath his shirt that looked terribly familiar.

"I am human," he said, though his gaze looked humorous suddenly, as though he could not commit to the lie.

She said nothing but remained on the other side of the single bed within the room, and continued to stare. It was as though she were trying to place where he came from, if anywhere at all.

After several painful moments, she gave up and took a deep breath, sinking atop the bed, removing her gloves from her hands. Without turning to eye him, she said, "I won't be meeting him tonight, will I?"

"It is...a long journey to his dwelling place, my Lady," he said.

She looked at him over a shoulder with his remark. "And he is really a Count? What would a Count want with me?"

He said nothing, but Arminius almost thought he was prepared to speak, the eagerness of the young man a few years before almost peeling through. It was then that he wondered why Dracula would choose the Vampire to watch over Alexandria Stone.

"I see," she said after a moment of silence. And with that, she lay atop the bed, her back to him, and shortly, surprisingly, drifted off to sleep.

Nicholai had waited but several moments before she'd entered a deep sleep, for he must have known the excitement of seeing a Count for a young woman would have tired her, until he stepped towards her.

Something about her seemed to alarm him, for his gaze had changed from austere control to utter disbelief. Arminius watched in bemusement as the Vampire ran a hand across her bare arm, and he was astonished when she didn't wake immediately, for he knew the touch of a Vampire...knew it well...

No, she remained asleep, and there was a gleam, a glow in his blue eyes that made Arminius let out a surprised gasp. *The* Vampure *knew magic*. Yes, he knew that glow, that concentrated glare, even if it were marred with disbelief...the Vampire knew magic and was using it to keep the woman subdued.

How curious, Arminius thought.

He watched in further wonder as the Vampire whispered something he could not catch, and then stepped from her, his gaze once more removed, his mission complete, the soldier returning...

The vision changed and soon Arminius stared at a furious Dracula, an apologetic Nicholai kneeling before him. They were in some secluded wood, the light of the sun shining clearly upon both their heads as they were in a clearing, although Arminius did not see a golden ring upon Nicholai's finger.

"...How could you let this happen?!" Dracula was screaming at the top of his lungs.

Nicholai never stood, nor did he lift his head. "I don't know what happened, your Grace," he said, his voice low, "I awoke and the woman was—"

"Do not tell me she is gone, Noble! I grabbed you up from the dregs of the sewers you ungrateful boy! I granted you the bloody name Noble, hoping that you would be the one to help! You would be the one—can I rely on no one?!"

"Your Grace, if you would just give me another chance—"

Dracula's eyes turned red in the light of the sun and then something happened that Arminius could not understand:

Dracula's face elongated, his chin becoming more pointed the more it grew, his ears pointed high on the sides of his head like an Elf, and his teeth, all of them, sharpened so that the two previous fangs that had sat within his mouth were indistinguishable from the many that now filled it.

He stretched out horribly pointed fingers, the nails much longer, much sharper than they were before; they were also black.

Arminius watched as the Dracula-Creature gripped tight Nicholai's throat and lifted him into the air, the sun shining brilliantly upon his handsome, horrified face.

"*You disappoint me, boy,*" the Dracula-Creature snarled, though his thin lips never moved.

Arminius soon realized the Creature was speaking through the mind.

"I," Nicholai choked, grasping at the long, large arm before him, "I—am sorry, y-your Grace. I did not mean—"

"*Yet you do it all the same!*" he roared, throwing Nicholai across the clearing, where he landed against a tree, his body limp. "*All of you—disappointments!*"

And as he began to stalk towards the unconscious Vampire, Arminius took a deep breath and shouted, "*Aven Nam Emmolis-Cora! Aven Nam Emmolis-Cora!*"

And the dark red air dispersed, the large cellar returned, the white orbs flittering calmly around them both, and Arminius stared in horror at the unconscious Vampire atop the table.

The memories had not seemed to cause a dent in the Vampire's state: his eyes still remained open, but unseeing, the medallion never lighting.

Arminius clutched his own medallion at his chest and let out a slow, haggard breath. He waved a shaking hand and a chair left its place and zoomed to him. He sat without a look back, his eyes wide, wet with oncoming tears, and as he stared at Nicholai, now eye-level with the body, he knew they, all of them, had been tricked, miserably, into working for a monster.

For he no longer feared the crushing aura of the Elite Creatures that reigned dominant outside the shop's walls, nor did he fear the paralyzing energy of the Phoenixes that filled every medallion along with Dracula's red light.

No, he feared the Creature he had just seen. The true face of the Great Vampire. And as he waved another hand, the light dispersing into nothingness, a tremendous fear filled him, and he hoped the others were moving, and quickly, to locate him, to save him, to save them all.

Chapter Five

TRAPPED

Christian Delacroix stared at her within the red carriage, feeling her eyes burrowing into him, feeling their judgmental, pressing gaze. "Paint a portrait," he said after a time, "it will last longer."

She did not remove her gaze. Instead, she said, "I'm sorry, I just cannot *believe* you went so long without blood."

"Well, thanks to you that is no longer an issue." And he stared daggers at her, never tearing his gaze from those brown-green eyes, for she had "allowed" him the...pleasure of feeding on a maid, under her watch, of course.

He had never been so humiliated in his life or death.

It was a deal under the implication that the maid's mind would be cleared once it was done, and of course he wasn't "allowed" to drain her to death (how he *needed* the blood), under Alexandria's watch.

He let out a loud laugh, ignoring her startled gaze, for it was preposterous that he was forced to feed under the watchful eye of a terribly cross human.

How far he had come from the one the humans feared...but of course a lot had changed in the two months since he had met Alexandria Stone.

"Do share with the class," she said, brow furrowed in deep thought.

He giggled as he realized how ridiculous he must have seemed to her. "I was just thinking about my breakfast. How restrictive it was."

She blinked. "Restrictive in the sense that you could not kill her?"

"Restrictive in the sense that a pair of un-seeable eyes kept themselves upon me, forbidding me the notion."

She scoffed. "Forgive me for wanting to ensure the young woman lived."

"Ah, like you, yourself are any judge of who shall live, when you shall be drinking from the maids about us soon enough."

The anger in her gaze could not be stilled. It was humorous in the way she had him on this proverbial leash. He could not feed freely in her presence, but much to his surprise, with her will, her words so clearly spoken, he had his thirst returned to him.

She can control far more than previously thought...

He had not yet decided whether or not this was desirable, for if she could control a Vampire with the mere word... But had she not controlled a Lycan with the same, forcing it to go?

It was then that he stared at her, taking in her anger, that gaze so sharp.

What a formidable Vampire she would make, he thought, for it was in that gaze, her voice, that he knew whatever was happening to her had just begun.

The carriage jolted to a stop and he pressed his hands to the doors on either side to keep himself from flying into her.

A door opened. A man stepped aside, bowing low as Alexandria took his hand without a look in his direction.

Once her shoes touched the dark stone of the sidewalk, Christian let himself leave the carriage, placing two coins into the pocket of the man's suit jacket. When he turned to eye her, she was staring at the sky, and his gaze followed suit. When they'd left the manor, the sky was slightly darker than is normal for a London morning, but now it was practically night, or as if a storm threatened to roll over them at any moment.

She pulled her light traveling cloak tighter around her shoulders, as if to keep at bay a wind that did not pass, and turned to him, her gaze expectant. "Is this where Lord Vonderheide said he would be meeting us?"

He looked up at the inn, squeezed between two tall buildings, and as the carriage pulled away behind them, he read the words that had been painted on a newly placed door:

The Dragon's Cavern

He extended an arm for Alexandria to take. She did so, and together they moved for the door.

The room beyond was dark: he could just make out the faint glow of small candles placed upon three tables spread out in the large hall.

Splinters of wood lined the dark floor, and as he stepped for the counter right across from the door, a serious-looking man appeared out of the darkness to stand just before them, dark hands splayed in a welcoming gesture, though by the look of his tattered cloak, his cruel black-eyed gaze, he was anything but welcoming.

"Welcome, Lord Delacroix, Miss Stone," he said, his voice deep against the dread-filled air of the place.

Christian felt Alexandria step behind him, then, and he thought she had good reason.

"Where is Victor?" Christian asked.

He rubbed the black hair that covered his chin, his strange eyes gleaming in the faint candlelight. "Victor will be arriving tomorrow."

Christian stepped closer to the man, sure to keep his gaze upon him. "Why tomorrow? I was under the impression my brother was in serious trouble."

The man reached for two keys in the many hide-a-way cabinets, and turned back to face them

Christian stepped up to the counter, well aware Alexandria remained near the door. He half-wondered how he was able to smell her blood, when he realized she was quite possibly letting him.

He ran a finger across the keys, staring the man in his eyes, wondering if he were a Lycan.

"If it cannot wait then why is he meeting us tomorrow? And we're to remain here until he's ready?" He lifted the keys to eye level.

The man's black eyes surveyed the keys for a minute. "Yes, your rooms are ready and waiting. And I cannot say why Master Vonderheide is meeting you tomorrow...nevertheless...your rooms." He gestured a sweeping arm towards an old dark staircase to the back of the room.

It led into complete darkness, not a speck of light shining down, and he felt a hand wrap around his arm. Looking down, he saw her, the uncertainty in her gaze, and he knew what she thought.

"You do understand this is quite odd," Christian began, staring at the man.

His head tilted to the side and he quite reminded Christian of a dog that looked upon something curious. It was the first time Christian saw the man's hair: long, black and sleek, it trailed behind his head blending into the darkness around them.

"Odd, Lord Delacroix?" the man repeated, his brow furrowed.

"Yes, yes, this is all quite odd. The letter Victor sent made it very clear that my brother was in grave danger and that he would be meeting us here—what is this about him returning tomorrow?"

"Exactly what I said, my Lord." The man's voice was rather forceful. "He implores you and the woman stay here for the night...it would be most convenient for him."

Christian, the sudden voice sounded through his mind as the hand squeezed tighter around his arm, *something's wrong here.*

The swirl of dread entered his gut with her words.

"I see," he said at last, trying his best to ignore Alexandria's continued thoughts of, *"Wrong, wrong, wrong."* For there *was* something wrong here, and terribly so. He began to think of Elite Creatures and Victor as well, when sense snapped into him through way of Alexandria's rapid breathing. "Well...let us just head to our rooms." And he began to steer her around the counter, towards the dark stairs, when the man called out:

"But, my Lord, you don't even know what numbers your rooms are."

"Oh?" he breathed, lifting the keys to his eyes, able to make out the numbers branded into the brass: 17 and 18.

"They are our best rooms," the man said, as he and Alexandria ascended into darkness, neither daring to chance a look back.

※

"Get back James!" Lillith yelled, shooting an arrow towards an approaching beast. It fell over onto its side with a whine, blowing up blades of grass and dirt into the air and Darien stepped beside her.

"Yaddley," he said, brown eyes on the still-wounded Vampire who was holding back a Lycan with a bleeding arm. His hand dug into the beast's hairy chest and Lillith thought he attempted to rip out its heart. "Finish this."

Lillith stared and Yaddley suddenly let out a loud snarl, veins appearing in his arm, and with a step he pushed his hand into the Lycan's chest and the Lycan let out a painful roar.

Her eyes widened. *What on Earth?*

She looked to Darien. He seemed calm, pleased, even. His brown eyes were shining with admiration in the scattered sunlight.

Yaddley threw a dagger at an approaching Lycan as Minerva appeared at his side, sharp nails poised to attack yet another beast when James, who had been trembling the moment they'd left the manor some minutes ago, snarled viciously.

She stared at him, the overwhelming scent of beast filling her senses, and she let another arrow fly towards a beast that had just bounded past a terrified Satyr. She barely noticed the beast fall out of the sky with a loud whinny and land roughly on the ground at her feet, for James had doubled over in pain, low groans protruding past his lips as his clothes ripped, and he grew larger, thick brown fur appearing atop his skin—

"No!"

Damion appeared just before her, blocking her gaze from the rest of James's transformation, and she could barely question what he was doing when she heard the familiar voice amidst the low snarls and loud growls.

"Damion. So lovely to see you again."

Lillith stepped from behind him, disbelief clawing at her mind. *It could not be.*

"Lore," Damion said, brandishing his sword. Beside him Darien tensed as well: he raised a long staff, curved blades finishing it on either end.

Lore stepped forward in human form, a dirty buttoned shirt covered his chest, frayed, tan breeches adorned his legs. His feet were bare as he stepped over the bleeding corpse of one of his beasts, his brown eyes only on Damion as he went on. "You can imagine my surprise when I followed my nose to your home. Again. You have an affinity for powerful humans." His gaze moved to James, something of a smile curling his lips. "But this one isn't human anymore, is he?"

"What is the meaning of this Lore?" Damion said with a snarl.

Darien raised a dark hand. All watched as he stepped forward, the staff swaying in a fist. Yaddley, who was fending off two Lycans at Lore's back broke away from his fight to watch his Master as well.

"You bit the human, yes?" Darien asked Lore.

"I did," the King of Lycans said coldly, "and it seems he's not just human."

Damion opened his mouth to speak, but Darien said it first: "Not just human?"

Lore smiled. "He holds blood similar to my own, blood that is Ancient in origin."

At this, both Vampires seemed to freeze, and then Lillith heard Darien whisper something into the air, something she could not catch but it made her feel strange all the same. Minerva, who had been beside Yaddley the entire time, disappeared in a soft breeze.

"Nonsense, Lore," Darien said, anger in his voice, "that boy wouldn't hold Ancient blood."

Lore glared at him. "Then how do you explain that scent? The fact the boy can change in sunlight? I wouldn't put it past Dracula to set this up, make a bloody Ancient descendant his Vampire's servant."

Neither Vampire said a word, and it wasn't until Lore chuckled that anyone said anything at all.

"I," James said, voice rough as it passed through his large throat, "it hurts."

"Yes, it would. The first complete transformation is always the hardest. I take it you have not fully transformed until now?" Lore asked.

James's paws padded the soft ground and Lillith thought he desired to walk, to move within his new form. *He's restless.*

"Never," James said, and she could almost see his mind turning with thought.

Lore clapped two rough hands together and Damion jumped. "Beautiful! You transformed so quickly, as though you've practice in the art! I cannot abandon these signs. You are my new heir, and with the state our world is in, I could surely use your help in restoring my lost power."

Darien moved before anyone could see it properly: He was standing beside Damion in one second, just before Lore in the next, the staff piercing the air, a well-aimed stab towards Lore's heart.

Lore fell back to the ground before the blade could pierce his skin, swung his legs against Darien's sending the Vampire to barrel back to the ground as well, but before he could do much more, Yaddley had a dagger to Lore's throat, crouched low over him, a threatening snarl leaving his lips. The other Lycans stared and Lillith thought it strange they did not move to defend their king.

Darien stabbed the ground with the staff, rising to stand, his gaze on Lore, when Lore let out a harsh laugh, and even from the distance, Lillith could tell he truly wasn't scared. "Do you see, James, how the Vampires treat we powerful Creatures? Do you see how they fear us? How they," and he waved a tan hand through the air, "keep us down? They'll do the same to you if you let them—if you stay."

"Silence beast!" Darien commanded. The blade of the staff joined Yaddley's dagger at Lore's throat. "Now you say this man is born of Ancient blood. How can that be possible?"

"How? He's a bloody Lycan in broad daylight, Darien, pay attention! And his blood, for another, drew my men to him—to Delacroix manor. They thought him me. And how can you ask me how when you, yourself, your brother, are born of the Ancients as well?!"

Many things happened all at once:

Darien pressed the staff's blade into Lore's throat, Yaddley stepped away as though burned, Lore transformed into a beast just before Darien's blade could touch him, and James charged for Darien, knocking him to the ground, the staff flying out of hand to land upon the bloodied grass.

And before Lillith could fire an arrow at anyone at all, Lore was on his large paws, his deep voice roaring as he turned tail and leapt over the multitude of bodies that littered the ground, back toward London: "Our bloodlines shall meet time and time again, Vampires, only yours shall not remain to be passed on. I shall see to it."

No one said a word as the two Lycans that remained watched Lore pass them before they reverted to human form, strange smiles upon their faces. Lillith blinked, not understanding. Damion whispered, "Damn," and they disappeared in a harrowing gust of blackened dread that sent the remaining Dark Creatures alive in the woods running in opposite directions.

"Elite Creatures?" Lillith asked. Yes, it was strange the Lycans appeared in their beastly forms in daylight—why hadn't they noticed it?

Darien rose to his feet once more as James moved away from him, reverting back into a human man. He remained on hands and knees, sweat dripping down his hair and face, and aside from being completely naked, there was a newness to him, a feral nature Lillith could not ignore. *Ancient blood?* she thought as Darien stepped to him, and much to her surprise, extended a hand for him to take.

It was not long before he did so. Darien pulled him close, staring him down with a ferociousness she had never seen in either him nor Damion, and said, "How did you come to work for Xavier Delacroix?"

James looked exhausted. "I...my aunt received the letter..."

"Letter?" Damion asked. "What letter?"

"The letter from a Count Dracul...she told me he'd sent it when I was just a baby." A cough escaped him. "My mother...died shortly after I was born. My aunt...believes my father killed her. But she won't...whenever I ask...she never—" And James fell to his knees at last, his head falling forward over his chest and Lillith realized with a start that he'd fallen asleep. Just like that.

Darien dropped his hand and looked to his brother. "How likely is it that Dracula had a bloody Ancient-born Lycan stay in Xavier's home for twenty-odd years?"

Damion said nothing for quite some time, and it wasn't until the loud flap of wings sounded from beyond the wall at his back that he said anything at all.

"Given what we've done for the Vampire, given to him, Darien, I'm hard-pressed to find this surprising, if it is, indeed, truth."

"That's what I feared," Darien said, looking back down upon James.

No one said a thing for a long while until the sound of hurried footsteps filled the air and they all looked up as one.

Ewer Caddenhall came bounding through the trees, his golden robes shimmering here and there amidst the sun's sparse light, his old face taut into unreadable emotion. Once he passed the last trees before the clearing, he said, "What's this about Lore? About James holding Ancient blood?"

Darien motioned with a hand for Yaddley to grab James before he turned for Ewer. "I wish we knew."

✳

Victor Vonderheide stared at her, her black eyes illuminated in the light of the many torches around the room.

He could not think when pressed with her gaze. It was the damning energy. The crushing, dread-inducing energy that would not allow one proper thought. It was Eleanor's scent in your nose, Eleanor's sultry voice in your head, Eleanor's touch on your skin the moment your mind would wander from her...

"Victor?" the low voice sounded pulling him from the dark thoughts.

He blinked, looking up at once, her dark eyes upon him with dimmed interest. "Something wrong?"

"Wrong? No, nothing, nothing. I was just...musing on the next plan to be set in motion. The Merpeople of Tolp, their waters churn with their unease. Trent believes they will be an easy attainment if we move fast before any opposing forces can get to them first."

"Ah," she gasped, her gaze relaxing in the light. She ran her slender fingers across the silver necklaces at her chest bringing his eyes there...how one settled in-between her breasts... "This is excellent, Victor."

His dead heart beat faster as her words echoed on in his mind long after she'd spoken. "*Excellent,*" he repeated dimly. It was not until she smiled reassuringly that he found his voice, "I am aware it is not where you truly desire to be."

"No," she said, her smile fading, "it is not. But Merpeople are essential to control of the waters, their Creatures...although grotesque, are easily untouchable. You have done well to heed Trent's words. Yet," and she stepped even closer, her long black hair flying out behind her the more she moved, "we need...better Creatures." And her voice took on such a low, heeding air that he could not help but lick his lips.

He merely stared, her dark eyes shining in the light of the torches as she gazed directly at him, and he knew what she meant, what she would do...

Her hand was in the air, her touch he did not feel until the dread, the darkness overtook his vision, and he let the sigh of relief, of sheer pleasure leave his lips.

"*Victor,*" her voice echoed on in nothingness, rendering his mind, already lost on thoughts quite dark, incapable of independent thought. All he knew was her, as it should be. "*Victor...you know who we need.*"

"Y-yes," he gasped, the dread filling his throat, making it hard to speak, the cold thickening, freezing, "I-I know."

"*Then why,*" the darkness continued, "*did you not return to me the moment you stilled those Creatures?*"

The dread thickened in his dead heart, but he knew it was not hers. *How could she know?* "I—I did not," he stammered before the darkness rippled just before his eyes, and the voice returned:

"*My reach extends to all my Creatures. I felt the medallion die. I felt my energy take its place. Where are these Creatures, Victor?*"

"They," he whispered, unable to still the thoughts, the stark fear that filled his mind; the fear that she would destroy him, indeed, "they—they escaped."

"*Did they?*"

"I—they did."

"*This cannot stand. I need those Creatures. One of them has been touched. He cannot be taken away from me. We must move forward. Do you understand?*"

The pull of dread that had been sitting in his throat pushed upwards, leaving his lips in a terrible rasp, and the moment it did, the darkness dispersed; she was before him again, her front illuminated in the orange glow of the torches as his eyes adjusted to the light.

"Eleanor," he began, unsure of what more to say, what could be said, but she merely smiled, and it was as if nothing had happened, as if she had not taken his sight, his will, his desire to speak clear from him.

"Find them, Victor, they cannot be allowed to be returned to Xavier, to those other...trinkets."

Question sparked in his mind the more he stared at her. Was he not to oversee Carvaca's castle? Was he not to painstakingly wait there until Xavier showed, stilling him from entering it? "You're demoting me to this meaningless task?" he asked before he could stop the words. *I did not leave Dracula to be cast aside again.*

"Meaningless? No, you misunderstand, dear Victor. This is not meaningless. This is progress. The kind of progress I have been waiting for since we left that damned City.

"The Creature's medallion that is now filled with my energy, my call—he will soon rise to do my bidding. I am aware they will try to stop the process from happening once they know what is going on, but this we cannot allow. We have grown stronger, yes, but they will soon follow behind," and she smiled again, her sharp fangs bathed in the glow of the torches, "and we must be untouchable before they can even muster the knowledge to do so."

Her eyes were red, her gaze placed upon him, and he knew she had given him his answer.

He stilled the feelings of anger that arose, the seeds of doubt that had sprouted the moment he agreed to fight alongside her, and he did what any sane Dark Creature would do when faced with a deadly, powerful force:

He kneeled.

Chapter Six

THE OLIVE BRANCH

He lifted himself from the bed: it far exceeded the tough bed he'd been given whilst in his tower, though he tried not to think of that if he could help it.

He reached out for the cold leather of the handle at his side and once his fingers touched it, he squeezed it, lifting the sword off the bed to appraise it.

"At least I kept you," he said, replacing it at his side. He swung his feet over the side of the bed and pressed them against the hard floor, staring at the peeling, cracked wood.

Far better than the wet stone, he thought with a smile, lifting from the green sheets.

His black hair fell in waves at his shoulders and back, and he moved across the room to reach the partially destroyed dresser where he kept what little he owned.

The medallion swaying against his chest, he opened the topmost drawer, revealing the thin buttoned shirt, stained with droplets of blood here and there along the sleeves, and the memory returned:

He carried her from the flames, not stopping in his swift steps until he reached the safety of a side road, never traversed in the dead of night. He placed her carefully atop the ground, staring upon her gentle frame, her face soft, even as her eyes remained closed, and he wished that they would open.

Such a fool, he thought, blinking upon the bloodied shirt. He threw it on, buttoning it, pulling on the simple black vest the Vampire had given him, the black traveling cloak as well.

"Awake Mister Black?" the voice beyond the old door called as he tucked the medallion beneath his shirt, hoping against great hope that it would not blare...not now, not here.

"Just," he called, sheathing the sword in the black leather wrap he'd fashioned one of those many dark nights, years before. He was settling it around his waist when the knob turned.

"I'm coming in," the man said, opening the door, "oh, you look far better than last night."

I had my full of your guests last night, he thought. Smiling his best, he said, "Sleep does wonders for the soul, or so I've heard." He watched the strange, small man stare at him, emotions he could not guess passing across the thin face.

It was a while before the man smiled back. "Quite," he said, "we're having beans and boar sausage if you're so inclined."

"I wouldn't miss it," he said, stepping behind the man, thinking only of the girl he'd saved, the medallion pulsing against his dead heart.

✳

His sword vibrated against his leg as he moved through the trees, mind gone on visions of Dracula storming through these very woods, these same Creatures at his heels. But, he reminded himself, Dracula did not have them at his back, not all at once, not like this, indeed.

"We will need to ask Evert the Ancient Elder what can be done about Arminius and Nicholai," Aleister was saying.

Xavier did not turn to eye them, even when Dragor responded with, "Agreed. That giant would surely know the business behind these medallions. What can be done with them, how far their...reach extends."

He stepped over several fallen branches, his thoughts clamoring on just what could have happened to the Elf, indeed. The note told them all nothing in way of what exactly happened, and none of them had any true ideas on what that could have been.

Elite Creatures attacking Members of the Order of the Dragon? He continued his walk even as the thought gained greater traction, a chilling thought rising up behind it. *Could she know they existed?*

No, he reasoned, stepping over the bones of what once had to be a small animal, *they could not know of this Order.* He, himself, had been reminded of him this very morning, before that their importance teeming at the back of his mind, but never truly surfacing. Yet still the dread in the air could not be denied, despite their ever increasing proximity to this enchanted castle...

He turned, his eyes locking on his father's as though they had known where to gaze. With two fingers, he motioned for the Vampire to leave the others and reach him, and once close enough, Xavier started, quite sure he was letting his mind get the better of him, "Eleanor...her men...*why* would they attack Arminius?"

The scarred Vampire looked upon him in hidden exasperation. "We've been over this, Xavier. Her men are everywhere—they would have stumbled upon Arminius and Nicholai sooner or later. Both Creatures are hardly known for keeping still, regardless of the times upon us."

He blinked. "It makes sense," he agreed, letting die the voice in his throat that would shout its ill ease at all that was around them now.

Perhaps, he thought, turning from his father with a curt nod of thanks, *I am letting her maddening energy get to me once more.*

He gripped the handle of the sword at his waist, knowing that could not be allowed to happen. Not again.

Shaking away the guilt at all he had caused almost a month before, he turned his attention to the many trees before them, the grass specked with the bones and corpses of the Creatures left over from the battle at the Council of Creatures Meeting.

"Xavier!"

He turned, the sword leaving his grip at the sight.

Two hooded figures stood in-between he and the battle-ready Creatures, their respective swords, daggers, and glowing hands raised high against the strange figures' backs.

Xavier eyed them, unable to see their eyes in the shadow of their low, tattered hoods. The more he stared, the more he noticed the dark splatters of black here and there along the rest of their cloaks: dried blood.

He raised a hand, the four Creatures behind them tensing at his movement, their medallions beginning to blare their red color beneath their cloaks.

"How did you get behind me without me knowing?" he asked the two Creatures, wondering how indeed they appeared without a burst of wind, a sweeping chill of utter dread...

Neither said a word, but swept both hands in a horizontal motion across their midsections, a surge of thick, black energy leaving their gloved palms, moving down to the grass at their blood-stained boots. Xavier watched in bewilderment as the blackness solidified until it formed a thick wall, and then one of them spoke, his voice a strange deepness that echoed on in the air, against the trees long after he had stopped:

"Xavier Delacroix is here."

And the small wall stretched and reached upwards, blocking his view of the two Creatures, the Order Members behind them.

Before he could say a word or do anything, the black wall formed a large door, opening against the late afternoon air, the Creature that appeared there staring upon him with unveiled glee: his black hair was short, swept atop his head, his eyes black, fanged smile wide.

"Amentias?" Xavier whispered, hand upon the Ascalon. He barely realized he felt no pulse from the sword when Amentias stepped forward, boot not making a sound upon the grass, a long-nailed hand reaching forward—

Xavier smelled the heavy scent of lilac and blood in the next moment, and she appeared in his mind's eye, beckoning, calling, long black hair whirling behind her head in a brazen wind—

The sharp pain of the long nails piercing his chest brought him out of his mind, away from her, and his eyes widened as he realized Amentias had grabbed onto the front of his traveling cloak, and was attempting to pull him into the swelling darkness of the portal he remained within.

"No!" he cried, feeling the emanating dread pulse against his front, burrowing into his skin, finding refuge within his mind.

"Xavier, do not resist me..."

No, not again.

And then it returned, the flash of sanctimonious air he had held while trapped in his mind those weeks before, her king, the Dark World fallen at their hand, the curious woman the only one not yet turned.

Christian's eyes filled his vision next, their hatred clear, and the spark of indignation filled his dead heart, for the Vampire had to know his place! And yet...he was the Vampire's very sibling, he would only do what was right...what was just...

A horrific sound pulled him from his reverie and he opened his eyes. Amentias was no longer clutching at his traveling cloak, he was now doubled over, a blood-dripping hand cradling the blade of a sword that jutted out of his midsection.

And then the voice spoke, its owner appearing behind the wounded Elite Creature, and Xavier felt his blood run cold in his veins:

"Xavier, how *sweet* of you to leave your beloved City, make it easier to find you."

He watched the tongue slither between the thin lips and he stifled the snarl that threatened to leave his throat. "Aciel."

"Yes," the Elite Creature said, stepping past Amentias, moving out of the dark portal to stand upon the grass, "it is I. Forgive my foolish friend here, Xavier, but we had to see you. We've spent weeks trying to track you down, reach you where is best."

He released the Ascalon, the silver blade gleaming in the sparse sunlight that beamed through the leaves, and he wondered just what the others were doing, for he could not see them beyond the door so vast, indeed, he realized with a pang of terror in his dead heart that he could not hear them at all. "You sought me?" he repeated, knowing this Creature couldn't be trusted.

He forced the lingering feeling of dread, confusion, and righteous indignation to leave his mind, for he knew the Creature before him was steeped in Eleanor's energy—his very presence would cause the memories of that most confusing night at Cedar Village to return.

But the more he stood there, staring upon him, the more he realized he felt nothing, no rush of dread, just a steady pulse of it, which came, he quickly gathered, from the door of darkness behind them.

"We sought you," Aciel repeated, calm, "and we merely ask you for your assistance. You see," he went on before Xavier could ask, "much has happened since we met at Cedar Village that...horrid night. We are changing, Xavier Delacroix, we don't know what in to, but we are aware we're losing the ability to hold each form as well as we would three weeks before."

The sword lowered in his hand. "What?"

"Her energy," Amentias coughed, bringing Xavier's gaze to him. He was still on his knees, sword still placed within his abdomen, "Her energy...you cannot feel it from us, can you?"

He nodded, unsure of what was truly happening. How could they lose the ability to turn from Vampire to human, to Lycan as they pleased?

"It..." Aciel said, bringing the attention back to himself, "was Dracula's sword. When we touched it while facing off against you, your Creatures, we were forever changed. I believe," he said with a pleasant smile, however wide it was, "we were imbued with a bit of the power Dracula's sword holds. It...interfered with Eleanor's carefully crafted power...and this," he waved a hand to Amentias at his side, "is the result."

He stared once more at the black-haired Creature who still bled from his wound. "What happened to him? Why did you stab him?"

"It needed to be done. To keep him...us...together as it were. We are...I believe we are dying, Xavier, Dracula's power unable to take over as Eleanor's fights it. Dracula's red light," and as he said this the same red light Xavier knew to blare from his sword, the medallions, filled Aciel's irises, "is within us, and it will not leave. We have tried various...ways to get it out, but...it is there.

"We discovered the act of consuming the blood of another Elite Creature keeps the more...undesirable symptoms under control.

"But you can understand why, after three weeks of drinking the blood of Eleanor's Creatures and then killing them discreetly some concern was caused amongst the others. We have been out of Eleanor's...graces since we touched the Ares...we do not smell like her, we do not truly hold her blood anymore...we are...essentially outcasts." And there was a quiet sadness in his strange gaze that

Xavier could, miraculously, understand. He could easily see both Creatures struggling to keep themselves together before her, their insides falling apart, their energy no longer what it used to be.

He stared at the dark-haired Creatures, discerning them closely, doing his best to feel any trace of dread upon them, any hint of a lie. There was none.

"What," he began, hesitating on replacing the Ascalon, "do you want from me?"

And Aciel gazed down at Amentias who returned the gaze wearily. "Simple," Aciel said, bringing his gaze back to Xavier, "we want to join you on your quest to end Eleanor and all she has wrought upon this World."

He swallowed the snort of disbelief, a wry smile turning up the corners of his lips. "I...I can't...you can't expect me to believe that you wish to abandon Eleanor and join me in taking her down," he said, "it's—this could very well be an elaborate trap if my past experiences with you, Aciel, are to be remembered."

And at this, Aciel's eyes widened in anger, his red eyes glowing brighter sending the sword to pulse at Xavier's side. "My world has been turned upside down! If this were a trap, Vampire, we would have killed you already. As it stands, we are hearing...a...voice in our heads, a voice that is *not* hers. You have no idea how dangerous that is—to not hear Eleanor's continuous call. The others are aware we are tainted, we can no longer go back to her; *we have no place there.*

"And besides," he went on, indignation spewing his words, "we *know* Eleanor's energy, we *know* her mind...what she would reveal to us, anyway, and we can give you this if you would only give us what we ask: protection."

His eyes widened as this realization reached his mind with a burst of red light at his hip. "You would truly give us her secrets?" he whispered, hardly daring to believe the information that was at his doorstep. To know her...to remember all that she had revealed while lost in his mind...to have the advantage over her deadly forces whose energies filled the air slowly dissolving Dark Creatures' energies.

"We would," Aciel said, red eyes glowing.

Xavier stared upon them, marveling at what he was told. And then the red light filled his vision, and the voice that had been whispering a steady stream in the back of his mind since he'd heard it once free from her hold, grew louder:

"Xavier, you must become greater than you are. Please listen to me—you need to be all you must for this world. With the power I have given you, you alone can do it—must do it."

And there it was again, how Dracula must have felt when faced with such a choice, for he was sure the Vampire faced something similar, though he could not know why.

"Xavier! My king, are you well!?" the harried shouts issued dimly from beyond the door.

"The portal is weakening, Xavier," Aciel said hurriedly, and indeed the black wall was beginning to fade, its edges becoming a wispy gray smoke. "We need an answer. We need it now. We either leave the portal for good or we return. And we cannot return."

And there he saw it: the pain and fear in the Creature's dark eyes.

"Xavier! What the bloody hell is going on?!" another frantic shout issued past the wall, this time louder than the last.

The sword gave out yet another pulse and his right arm flew upwards, Aciel stepping forward and grasping it immediately. He gave it a firm shake, and the portal behind him let out a red flash of light and dispersed in a large wisp of black smoke.

And before Xavier could say or do a thing, Aciel and Amentias, now rising to his feet, turned to eye the two Elite Creatures that had opened the portal, the Order of the Dragon beyond them staring in alarm, swords, daggers, and glowing hands raised tentatively.

Aciel raised a hand and Amentias let out a vicious snarl, a sweep of cold wind pressing against them all, and Xavier knew he had turned into a Vampire.

A beam of blue light left Aciel's palm and hit the hooded Elite, rendering him immobile. He did not move or lift a finger even as the Elite at his side raised his own hands in an attempt to keep Amentias at bay.

Amentias did not let this phase him. He pressed himself up against the hooded figure, pushing the sword into the Creature's abdomen, and while they both bled, he grabbed the Creature's head and sunk his fangs into the Creature's neck.

"What the bloody hell?" Aurora gasped, as the Creature let out a high-pitched scream, Amentias covering him as they fell to the ground, blood spilling onto the grass.

Dragor pointed his sword at Aciel who had just stepped towards the Elite Creature he had frozen, and merely extended a hand to press the Creature's head to the side, revealing the Creature's neck, his hood falling, revealing a bright head of red hair.

Before Dragor could move, Aciel had lowered his own fangs into the Creature's neck, drinking his blood.

The gargled sounds of screams not able to rise past bloodied lips was all that was heard as the Creatures continued to drink, and then Amentias was the first to rise.

The handle of the sword protruding out of his back, Xavier had half a mind to walk over and remove it, but Aciel was on his feet in a matter of minutes, removing it himself.

"Many thanks," Amentias told the thin-lipped Creature. Both their eyes were glowing the same red that left the medallions around the four Creatures' necks, although dimly now.

"Xavier," Aleister said, bringing all eyes to him, Xavier able to see the three daggers within a hand, poised to strike either Amentias or Aciel if the scarred Vampire so pleased, "did they harm you?"

He opened his mouth to speak but Aciel asked, "Why ever in the world would we harm our new king?"

✻

The wave of darkness filled the old room and Alexandria shivered. She drew the old, hard sheets over her body to still the cold, but found the thin fabric disappointing: it let in air through the patches of holes throughout its body.

Best rooms, she thought, scoffing as she stared around the small, dusty room. It was as though nothing had been cleaned in months: cobwebs hanging from the corners glistened in the afternoon light.

She sighed.

Although Christian remained right next door, she found it difficult to muster any feeling of true safety. Her mind ran through thoughts of blood-covered beasts, blood-hungry Vampires, startling dreams, and perhaps worst of all, memories most disturbing.

Yes, the vision of the strange Vampire locked in a room with her that night she was to meet the elusive Count sprang to mind, and she found herself recounting his features. Indeed, what was once, perhaps, a look of stoic necessity upon his countenance, had in fact been a twinge of fear. She had stared upon Christian enough to know the slightest changes to the Vampire's face, the blankness wasn't all blank it turned out.

But that Vampire, that Nicholai Noble...he had not left the wall, and those blue eyes had not left her frame. But yes, in her own fear she had not seen his.

He had been scared.

A Vampire, she remarked in slight amusement, *scared of me.*

But shouldn't they be?

And she lifted a hand against the red light of the sun, staring upon the veins that showed themselves on the back of her hand. The glow was faint, but it was there, red and pulsing.

"The power to still their urges," she whispered, focusing on her hand. It was not long before the red light grew in her veins, expanding until it covered her whole hand. She felt the warming heat around her hand and, besides herself, smiled. "The power to still their urges," she repeated, this time louder, with more conviction.

She had sent Lore running both times, though she had not been able to save James Addison's life—the last she'd heard he'd been living with the unsettling Damion Nicodemeus. She had thought of him often when awake, and since she had not heard of his standing she had assumed the worst...

The bite had been horrible, she remembered, the moon shining down upon it, the gaping wound in his leg...his penetrating screams of pain...

And Christian, he had been brilliant in moving to see what could be done, in talking to those strange Vampires that had appeared.

Christian...

The smile returned as she recalled how...easy it had been to... allow him the desire to drink. She hadn't the slightest idea that she was stilling them this whole time. She marveled at the fact that he had gone without blood for three weeks, yes, he did look terrible, horribly sleep-laden, the dark circles under his eyes only slightly gone with the blood he'd taken from the maid.

Another pulse of cold filled the room and she drew the sheets up over her arms, the sleeves of her dress only reaching her elbows.

"Why's it so bloody cold?" she whispered, staring at the old door. The bottom of it did not touch the floor so that a draft could surely pass through, but this much cold...

She turned her gaze to the window, observing it closely. Even that remained tightly sealed. So what on Earth could be causing such freezing wind?

"Pretty, pretty..." the voice drifted along the breeze. *"What a beautiful...what are you?"*

She slowly rose from the bed, releasing the sheets, staring around at the old room, quite aware the red of the setting sun was slowly dimming. But she looked at the window, brow furrowing: the sun was still sinking behind the tops of buildings. *That can't be right.*

"No, no," the voice went on, pulling her gaze from the window to stare upon the growing darkness that was forming in the center of the room just before the end of the bed, "I'm right here."

And as she watched, the darkness solidified until it took the form of the man from downstairs.

"Right," she breathed, blinking rapidly. No: when she opened her eyes, he was still there, grinning though his black beard.

"My," he gasped, a gloved hand going to his heart. As he moved, she saw the multitude of daggers against his chest, his long cloak hiding them from view as he dropped his hand. "My, you are stunning."

She said nothing, not daring to speak against his dread: it filled the room, and she felt her red light flare in response. Her heart beat quickly, but not with fear: it warmed as though bathed in a pleasant fire.

The Elite Creature's eyes flashed with her silence, and he took a simple step forward. "You beautiful Creature," he went on, "I was not meant to intrude, and so soon, but I could not resist the smell of your blood."

"My blood?" she repeated in bemusement despite herself.

The red light multiplied as she felt the dread expand even more. It was as though the light served as a shield against it.

He took another step around the bed, but she did not move. "Your blood," he answered. "It is unlike anything I have ever—" But he stopped suddenly, his brow furrowed in confused contemplation. "Ah," he gasped, watching her in renewed wonder, "*ahh.* This is what

Lord Vondeheide meant. You are dangerous, aren't you? You almost made me forget my purpose." And he clenched and unclenched his hands at his sides. "Almost. But her Grace will get what she wants, yet."

With that, he turned. His cloak flew out behind him, whirling up darkness in his wake. With her next blink, he was gone.

She exhaled, the red light leaving her lips, dispersing in the cold air of the room that was now fading, but the darkness still remained.

She found no fear to exist within her, as strange as it was, but she was quite glad for it. She was sure she had enough of fear to last a lifetime. This...pleasant heat, this red light...it was soothing, comforting at least. She found reason could exist within her mind now, no cloud of fear to fog her brain.

And it was with this that she stepped quickly, moving around the bed, feeling the red light fill her, sway against her skin as she stepped for the door.

She opened it, met with a thick wave of dread, the red light surging up to repel it.

Still no fear.

Remarking on how strange it was, the red light shielding her from feeling the effects of the dread, she moved to the left, pressing against the strange cold to reach the Vampire's door.

Once she graced the handle, she whispered, "Christian— Christian, are you in there?"

Silence pressed against the door.

"Christian, please!" she tried again, the red light pulsing in her heart, keeping the fear at bay. But her gaze still ventured down the hall, waiting for any strange ripple in the darkness, waiting for another dark form to materialize, for the grin to peer at her from within the curtain of black—

The door opened and she stepped back, eyes wide upon the Vampire's frame: His hair looked slightly disheveled as it trailed behind his back, his black eyes unreadable as they purveyed her. She thought for a moment that he couldn't see her at all.

Turning her thoughts from what on Earth he'd been doing, she began, "Christian—the Creature from downstairs—he appeared in my room."

The Vampire blinked as though he had heard something he could not comprehend. "He *what?*"

"And he—"

"Did he hurt you?"

"No—no," she whispered, waving a hand, "but he mentioned Lord Vonderheide—"

The Vampire started, placing a cold hand upon her back, gently pushing her into the room. It was with a flourish that he closed the door behind them, his gaze serious: there was no darkness here to hide his gaze.

"What of Victor?" Christian asked, and she could hear the fear in his voice even if his eyes would not show it.

She turned her gaze to the only window, confused to see a sun almost finished setting: a natural purple light began to fill the sky.

The hand was on her cheek gently guiding her face back to him before she could realize it. "Alexandria," he said, the urgency full in his voice, *"what of Victor?"*

"Th-the Creature mentioned my blood," she said, doing her best to ignore the cold of his hand, "said it drew him to me before it was supposed to. He began to approach me when he mentioned Victor—that Victor said my blood would be—"

But she could not continue. *Victor Vonderheide told an Elite Creature about my blood?* she thought, a sudden burst of horror filling her, the red light unable to shield it this time.

"Alexandria?" the Vampire before her repeated, impatient.

She remembered with a low sigh the feeling that Xavier was not harmed, how strong it had been, how clear... She had no idea why, but she felt it was as clear and pure a feeling as her red light, how it filled her now, and even with the dread all around them, filling the sky, she knew none to reach her within.

She stared into the Vampire's black, worried eyes, and her own brow furrowed. "Christian," she said seriously, knowing it to seem crazy to the Vampire when it was uttered, "I believe...I believe Lord Vonderheide is—is an Elite Creature."

He said nothing.

"I knew it was strange that you received such a letter, and even if we've received no word from your brother for the past month, we still would have been...alerted much sooner if Xavier—the king of this bloody world—was truly hurt—in anyway.

"And—and I know it will sound stranger still, Christian," she went on, staring him still in his unreadable eyes, "but when you told me the contents of the letter...I did not believe it true. It did not *feel* true."

And he opened his mouth, but the words that left his lips were not the ones she was expecting to hear: "Why did you not tell me this sooner? That you had this feeling?"

"I...I wasn't sure it was relevant. But with an Elite Creature speaking his name so comfortably...we've been led into a trap."

She watched as he stared around the small room, his eyes lingering on the window as night fell fully now. He turned his gaze to a lone candle atop the old dresser and waved a hand across it. The candle's low light cast a small orange glow across his face, casting the left of it in shadow.

"It felt as such," he said, seemingly more to himself than to her. "But why would that Creature come to you if Victor was supposed to get to you first?"

She remembered his hungry gaze. "I believe he couldn't...still himself. He smelled my blood."

And his eyes gleamed in the light, a look crossing his face so suddenly, she could not place it. "Did he?"

Her brow furrowed. "You can't?"

"Only," he sighed, "when you allow me the torture, it seems. Tell me, what were you thinking when he showed up?"

The surge of power reclaimed her with the memory, but she would not let slip that she had started to welcome what it was she was she had been gifted. The ability to control the senses of these Creatures had saved her life, and many others, perhaps, time and time again.

"I thought on the red light," she answered.

He waited. "What of it?" he asked after a time of staring upon her.

She opened her mouth to speak when the voice entered her mind, warm and soothing: *"You are the key against the beasts: the blood-stiller."*

Dracula. The image of the tall, lean Vampire appearing from darkness slid into her mind's eyes: His brown eyes, although cold, appeared to hold some semblance of warmth as he gazed upon her, his long white hair blowing gently in a low wind.

The cold hand was upon her cheek again and she blinked, staring upon Christian, confusion marring her mind. "Are you all right?" he asked in concern.

"I—yes," she said, unsure if that were true. "My red light can— it can protect us."

"Protect—"

"Yes—I can...feel it around me, filling me...it keeps the dread at bay."

"How convenient."

"And I know when Vampires, Lycans...Eleanor Black's Creatures are near," she continued, the brown eyes still glaring at her in her mind's eye.

The Vampire just before her shifted his footing. "How?"

She looked up at him, the red light growing stronger in her heart. "Because her Creatures are near," she said, "and they are almost here."

✻

The night sky swirled with the tumultuous energy, and Aleister stared at them, the hand that had held the three daggers now numb, but he hardly cared. Ever since they appeared, the Members of the Order had been exceptionally wary. The only one, it seemed, who welcomed this sudden change was Xavier.

Aleister watched the Elite Creatures: they stood beside a particularly thin tree, its branches twisting out towards the sky in strange spirals. He let the deep sigh escape his lungs. They were bloody Elite Creatures only a day ago, no matter what they said.

He remembered the sight of the Creature named Aciel as he taunted Xavier that wild night at Cedar Village. The snake-like grin... no, the Creature couldn't have changed that much, outsider he may be to Eleanor's Creatures...or so they claimed.

He turned from the sight of them, replacing his daggers, and stepped briskly for the woman amongst them, the only one that could quell his troubled mind.

Aurora sat beneath a dark tree farther away from the others, golden book in her hands. The pages appeared to spark and leap with all manner of color, the light sending brief bursts of red and blue to shine against her black hair which fell easily down her shoulders and back. As he approached, she looked up, her black eyes shining with seriousness.

Before he could speak, she closed the book, darkness falling over her face, and said, "I know how you feel about it, but we cannot move. If they say there are traps within these woods to still us..."

and she eyed the churning sky, a shiver escaping her, "her forces are indeed all around us."

"As they have been," he said before he could stop it. The stare she placed him with forced his tongue to still, and it was with apology that he sighed, kneeling beside her. "Forgive me," he said, prying her fingers from the book to grasp them gently in his hands, "this has been hard—on all of us I know, but especially me. When those Creatures appeared and that wall went up, I thought I'd lost him all over again."

Her gaze softened. "Oh, Aleister." And she openly grasped his scarred hands, gently caressing them. "You simply cannot destroy yourself over all that happens to him. He has died by your hand already, and in doing so you have saved his life. Yes, I agree, this path he walks—we all walk—is not desirable in the least, but it is the lot Dracula has left us. Xavier was right, if you ask me, in moving as soon as he did for Carvaca's castle. It is what we should have done weeks ago. Arminius was right, as usual."

He smiled. "Aurora," he said quietly, removing a hand from her hold to push back a tendril of her hair, "your words are a comfort. I was a fool, indeed, to keep from them my truth. And now that the truth has been released, I do feel lighter. But I'm afraid I can never still in my worry for my boys. Xavier most of all."

The hand guided his face back. "I know I can't still that," she said, the smile upon her lips, and he marveled at her ability to smile within the dread that encompassed all, "but I can lessen it, if you would let me."

He kissed her forehead. "I welcome it."

"We should move soon, your Grace," the voice of Amentias sounded through the trees, pulling him from her.

He grasped her hand, guiding her to stand as he rose to his own boots.

"Looks like the rest is over," she said, shoving the book in a black satchel draped across her shoulder.

He stared back the way he had come, watching Peroneous and Dragor move to their feet, away from the trees they had been sitting against. He turned his gaze to the Elite Creatures now surrounding a standing Xavier.

He stepped to them, anticipation fueling his heart for what they would now do; he knew it was only a matter of time before they acted as they were meant to... Stuck to her hand as all of her Creatures must be, regardless of what they said.

"...Can only move when her forces are thinnest, I'm afraid," Aciel was telling Xavier. "She has groups of men in this area on rotation."

"So we move at night," Xavier concluded, a hand on the handle of the sword.

"It is best," Amentias said, sweat forming on his brow. Aleister marveled at the fact that he was not in either Vampire or Lycan form. How could he withstand the bloody darkness if he was truly not one of hers any longer? "We can sense them before they can sense you, your Grace. There shall be fewer than normal—last we heard she had something big planned for the Elves of Gardenia."

At this Aleister started. "The Gabbling Elves?" he asked in astonishment, remembering when he'd taken Xavier to them much against his will to get Eleanor's influence out of his head. "What does she plan on doing to them?"

Aciel stared at him, Aleister seeing his eyes were a seething red. "She plans to turn them to her side, obviously." Abruptly turning back to an equally flustered Xavier before Aleister could retort, he said, "We must move, your Grace," and he moved, his cloak parting, revealing a slew of blood-stained blades at his hip, "if we are to aid you, it would be best..." He gestured with a pale hand through the trees.

Aleister placed his hand on Aciel's shoulder, whirling him around. The Creature's eyes widened, but he could not utter a word before Aleister asked, "Where'd you get those blades?"

"I—beg your pardon?" Aciel responded. He wiped Aleister's hand from his shoulder, and stepped back.

He felt all eyes upon him, even heard the gasp of Aurora at his side. The Creature was hiding something, for Aleister was certain he did not have the blades upon him when he'd taken the blood of the Elite Creature earlier.

"Those blades," he repeated, brandishing his own daggers, sending gasps to ripple through the small crowd, "you did not have them on you earlier, Creature."

The slow grin formed, sending a dark chill down his spine, and he raised the daggers in hand. "Aleister! Still yourself!" Xavier shouted, a hand up to still him.

"No," he countered, glaring at Aciel, "no, he didn't have the bloody daggers on him before, Xavier!"

"So I produced some protection," Aciel said, the smile not fading, "you would fault me for that, Vampire?"

Aleister's eyes widened as he realized the blades were indeed surrounded in the same black smoke that had formed the portal. "Produced? So you still have her...gifts—you both still are *of* her!"

Xavier's hand, still raised as though to still him, twitched the slightest, and Aciel's smile widened even further. "Look, Amentias, we are not believed."

Amentias merely stared and said nothing.

"If you Vampires do not believe us," Aciel whispered, a low wind beginning to stir around them, "then see our actions as proof. The more we move through these trees, the more her Creatures will appear, and the more they do," and he shared a knowing glance with Amentias, "the more we will have our blood to keep us alive."

"You don't—" Aleister began, Xavier stepping in front of him, stilling his words.

"Enough, father," Xavier said. "We cannot afford you to still us even more than you already have."

He opened his mouth, but the words would not find the tip of his tongue.

"Your Grace—" Aurora began, silenced by a scathing glance in her direction.

Xavier's green eyes narrowed upon them, and it was in his presence that Aleister saw his truth: the Vampire believed the Creatures would not harm them. Believed it so readily, but how? And then he saw the faint red glow atop the sword at the Vampire's side, and his eyes widened.

Was Dracula behind this?

"Let us not question them, they offer us answers to her power, they offer us her secrets, and as we are knee deep in her energy, her Creatures as it is, we have no choice but to accept their help," Xavier said, pulling Aleister out of his thoughts. "Do I make myself clear?"

He did not dare turn his gaze to the others. Instead, he closed his eyes and sighed, exhaling the dread that had filled his lungs when he had yelled. "Crystal," he said.

Xavier said nothing more, and turned, stepping for the trees lost to the dark of the night before them, Amentias, and a still-grinning Aciel following in his wake.

Aleister heard Dragor, Peroneous, and Aurora step to his sides, but he did not turn to eye them: his gaze was held on the Vampire whose back was now devoured in the darkness of her thickening energy.

The medallions began to glow, a low hum accompanying them, but no one reached beneath their shirts to pull them out against the night.

"We share your sentiments, Aleister," Dragor said from beside the dark Enchanter.

"We will do what we can to watch them closely. We are well aware this could be a trap," Peroneous said.

The slender hand was placed upon his shoulder, and he turned his gaze from the darkness ahead to eye her. "We are with you," she said, her eyes dark with her concern, gently glowing in the light of the medallions.

Aleister stared at her, feeling the medallion against his chest burn with a gentle heat.

Damn you, Dracula, he thought, motioning for the Creatures to step ahead and follow in the wake of the king. He stared after them as they moved, feeling the dread thickening around him.

Chapter Seven

THE INVITATION

The office door opened and Nathanial Vivery rose from the chair, staring at the figure that stood in the doorway. He wore a dark cloak, wet with what smelled like rain water, his long brown hair stuck to his face as he extended a wet glove, between two fingers a damp envelope.

"The king has stepped out on business," Nathanial said, repeating what he told several Vampires hours before.

"For you, Mister Vivery," the Vampire said, shaking the envelope.

He stepped forward and took it, thanking the Vampire before closing the door. The damp envelope smelled of burned paper, and Nathanial thought even more of Eleanor's Creatures were ruining another Vampire town or city.

Without preamble, he slid open the top of the envelope with a fingernail, pulled out the paper within, peeled it open, and read the tightly penned words upon the page:

Nathanial Igorian Vivery,

It is with a heavy heart that the Enchanters Guild of Lane call for your immediate attendance to an Enchanter Summit being held currently in Equis Equinox's estate. The Greatness has been most kind to grant all Enchanters freedom about his home—it would call to the strange times that are upon us.

With the lack of magic available to us, even His Lord Equinox is effected, and wants us all to come together to do something about it.

Do not bother sending word, Mister Vivery, we will know when you have read this, and we will expect your arrival here shortly thereafter.

The directions, are, I imagine, now appearing in your Book of the Arts.

Do take a look, dear.

Oldest Friend,

Madame Mastcourt

Madame Mastcourt? he thought, staring at the large, curving M signed at the bottom of the page. The *Madame Mastcourt?*

He'd met her once on one of his many journeys through the Dark World at Dracula's side, the meeting brief, why, he'd never even given her his name. So how did she remember he existed?

He looked over the letter again, this time focusing on the words, "*Summit...Enchanter...Equis Equinox,*" and ran a hand over his mouth in exasperation.

While it was true magic had begun to weaken, he was not certain gathering lots of Enchanters in one place to speak on it would help. For one, that would remove skilled Enchanters from their positions in their Guilds around the Dark World, and with Eleanor's Creatures roaming about, it made it impossible to successfully defend the other Creatures.

Images of Fae, Gnomes, Satyrs, and Goblins filled his mind the more he thought on it, and he let out a groan.

"Xavier, hurry back," he said to the note, staring upon it with seriousness, reading over the end of it.

A map?

He dropped the letter atop the desk and turned to the satchel slung over the back of the high chair. He undid the latch and removed the golden book, feeling the faint hum that left it as he placed it atop the letter. With a deep sigh, he opened it, the trapped spells and charms flittering from the pages in streams of blue and orange light, fading once they touched the cold air. He'd gathered it once able to return to Scylla a week before.

He slid his finger against the pages until he reached the very last page, and sure enough, what was once blank and dog-eared, now showed a very detailed map, outlining his exact location, and trailing, with a red fingertip of a very slender-fingered person, across the back of the book to a red "X" atop a brilliantly drawn castle.

Underneath were the words, *"Equis Equinox,"* scrawled in the same tightly penned script.

Nathanial Vivery stared at the page for a few moments, pulling the letter out from beneath the book, placing it atop the map.

Equis Equinox called the Summit, the creator of magic as all in the Dark World knew it, and though he still lived, had lived for what was argued, a very long time, not many had ever seen him. Nathanial certainly hadn't before.

So why hold a Summit for all Enchanters?

And what was more, he thought, staring over the desk to eye the empty grate within the fireplace, dark and cold as it had died when Xavier had left to journey to Carvaca's castle, he would not be able to do a thing until Xavier returned.

He rose from the chair and stepped around the desk, eyeing the large portrait high upon the wall. The green eyes stared down at him in their perfect coldness, and Nathanial thought the Vampire had quite the journey ahead of him if Dracula's hold over magic was truly beginning to die.

✳

Darien Nicodemeus paced the large room. The fire burned brightly in its grate, his brother sitting in an armchair just before it, but he did not say a word until he stood just before the tall bookshelf and it was to his brother he spoke. "Our mother would be sorely disappointed in how we've let things happen in her home, brother."

"On that we are agreed," Damion said from the chair, a glass of blood cradled in a hand. "But truly—James Addison, a descendant of the Ancients?"

He scoffed, staring at the spine of an orange book. "What else can we think? If Lore was so adamant to send...bloody Elite Creatures to our door—what can we think?"

At this Damion stood, taking one last swig of blood before letting the glass fall to the floor. It shattered at his feet but he paid no a mind to it as he turned to Darien. "But if this is true, Dracula placed the boy there, in Xavier's home since birth. For what? To what end? The boy never shed a scent of Lycan blood until this incident."

He turned, Damion's front cast in shadow. "My sense tells me it was magic. After all, we know Dracula commanded the art magnificently."

"He what?"

"Commanded the art of Enchanting, Damion. Given precise power over its exactness. Now that he is dead, it shall all dwindle, surely."

Damion stepped around the chair, closer to him, his dark stare wide. "What are you saying?"

He stared, realization beckoning. "You did not know, did you? That Dracula commanded control of magic from Equis Equinox."

"The Enchanting Elder?"

"The very same. I swore you knew this, brother—once you were inducted did Dracula not tell you?"

"He t-told me nothing of this—so if that is true—h-how—what— his weapons, surely, must be imbued with his magical knowledge..."

His brow furrowed. "I suppose. But we must remain on point, Damion. If James Addison is the descendant of an Ancient Creature, and Lore knew of *our* blood, we cannot remain complacent."

Damion's mouth opened and closed. At last he said, "What do you mean?"

"We must move for Xavier Delacroix, help him where we are meant to. With Dracula dead it is only a matter of time before more of his secrets will be exposed to this world, and we must make sure Xavier hears the truth of them as only he is meant to. And where Xavier is, his brother will be, and in association, Alexandria Stone."

"Now wait just one minute. I cannot go off and aid that Vampire, his bloody family! I have my own...my own ventures."

"You mean that Vampire you kept in Caddenhall manor," he said. "Tell me, what did you uncover from him? Anything noteworthy? Anything to help further your ridiculous plans?"

"They are not ridiculous!" He pressed a finger to Darien's chest, anger burning in his eyes. "They are just! Lucien and I are on the cusp of great power—I don't need to get wrapped up in whatever nonsense Xavier goddamned Delacroix gets himself caught up in!"

Lucien. He crossed his arms. "Where is your charge, Damion? Last I saw of him he was telling me about *The Immortal's Guide* after tending to your prisoner. What harebrained scheme do you use the young one for, Damion?"

He turned away and Darien knew he struck a nerve. He stepped to his brother's back, the seething anger that had been burning in his blood blooming to full anger. If the Vampire ruined all Dracula had worked for—

The pain returned in a sweep of heat and Darien was on his knees again, the scream threatening to tear itself from his lips, but all that lingered on the air was the strangled, "Blood. I need...the dagger. G-get Ewer—"

Damion turned and sank beside him, and Darien felt the hand on his shoulder. He could not look up to see what he was sure was the confused gaze the Vampire must have spared him. And suddenly he felt terrible for a different reason: Damion had never seen him in this state, had not seen him, truly, since he left the book. Damion had not known the plights that befell him.

"Darien, what's wrong?" Damion asked.

"I," and the pain was unbearable, a burning heat in his blood, a fight between what he was and what he would become, "get Ewer. I need—I need the blade."

And he did not look up as Damion left his side, pressing for the door to the rest of the manor. Now alone, the colors that flashed before his eyes gave way to shape, the sharp pain cutting his skull as the memory returned with vividness.

Yes, there she was, her serious brown eyes filled with tears, her straight brown hair falling around her face, and there was Dracula at her side, holding her arm out for him take—

A gasp seized him and the pain grew, the memory blanketing his mind with terrible pain.

He had searched Dracula's eyes for reassurance, had found it, had continued until—

"Master Darien!" Ewer's old voice sounded in alarm somewhere around him.

He heard several footsteps approach him but could not open his eyes to look—his eyes were glued shut with his pain. And then the hand was in his hair, holding his head up, and his throat was cut, the blood on the blade mixing with his own.

He gasped as he heard the others muttering anxiously amongst themselves, his brother's voice the loudest amidst the din: "If this is what Dracula's secrets have rent upon your head, Darien, you cannot call me a fool for seeking my own way to power."

※

Victor walked past the many shops, noting how many of them had changed entirely, now selling magically-enchanted trinkets and precautions, and yes, as he turned a sharp corner, he was surprised to find that a well-known restaurant had now become, as it appeared with a quick look through the glass, a Vampire-only inn.

Oh, but he was sure humans ventured in. He was not entirely sure they ventured out.

How vastly the Dark World is changing, he remarked, knowing the death of the Vampire who turned him to be the cause.

The Vampire who held such tight restraints on all his Creatures would never have allowed this free mingling with the humans.

But the humans, ever oblivious to their surroundings, had not noticed.

At least not yet.

For he knew, as did the rest of her Creatures, that magic was beginning to fade.

Eleanor, of course, thought it to be because of her ever-growing power. The more Creatures she turned, the more the dread in the air would spread.

But Victor was not sure how much he believed her energy was causing the lack of magic.

She was powerful, yes, as were all who stood by her side, transformed or not, but her power would not be able to kill magic, at least, as much as he understood of it, would not be able to kill it within a mere month.

No, he had a thought that another Creature was responsible for it.

But he would not dare voice it aloud unless he was absolutely certain. For he no longer held ties to the Vampire.

Xavier Delacroix, however, did.

And he hoped the new "king" did not realize the truth of the old king's reach...how far it extended, indeed.

He stepped directly under the hanging sign of the inn, squeezed in-between two buildings, the smell of stifling dread, and warm, sweet blood filling his nose the moment he did so.

"Ah," he breathed as the door opened and the Elite Creature bowed low, "the cavalry has arrived."

"Only just an hour ago," the darkly-bearded Elite Creature said, stepping backwards to stand beside the others. The hoods were upon their heads, their tattered cloaks illuminated in the faint light of the sparse candles that remained upon brass holders atop the few tables still standing.

As he stepped further into the room and closed the door behind him, letting out the cold of the night, he said, "I am happy to see you all."

They bowed in unison.

"Though it would aid me," he said, sending them all to rise, "if I knew the faces of the ones that have agreed to help me in my endeavor."

And one by one the hoods fell, revealing all manner of young and old faces, men and women, their eyes bright despite the colors, their excitement full on the dread-filled air.

"You are all here," he began, watching their anticipation grow with his words, "to help me...ensure the successful coercion of a dear friend of mine and his companion to our side."

The Elite Creature that had opened the door stepped forward, bringing Victor's eyes to him. This Creature's thick, black beard stood prominent against his chin, but when he spoke, it was his deep, entrancing voice that Victor found curious. "If you would, my Lord, they are aware I am not a Dark Creature."

He stared at him, seeing the strange gleam in his dark eyes. It was a while before he said, "And how would they know this?"

The Creature cleared his throat and looked at the floor. "Gregory, my Lord," he said, the faint glow of candles illuminating the guilt in his eyes. "They would know it because of me...I...faltered in keeping myself from the woman. I had to see her for myself, my Lord."

"What did you do?" Victor asked, eyes searching the ceiling as though he could see the woman there.

"I...nothing, my Lord. I was drawn to her...her blood was much stronger than it is now," and he fell silent in the light of Victor's gaze.

"You spoke to her?"

"Yes, my Lord."

"What was said?"

"I...nothing, my Lord."

"Truly?"

"Yes."

Victor stared at him, noticing the faint smell of the human's blood had diminished in power, indeed.

He waved a hand emphatically through the air, sending the line to part in the middle, the Creatures to give him leeway to the dark staircase to the back of the room. "If you will," he began, stepping past them to reach the stairs, "I would like to speak to our guests myself for the moment. You will know when you are needed."

And he did not wait for the less-than-enthusiastic murmurs before he ascended the steps, the weight of his boots he allowed to press upon the old wood sending it to creak with every step.

He did not care.

The Creature had already alerted them to his true nature...he was almost certain Christian and Alexandria had known it was he that called the little meeting. If it were not in the Elite Creature's words, surely, then it had to be in his own blood. He knew, despite the thick of Eleanor's energy that his own very Vampire blood stood out miraculously the moment he'd neared the inn.

Yes, they would know he, Victor, was here, but he was sure they would not know why.

He reached the landing and stared down the long, dark hallway, allowing his senses to lead him to the cold, familiar scent of Vampire blood, the vague, sweet scent of human blood very near it...

He reached the second to last door on the right where the blood was strongest, and he felt his own blood run even colder in his veins. He eyed the dark wood of the old door, the old handle quite ready to fall out of it, but he would not touch it.

He would see me as a traitor, he thought, having seen this moment in nightmares. Christian would not take it in kind, surely, that he had sided with the enigmatic Eleanor, left Xavier's side.

But he would understand, Victor thought, regaining his composure. He had wanted to reach them before Eleanor did, and he had. It was up to him to get them to see sense before she forced her hand...

With a deep sigh, he grasped the handle of the door, surprised to find it unlocked. With a gentle turn, he pushed.

A single candle remained lit atop a dark dresser, the more the door opened, the more he was able to see the rest of the small, shabby room. The faint light cast more shadow than it did light, the walls peeling, cracked here and there: a smattering of dirt and unknown stains covering the wallpaper.

He stepped inside and looked to his right, the black-haired Vampire standing beside the bed, looking down at the sleeping woman who lay atop it. She was dressed in a fitting light day dress. Her eyes were closed, the faint red glow surrounding her softly bathing the old bed in its illumination.

"Christian," Victor said.

He looked up, and there was nothing to read upon his face, within his eyes so black, quite unlike his brother's.

"Victor," he said, turning from her, "we weren't expecting you 'till the morning."

He smiled, stepping forward, embracing the Vampire in a quick hug, his eyes on the woman as he did so. "I did not want to leave you waiting, naturally," he said, though his eyes were cold.

Christian pulled from the hug and smiled, though Victor noticed it did not reach his eyes. "Naturally," he said. "What has happened to Xavier?"

Victor replaced his smile with a look of somberness. "Ah, Christian," he said, voice low for added effect, "it is most...grave. He took an attack from a group of Eleanor's Creatures only three days before. Despite his training, his fortitude, he was badly injured. I figured it'd be best to gather you two away from the manor—I feared they would be coming after you next."

Christian looked quite despondent, though Victor could not help but feel it was not genuine. He eyed Alexandria atop the bed again, red light glowing faintly, and he felt a sliver of unease. *Was it possible?*

"It is alarming how quickly their powers have grown in the mere month since Dracula was killed," Christian said, jarring Victor where he stood.

"I—what?"

"Eleanor's Creatures," Christian repeated, a look of concern upon his face. "Their power. How it spreads, darkens whatever it touches."

"Yes," Victor said, playing along, "yes, it is most...most alarming, damaging." He waved a dismissive hand. "Listen, Christian, you must come with me—you and Miss Stone. It is not safe in London, I daresay it hasn't been for a long time, even with the spell placed upon the city to have them forget the devastation."

"That *was* horrible, wasn't it?" Christian remarked, and Victor could not deny the accusatory tone that lined his voice.

He stared at the Vampire, and then his gaze traveled to the woman. She still slept, the red light faint as ever...but he stared closer, noticing the single line of red light that left her stocking-covered foot, how it trailed off the bed, towards Christian's hand...his ring to be exact.

Victor could not stifle the smile that arose. The ring was cracked. The red light, although faint, seemed to be holding it together, keeping the clamps from falling out of his finger, releasing his power.

But why?

And how was she able to do it?

They are smarter than I accounted for, he thought, feeling the air in the room change. Christian's unreadable, black expression suddenly became hidden, protective. *They know.*

He sighed. "I will not waste your time, Christian," he said, dispelling all notion of pretense: his eyes darkened as he stared at the Vampire. "I extend an invitation on behalf of Eleanor Black. Please, come with me now and you will not be hunted down and harmed when she decides to gather you for her own means."

At this the ring fell from his finger, clanking loudly to the floor in the silence that stretched through the room, the red light dispersed, and Alexandria opened her eyes.

Victor stared at her, Christian whirling to eye her as well. She sat up in the bed, and Victor took a step back. Her gaze was quite pressing as she glared at him; he was wholly reminded of the damning presence of the Vampire that had shared that same glare, those same eyes...

The pain was stifled before it could be fully felt, and he blinked, swallowing the tears that desired to rise.

His damned granddaughter.

He waved a hand before either of them could make a move.

In the next moment there appeared the several Creatures from downstairs, their wind a collective culmination of dread.

He ceased his breathing as he watched Christian and Alexandria tense, fear full in their eyes as they surveyed the many Creatures who stood on either side of he, Victor, filling the room.

"Take them to Eleanor," Victor said, seeing the hatred upon Christian's face, reminded wholly of Xavier's haughty air. Anger fueled him, the grief spurring within his dead heart as well. He stifled a snarl, turning for the door. "I will not be coming with you—her Grace has tasked me with another mission."

He smiled as he opened the door and stepped through, Christian's voice shouting after him over the rush of Eleanor's dread that left with him, "Victor, you bloody traitor!"

Yes, traitor, he agreed, stepping down the dark hallway, the sounds of scuffling boots and shrieks following him, *but it is right.*

As he descended the steps, his mind turning to the Elf, the Vampire he had let slip away, he was met with a sudden silence, a burst of Eleanor's energy pressing past him.

"My ascent to madness is assured," he whispered to the darkness.

Chapter Eight

MOVEMENT

Her darkness filled the sky, thickest, it seemed, over the burning town several thousand miles from Cedar Village. It had remained empty for a day now, many of its inhabitants called away to a Summit in the home of Equis Equinox, a call they had all taken up with glee, glad to be rid of the place they called home.

It was because of the strange new Dark Creature that had appeared a few days ago; he had resided in the store of the town's most beloved Enchanters, Terch and Terry Tilling. But with the arrival of this most suspicious long-eared guest, it seemed even the beloved enchantment shop had become tainted.

A strange energy left the shop whenever anyone would dare pass it, and many agreed it was not Eleanor Black's energy, but something peculiar and unsettling all the same.

It was why Arminius the Elf would think the previous inhabitants would have been pleased to know their beloved town was now burning high in the night, more to blame he and Nicholai's time there for its current downfall.

And he could not fault them, for it was the truth:

117

The Elite Creatures had arrived in Wingdale.

He had been pushed out of the shop several hours before by a harrowing laugh, a burst of her most dreadful energy, and a frightful scream.

The Elites had set fire to the old Enchanter, the withering magic granted all magic-enabled Creatures failing him in providing the proper counter-spell.

It was a horrible scene to watch, but watch Arminius did, before journeying back down to where Nicholai lay atop the table, medallion now black, and placing (with all the energy he could muster), a resolute protection spell upon him.

He now stepped gingerly on his bad leg, moving with his cane for the outside where flames danced high around the buildings that were once the homes and shops of many Enchanters, Elves.

A groan left his throat at the damage that was done, and he shook his head, fearful.

"There he is!"

He looked up, eyeing the Creature that had spoken, low tattered hood atop his head billowing in the brazen wind that filled the air.

Arminius blinked, seeing even more of her Creatures hovering in the sky, some with their hoods aloft, others with their hoods down, dark eyes gleaming in the destruction created.

"Ah," he breathed, wondering how on Earth they managed to find him, but then, he thought as he stepped further out of the shop, stepping onto the hard sidewalk, it was only a matter of time. Only a matter of time, indeed.

A wave of hot wind began to barrel down upon him in the next second and he returned his gaze to the skies, not surprised at all to see the bolts of red and blue fire tunneling fast through the sky, heading straight for him.

The flurry of fear rose in his chest, but the medallion glowed, stamping it down.

Hardly thinking on this strange occurrence, he waved a hand just as the bolts of fire reached his head, and they froze in the sky, their pulsing heat still felt beyond his invisible wall, but it would not crack, not now, not yet...

He stepped from underneath the balls, his cane clicking against the ground, and even as the high flames rent the air, the Elites watched, he felt the medallion's heat grow brilliantly against his chest, saw the red light shine a beacon of light across the road, shining against a building that was burning, its foundation crumbling as the fire filled the dread.

"How'd he do that?" one of the Elites could be heard asking the others in the sky.

"Who cares? He's got a medallion—the other one must be somewhere!"

"No, no," Arminius called, feeling the medallion guide him forward, the fear dissipating as he moved, "you will not harm another, not today."

Shouts of anger left the Elites, but Arminius did not mind them: the medallion burned with a great, sweltering heat, greater than the flame around him. He could not know what caused it, nor did he truthfully care, all he knew was that it was protecting him, helping him, and as he hobbled across the road towards the building that was nearly gone now, he felt the wind change.

At his back there came several shouts, but he did not tear his gaze from the building, whatever it held, whatever burned within it was attracting the beacon, and he could do nothing but reach it, he could do nothing but walk—

"Stop!" a Creature called from behind him.

A shout of anger filled the air when he did not obey.

The thunderous chorus of *"Protect the Dragon! Protect the Dragon!"* filling his mind the more he moved.

"He must be there, then! The Vampire that the Queen desires!" a woman shouted now.

Murmurs of assent filled the night behind him, and the smile was small upon his lips as he knew he was being guided, but he could not know how...not truly, for he had never faced this kind of enchantment, this kind of magic before, if indeed that was what it was.

He stopped just before the burning door to where the medallion shined and waited patiently for the Elite Creatures to take the bait.

It was not long before they did.

He watched as they moved past him along the air and with a wave of collective hands, they removed the fire from the building, a restaurant Arminius knew from his previous journeys there.

He said nothing as they tore down the already smoking door and found their way inside, the sounds of them moving about the large room within reaching him from the street.

The smile remained as the words repeated their tumultuous call, and then the medallion's light faded just the slightest, and he knew the dread, his underlying fear to return.

But why?

He knew not what had happened to him, but he had welcomed it, and now that the Creatures had taken the bait, had entered the restaurant what else could he do to still them? Magic was all but null and void, at least for Creatures that were not hers, but...

He turned, eyeing the bolts of fire that still hovered in the air, frozen against the shield he had conjured. His eyes narrowed: *That spell should not still remain.*

No sooner had he thought this did a high cry fill the sky, and for a moment it seemed the darkness dispersed, the dread gone, for it was such a beautiful sound to fill his tall ears.

He looked up, watching the dread as it lessened, the black night fading just a little showing the tint of dark violet that remained underneath.

And then the large bird, white wings spread wide, flew across the sky, just over where he stood surrounded by flame, and the gasp left his lips.

The bird was large, its long beak appearing gold against the night.

Arminius watched it for a moment, until it disappeared towards Cedar Village, elation filling him the more he stared after it, and all at once he knew what he had to do.

He raised a free hand against the heat of flame, what little dread remained along the ground, and shouted, *"Sacrade Elipsum!"*

The energy pulled from the red light, a surge of Phoenix energy and his own, his hand trembling with the power, but he did not falter, he focused as best he could on the badly burned restaurant where her Creatures still remained, still moved about hoping to find Nicholai.

And he felt his mind go, the energy riding through every vein in his body, pulling him, guiding him just as the medallion had done.

The burst of black and red light left his palm and covered the building completely; he could feel the spell thicken and grow, finding the hearts of the Creatures inside, sending them to burst—

Horrified screams rent the air, but he did not drop his hand until he could no longer feel their hearts beat their rhythmic motion.

The slow breath left him, his eyes closing as the exhaustion overtook him: he fell to his knees, a hand sliding down the cane, but he still held it upright.

Sweat had formed at his hair, sliding down his face as he gasped for breath, for air that was not her damned dread.

He could only stare at the crumbling building before him, knowing all inside were dead, splattered across the walls and ceilings, what remained of their hearts joined with the rest of their bodies.

He could barely question what he had done, how he had gathered the power to do it, when footsteps sounded from behind him.

He turned his head, the shaky smile lifting his lips as he stared at the Vampire who remained there, serious face broken into an astonished glare, his blue robes drenched with what could only be sweat, although Arminius knew the Vampire was incapable of the feat.

"What's happened here, Elf?" Nicholai asked over the roar of fire on either side of him.

Arminius rose to his feet, leaning on the cane as he did so, and turned to eye the tall Vampire, seeing that he stood just beneath the frozen bolts of flame.

"Her Creatures," he said, quite surprised to find his voice almost gone from him. *The spell must have taken more than I thought...*

"Her Creatures?" he repeated, blue eyes thoughtful. Arminius let relief wash over him as the Vampire stepped from under the balls of fire and moved closer to him. "Whose Creatures?"

His eyes narrowed. "You can't be serious?" he asked, hand at his heart, for it suddenly felt as though it were being ripped apart. "*Her* Creatures. Eleanor Black's creations? They were here just moments ago—here for you."

Nicholai said nothing but stared at him, and Arminius felt rather strange underneath that gaze. *What more could Eleanor's energy have done to him, the medallion?* For he stared at it now, still seeing it black against the light of orange and red that filled the sky. *Black. Not good.*

He stared at the silent Vampire for moments more when a wave of fresh dread reached him and he instinctively looked up at the darkening sky.

Damn.

Her Creatures filled the air, coming from the direction opposite Cedar Village, a great line of them headed straight for Wingdale.

He turned his gaze back to the Vampire that watched the approaching Creatures in bemusement. "Quickly, Nicholai, we must leave!" he said, beginning to limp towards the Vampire.

"Why?" Nicholai asked, eyeing Arminius again.

"Why?!" he repeated, incredulous. *What more has she done to you?* He let out an aggrieved sigh, moving quicker still for the Vampire and once he was just before him, he grasped his arm with his free hand. "Because we must reach Xavier and the others, we must protect the king—protect the Dragon! Don't you remember?"

"I—"

But before he could get very far a raucous shout filled the air: "There they are!"

"Come!" Arminius hissed, beginning to move unevenly in the direction opposite the approaching Creatures, pulling the bemused Nicholai along in his wake.

He ignored the continued questions the formidable Vampire asked at length as he hobbled along, feeling the great wind at his back press his cloak, robes, and hair against his body: They had landed.

"Stop right there, Elf!" one of them called.

The wave of dread was thick, so thick he found it inescapable, his medallion's light faded fast. *C'mon*, he goaded, *not now—work a little longer—get us away from them!*

And as if on cue, its light increased just the slightest, and Arminius did not waste any time in whirling with a curious Nicholai to wave a hand through the miserable air, sending the three bolts of fire to hit the ground brusquely, shards of stone and earth lifting up to blind the Creatures from moving forward.

As their screams and shouts filled his ears, he turned, the smile upon his lips, and although his hand shook, he grasped the Vampire's sleeve once more, and focused as best he could on where it was the king remained.

He had been saved, he knew, by something far greater than himself, and as he traveled on the wind, the Vampire at his side silent in his unending curiosity, he found peace in the fact that her energy, magic, *could* be overcome.

Not all was lost, he thought with joy, swept up in the crushing darkness, disappearing from the burning street where her Creatures were recovering, wiping dust and smoke from their eyes.

✳

"We cannot just stay here, Aciel!" Aurora shouted at the thin-lipped Creature.

"Lower your bloody voice!" he whispered, motioning towards Peroneous.

The dark Enchanter lifted his hands and sent the blue mist through the trees, blanketing the darkness in its shimmering strangeness.

Xavier watched as the Elite Creatures a few feet ahead walked into the mist, their eyes bulging the moment they met it, hands clawing at their throats as their ability to breathe was taken from them.

"Unknowable magic," Xavier heard Aleister whisper. He turned, eyeing the Vampire who did not remain behind a tree like everyone else, his green eyes wide in horror.

Xavier stared. "What do you mean?" he whispered.

"What do you mean, 'what do you mean?'" he said, incredulous. "That's the Barely Breathing Blue Air, completely unforgiving, banned in the Enchanters' books."

"Yes," Peroneous said, lowering his hands as the last Creature fell to the ground, unmoving, "quite dangerous."

"How in all of the Dark World do you have the authorization to use it?" Aurora asked. Xavier thought he noticed anger on her words.

The dark Enchanter lifted the purple hood over his bald head. "Why are any of us here?" he countered.

Aleister and Aurora stepped to him and Xavier moved from around the tree to near them as well.

"Dracula authorized the use of that spell?" Aurora asked in disbelief.

"What do you think, Aurora?" Peroneous said, his mouth curling into a frown beneath the hood. "He granted me the authority after I'd...bequeathed unto him that bloody spell."

"What?" Aleister and Aurora said together.

Xavier stared at them, marveling at the disbelief in their expressions. What did it matter what spell Dracula gave what Enchanter?

He blinked at his own question.

Could Dracula even bequeath spells unto others?

Peroneous opened his mouth to respond, when Amentias shouted, "We can be upset later, don't you think? The spell's wearing off!"

And sure enough, when Xavier looked at the blue mist, he saw it thinned. The bodies upon the ground remained, dark silhouettes of decay, and further away, the sound of footsteps approaching neared.

Dragor wiped blood off his sword with a sleeve, bringing Xavier's eyes to him. "I agree," he said, not bothering to sheath the sword. He stepped past Peroneous and moved for the bodies ahead, Aciel watching him move.

"Your Grace," Amentias said, stepping for him, "we must take the blood of the Creatures approaching. They must not be killed outright."

"Fine," Xavier said, unsheathing the Ascalon. He eyed Peroneous, Aurora, and Aleister. "We should move. We can talk about this later."

He stepped from them before they could word their bemusement, and with Aciel, he followed in the wake of Dragor and Amentias. Both of whom had reached the dead Elites, the blue mist gone, and had raised their swords, prepared to strike the Elite Creatures that appeared through the trees, their cloud of darkness thickening through the trees.

When it reached Xavier, the sword in hand began to glow a vibrant red, and he felt it buzz with the energy, Dracula's energy.

The words of the dead Vampire repeated in his mind, and even as Aciel lifted a wispy, black dagger from his chest, prepared to send it into the chest of an Elite, Xavier felt the very strange sensation of being warm.

As the thin-lipped Creature sent a dagger into the neck of a snarling Elite Creature, Xavier stared as Dragor sliced through a woman with his sword, and Amentias dodged blows from a larger Creature. But he was not seeing them at all.

The red light had covered his arm since it appeared just moments ago, with it, the heat traveling as well. And he had the strangest feeling that he was being watched.

Yes, the large, penetrating eyes bore into his back, just there, sending an uncomfortable tinge of transparency to cover him.

This thing that watched him knew all there was to know about him...knew his every fear, his every desire, indeed...

Streams of blue and green light passed right by his head, sending his black hair to billow over his shoulder in the wind.

He watched the streams intertwine and smash right into several Elite Creatures's chests, sending them falling back into the grass.

Aleister appeared at his side in the next moment. "Everything all right, your Grace?"

The heat remained, nearly covering his whole body. He eyed his father, staring at the scars embedded in his face, the sounds of battle stretching ever onwards in front of them.

He thought, briefly, of telling the Vampire of the strange feeling he still felt, even thought of telling him how strange it was that he welcomed Aciel and Amentias to his side without a second thought, but something ceased his tongue from moving.

He merely nodded, a small smile upon his face, and stepped from him without a word, moving through the trees to join the battle of dread and dirt.

✳

Christopher Black walked the streets, the sun's light beaming down upon his back, and he breathed the dread-filled air, eyes rapt on his surroundings. People, dogs, cats, endless people, horses. The world was filled with life, vibrant life, and what had Dracula done to it?

For he recognized the Vampires he passed along the street, golden rings upon their fingers. They eyed him with little interest, their hands full with various bags or trinkets, and he wondered where they traveled, what preoccupied their brown or black eyes so.

They had had a freedom he could only dream of for years, they had lives, perhaps owned shops, sold goods, and where had he been? Staring at a black stone wall, tugging at the gold chain around his neck, ushered blood every night from a trap door within the damaged wood floor; taken care of by the one who had taken him from his mother, who had very nearly killed him, turned him, trained him.

Dracula.

He clutched the sword at his waist, not feeling at all secure. It was not what he was trained in, not at all, but he'd taken it off the first Creature he saw once he left the tower, Dracula's death lifting the heavy spell that'd left him there.

He cursed the Vampire for a third time that day, mind lost on all he had survived once left on his own to face this strange world.

The world Dracula had not bothered to explain.

Anger burned in his dead heart, and he felt his steps harden atop the cement. Left with nothing, hand held only when the Great Vampire thought it convenient. He was dispensable, he had known it, but to be locked away and still not know the true reason for at least that?!

The Vampire had only told him that he had saved his life, by killing him, turning him into a Vampire, he had only told him that he, Christopher, needed to be locked away, kept safe, for there were Creatures out there that would kill him had they known he existed. Their plans being put into motion that needed his, Christopher's hand.

And he, young as he was, had taken it all at face value, he had believed resolutely that the Vampire had his best interests at heart!

Oh, what a fool he had been.

Left to his own devices now, no guidance, nothing to propel him but the smell of her blood—

Her blood.

It was why he walked the streets at all so early in the morning, it was why he moved as quickly as he did, following the wisps of her sweet scent that drifted to his nose with every passing breeze.

But he found it stifling when he smelled another scent, this one horrid, dread-filled as it filled his nose between every intake of breath that was not Lillith Crane's.

He found it most puzzling, this strange scent, how thick it was in the air, filling his every sense with no remorse. He had wondered what it was many a time, hearing only whispers that it belonged to those strange pale, gleaming-eyed men the humans referred to on the off chance they would not be heard.

He hardly thought on the humans, their well-deserved fear of Vampires, Lycans, as he only kept their presence in mind when he desired to feed. But it could not be denied, not in any way, that the humans were not catching on to this free mixing of Vampire and human—not counting the Vampires he had directly passed, he recognized about thirty, if not from meeting them a few weeks before, then from their cold expressions, their piercing eyes, the way they carried themselves with the utmost pride.

Yes, they were not invisible like Dracula had shared with him some moons ago, in fact, he remarked, looking around the street more, nothing was invisible. The cleverly disguised magic-people were sending faint sparks to leave their hands even as normal humans passed them on the sidewalk, all the unaware. And there, directly across the street was a man who held an impossibly long scroll in his grip, the bottom of which graced the ground, and with a loud, fear-filled voice he was shouting, "Alert! Alert! The Highest Grace of Enchanting Arts, His Greatness, Equis Equinox has called for a Summit for all Enchanters, and few magically-gifted Creatures! Alert! Alert! All secluded Guilds are to report to His Greatness's palace atop the Mountains of Merriwall where your Heads are currently convening to speak on matters most important to the Dark World!"

Christopher's eyes widened at these words so loudly spoken, and he wondered if any human would realize what this man shouted, realize what manner of Creature walked amongst them. No one did. The more he stared, the more he realized only other Enchanters, Vampires, indeed, long-eared men he figured to be the famous Elves Dracula had mentioned once, were stepping across the street, stopping whatever they were doing to approach the Enchanter.

Once a group of these Creatures had circled around the man (blocking quite a bit of traffic in the process), Christopher left the sidewalk, avoiding the horses' hooves, and stood just on the outskirts of the group, where he could hear various Creatures speaking all at once:

"What's this about a Summit?"

"Why are they grouping there? Are Vampires allowed at this gathering?"

"What about we Elves? Are we worthy of the great and noble Equis?"

"What's being done about Eleanor Black's Creatures?"

"Yes, what's being done about the Enchanters that have already joined her side?"

He peered over the heads of the smaller robed men and woman, to eye the now flustered Enchanter who had hastily rolled up the scroll, and wiped at his brow with an already damp handkerchief.

"Eleanor Black," the man began, gray whiskers shaking the more he blinked, "and her Creatures are being subdued by our new king, Xavier Delacroix. As for the Summit," he smiled, "only the Enchanter Guilds are allowed the journey. Everyone else, I am sure your respective Heads of your departments will issue you your tasks. The Enchanters meet, I assure you, for the good of the Dark World— and the humans—everywhere." And with that, he gave a stiff little bow and retreated into an old shack wedged between two high buildings.

An uproarious din boomed as the door closed, the Creatures not pleased with these answers, and it was not long at all before the crowd dispersed, displeasure furrowing their individual brows, furious mutters escaping their tight lips.

"A bloody Summit?" one Vampire could be heard nearby, his blue eyes narrowed on the Enchanter he spoke to. They were a-ways off, further down the street, but the Vampire's voice carried, and Christopher, interest certainly piqued now, stepped closer to them. "Demetrius Bane never told us about a bloody Summit, and were we not his consorts in Lane? You'd think the Head Alliance for All Dark Creatures would know about this meeting to gather all the Enchanters up—did you know about it, Cyrius?"

The dark Enchanter called Cyrius donned his hood as though it would protect him. "Didn't know a thing—guess that says more about Demetrius than it does us, eh? We're here, mucking about in

London because Lane is destroyed. Demetrius hasn't been back to Lane—not that I've heard of, anyway—since before the attack.

"But I have heard," and at this his voice got low, causing both Christopher and the Vampire to move closer, "that his name isn't Demetrius Bane at all, but that he's Darien Nicodemeus—and an Invader at that!"

"Darien Nico... That's nonsense, isn't it? Demetrius can't be a Nicodemeus brother—they've been in the Vampire City this whole time."

"But have you ever *seen* Demetrius Bane?"

A long silence met this question, and it was not long at all before the Vampire gasped.

"How're they pulling this off, then?" he asked, once he'd recovered. "He sends his little Caddenhall to the meetings, never shows his face so we won't know it's him? But why would Darien Nicodemeus do that?"

"Because he's an Invader, Riley!" Cyrius said in exasperation. "You haven't seen his brother around in the Vampire City, have you?"

Riley narrowed his eyes. "No, no, can't say I have, not since Eleanor destroyed—"

"Yes, well, that's because—and this is my educated guess—those Vampires are in cahoots. The Caddenhall Curse Givers—the Invaders. With Xavier as king, why would they stick around the castle? Especially Damion? No one likes him. I figure he's buggered off in his home. Hell, last I heard he and his brother were watching that young one—what's her name? Ah, Lillith Crane."

"The Princess?" Riley said in surprise. "But isn't that...well... not done? Two brothers watching over of one so young? I wouldn't put it past Damion to have been taking a little more than care with Dracula's secret."

He almost stepped forward when the Enchanter said, "Don't be disgusting, Riley. The girl has prowess, last I heard."

"I wonder what goes on there," the Vampire said, "I really do."

"I'd be more concerned with what our new king is doing—if he's really taking down Eleanor like our town crier over there said."

"Doesn't matter does it? It's only a matter of time before we're all her Creatures..."

He watched them as they began to walk away from him, their conversation lost to the madness of the London street. *Damion and Darien Nicodemeus*, he thought, wondering who those Vampires were just as the dread-filled scent entered his nose.

Eleanor Black, he thought, beginning to step along the street again, *was it her energy?* Dracula *had* let slip that the brilliant woman had been gaining forbidden knowledge, but he had hardly paid attention, so consumed was he, on the blood of the sweet Vampire he had turned only a few years before, then.

But now he was paying attention. That stifling dread. It was everywhere. And the fact that she was his sister...had gained such knowledge...he was not sure what it meant for him, but before he moved for her, focused on the annoying, glowing medallion at his chest, he knew he had to get to Lillith Crane.

Chapter Nine

A GIFT ON A DARK DOORSTEP

He had not moved for her home, not yet. And he could not know what kept him in place.

It could have been Darien's plight, he thought, recalling the Vampire's bulging eyes as he groveled on the floor in pain. It was a burden Damion had not realized his brother suffered. Once removed from the Order, Damion was bidden to his work, lost in the world of Dracula and Xavier Delacroix to ever track down his foolhardy brother. Now he wished he had. If only to see what more plagued him, what more he'd gained from Dracula's book.

"We must move," he said cradling the full cup in his dark hands though he would not drink. Not after what he'd seen mere hours before. Lore knew of James, claimed the Lycan had Ancient blood— knew he and Darien held it as well. *But* how *could he know?*

Lucien Caddenhall shifted his footing and Damion felt the stare press against his back. "Master? Shall we make another attempt at her cave?" Lucien asked.

At this, he moved, feeling the blood in his cup sway, its scent filling his nose. He eyed Lucien, gaze red. "Yes, yes," he said, "we must move for her again...but I wonder if I will find my answer to Dracula's numerous secrets in my brother's predicament."

"Master Darien?" the young Vampire queried. "What—"

"Never you mind. You will wait for my word, Lucien, do you understand?"

"I—no."

An eyebrow rose as he lifted the cup to his lips and drank. Once sated, feeling the weakness that had permeated his veins wane, he said, "No? What do you not understand?"

His mouth opened and closed, a shadow falling over his brown eyes. "We've been scouting Eleanor's cave for weeks looking for a way in past their barrier and I believe we're close. If it's the sword you want, it is there!"

"I know where it is!" The blood flew out of his hand and landed with a crash against the long table behind Lucien. "I just wonder if there is more to Dracula's power than I have been led to believe."

"In your brother, my Lord? He is not like the rest of us—he has been changed by going through that book. You said it yourself! Forgive me for speaking out of turn, but it is the sword you have desired for years, all the plans laid have been for it. I am bound to do your bidding—I share your desires. Now please," Lucien Caddenhall said, brown eyes alive with anger, "let us move for the sword!"

Damion's red gaze fell upon the bits of glass and blood along the dining room table behind Lucien and he inhaled the human scent, knowing what kept him from moving as he should. Ewer's words to him in this very house returned with a needless breath and he saw it as if it just happened:

Ewer stood just beside the brown curtains in the cozy living room, his back to the basement door, and as Damion watched he emerged from the basement, and the Vampire said the words, *Eleanor Black has the sword, Lord Damion.*

Eleanor Black.

Being surrounded in her energy like he was since she'd attacked London, grew stronger, he found it most difficult to move forward with his plan. *She has the sword.* And barring that end, he knew she would not give it.

He eyed Lucien again, remembering when he'd returned speaking of the way Eleanor's men shrank from the sword, feared it as though it held some terrible power that would do more than harm them. But he smiled. The sword's power, as he'd witnessed it many years ago, would not harm *him*.

Nor, he thought, reaching into a pocket of his cloak, brandishing the black cloth, *would it harm Lucien.*

He handed it to the Vampire, watching as he grasped it, understanding lining his brown eyes. "You are right, Lucien," he said, turning to watch the darkness beyond the windows once more. "We must do what has already been prepared for. We cannot waste it. Thank you," he said with a sigh, seeing the plains roll against the wind. "You will move for her cave."

He heard the footsteps shift behind him. "Just me, my Lord?"

"Yes, Lucien, just you. You have been there before, you are best... suited to reach her abode unharmed," he said before the Vampire could say a word. "You will, of course, use what I have given you to grasp it."

The wind blew against the old walls and Damion thought of the magic that held it upright.

"I will do as you desire, Master," the voice sounded against the wind.

"Yes," Damion Nicodemeus said, "yes, you will."

※

Eleanor Black opened her eyes, allowing the feel of the hands upon her body to fade as consciousness reared its undesired head.

"Eleanor!" the voice from beyond the marble door called.

She sat up within the large bed, running an absent hand over the colder side of the black sheets, grief filling her warm heart with the thought it spurred.

Ignoring it, she cleared her throat, rubbed her eyes, and said, "Javier, you have the distinct displeasure of addressing me by my first name when it hardly calls for it."

The large door opened and he was there, his white and gold robes framing his body, and she thought on how odd it was he had not yet reached his Age.

He bowed. "I would not be here if it were not for you," and he winked, closing the door behind him. "As it stands, the power you've given me warrants us a first-name familiarity, does it not?"

She stared, recalling the attempted transformation the Vampire underwent a week before. He had failed in gaining a Lycan form, but had a knack, it seemed, for keeping the human one. She found it made him brash. Gone was the naïve, young Vampire emerged from Dracula's training room, he was now at least aware of the power the Elite Creature could hold.

"Do not speak so freely," she said, removing the sheets from her legs, the black slip she wore stopping at her thighs. She did not bat an eye as she strode to him, the many necklaces atop the stone bedside table forgotten. She shivered in the cold he exuded. "I have overseen your abysmal transformation, I fed you from the humans gained, watched you, trained you in battle, undid the mess Dracula filled your head with, and still you speak so bloody freely."

He smiled, the fangs showing themselves clearly in the light of the six torches lined around the stone room, the only things warming her blood.

"I beg your favor, your Grace," he said after a long moment, the smile not fading. "I do hope you desire to know why I've woken you."

She held down the longing to tell him he had not been the one to wake him. "Out with it, Javier. It is only morning and already I grow weary."

"The darkness grows, it spreads to the withering hills of Rore, to the shores of distant lands. This, I believe you shall be happy in knowing, your Grace."

She merely stared.

"As it stands," he went on, "you've gained a considerable number of Creatures—all of which heed your call."

"All these things I am already aware of, Javier."

"Yes, yes, but you were not aware of the illuminating fact that Victor Vonderheide has moved on his own."

At this, her brown eyes widened. "Speak."

The smile returned. "Just last night, your Grace," he began, "the Vampire was seen venturing towards an inn called *The Dragon's Cavern* in London. I was not aware of what happened, as I'd sent a few of my own Creatures to observe the Vampire—my own precaution, duly warranted—and they saw him leave a little over an hour later, several of your own Elite Creatures, your Grace, and the brother to the false king and that woman following shortly afterward."

Her blood ran cold, the warmth of the torches fading as the arctic cold claimed her skin. She allowed her gaze their hungry redness, interest more than sparked.

"Continue," she said, turning from him with a flip of her long black hair, stepping to a wardrobe fashioned out of the same dark stone that lined the room. She opened it and withdrew a long, thin housecoat, wrapping it around her body as the Vampire spoke.

"...Followed them to the outside of the city. Your Creatures stopped in the forest where the Vampire City is located, and then they veered past it. I believe they move for us."

"The woman and the Vampire will not be able to cross the barrier, surely their energy is not—"

"Precisely," he interjected, "it is why I have taken the liberty, your Grace, of releasing the barrier, just for the moment."

Dread filled the room in the next second, and she glared upon him in the darkness: the torches had been extinguished in her anger. "You bloody fool!"

"It is only for the moment—"

She silenced him with a breath, and through those brown eyes so filled with fear, she entered his mind, traveling along the waves that sparked, although more dully than one fully alive, and killed the thought of overtaking Victor that remained in the far reaches of his mind.

"P-please, Eleanor!" he cried. "I'm sorry—I won't do it again! I won't move without your word!"

You will not.

And he was brought to his knees in the next second, her pull filling his mind, rending him silent in the haze of her. As it should be.

She closed her eyes, tilting her head back, reveling in her control over those who shared her blood. Her own, her puppets, her men...

She did not release the hold until she was sure he had all desire to undermine Victor Vonderheide removed completely from his gifted, although jumbled, mind.

She sighed deeply, opening her eyes, staring down upon him, able to see him perfectly in the dark. Another gift she would not pass to her own.

They, she thought, staring down upon the fragile boy who now cowered on his knees, *could not take true power.*

She turned her thoughts from Victor's acquirement of Christian Delacroix and Alexandria Stone, pushing aside the pride she felt at his independent movement, and turned her gaze to the only other Creature who held Dracula's blood in his veins.

He would surely be able to take the transformation, and not move from me, she thought, the smile replacing her grimace. She was gaining all Creatures, all pawns in Dracula's dead hands, his untouchable sword aside.

And she saw it clearly, Xavier on his knees before her, just like Javier was now, but not in fear, in compliance, in beautiful surrender.

He would know my love again, she thought the smile returning, and she stepped from around Javier, leaving him to his mind, prepared to face Xavier's brother, prepared to gather the greatest threat to her power, Alexandria Stone.

Chapter Ten

EVERT THE ANCIENT ELDER

Darien was tired. The day before, beyond being exhausting, filled his mind to no end, and he sank deeper into the armchair, his gaze on the fire. He marveled, for the millionth time, how it felt upon his skin, the heat.

The warmth of flame. He smiled, though it did not reach his heart. *I am no longer a Vampire.*

But what he was, he could not give it a name. The longer he went without the human's blood, the worse his condition became. The blood upon the dagger was only temporary, would only keep at bay the effects of his imminent...demise? No, he did not think he could call it a demise, but he felt as though parts of him were changing, indeed.

The door to his left opened and in entered a solemn Ewer Caddenhall, the smell of Lycan following with him. He took two steps, the door closing behind him, sealing off the smell of James, sending him to snarl. "My very few spies about the Dark World, my Lord," Ewer said, "have said the Enchanters move for a Summit in Equis's home. And Xavier Delacroix...he moves for Carvaca's castle."

Darien raised an eyebrow, rising from the chair. "Spies? When'd you get spies?"

His mouth formed a thin line, and then he said, "You cannot expect me to rely on the boy and his sister, can you? They are unreliable most times at best, and Minerva has not reached her Age. My Lord, there are very few Creatures who have seen it lucrative to aid me in my pursuits. At my humble age, it is not easy for me to get around. And a Vampire that is supposed to be long dead with the rest of his family?"

Darien smiled, appreciation filling his eyes, dark thoughts leaving him. "That is how you found out Dracula had died, isn't it?"

He nodded, his long blond hair swaying as he did. "Yes."

"Beautiful, Ewer," Darien said, stepping towards the Vampire, the warmth of the fire fading from his back, "beautiful. But to the matter at hand...Xavier Delacroix moves for Carvaca's castle this very moment?"

"He does. But the way is heavily blocked by Elite Creatures, my Lord. And your condition—"

The flare of anger rose in his heart. "My condition?"

An apologetic frown found Ewer's wrinkled face. "You must be smart, my Lord. Her Creatures have grown in power, and yours weakens. It is not wise to join Xavier Delacroix and the others now."

Darien turned and moved to the long staff that leaned against the back of the armchair and grabbed it. "I can fight," he said to the staff, feeling the eyes upon him. "I can still do that."

"My Lord—" Ewer started when the terribly loud crash reverberated against the high walls.

"What the Devil?" Darien whispered just as the loud roar sounded from somewhere further in the manor.

"It's the boy!" Ewer shouted.

The doors blew open and Darien turned with the staff, tensing, prepared to strike when in a gust of wind Ewer brandished a dagger from within his robes and threw it at the Lycan that was running towards them, leaving long scratches in the hard floor.

The blade barely grazed the beast, and just as he raised the staff, the blonde woman appeared before him, white arrow raised in her long bow. She let it fly, but it missed, and the beast was upon her.

Darien jumped back, avoiding the blow, staring in bewilderment as they slid along the floor, the large claws digging into her shoulders. He heard bones crack, and watched in horror as the long snout snapped at her face, thick rolls of saliva leaving its many rows of teeth, falling onto her panicked face.

"James!" he shouted.

It looked up, a menacing growl leaving its snout, and with a painful scream from Lillith's lips, it leapt.

He raised the staff, catching the Lycan's sharp teeth against the black wood. He slid against the floor as James attempted to snap and press forward, but he would not be deterred. He'd known from the moment they arrived on his doorstep that having a Lycan in his home was madness, that it would not end well, but he had sidestepped his reservations for having the woman safe.

Look at what that has wrought.

With a snarl, he lunged forward, pushing the beast away, and as James attempted to recover, he twirled the staff in hand and jabbed the blade towards him—

The blinding pain cut through all manner of sense and he sunk to his knees, unable to see a thing. He barely felt the staff fall out of his hand, hardly heard the muffled shouts and loud thuds as the Creatures moved about within the large living room, for he was elsewhere.

The darkness was present all around him, familiar though it was, it was still maddening. The woman stood some ways off, the white hair of the familiar Vampire fluttering in an unseen wind.

Dracula stood behind her, two pale, long-fingered hands upon her shoulders, the smile barely present behind his hair.

"*Darien,*" he said, and the woman shivered at his voice, "*come. Drink. Take, so that you may remain here long enough to do what must be done.*"

He rose to his feet, but the moment he did, they gave way and he was upon his knees again; the pain far too much to bear now. "*I cannot—*"

"*Do not tell me what you can and cannot do! I have placed my trust in you—you will move for her and you will remain until my replacement can move. You will do what must be done.*"

"Darien! Master Darien!" the familiar voice called, and he opened his eyes against the pain.

He stared up into the blue eyes of Ewer Caddenhall.

"Ewer," he breathed, the pain pulling at his mind, fainter now it seemed, "what—where is James?"

Ewer looked back towards the doors and Darien followed suit. They were wide open, hanging off their hinges, and the Lycan was gone. Books littered the entrance hall, and shards of wood from a desk joined the debris atop the white floor. "He ran, Master," Ewer said, staring back at him. "Once you were...overcome, he fled as though bidden. But we must move, my Lord—it is the girl."

And Ewer rose to his feet and swept to the left where Lillith Crane lay, blood pouring from her shoulders, her bow several feet from his boots. Her eyes were not open, but despite this, Darien knew she was not dead. He could not smell her blood (how strange), but he knew she was not dead.

With a groan, he attempted to sit up, but found he could not attempt even that. With all the determination he could muster, he pulled himself towards her, despite Ewer's bewildered gaze and the pain that coursed through his veins... *Blood, I need her blood.*

But that woman wasn't here, and Lillith Crane was. The girl didn't deserve this pain. And she was not at her Age...her wounds would not heal, not at the amount of blood that spilled along the floor.

He was just near her when Ewer's voice filled the void that was his focus, but he ignored him. He didn't need to hear that he was acting wildly, that he should rest, receive the dagger to regain himself. *I am already dead*, he thought, lifting a shaking fingernail against his wrist and pressing down, *I see no reason she should die as well.*

As his blood spilled down his arm, he heard Ewer's gasp, but did not look up to see the disbelief that would be upon that old face, he merely pressed through the puddle of blood at her head and swung his wrist onto her lips, pressing down to part them, and waited.

Nothing happened for quite some time, and he had almost thought he was far too late when she began to suck, her eyes never opening against her desire.

"My Lord," Ewer breathed overhead.

He did not tear his gaze from her face, waiting for her red eyes to show themselves beneath the lids as he said, "We must move for Xavier Delacroix, Ewer. Gather Minerva and Yaddley."

"But they are—"

"I do not care! Gather Minerva and Yaddley, we must move, Lycans be damned." And the words of Dracula returned in a rush of heat he was alarmed to feel as strongly as he did, "*You will do what must be done.*"

There was a terribly long silence and then Ewer said, voice low, "Aye, Master Darien. We move for Xavier."

※

Xavier raised a hand against the cloud of thick smoke that surrounded him, only able to make out shadows of running figures moving here and there when closest to him.

But none stopped to eye him, nor did any shout out his name.

He turned his senses to smell, dread the only thing reaching his nose.

Too far removed from my own, he thought, swinging the sword threateningly in hand. *Let any of her Creatures try and get near...*

The blast from Peroneous's most awesome spell could not prevent the spray of dirt, blood, and limbs from filling the air.

And now all manner of the world was lost, and it seemed even her Creatures were bewildered in the remnants of the dark Enchanter's power.

How had *he gathered such power?*

Xavier thought on the Enchanter's significance.

Was it possible he was truly given such reckless authority by Dracula to use these strange new spells at will?

What was the alternative? For he had never truly asked Aurora or Nathanial what the ramifications for using certain spells was. He had not even known there were spells they were not *allowed* to use.

He thought back to Aurora and Aleister's alarm at Peroneous's mist spell, how both Creatures seemed bewildered at the thought that Dracula could give him authority over magic.

It begged the thought, did the Vampire have authority over magic?

Had he used far more than he had ever shown or told?

Xavier felt the ground soften near him and he swung the Ascalon, striking the Creature clear in the midsection.

He continued the swing, bringing the blade through its body, and he could see the Elite's horrified red eyes, its Vampire form fading fast. The smell of cold blood and dread filled his nose as he let out a roar, finishing the swing, sending the Creature's legs to fall to the ground, the torso to fall to the side, a cry of fright leaving its mouth.

He stared at it for a moment, waiting for it to turn to ash.

The red eyes merely stared at him in blank alarm, and he snarled at it, confusion filling him.

They did not turn to ash?

He could have sworn they did, having felled countless of their kind. They always were reduced to ash regardless of what form they held.

What, he wondered, staring down at the Creature in bemusement, *changed now?*

"Xavier!" someone shouted from nearby.

He looked around, the smoke fading. He narrowed his eyes upon the approaching figure, listening as it drew near.

"Xavier, the castle! Go! Go now!" It was Aleister, green eyes filled with fear.

He turned to follow his father's gaze.

The castle loomed in the distance, the blanket of snow atop it and upon the field just before it now gone. Green blades of glass littered with what looked to be bodies, bone, and blood shined in the open sunlight that pressed against the clearing.

The castle no longer hovered over the ground, it now settled upon the grass as if dropped out of the sky, the spell in place to support it perhaps dead along with the Vampire that cast it.

"Xavier!" Dragor shouted, sending his sword through several Elites at once. "Go! Get to the Elder!"

He moved, running past the Vampire, evading lunges from nearby Elites, and then he felt a hand upon his back, strong and unyielding.

"Do not stop, your Grace," the voice of Aurora Borealis sounded from beside his right ear. "You must reach him, even if we do not."

And he felt her fingers dig into his back, through the thickness of his cloak, and he wondered how on Earth she kept up with him, keeping his speed.

A spell, surely, he thought.

She pushed him clear into the middle of the large clearing, and he flew over the heads of bewildered Elites, their eyes, red and black, following him, and he could see how many more streamed out of the large doors of the castle.

There were thousands, all dressed in equally tattered, dark cloaks, stains of blood covering them here and there, and yes, even in the morning air, many of these cloaks were being ripped as the Creatures that wore them turned into Lycans.

The sword pulsed in his hand as he landed atop a Vampire, his screech filling Xavier's ears, much to his displeasure. He sank the sword into the Creature's throat, killing the scream immediately.

The smell of his blood reached his nose, and found his gaze to turn red, her smell thick on that dread.

Eleanor.

He moved for a woman that was running towards him shouting obscenities into the air, and placed the glowing Ascalon through her midsection, a groan leaving her lips as the light in her eyes died.

He released the sword and continued on, slicing through the coming Elites, the smell of her blood strengthening in his nose with every cut made on their skin. *Damn, damn, damn.* The sword continued to glow brighter and brighter, spreading its buzzing energy through his arm, and it was almost as if it had a mind of its own: it slashed and cut through the coming Elite Creatures, sending their blood to spray over his clothes, his face, his hair—

"Your Grace!"

He continued on, not stopping, the smell of her blood burning itself into his mind: *lilac and fresh blood, dread, lilac and fresh blood...* And he could see her, she was beginning to form in his mind's eye, her beautiful smile ever so inviting...the righteousness returning in the seed of his dead heart...

"Your Grace!"

Yes, this was right, they would fall to my hand, and my hand alone. They will not strike me...and I would be joined with her again—

"Xavier!"

The glow died as quickly as it had come, and he felt his arm, once so warm with the glow of the red light, now run cold with the nature of his blood. The righteousness died, she faded, and the red from his vision was gone now, the gasp leaving his throat:

He stood just before the tall double doors of the castle, the sea of bodies littering the ground at his blood-drenched boots.

Aleister, Aurora, and Peroneous stood in the line of trees far on the other side of the clearing their stares upon him in utter bemusement. Beyond them, he could hear the faint sounds of Dragor doing battle with the few remaining Elite Creatures, and Xavier heard the sounds of Dracula in his mind once more, quiet now, but there nonetheless.

Guilt crashed upon him in a wave, what he'd done replaying in his mind the more he stared at the blood, the unseeing eyes, her dread still there, but not as strong...

The Creatures started forward, moving swiftly over the bodies to reach him, and he merely remained there, unable to move.

How could this have happened? He had been so focused, so content on his place as king those three weeks holed up in his office. Yes, he had smelled her dread, had had the errant thought take over, but he had always regained control, he had always returned his mind to the tasks at hand.

So what now? The thoughts of her returning so forcefully... would it happen again now that he was out in the world? Would it mar his mind to move forward, to see Evert, to finish this task set about him to recover these Artifacts?

Doubt weighed heavily on his mind, and as Xavier stared at the ever approaching Creatures, he thought he saw that same doubt mirrored in their own eyes.

"Xavier, what the bloody hell?" Aleister said as soon as he was within earshot. His daggers were all gone, Xavier saw, his traveling cloak shed, lost somewhere in the blood and death, he knew.

"I don't know what happened," he lied, the words leaving his lips with an ease that scared him. He sheathed the Ascalon with a shaking hand, placing it behind his back to keep them from seeing it, his fear. *Am I losing my mind again?* "The sword began to pulse and then it moved of its own accord."

Aurora and Peroneous shared curious glances, and then Aurora said, "Your Grace, forgive me, but you moved as though possessed—"

"It was almost as if you were lost to Eleanor again," Aleister interrupted, not missing a beat.

Xavier stared him, seeing the fear and growing disappointment fill the green eyes.

He looked away, staring past him to see a bloodied, but smiling Dragor begin to step over the bodies of the dead towards them.

"I won't ever be lost to her again," he lied again, turning his gaze to Peroneous who looked remarkably tired: dark circles rested beneath his black eyes. "Come," he said, turning from them, stepping into the large castle, trying to forget the sight of her slinking towards him, hand outstretched, asking plainly if he would join her at last, "we cannot keep him waiting."

As he moved, he heard the small cry of fright and turned, Aurora with a glowing blue hand pointed at a smiling, but bloody-mouthed Aciel, and a fresh-faced Amentias, also with blood upon his chin. They stood behind the three Creatures, who had yet to move into the castle, and Xavier figured they had to have appeared there.

"Seems we missed a hell of a fight," Amentias said coolly, stepping past Peroneous and Dragor, who had just arrived.

"You don't know the half of it," Xavier told him, as they walked through the tall hallway, passing the doors where Xavier remained before the Council of Creatures Meeting, and the doors where he'd been named King of All Creatures...

He heard the other Creatures begin to follow in their wake, a gentle wind from outside blowing in past the large double doors, pressing his hair past his face. With it, the small wisp of dread reached his nose, and he realized it came from the Creature at his side.

He had wondered how much they were truly not of Eleanor, but they had shown nothing but support, indeed, since they arrived yesterday morning. And they had already let slip her plans to keep he, Xavier, from reaching the castle, had they not? They had even helped in dispersing with the Creatures, of course taking their blood when it suited them.

He had not known for certain why he had taken Aciel's hand when the Creature extended it. The sword, much as it did just moments before, had moved on its own, red light propelling him.

It was this that made him wonder just how much of the red light was Dracula's will, indeed.

Xavier climbed the stairs first, Amentias trailing behind him, the others following suit. It was not until he reached the landing, and stared down the long hallway, the many rows of doors hiding their interestingly large rooms, that he felt the immense weight of what he was tasked to do once more.

Dracula, he thought, and even as he moved, visions of her, ever faint, ever looming, swam in his mind, *I don't know if I can do this.*

But the hand was on his shoulder in the next moment, and he recognized the gruff, heaviness of it. He placed his own hand atop it, feeling the scars embedded into the skin. "Thank you," he whispered.

The scarred Vampire smiled. "We are right behind you, your Grace."

And with this, he stepped forward, moving for the door whose handle was the head of a Dragon. It let out a hiss as he grasped it and turned.

The brilliance of the sun shined through all the tall windows just opposite them, and as they entered, Xavier looked to his right, glad to see the large, golden bed still there, the long, graceful Creature atop it resting peacefully.

A sound very much like a door being shut sounded quite loudly then, and Xavier turned, as did everyone else, to watch in confusion as Amentias and Aciel stood outside the door, expressions belaying the confusion they must have been feeling.

"The Elites didn't touch Evert," Dragor offered, sword now stowed in his sheath; he too held flecks of blood upon his slightly older face, "because they could not enter the room. Spelled, most likely by something...we Creatures cannot understand."

And, indeed, Xavier could feel the sword begin to glow its warm heat again, although this time he did not grasp it.

The figure atop the bed sat up, a low gasp leaving his lips, and Xavier watched, for a second time, as the long golden hair spilled out around him, leaving the pillow, and once again he thought them the sheets.

Evert rose to his bare feet, and Xavier stared up at him, feeling remarkably small still. *Not much had changed since I'd been here last*, he thought, remembering how lost he had felt those moments after Dracula had fallen, how sure Nathanial had been in moving. And now he, Xavier ruled an entire world that was falling to the hands of Eleanor Black.

Evert swept two long arms forward, and Xavier eyed the Creatures at his sides as they immediately fell to their knees, medallions glowing a steady red light, bathing them and the floor in it.

He half thought he should kneel when Evert opened his mouth and said, in a voice as timeless as the sky, "Xavier Delacroix, you are back. I trust you have learned much in your time venturing through *The Immortal's Guide*?"

And all at once it flooded back to him, rising from the ground, no sword at his hip, hopelessly human...how he had ventured through that strange world beside those two strange Creatures...

"I have learned...what little Dracula would reveal to me within the book," he said, unable to speak louder against the presence that was this Ancient Creature.

"And you know, now, what the first Dracula desired for you, his underling, to accomplish?" the great voice went on.

He hesitated, not sure why he was doing so. "I know that Dracula desired for me to drink from the Goblet of Existence...to render the Lycans, the Vampires, human. To have peace in this Dark World."

Evert nodded, his deep blue eyes staring only upon Xavier. And he thought, briefly, on the battle just outside the castle, how he had felt two piercing eyes upon his back... "You are the only Dracula that remains in this world now, Xavier. And yet, I do not get the sense that you understand what this means. Did the Knights of the Order not tell you what must be?"

"They...did not have the opportunity to share all they desired, I'm sure," he answered, feeling the Ascalon pulse strongly against him, "we fought off many of Eleanor Black's Creatures to arrive here."

"I know. But there was always time. Always time to share what must be shared." And Xavier felt these words were directed at the Creatures on either side of him, though he still felt the humiliating sting. "I suppose I must be the one to share it."

And then he gasped, a long strenuous breath that made Xavier wonder just how long he'd lived on the Earth.

He dropped his long-fingered hands to his sides and sat atop the bed once more, though seated, he reached Xavier's height in full. The blue eyes never left Xavier's green ones.

The Ancient began:

"You have been graced the title of Dracula, Xavier Delacroix. You were given it when named King of this World, you were given it when you took the old Dracula's blood. Yes, you were always Dracula, Vampire. It is not a name, but a right given to the Creature that has proven his or herself courageous enough to take up the mantle of power afforded to the one that desires to see the status quo changed.

"You Creatures, Vampires, your counterparts, the Lycans, were created of death, of rage. My brothers in the skies cried for their creations, how easily they had slipped from their hands, but they would not move to correct it.

"They would not step foot in this World that they helped create, for it had become something untouchable. They cannot grace this land for the terrible power the previous Dracula showed in his original form."

Xavier opened his mouth to ask what this original form was, but Evert gave him a cutting stare and he closed it abruptly.

"The original Vampires were fearsome Creatures...blood-desiring, and when Lore was created, the battles that would take place were gruesome. The Phoenixes did their best to shield their creations from the darkness, but the original Dracula's creation made this impossible.

"He spread a shadow over the world, a shadow I am sure you are not aware of. But those of us from before...we remember. And we were scared. They ruled over the land, winged aberrations, their power unyielding in the face of what we," and he placed a large hand over his heart, "were.

"We could not touch them, we recoiled. Tremor sent his own to fight them, but of course, they were all felled. And soon his power waned."

Xavier, who had listened to this with darkened eyes, said, "Winged aberrations? I'm sorry, I don't understand."

Peroneous rose to his feet, both Xavier and Evert eyeing him in confusion.

The red light blared from his medallion, bathing his dark face in its red glow. Xavier almost thought he looked murderous. "Winged aberrations," he repeated, his voice lower than Xavier had ever heard him use it before. "I was scared," he went on, Evert letting out an impatient sigh, "I was terrified when that thing came for me. It did not speak with its horrid mouth, its many fangs glistening with the blood of its prey, it spoke with its mind." And he stared at Xavier, as though begging him to understand something that could not be understood.

"It begged me at first, to make it anything—anything resembling human. I had heard of its terror; I had heard of the new...monsters plaguing themselves in the world. But they were...to me they were mere myths. I had felt the change of the air, the smell of the wind, but forgive me, I did not know the *truth* to the stories.

"It had no name. It only took the title of Dracula once it ventured to the Nest to beseech the Phoenixes for their help. But when it came to me, it had no name. When I would not submit to its desires, it turned hostile, its wings spread wide as it glided for me in my own home, ruining my apothecary. It moved for me, its beady black eyes nothing one would call human.

"I...I promised it I would do my best after it had stabbed me in my gut," he went on, anger dripping with his every word, "and when it had gone out a window, I healed myself, and too scared to call for my Guild, I began to work on a spell rendering inhuman...beasts... human. I eventually found a way. Through the blood."

"It is most unthinkable magic," Aurora said quietly from her knee. She never raised her head.

"But necessary," Peroneous snapped. "Think! If I had not given that...monster that concoction, he would surely have convinced another of our kind to do it! As it stood, I hoped it killed him! But the damned thing survived and what emerged was more beautiful than any human could hope to be! His cunning outmatched mine, outmatched any Enchanters' I daresay! I did what I could! I cannot say the same for you, can I, Madame?"

"Enough!" Evert yelled, his voice loud enough to drown out Peroneous's shouts, the ring in the air of Aurora's lost words.

Xavier eyed the Ancient Creature again—his blue eyes were angry, long chest heaving with his displeasure. "No more! You, Peroneous Antiquitus Doe, have played your part in the previous Dracula's ascension to the Vampire Creature we have come to know today, and for that you are thanked by we Ancients, I assure you. No more shall we shed on that dark time. We move forward—" and he froze as though a strange new thought had just reached his brilliant mind.

"Where," he began carefully, scanning the room, "are the others? The Elf, the Vampire?"

And Peroneous said, anger still clear in his voice, "Gone, Evert. Lost to us for the moment. They were moving here six days ago...we believe they were detoured by Elite Creatures."

"Not good," he whispered, seemingly to himself, "never good. Nevertheless," and he eyed Xavier again, "Dracula, you must secure the original Dracula's sword. He kept it, knowing he would meet his end, but he had desired, as I understand it, to give to your kin. He told me of his plans to give it to your brother once you both ventured back from a meeting with Eleanor Black some moons ago. This has not happened."

Xavier felt his heart pulse just once. *What? Dracula...the old Dracula wanted to give his sword to Christian? The night Eleanor died?*

"There is special power in that sword," Evert went on, "the gem in the guard of the Ares holds the blood of the Creature that has been slain by it. Useful in creating new spells," he waved a long hand to Peroneous, "or merely in ferrying the lost soul to *The Immortal's Guide*...ah, where is the book, Dracula?"

Xavier blinked. And then he realized Evert had meant him. "It—it burned, Evert," he said quickly, "soon after I had left it.

The Phoenixes were coming for me within it and I was not yet a Vampire—"

"Burned?" he repeated in bemusement. "Burned? Destroyed?"

"Yes."

"How hopelessly mad. So he must have thought you were the one. Regardless, you *are* the one that must bring peace to this world. I grow tired of inhaling this putrid air." He waved another long-fingered hand. "Gather the sword for your brother, Dracula, he shall need it in the coming years, I fear."

"But that's...I don't have the sword."

"Who does?"

"Eleanor Black."

He was silent for a moment and then, "It seems that woman will be a much bigger problem than we thought."

※

Thomas Montague walked slowly through the high stone hallways of the cavern, having lost himself in them some weeks before. He had not given up looking for the woman, no, he had merely gotten distracted.

Eleanor had gained in Creatures, yes, she had, but with every transformation, every fresh-faced, hungry Elite, there was more dread in the air, more stifling to breathe, less of Alexandria Stone's blood to smell.

She could not be tracked, much to his dismay, without Eleanor Black's suffocating energy filling his every sense, covering his every thought.

Miss Stone, he thought, pushing away Eleanor's name as it drifted on the back of his mind, *I will have you, yet.*

He ran a hand over the cold golden ring within a pocket of his vest, gently pondering its significance. He had known the Vampires wore it to walk along the surface, but he had a strange feeling, as he passed other Elite Creatures in the hallways, his destination unclear, it also bore another, much more helpful power...

"Have you heard? General Vonderheide's men have just returned with a Vampire and a human woman!" a passing Elite whispered in strained amusement to another.

Thomas watched as they passed, their continued whispers on the strange occurrence filling the hallway. He looked around, drawing himself out of his revere. Yes, all Elites, those hooded and not, seemed feverish, excited about something. It was in the air.

And then he realized it.

The barrier was down. Yes, he could not feel the solidifying weight of her energy anymore. Indeed, what he had felt before was merely her energy, but was much less than it had been since she'd gathered so many new Creatures.

Could it be?

He turned back, heading the way he had come, following in the trail of the dirtied cloaks the Elites ahead wore. They walked past several stone doors, their inhabitants surely the newer recruits, for this was where they were kept. Given a cot, their cloak, and paired with another that would watch over them until they were assigned to one of the many groups of Elite Creatures that Eleanor had begun to call her "armies."

Thomas did not have one, no, he had not seen Eleanor Black since he returned from his rather pointless journey across the Dark World to track the woman down. He could not bear to eye her. And it was not just because he no longer felt as tied to her as he once did, it was because Alexandria Stone entered his dreams, filled his soul, and in her presence he was given his late wife.

Mara would join this strange woman, and in those dreams he would be with her again.

Nothing could compare to the feel of her skin...

And then he would waken, slapped once more with the harsh cold of Eleanor's hovel, the nasty scent of dread regardless of how far you would run from it.

The Creatures rounded a corner and he did the same, not losing sight of them. Their whispers of their excitement over a normal Vampire remaining inside the cave reached his ears, but he did not listen to them. He was far too focused on catching sight of her...

They soon reached a group of heavily cloaked Elites that filled the hallway, making it impossible to move further, and Thomas cleared his throat, sending the few Creatures just before him to part, making way for him to pass.

He pressed past them, placing a hand upon the next Creature's back to beg him or her pardon. They stepped aside with ease, once seeing who it was, and he reached the center of the crowd in short time, a slow smile spreading across his face once he did so.

Hands of four Elite Creatures, respectively, were on the arms of an angry Christian Delacroix, in the center of the excited circle, beside him a bedraggled looking Alexandria Stone.

She wore a long, light day dress that had been ripped in several places, her brown hair in wild, loose waves that fell around her shoulders. She had struggled, indeed. *A far cry*, he thought, *from the vision of my dreams...*

He stepped forward and Alexandria, who had been looking elsewhere, stared at him, recognition filling her eyes as well as tears. *How interesting that she be brought to me, brought here of all places.* He lifted a hand to stroke her cheek, when the thought reached his mind: *Why had she been brought here?*

"Don't you dare touch her!" the Vampire at her side snarled, attempting to move. The Elites that held him dug their fingers into his arms to keep him still. Thomas surveyed him fully for the first time since he'd entered the circle:

The Vampire's eyes held slightly dark circles beneath them, his pale skin showing his veins, and quickly eyeing both the Vampire's hands, he saw no ring remained on any finger.

"Unguarded," he said aloud sending Christian's brow to furrow. Turning to him, he went on, the question sparking his mind, "Your ring. Where is it?"

He snarled. "What?" he spat, straining against the Elites' hands.

Thomas felt her dread thicken in the long hallway and saw visions of her fill his mind. *Damnit, she's coming.* "Where is your ring?" he repeated, needing to know the answer. If he knew, perhaps it would help him learn how to better use the ring he kept.

Christian's black eyes moved to Alexandria in clear confusion. "What the bloody hell are you talking about? Let me go!" he yelled.

"Now," a new voice sounded through the hallway, rendering all who stood within it deathly silent. A few Elite Creatures stirred behind Christian and Alexandria, and Thomas stared, feeling his heart triple in its beating with a dread all his own. "We can't have you leaving us after just having arrived," the voice continued.

It was not long at all, much to Thomas's dismay, until the crowd parted fully, revealing the woman who was walking towards them, Javier Theron at her back.

He stared, much against his will, eyeing the smile so beautifully placed upon her face, the ruffled blouse she wore, beneath it the black breeches that hugged her legs. *She always did favor the clothes of a man*, he thought. The many silver necklaces at her chest clinked against each other, dipping in-between her breasts.

She entered the circle, and Thomas stared as the Elites moved quickly to close it once more.

He watched as she swept two arms majestically through the air and Thomas practically felt the Creatures around them sigh in anticipation. "Christian," Eleanor said, and it was as though she spoke to a dear friend, "it has been far too long."

He said nothing to her but merely stared, and Thomas thought he saw a flicker of terrible fear in those eyes so black. It even seemed the Vampire slackened in the Elites' grips as though he could not keep himself upright any longer. He thought it strange: had the Vampire not faced her Creatures before?

But, he quickly corrected himself, *she was not like the rest of us.*

"No words?" Eleanor said with a content sigh. The smile would not leave her lips, and Thomas could practically feel her joy. "Very well," she went on, turning to Alexandria.

Christian sparked to life at this movement, pressing against the Elites, but he could not leave their grip. Thomas thought this strange. Was he not like his damned brother? Powerful above all else?

Alexandria tensed as Eleanor's eyes fell upon her, and Thomas could not blame her: the gaze Eleanor gave the woman quite made him think she desired to devour her, eyes and all.

"The elusive woman," Eleanor whispered, and she stepped up to Alexandria, Christian let out a vicious snarl, his eyes turning a bloody red. "Oh," Eleanor gasped, eyeing him with faint amusement, "am I not allowed to touch her? Is that it, Christian? Will you hurt me if I touch her? If I rip her apart?"

"You cannot touch her," Christian yelled, and many Elites let out laughs.

Eleanor smiled, dropping the slender hand that was prepared to grasp Alexandria's cheek. She turned again to eye Christian fully, and instead touched him, running a finger clear across his cheek. He turned away, but Thomas could see the shudder that ran through him with her touch. Freezing and burning all at once, a simple touch to muddle your mind...make you hers, yes, he knew it all too well.

"Christian!" Alexandria shouted, the Elite Creatures that held her arms keeping her in place.

"Now, now," Eleanor crooned, still staring upon the Vampire whose eyes had closed at her touch, "best not to wake him. I don't need him trying to stop what I plan to do," and she turned to the woman whose tears ran down her cheeks, "to you."

Thomas stepped forward, bringing Eleanor's eyes to him. There was a flash of recognition across her face for the briefest of moments, and then it died, a cold blankness replacing it.

"You," she said in astonishment, her eyes wide.

"Hello, Eleanor."

Javier stepped from the line of the circle and stood beside Eleanor, a hand upon the sword at his back.

Thomas waved him away. "No need for that, fresh blood," he said, "I only desire to know what our Queen intends to do with the woman."

She laughed and a few nervous laughs left the Creatures that lined the circle. "Oh my goodness, Thomas. You lurk around my halls for a month, doing who knows what, and now you show when we've guests? Ah," she gasped, sudden thought sending the spark in her eyes to flash, "the woman. You want her, don't you? Yes, of course, that's all you've wanted. And when I sent you to gather her," she said, something of a bite filling her words, "you moved for her, but, and this I assume, help me if I'm wrong, when you could not gather her, you returned here without consulting me, set about to sulk."

He felt the anger fill his veins, his blood running warm. "You only desired her to kill her before she can be turned by the hands of Xavier," he said, many affronted gasps leaving the Elites around them. "You don't know the power she holds!"

Javier's hand twitched on the handle of the sword, but Eleanor held out a hand, stilling him.

She eyed Thomas solemnly.

"The power, Thomas?" she asked, her voice quiet, pleading, and he knew what she was doing.

He would not fall for it. Not today. Not bloody today.

"What power?" she went on.

"No," he said just as quietly, the visions of Mara swimming in his mind, and he could feel Alexandria's beautiful presence fall over him in a wave, "no, no, no, I will not aid you anymore, Eleanor."

"Whatever," she said, feigning confusion, "do you mean, Thomas? What power does this woman hold? What has she done to you?"

He stared at the terrified woman still in the Elite Creatures' hold, hoping she would know him, would recognize him as the one chosen, the one that could give her the bloody sword, the one that would be worthy enough to receive his wife. None of this came, she merely held his gaze, a haze of fear covering her brown-green eyes, the tears endless within them.

"Thomas," Eleanor repeated.

He eyed her. "She's freed me," he said, feeling his own tears begin to well in his eyes, his heart fresh with his grief, "freed me from your binds. And I see now, you beside her...you against her brilliance, how remarkably you pale in comparison—"

"Watch your words!" Javier shouted, releasing the sword from his back even while many jeers left the Elite Creatures that watched them all.

Eleanor lifted a hand again and all fell silent. She stepped towards him, right past Alexandria, and once she stood just before him, she extended a hand to grasp his arm before he could know it happened.

The familiar dread filled him at her touch, the many voices whispering in his mind, and then another voice sounded, one he had only known in his dreams:

"Thomas...the sword. Get me the sword, and I will give you your wife."

And then something happened that he had not been expecting.

A brilliant red light left Alexandria, sending the Elite Creatures to release her and to stumble away as though burned. The red light moved to where Eleanor grasped his arm, and as soon as it reached it, she released him with a cry, black smoke leaving her hand with a hiss.

"What—"

But the red light filled his arm, and everyone watched as it moved up his shoulder and filled his heart, Eleanor's dread dispersing in his blood as the red light quickly replaced it.

"He's glowing!" an Elite from the crowd shouted in alarm, many other gasps and cries of bewilderment leaving the others. The sound of their voices rippled through the crowd, growing louder and louder until it was a maddeningly loud buzz in his ears.

"Thomas, what on Earth—" Eleanor began when the voice entered his mind again:

"*The sword,*" it said gently, "*get the sword.*"

He stared down at the red light that softly left his body, feeling the warmth pass through him, and he knew.

His eyes found hers, and through the growing anger of the crowd that had begun to realize something was terribly wrong, he could see the brilliance that was at her core. She was something magnificent, oh yes, he could see it clearly, and all at once he knew he needed to help her in any way he could.

He turned from them all and watched as the Elite Creatures at his back created a path for him to walk through, none of them seemingly wanting to touch him.

"Where are you going?" Eleanor asked, and he could feel the confusion leak off her in droves. *She was lost, she had lost, she had no true idea, none at all!*

He did not answer as he moved through the crowd and turned left, heading for the cages where they kept those who did not want to turn. He vaguely wondered why Victor Vonderheide was not kept there.

There was a room down there where she kept all the important things, yes, he would get the sword and give it to her...

The voice of the young Elite sounded down the hallway, and he could hear it clearly over the angry shouts of the many Elites: "He's heading for the room!"

"Get Aciel and Amentias!" Eleanor could be heard shouting. "Stop him!"

He did not slow in his run as he passed many other chambers, moving past them without a look back.

The sword, the sword, the bloody sword was here the whole time! And what was I doing?!

The hurried sounds of many footsteps pressing against the ground behind him forbid him the notion of anymore thought, and he let his mind go, moving on the warm air that was the red light.

Chapter Eleven

REGRET

Philistia Mastcourt turned to the man in the high blue chair, her large brown eyes warm as she eyed him. "Your Greatness," she said carefully, knowing it a touching subject for them both, for of course the Enchanting World had not known such an anomaly aside from the first Vampire...and she had invited him here.

He shifted in his seat, but his eyes remained closed, and she knew he was pretending. *Always pretending, Equis,* she thought with a smile. *Always pretending but not the pretender...*

"Your Greatness," she said louder this time, turning fully to watch him continue to feign deafness. She caught the eye of the woman beside his chair and squared her shoulders as heat filled her cheeks, and she thanked the Phoenixes her dark skin kept the blush from being seen. "Your—Greatness—*Equis,*" she repeated louder still, stamping her heeled foot with every word.

At this he started, a flutter of his eyes and clearing of his throat signaling that he had awoken, that he no longer, she knew, desired to pretend. His long black hair, silken as it was, rested over his gold-encrusted shoulders, the long red cloak he wore embroidered with the shimmering metal. Flecks of it shined through his hair.

He sat forward in his tall chair, removing his fist from his slightly pointed chin, and he stared upon her, a sad smile upon his face.

"I beg your pardon," he began, rubbing his eyes with a gloved hand, "you know I have grown weary, Philistia."

"You've reminded me endlessly, your Greatness," she said, smiling despite herself. She bowed low, the folds of her many layered robes swaying around her heels as she did so. "The Vampire has received," she said, waving a similarly gloved hand, a roll of parchment appearing in it as she did, "the request to join us."

He stared. "And you think he will come?"

She eyed the woman who stood beside him, hesitation keeping her from speaking further.

He seemed to have sensed this for he waved a hand and she moved from him, walking to a large white door, disappearing through it in another second. He turned back to eye her once she was gone, and stood from the chair, his tall, lean frame towering over her as he stood atop the marble dais his chair was placed upon.

She watched him, smiling at his youth, his beauty, for he was, and she knew, as old as time.

"Your Greatness," she said, bowing once more, for it was hard to remain staring upon an Ancient Creature, this she knew firsthand.

She heard him approach, his boots pressing against the marble of the floor, and the slight tremble over took her. She nearly lost her breath when the hand graced her shoulder.

"Philistia," the voice overhead said, and how gentle it was, "do you believe the Vampire to join us?"

"It is...hard to say," she whispered, rising to stand, the hand sliding off her shoulder, but still she would not gaze upon him anymore: It was known for a while by those closest to him that the spell worked to keep him young, able to remain in the presence of

Enchanters was fading, and steadily. "He is a Vampire turned by his father to ensure the bloodline remains...but with what Dracula has done to him, he is very much an Enchanter by your very standards."

"So he knows all the Spells, Enchantments, Potions?"

"To the letter, your Greatness. And he has been most skilled in protecting Dracula when taken on those quests for the Artifacts, as it has been understood...it is only...which side he feels most...akin to joining in this war."

He shifted his footing and she could not help but watch his face: he looked most troubled, his brow furrowed.

"I see," he said, "though it cannot be argued it would be desirable to have him here, close by. The illusion of magic is, indeed, beginning to fall...and I cannot help but wonder if I have not caused it by granting that Vampire his immunity."

She stared, mouth open in shock. "Do not speak like that— that Vampire was given grace by the Phoenixes—there was hardly anything you could do, your Greatness," she said once indignation forced her tongue, "what happens now...what happens now..." But she could not find the words, for it was true.

The process of granting Dracula the magical blood rendered the art impure. It had only been a matter of time, indeed, before magic began to fall.

It had been, as Equis had told her the Phoenixes had instructed, a necessary evil to ensure the end to the curse that were the Vampire and Lycan Creatures.

But she wondered now just how much it would help.

The Art of Enchanting was so necessary to keeping the humans subdued, safe, from keeping certain Faes protected, from keeping the Vampires in order...and now...it was all falling apart.

And the world that would emerge once Enchanting was gone would be one of madness, she knew.

"I have given the Vampire too much power," Equis went on, and she watched him stride to one of the many long windows in the great blue hall. She could see the tips of the high trees even from where she stood in the center of the room. "And even if my brothers above have granted it, unable to move down here like we that chose to stay...it has dwindled my power...our power." And he swept a hand to her. "Do you wonder, Madame, what would happen if we removed our gloves?"

She placed a hand instinctively over another. "I...I have wondered, although I know it is most undesired to do so," she answered quietly.

He smiled. "Quite," and with a flourish he removed the black glove from his hand, and she gasped, stepping away despite the great distance already in-between them. "No, no, do not flee," he begged, "see? Our powers are so much less than what they were mere weeks ago." And she stared, indeed, seeing his hand against the light of the low sun that was beginning to set behind him.

No sparks or beams of light left his hand, indeed, its light fluttered as though it could barely keep itself together.

She narrowed her eyes, unable to believe what she saw. "Your Greatness, you should have killed me when you removed the glove."

"Yes," he agreed, "but that has not happened. We are losing the battle, Philistia, and the Enchanters below us look to us to keep the order, to explain what is happening, but we cannot. We do not have the benefit of the Phoenix Fyre to restore our powers. We are," and he sighed, replacing the glove upon his hand, "a dying breed of Creature."

"And what," she thought aloud, "does Nathanial Vivery have to do with our survival?"

He stared at her, his gaze palpable in its darkness as the thought reached her mind before his lips moved, "We need his blood."

And before she could say a word, he went on, "To restore the magic that has been lost, we need to reverse what Peroneous Doe has

done to Dracula, and we can do it through the Vampire he has trained
to take in the Enchanting Arts."

"But you're talking of taking a Vampire's blood—"

"Yes, and when I drink it, it will undo what has been done."

"But the Vampires' immortality—"

"They are *not* truly immortal. The Phoenixes would not give
them *true* power, do not be *simple*, Philistia. The immortality is only
to keep them living if only several years longer than the normal
Enchanters do. It was *only* to ensure Dracula could uncover the
Artifacts...but when he died...a successor had to take his place... The
Vampires have always needed the blood of humans to continue their
life; that will not change with or without the curse within their blood."

She merely stared, fear covering her heart. "You speak, your
Greatness, o-of, of ending the Vampires' existence to regain what
was lost..."

He stepped to her, and she had to resist the urge to run: his
energy, despite the glove upon his hand once more, was immense,
even for an Enchanter of her skill. "And would it not save us? The
Vampires will die eventually, would they not? Even if they do reach
this elusive Goblet forged in the Fyres of the Nest, they will die.
They will become human, and they will die. Or they will remain
Vampires," he said matter-of-factly, "and die. Those...Elite Creatures
roaming the world will see to that."

"But Xavier Delacroix moves to still those Creatures, as I
understand it," she said, regaining some semblance of order; it would
not do to let emotion cloud her judgment, especially in this time,
"can we not just let him do it—reach the Goblet and wait for them to
turn themselves human?"

"And how long do you deem that will take, Madame?" he asked,
something like anger lingering on his words. "We cannot afford to wait
and let the Vampires sort this out. No," he continued, and she saw it
in him, then, far more than she ever had before, the presence of the

Creature he truly was. "We will move on our own and not be pawns to lesser Creatures anymore. I never intended that for any of you."

And he bowed, a hand over his stomach, and she knew she was to take her leave.

She curtsied, letting the words linger on her tongue. It would not do to speak so freely, she knew, it would not do to anger him further. For when an Ancient Elder was pressed to it, as it was said, the world could burn.

She stepped backwards, moving against the warm air, never turning her gaze from him. It was not until her back tapped against a door that she curtsied again and turned, pulling the golden knob and turning it.

She pressed herself through the doorway and closed it quietly behind her, a sigh leaving her lips with her fear.

He was angry and the world would pay because of it, of this she was certain.

For if any Ancient Creature's anger was one to avoid, it was the anger of Equis Equinox, indeed.

✳

Alexandria Stone screamed as the cold steel of the dagger was plunged into her abdomen. Her waist cincher had been torn off leaving the thin chemise she'd worn underneath the only thing to cover her body after her many skirts were viciously removed from her legs.

Tears left her eyes in droves as another cry left her lips, the Creatures on either side of her holding her arms still, keeping her in place as the woman before her did as she pleased.

"What power?" Eleanor asked for a third time, removing the dagger with ease, moving it to hover over her heart. "What power do you hold?"

"I don't know!" she screamed, her vision blurring as the blood left her wounds in droves. She was vaguely aware her toes could not touch the cold wetness of the dirt.

"You lie!"

The warmth of her blood returned to her with a stab to her breast, and the cry left her mindlessly: "I don't! I don't! I don't know what he was talking about!" And the sob left her throat, the numbness beginning to claim her, yet she braced herself for another pierce of blade all the same.

She opened her eyes a sliver when it did not come, staring around through her tears.

The room she'd been taken to was large, her screams bouncing against the stone walls in haunting echoes, several torches placed around the room offering her the only warmth she would feel whilst held here, she knew.

Eleanor had turned from her, her long black hair swaying as she stood before one of the large stone doors that was open now, a blurry figure talking to her in low tones.

Alexandria tried her best to hear what was said, but she could not release the sobs that left her throat, the pain spreading from her wounds.

I'm going to die, she thought, *I'm going to die by her hands and there's nothing I can do...*

For she had thought it strange that her red light hadn't sparked when the Elite Creatures had arrived in their room, protecting them. But then, she felt she had used a lot of it keeping Christian's broken ring atop his finger. They had thought it best to make it seem as though everything was normal, indeed, but the Vampire must have seen through the charade.

She had felt it was a lost plan, but she would not forgive herself if she did not try something with the light that could afford her control over the Lycans, the Vampires' urges.

Brilliant job, she admonished herself, tensing as best she could: Eleanor had turned back around, slender fingers intertwined before herself.

"Change of plans, Alexandria Stone," Eleanor said, releasing a hand from the other, waving it through the air.

Alexandria watched in confusion as a trail of black energy left Eleanor's fingers and traveled to her wounds, seeping into them, filling them. She felt them begin to repair her organs and skin, her confusion growing greater.

"You will be kept alive," Eleanor went on, "long enough for me to return from what I must do and kill you." And then to the Creatures on either side of her, "Make sure you feed her, I do not want her dying from starvation before I return."

Both Creatures nodded, never releasing her arms, and Alexandria watched in relief as Eleanor stepped from them and slipped past the still open door.

Christian, she thought as the Creatures hands released her arms, the blood rushing to them, *what did they do to Christian?*

✻

Lucien Caddenhall appeared behind a tree, the entrance to the low cave just there, several feet before him. With a deep, needless breath, he moved forward, prepared to feel the invisible wall that would keep him from stepping further.

He took a step, surprised to find nothing impeded his movement.

With a tentative hand, he reached out to grasp the lock on the black gates, when it unlocked and swung forward on its own.

I shouldn't go further, he thought, allowing his curse to wrap itself around him, rendering him invisible, but he knew the Vampire would be most displeased if he did not follow through.

Gritting his teeth, he took a step down the stone stairs, exhaling as he took another. When nothing happened he took another, confusion gripping him as he moved, prepared to be blasted back, away from the long tunnel that stretched out before him. He felt the surge of disappointment fill his dead heart when this did not happen.

Once he reached the bottom of the stairs, he closed his eyes, very aware he was entering a place no sane Creature would dare tread.

And yet, here I am.

He opened his eyes and began to walk down the long tunnel, unnerved that it was remarkably empty. He remembered when he had been here before, how freely the Elites walked about the hallways...

What changed?

He reached the dark wall, and turning his attention to the sword, he turned right, met with a much longer tunnel, the torches placed high above his head every few steps he took.

Again he was met with no one, and this scared him far more than Damion's wrath ever could.

Something was terribly wrong.

But still he walked, until he could not stand it, the presence of the sword reaching his curse, begging him forward, and he sprang into a steady run.

He turned another corner, met with still a strange emptiness, the sword's call getting stronger...

The woman and man appeared, Lucien ceasing abruptly to keep from walking straight into them. Their eyes were placed far past him as he pressed himself up against a wall, clear of their steps. "Find them, Trent," the woman was saying as she swung a long cloak around her shoulders, hiding her long hair. "I did think it strange they did not come when called..."

Her words were full of concern, but he moved in the opposite direction, continuing down the long hallways until one dipped down at a slight angle, going further into ground, and he knew he was close.

The more he moved, the torches' light shining their orange flames upon the walls, the ground before him, he saw the large stone door emerge from darkness at the very end of the hall.

Before he could reach it, it opened, a sound like a heavy groan emerging from behind it.

He stared in alarm as the man appeared holding a sword in a sweaty grip, a red glow about his body. There was blood all across his face and torso, the marks of bloody hand prints trailing down his arms. Lucien watched in alarm as the man ran a hand through damp brown hair, smattering it with this blood, and started forward, eyes weary the more he approached.

Lucien narrowed his eyes on the long blade held tight in his grip. *The sword.*

He started forward, the call the loudest in his shadow, his heart, and he reached out a hand to grasp it, to pry it from the man's hand, the cloth Damion had given him held aloft in his palm—

He felt his darkness lift off him with a strange, hot wind.

The man stopped dead in his tracks, staring upon him in frightened alarm, and Lucien stared at the sword, the cloth falling quietly out of his hand, knowing what would happen before it did.

Chapter Twelve

THE BLOOD-STILLER

Thomas lifted it, the red light propelling him; he could barely question from where on Earth the Vampire appeared when the sword moved, cutting through the Vampire's neck with surprising ease.

He watched the blonde head of the Vampire roll over the shoulder, and fall to the floor, before it turned to ash, the rest of the body shortly following suit.

He stared at the ash for another moment before moving, the warmth within guiding him down the tunnel with every step he took, and indeed, the moment he'd grasped the sword the heat grew until it was all he could feel.

He reached the end of the tunnel, turning right to enter another, the red glow of his light, the sword's brightening his way. He ran mindlessly, not stopping as he passed various doors, until he reached the large stone ones that blended into the walls around them. Eleanor's throne room.

He banged his fist against the stone, waiting patiently as the Creatures moved to open it. The moment the orange light passed through the doors, Thomas lifted the sword, sending it straight through the Creature's head.

He removed it, the Creature falling to the floor as another let out a cry of alarm, and he swung the door open with his free hand.

A woman's scream filled his ears, and then he could see, the Elite just before him now raising a sword, prepared to bring it down over his head.

He ducked, sending his shoulder into the Creature's chest, the grunt leaving the Creature's throat, the sound of the sword he'd held sliding against the stone floor.

The woman's screams continued somewhere nearby, and Thomas landed atop the Creature who had flew against the air with him, sending the Ares into the Creature's neck before the Creature could let out a scream.

As the blood poured from the Creature's neck, Thomas stood, looking around the room with wide eyes until he saw her. Standing just beside the throne, a tentative hand upon it as if to steady her trembling frame was Alexandria Stone, her fear one he could greatly smell.

He stepped for her, and she stepped away, nearly stumbling down the steps from the throne, her brown-green eyes wide with tears, a shaking head before her as if to keep him at bay. "P-please," she whispered frantically, "please—s-stay away!"

"But why?" he said quietly, sweat covering his shirt now: the heat remarkable with how it sweltered and filled him. "You wanted me—your chosen—to-to hand you the sword, and here I have it!" And he waved the Ares through the air, a shriek leaving her lips. "Why won't you take it—give me my Mara back?"

"I—I don't know what you're talking about!" she whispered, having stopped stepping away from him.

He narrowed his eyes upon her taking in her fear, her tears. "But you do," he went on, "you *do* know! You have filled my dreams, even now you fill me with this red light—your red light!"

"I-it's not—it's not m-mine," she stammered, and it was so wildly she looked around as though searching for elsewhere to run, "it's Dra-Dracula's—"

"*Him?*" he interjected. The laugh soon left his throat. "No, no, it is you—the woman in red—the one who can save me, give me back my life—"

"I have no idea what you're talking about!" she screamed, sobs leaving her throat in earnest. "I have no idea who your wife is—why you think I can—I can give her to you!"

"Because you have said it!" he shouted back, brandishing the sword upon her, though not entirely meaning to. He stepped for her, watching as she stepped away with his movement, a careful dance. "You have said it to me over and over for the past month! 'Get me the sword, give me the sword,' you wanted nothing else! So what now has changed? What now has rendered you incapable of grasping it?!" And he threw it at her feet, a cry of fright leaving her lips at the movement. She merely stared, the tip of it pointing at her, the gem in the middle of the guard a beautiful crimson. Even it glowed.

"Go on," he encouraged, watching her, waiting, indeed, for her to turn pale, the spark of red to fill her eyes, "go on—take it. Give me back my wife."

She hesitated for just the slightest of seconds before she dove for it, grasping the handle in hand.

A steady stream of red light left her then, much like it had done when it had entered his arm, and filled the sword, the red light blinding him so...

A terrible scream filled the air as the sword clanked against the floor, and when he lowered a blood-covered arm, his eyes widened in surprise:

She was on the floor, eyes closed, the sword inches from her finger tips, the steady stream of red light filling the entire sword; the red gem in the guard glowing brilliantly against the now faint light of the torches.

And he heard it, the low voice in the back of his mind, a rousing call pushing one to immediate action:

"Protect the Dragon!"

But he could not move.

The enigmatic vision from his dreams, the pale skin, the Vampire that whispered in his ear every night was not this woman. She was, why she was utterly *normal*, save for that red light; she had claimed to not know what it was he spoke of. And he thought, for the first time since he'd laid eyes upon her, she truly had no idea what it was she did whilst in his dreams.

"Protect the Dragon!"

He turned from her only when the figure appeared in the open doorway, her red eyes wide in her anger as she glared around the room.

"Thomas," Eleanor said, stepping straight for him, "you continue to astonish me."

He said nothing, the red light continuing to fill him, surround him, the low voice continuing to call...

"To," and she waved a hand to the sword, Alexandria beside the throne, "render the woman unconscious...to keep her from running... you have done...beautifully..."

"I did not do it for you," he said quickly, the words in his mind growing louder the more he stood there.

Eleanor's face dropped with her upset. "Oh?" she breathed, "then who," and she eyed Alexandria's unconscious state in distaste, "did you do it for?"

"Myself," he said, moving for the sword before she could know it happened. He picked it up without a word, darting for Eleanor, the tip of the sword pointing for her heart, when she let out a strange laugh, and waved a hand.

Thomas stopped just before her, staring at it in alarm, for it was large, immensely so, her fingers now resembling long claws, the bone beneath apparent through the skin quite thin.

He tore his gaze from the hand, watching Eleanor stare at the hand with equal alarm, something like fear covering her face.

"Damn," she whispered, placing the large hand behind her back quickly.

"Eleanor," he breathed, fear not reaching him even as he eyed the sharp nails not hidden behind her back. *What is that?*

"You've seen nothing, Thomas," she said, her desire to erase what happened clear in her voice, "nothing. Now leave me, I must tend to—"

But even as she spoke her voice died, and her gaze, Thomas saw in continued alarm, was placed on something behind him.

✳

The eyes remained closed, but the woman stood, her face pointed in her direction as though she stared upon them.

And Eleanor could feel that glare. Through the eyelids, she could feel that glare, and how penetrating it was: Eleanor quite felt as though she would be consumed by that unseeing gaze.

Alexandria raised a hand and all at once, Eleanor felt her own hand return to normal, and with it, knew her skin to resume its blood-filled glow, her red gaze to disperse in its hue.

She was human.

"I," she began, not sure what more to say, for indeed, Thomas turned to eye Alexandria as well, a gasp leaving his lips, the sword lowering in hand.

"I'm yours," Eleanor could hear him whisper over the red glow, "please, let me be yours—I will do anything if you will give me back my wife..."

Alexandria turned her face to him, and the smile lifted her lips though her eyes remained closed. "You are not the one," she said quietly, "to hold the sword. Leave me." And without another word, her red light pulsed just once and Thomas turned on a heel, the sword hitting the floor with a loud clank. He moved silently past Eleanor, stepping out of the room.

She merely stared after him, marveling at the woman's ability to influence the man so easily.

Dracula's blood, she thought in wonder, *of course he would give this woman such power. Of course he would subject his own to his protection even in his death...*

"You are a brilliant tactician," Eleanor said aloud, finding her voice amidst the glowing woman's presence, returning her gaze to her, "to...reduce my men to stammering idiots, unaware of my hold..."

Alexandria said nothing, but remained standing, her chemise reaching down to her thighs, keeping her under garments hidden. Her hand was still before her, and Eleanor watched as a finger crooked, and she almost laughed, bemusement filling her mind.

Was she calling me to her?

She hesitated, greatly aware she could not feel her blood in her veins, could not smell her dread, could not smell her chosen perfume of lilac petals, the fresh blood she would consume as a Vampire. *I am human*, she thought with concern, *and that woman...is something else.*

Something she was not certain she should be near, indeed, for it was so easy the woman made Thomas do her bidding...

Such power. Such ease.

Was her power truly greater in its hold? Could she really undo the Elite Creatures' desire with just a flick of a finger?

"Come here," Alexandria Stone said, her eyes still closed.

"Why?"

"You keep the chosen from fulfilling his duty to the Dark World... Come here. We must talk."

"Talk?" She did not move. "You must be...joking."

She said nothing.

"Xavier Delacroix deserves to know the truth to Dracula...to your power," Eleanor said, not able to still her voice, "he deserves to be with someone that will understand the greatness he can achieve if released from the shackles that bind him."

"Oh?" Alexandria breathed. "You mean these shackles?" And she raised both arms, the red light glowing brilliantly there. "This light does not hold him back...it propels him forward. It is your dread that stills him."

"No! It is that bloody light that keeps him from me, from seeing the truth! Even Victor has agreed to my way—to what I have uncovered in that book!"

"Victor doubts just as you do."

"What?" she spat, anger sending her chest to heave, her heart to beat wildly. "I do not doubt what I have done—what I've become!"

"And what have you become?"

Her mouth closed abruptly and she found she could not answer. Not that question.

Instead she let out a deep breath and replaced her frown with a smile. *I will not be outsmarted.*

"I am...what we Creatures should have always been," she said plainly, "what Dracula...fool he was...kept for himself. I saw his heart...in that book. His heart screamed of fear for the...brilliance he once was."

"And what was that?" Alexandria asked, her voice just as calm as it had always been, eyes still closed.

Eleanor smiled, despite herself, and said, "He was scared of the true face of the Vampire. He wished to erase it, to be as his mother."

"And are you not scared as well, Creature?"

"What do you mean?"

"Your hand."

"My—"

"You hid it as though you, yourself, were terrified of it. Could it be," she went on much to Eleanor's dismay, "that you were scared of what it means?"

She blinked. "What are you talking about?"

And her eyes opened, the brown-green gaze boring into hers, no trace of fear, of recognition showing itself in them. Eleanor thought it the gaze of one who slept-walked. "You know what it means," she said, "he said it himself, after all. 'You are a curse.' A curse. And as with every curse comes consequence."

"What the hell are you—"

"You are turning into the very Creature you desire to be...but it is not happening as you expected it to, is it? You cannot control when it rears itself, for instance, your hand...you cannot control what is happening to you, what will, in the end, consume you."

Anger filled her but she knew she could do nothing against this glowing woman, this woman that spoke so knowingly... "You know nothing of what I have unleashed! I control it all!"

"Do you?"

She opened her mouth to retort when the hurried footsteps neared the doors, propelling her words to the bottom of her throat.

She did not turn to eye who it was, for the woman before her held her attention immeasurably. *She stopped the transformation, ceased my Lycan and Vampire blood, reduced me to humanity?*

"My Lady!" Thomas's voice issued from the doors.

Eleanor whirled despite herself to eye a sweat-laden Thomas who held up a beaten, bedraggled, *awake*, Christian Delacroix. She stared at him, not daring to believe he stood there.

"You...how are you up?" she asked dimly, both Creatures stepping into the room, moving past her to stand beside Alexandria, a place the black-haired Vampire had stared in relieved astonishment since he'd arrived.

Thomas, however, smiled as though he would finally get what he desired.

"I have done as you asked, my Lady," he said to Alexandria.

Alexandria stared at him, then eyed Christian. "Indeed. Now, my chosen," she said to Christian whose shirt was ripped in various places, the cuts made there already healed, "take your prize." And she waved a red hand towards the sword behind Eleanor.

Eleanor started, stepping for the sword before Christian could move, the red gem gleaming in the red light of Alexandria, the torches still about the room.

"I can hold it," she said in surprise.

Alexandria's lip pursed, disappointment lining her face. "I had hoped," she began, "you would not think to grasp it."

"Then you are daft," Eleanor said, pointing the sword at her, "I don't care what form I hold, however disgusting it is, I know my place, what I deserve!"

And much to her surprise Alexandria smiled, slowly, knowingly she smiled, and Eleanor lowered the sword in hand. "What?" she asked. "What more do you know?"

And Alexandria stepped past her, motioning for Christian to follow. He did so without haste. "Enjoy your ability to hold which evades you," she said, and Eleanor could smell the blood of Dracula as she passed, "you will not be able to hold it for long."

Not daring to believe she smelled what she had, she swung the sword, turning with it to eye the beheaded woman, quite sure she had ended the annoyance that had plagued her save Dracula when he still lived...

She blinked, the sword falling in her hand: the woman was gone, as was Christian Delacroix.

Before she could ask the walls what on Earth had just happened, a very bewildered voice sounded from near the throne.

"She—she left me."

She eyed him in alarm: she had almost forgotten anyone remained in the room with her. He looked incredibly lost the more she stared: his brown eyes were filling with tears.

"Wh-where did she—why would she leave me—a-again?" And then he moved, stepping straight up to her, delirium clawing at his mind: his eyes turned black and she could feel the rage of the Lycan warm his blood as he grabbed her arms, shaking her angrily. "Wh-why would she? She said she would, she would—I need my Mara!"

Eleanor merely stared at him, unable to speak, for she, herself had no idea what in the world just happened, how easily it was the woman had left the cavern...and indeed, she didn't know how far they had gotten.

The sword let out a burst of red light and flew out of her hand landing on a step just before the throne, and Thomas stepped from her as though pained.

She stared at him; tears still left his eyes, but he looked solemn, the anger apparently having left him.

"Thomas," she began, not sure what to say, and even as she said his name, she began to feel the pull of the air against her skin, how cold, devoid of life. She stared at him, the red overtaking her vision against her will, the thirst drying her throat, and then, with a cold breath, the fangs tore through her gums. It was as though the woman had not interrupted her Vampire form at all.

"She's gone," Thomas said, as though at peace with the truth. His stare was upon the sword as though it would rise from the floor and plant itself within him. "She's gone—it's why...you can regain your forms...the sword cannot be held by you again."

The thirst consumed her, but she turned her thoughts to more important things, her mind turning with how she could use what just happened to her advantage. For of course, there had to be a turn. "It can be held by you, though, Thomas" she said, intrigue fueling her. Her own gaze moved quickly from the sword to him and back. If the woman's pull was gone from around them surely he would be able...

He eyed her as though he'd been slapped. "I will never..."

"But you must!"

He continued to eye her in bewilderment.

"Thomas!" she hissed, seeing her chance to regain what was lost. "Think! You gave her what she desired—the Vampire, did you not? You gave her the sword! And what did she do? She left with him, and she was to leave with the sword if I had not grabbed it! *She used you*, Thomas," emphasizing the last few words, "used you and now she is off with that Vampire to further evade me, to keep me from my goals. Will you allow this? Allow her to get away with making a fool of you?"

And she waited what seemed an eternity, the gears working in the man's mind, before a darkness filled his eyes, and he said, conviction clear on his words, "I will end Alexandria Stone, if it is what you desire...my Queen."

"It is," she said, glad she had at least one of her men back to his senses: the damned woman had at least given her that.

Chapter Thirteen

PARDON

They landed on their knees in a swirl of his darkness, and he'd barely grasped the grass before the blood left his lips.

"Make way! Move!" Ewer Caddenhall's voice sounded over his head; he could smell the blood as the Vampire neared.

The dagger was at his throat in the next second, and he gasped, the pain leaving him.

"If I have to do that one more time," Ewer said, and Darien could hear him replacing the dagger in its place at his side, "you'll be a dead Vampire. Permanently."

He looked up from his knees to eye the old Vampire. "I had to move us—we would have been killed—"

"Yes," Ewer snapped in exasperation, "we would have been murdered by the three measly Elite Creatures, one all but frozen thanks to the girl's arrow!"

He scowled, rising to his knees, unnerved when he fell to them again. "Whatever the circumstance," he said from the ground, "we are closer to our destination." And he stared ahead at the large lake just before them, its water dark against the setting sun.

Oh damn, he thought, attempting to rise to his feet again, *we do not have the strength to swim through Merpeople's waters.*

Ewer's hand was on his shoulder in the next second, the long fingers gripping it, holding him upright. "I agree," he said, not doing a thing to hide his displeasure at being made to move, and in this time. "Which is why we should wait until you are...better," but even as he spoke, his voice faded and Darien knew what he thought.

I will never be better.

He shrugged off the hand, and turned from him, his knees shaking as he eyed the water, yet he found he could remain standing.

"Darien," a voice said from his right. He turned his head against the voice, sending a piercing pain to slice through it, and he grimaced. She was walking towards him, limping slightly, in a hand one of her arrows, the large white bow in the other. "Where are we?"

"The Forest of Yielding," he said before Ewer could respond, willing away the steady headache that threatened to fill his mind the more he stared at her. Closer now he could see her blonde hair loose, wavy as it fell around her face, and her blue eyes, even in the growing darkness were wide and clear. She was not scared. *Did my blood do that?* "It is only a few days travel to the castle where we will meet the king."

Ewer snorted bringing all eyes to him. "And in the dark," he said, waving a hand around at the night that was swiftly falling, brandishing all things in shadow, "it will become a much longer travel. And there are still the waters we must swim. Did you not think this through, Master Darien? Or perhaps," he went on, despite Darien's displeasure, "you only moved, thinking of the last time you had been with the woman. It was here, was it not? That you last traveled with Eleanor Black—"

He'd grasped the bladed staff at his feet and had placed a blade dangerously close to the tall Vampire's neck, rendering him most silent. "Do not speak of her, do not speak of what you do not understand."

His blue eyes widened, but Darien knew he was not scared. Ewer Caddenhall was never truly scared of him, only bound, regretfully, by the curse placed upon him. "I understand," he said slowly, "that you were here when Eleanor moved to confront Xavier Delacroix." Darien narrowed his eyes. "Ah," Ewer breathed, "you do not think the curse is merely one-sided? With the dwindling of the Enchanting Arts, Master, it seems spells are being undone, curses expunged...I can access your thoughts, know your locations just as you can mine."

He removed the staff, a tired breath leaving his throat. The hand that held it shook terribly and he dropped it at his boots, his gaze only upon the Vampire. *Of course*, he thought, staring into the wise eyes that had known this for a while, *of bloody course*. "You claim," he started, feeling Lillith's eyes upon him, heard the questions that filled her mind, "to know my intentions, my thoughts. I was here, yes, but it was not to aid her. I deemed to stop her. Yet she knows me, knows how to use my journey through the book against me. She went on with her men, and I...I was left to face a Dragon."

"Yet there are no Dragons—"

"And why do you think that is?"

A spark of recognition filled his eyes, and Ewer's mouth formed a thin line at last.

Darien turned from him and watched her. "What we face," he told her, the pain returning as the brief rush of adrenaline began to fade, "belongs to all Dark Cre—"

"Darien," Ewer said, his voice high, and Darien eyed him: he stared across the lake, his blue eyes wide with disbelief.

He followed the gaze, his own eyes widening. There stood Xavier Delacroix, dark splatters adorning his face and clothes, beside him were several Creatures, only one Darien had met before in his life.

✵

Xavier narrowed his eyes. The dark figures that stood on the edge of the lake appeared to be facing them, but he could not be sure they were who he thought they were. Indeed, the strange darkness blanketed the sky, making it terribly difficult to see anything beyond a few miles.

Aurora waved a hand, a ball of light appearing in her palm. Xavier watched as it moved across the lake, shedding its light over the black water, the light not passing the black surface. And then the water rippled, its rippling following the trail of light, and it was as though a being beneath the surface followed it.

He heard the Vampire beside him let out a steadying, needless breath. "We've awoken the sea-beasts," he said, a hint of amusement on his words, but when Xavier turned to eye him, he saw the Vampire's blue eyes were shining with fear.

Something appeared out of the corner of his eye before he could respond, and when Xavier turned to watch the lake, he saw the upper body of a very slender woman, long black hair slick to her head and naked back. She reached up to the light with terribly pale, webbed claws, and snatched it as though it were a ball, and submerged with it close to her chest, a horrible screech filling the sky as she did so.

"They won't allow us to swim their waters," Amentias said from beside Aciel as darkness resumed over the water, both Creatures' eyes red as they surveyed the lake; their skin appeared to pale in the vague moonlight. Xavier knew they needed more blood of the Elite Creatures to maintain their forms, but as it were, if they did not get it, then they would die, wouldn't they? And he needed to know what they knew of Eleanor Black's secrets—her power—they had yet to share that.

"And we don't have pardon," Peroneous Doe added, his own brown gaze eyeing the waters with a mixture of fear and anger:

Xavier half thought he still resented telling his truth to Dracula's creation as they had come to know him, but he would not speak on it again, regardless of the many times Xavier had asked once they left Evert's room.

"What do you mean, pardon?" Aciel asked.

Xavier did not fail in catching the surreptitious glance Aleister and Aurora stole before Aurora said, "The only ones that can allow a Creature passage, any other way around or over or through Merpeople's waters are the Phoenixes...and the former Dracula."

He stared, remembering clearly when he'd been here before, watching Dracula fly easily over the water to reach this very bank. He blinked, returning to the present. "But you were able to cast some spell after I'd saved Aleister when he went under at the lake before, can you not do so again?"

And he could not imagine away her discomfort: her black eyes were downcast, and as he stared around at Aleister, Dragor, he saw all their gazes were avoiding his.

"No, we will not do this," he said, "you claim to fight for me," and he eyed Aleister, forcing the Vampire's gaze up to his, "to be right behind me? How can you claim this and still keep things from me? Explain this 'pardon.' Why do we need it to be able to pass across Merpeople's waters? And how can we get it? Do I have it now that I am...now that I took his place?"

An unsettling wind passed them all, and Xavier did not remove his gaze from the three Creatures.

It was not until a voice beyond the lake sounded that anyone did anything.

Peroneous stepped up to him and said, tersely, as though to say it slowly would harm him, "Whatever spell Aurora was able to cast was because of the Phoenixes. I, myself, have only just learned of their involvement in our world, however removed. They watched you," and he eyed Aleister, Aurora, and Dragor in apparent disappointment, "while you roamed the Dark World for the book, your Grace. To... protect you, to ensure you reached it safely."

Aleister placed a scarred hand on Peroneous's shoulder, bringing all eyes to him. "You speak too bloody freely!" he shouted. "He needn't know about the signal!"

"Wait," Xavier said, a snarl escaping his throat with his frustration. "You're telling me that the Phoenixes had *signals*? What bloody signals?" And as he spoke he felt the red light rise in his blood, the dread on the night air pushing against it, threatening to take over once more.

"But that is precisely why we did not tell you," Aleister said amidst the rush of blood in his ears. Xavier watched him shove Peroneous rudely to the side and step up to him, a pleading darkness in his eyes. "You were lost to her, Xavier. We could not risk you..." His voice faltered, and it was as though he could not find the words to finish.

He felt his annoyance grow, the dread penetrating his blood, and how faint Dracula's voice was becoming. "Risk me *what?*" he snapped, sending Aleister to jump.

At this Dragor stepped forward, and the strange shouts from beyond the lake could not reach Xavier's ears as he watched the gruff Vampire open and close his mouth, the words escaping him.

"I swear on a Lycan's tail, if you bloody Creatures won't tell me what's going on—!"

"We could not risk you getting captured by the Phoenixes before you were ready to meet them," Peroneous finished, the muffled screams having stopped a minute before.

As Xavier watched him in confusion, he caught Dragor's eyes and went on, "They protected you, kept you going as best they could to reach the book, but it is believed...it is believed that they only desired you to force your hand..."

"I don't understand."

Peroneous cleared his throat. "In the book," he said, is voice strained as though it hurt to say the words, "you should have met Dracula—you did, yes?"

He nodded, the rush of blood growing louder in his ears...

"And you would have been led...to where it was Dracula, in the book, remained, yes?"

He nodded again, fighting the desire to tear the Enchanter's head off as the dread seeped into his skin, the righteousness returning...

"You would have...been told the various secrets Dracula kept close to his dead heart..."

The anger surged despite his best attempts to keep it at bay. It must have shown on his face, then, for Peroneous and the rest stepped away, looking bemused, their medallions letting out steady glows of red light against their chests as though to keep him away.

"I was told nothing of true merit," Xavier almost shouted, the anger burning in his dead heart. He remembered the sight of the Vampire sitting atop his chair, lying to him even at the last hour... *Bloody liar.*

"But you were surely told what you were meant to do? The truth of—of the Phoenixes—the power of the Vampire?" Dragor asked next, a hand on the sword at his waist.

Xavier eyed him in slight amusement. "Whatever truth this threatens to be, I daresay, Vampire," he said, the words sliding out of mouth as the rage grew, "I know not of it. Dracula only expanded upon the lies he readily deemed it appropriate to share. And then he bit me when the Phoenixes approached, turned me back into a Vampire—"

"What?" all three Creatures said together, pushing him into silence.

Xavier let out a low snarl. Why was it so bloody hard to keep the meaning of words together? "I said," he started with a sigh, "he turned me back into a Vampire."

"Well, that means," Aleister said, as though he couldn't believe the words he spoke, "you were a human—in the book."

"Yes," he said. "What? Weren't you all told this by Evert?"

"No," they said together.

And before he could open his mouth to ask just what they *were* told by the Ancient Elder, a particularly loud scream issued from beyond the lake.

He whirled, the large yellow Dragon hovering in the sky over the three Creatures that stood beneath it, apparent shock keeping them in place.

"A bloody Dragon?!" Dragor said from behind him.

He kept his gaze on the blonde-haired Vampire, her hair swirling in the wind the Dragon's large wings swept up in their continued beating. *Lillith*, he thought, her bow rising in her hand. He watched in alarm as she lifted an arrow from her back.

"That girl isn't going to—" Aurora began, when the arrow flew through the dark air, the Dragon's red eyes trained on it. It hit the Creature's massive underbelly with a dull thunk.

"What's a bloody Dragon doing here?!" Peroneous shouted in anger, a dark hand waving across the lake.

Xavier heard someone snarl behind him. "Pay attention," Aleister said next, "the air is filled with her energy, and so is that Dragon."

"But how would she know we're here?" Amentias asked, and Xavier could hear the worry on his voice, but he would not turn to eye him: he was too focused on the large winged beast that filled the sky.

"Precautionary measures," Aciel responded. "None of her men returned from being sent here—of course she would send another even greater threat to still Xavier."

"But a bloody *Dragon?!*" Peroneous shouted again.

Xavier watched the large beast flap into the air, its large tail swaying dangerously close to the head of the Creature beside Lillith: the black-haired Creature ducked to avoid it, and then fell to his knees along the ground.

He narrowed his eyes, unable to smell anything other than Eleanor's dread...and how persistently it pushed against the red light of the sword: he felt the heat surge against his thigh. "That can't be," he began, not daring to believe it, "that can't be Darien Nicodemeus? And Ewer—Ewer Caddenhall?!" For he saw the particularly tall Vampire move swiftly to help Darien up to his feet.

Dragor brandished his sword. "A traitor and a Caddenhall?" he repeated, staring over the dark water as well. "We'll deal with them, your Grace—"

"How?" Peroneous shouted, staring at the water even as the Dragon continued doing somersaults in the air, a great wind blowing across the lake, sweeping their hair and cloaks away from their bodies.

And even as the wind blew, the water rippled again, but this time in several places: several dark heads rose from the blackness.

Xavier continued to stare, a hand on the Ascalon even though it burned, as the heads surfaced even more, slowly becoming the wet, bare shoulders of men and women, their hair slick to their backs as they appeared to watch the Dragon.

And then, without preamble, the Dragon let out a ferocious roar and swept low over the land, large mouth open, and Xavier realized what would happen before it did.

"Move!" he cried, jumping out of the way as the Dragon's long mouth graced the water, attempting to gather a Merperson between its teeth.

He landed roughly atop the grass, just atop his sword, and the curse left him as the burning hilt dug into his hip, burning, he could smell, through his shirt.

He rolled onto his back, a hand grasping his hip where the metal sizzled against his skin, and he pried it away with a groan, Eleanor's dread dispersing within him as he did so.

He exhaled a cold breath as the Creatures were on their feet, eyes on the air, and he followed their gaze:

The Dragon had succeeded in gathering his prey, for a black-scaled tail, its two large black fins slapping wildly in the air, was stuck in-between the Dragon's long, many-rowed teeth. It chomped happily, sweeping back around to return to the lake.

"Your Grace!" Aleister shouted from nearby, scarred hands grasping at his collar, pulling him away from the water.

Xavier could not say a word as the Dragon dove again, this time submerging headfirst completely into the black water, an eerie silence falling across them all.

It was a long time before the water began to form small waves, and it was as though something large was attempting to rise from its depths.

"Why would a Dragon do that?" the terribly scared voice of Peroneous Doe could be heard whispering nearby.

He thought immediately of when he was last here, the sight of the large Dragon swallowing whole an entire Mermaid passing through his mind.

They loved to feast on the Merpeople, he thought.

"Let's see if it's able to get out," Dragor said.

And they waited, Aurora and Peroneous the only ones breathing, until the waves grew larger, yellow scales beginning to emerge from the middle of the water...

"That's impossible!" Aleister whispered, hands still gripped on Xavier's collar, and Xavier felt the belt at the back of his head and knew the Vampire knelt behind him.

But the more they watched, the more nothing else surfaced, and then a new color began to overtake the blackness.

"Merpeople killed a Dragon?" Dragor whispered in disbelief, and indeed, the red blood spread to the shore, Xavier staring at it in astonishment as it lapped at the dirt.

What just happened?

Slowly climbing to his feet, eyes still on the water, he grasped the hilt of the Ascalon surprised to feel it no longer burned with heat: it remained strangely cold to the touch as though it were a normal sword...

The black heads emerged from the water once more, this time facing them, their eyes completely black, their hair and pale skin covered with the blood of the Dragon. A Merwoman, one closest to the edge of the lake, lifted a webbed claw towards him, and Aleister nudged him forward.

"What—" he began, turning to eye the Vampire, but he saw all Creatures, save Aciel and Amentias were kneeling before him, their medallions letting out feeble red glows against the night.

And he remembered when Aleister had moved forward into Merpeople's waters only to get pulled under...

He hesitated as he turned back to the black, watchful eyes peering at him from behind long strings of black hair, and someone behind him whispered:

"You are the Speaker for Us All, your Grace—you must go."

Speaker for Us—

But the Merwoman let out a shrill screech, her hand shaking impatiently, still outstretched, and it was clear she waited for him.

"It is fine! Go! You are recognized," and he knew this voice was Aleister.

Squaring his shoulders, he stepped forward with his right leg, his hip letting out a searing pain. He doubled over, a hand atop the burn, and Aurora whispered, loud enough so he would hear: "Do not show weakness! Whatever ails you, fight it! You must move forward!"

Gritting his teeth, he stood upright and removed his hand from the wound, the black eyes glaring at him impatiently from the bloody water.

He moved, swallowing the pain with every step on his right leg, and at last he reached the edge of the ground, and he kneeled, not sure what more to do.

The Merwoman moved forward in the water, her hand gracing his cheek.

He swallowed a gasp, surprised at how cold her hand was against his skin. *This shouldn't be possible,* he thought as she searched his eyes with her terribly black ones, and then, and at last, a sweet voice entered his mind, and he felt, strangely, as though he were being pulled deep under water...

"We welcome you, our new king," the voice said. *"We will aid you just as we did the king before."*

And with that, she released her hand, and swam backwards, the rest of the Merpeople following suit, pushing back the bloody corpse of the Dragon against the other side of the lake.

He shook his head, feeling as though he needed to gasp for air, when they passed him, Aleister, Aurora, Peroneous, and Dragor, without a look back, and he watched in bemusement as they gently propelled themselves into the sky, moving as one, and pushed forward over the water.

He was still shaking imaginary water out of his ears when Aciel and Amentias stepped beside him, and Aciel said, a strange gaze over the bloody water, "You gain this lake, these Creatures, your Grace," and he placed a hand on his shoulder, and Xavier thought it an incredibly strange feeling, "but know that she has already gained so much more," and he waved another hand to the Dragon behind the line of Merpeople.

They walked to the edge of the lake before he could respond, their red eyes bright against the dark, and Xavier watched as they dove into it, their heads and arms the only things that could be seen as they swam through the blood, moving to reach the other side.

Xavier waited until the Merpeople parted, allowing them to pass, and the Elite joined the rest of the Creatures on the other side of the lake, before he started forward, the pain at his hip growing with every step.

He grimaced as he stepped into the water, the blood of the Dragon parting around him, and then he pressed forward just as Amentias and Aciel had done, swimming to the other side of the lake.

Chapter Fourteen

FORBIDDEN BLOOD

A low wind blew past him as he held her, unable to look away despite his great need for blood: his knees buckled and he fell to the ground, the faraway voices of the Creatures moving on the wind towards him.

He ignored the pounding in his ears, the pain that covered every surface of his skin, and he stared at her, unable to believe what just happened.

She had overcome Eleanor Black, sent Thomas Montague to aid me?

He had wondered how it was possible for her to be awake whilst covered in the light, so controlled...

"I smell something," a voice sounded through the trees, bringing his eyes away from her at last.

I must move, he thought, quite aware he had no energy, no blood to fly or run. He rose to his feet, her head rolling back in his arms, eyes still closed as he let out a snarl of pain, his legs holding up his weight in full.

"God," he whispered beneath the dull pounding in his ears, stepping in the direction opposite the voices, trying to keep his vision from blurring completely.

He walked for what he deemed an eternity, the voices ever closer against the strange night air...but it was no longer as strange as it once was.

Yes, he smelled the air as he moved, knowing the dread to have lessened in the sky, and he wondered if Alexandria had done that as well.

"A Vampire," a voice said from somewhere behind him, "moves through those trees."

He sped up, moving as quickly as he could against the pain that sent his knees to shake, made his every step an uncertain one.

He felt her back expand and retract gently and he thanked the sky she still breathed. Still breathed, but not awake, not eyeing him with her knowing gaze...

"There!" another voice sounded through the trees. "I think I see someone!"

The curse left his lips as he stumbled over the sparse twigs that littered the hard ground. His vision darkening, though he knew it was not the night sending the sight of the trees to get lost in the enclosing blackness.

He fell to his knees as the black covered his eyes in full, the stark need for blood ripping at his throat, sending his tongue to dry.

He heard the footsteps, their movement nearing ever closer, and he knew complete nothingness to claim him at last—

The pulse was strong in his arms. So much so he jerked away from it, hearing her body hit the ground brusquely.

And then he could see her, see the lines of her veins, the many tubes of blood that granted her life, and he watched in awe, the red light pulsing in those veins, the only thing he was able to see against the complete black.

And then a brighter light surfaced: her heart. He watched it in wonder, seeing it convulse, grow and shrink, the sound beating a rhythmic pulse in his ears.

And he knew.

Without preamble, he bent low, eyeing a vein in her neck, its steady pulsing pulling at his need with stark desire. And then he smelled it, the voices behind him fainter than they'd ever been before.

Her blood rose in his nose, a swirling wind of need and strange sweetness. Foreign, dangerous, compelling, forbidden...but blood all the same.

He knew nothing else but the liquid, the voice of Xavier a distant memory somewhere in his mind.

He could not truly hear it over the rush of his blood pounding in his ears, dulling all else.

Another voice, this one louder, sounded from somewhere around him, but he could not care.

He pressed his fangs against her skin, something like a rush of wind he could actually *feel* brushing past his face as he did so.

But before he could sink any deeper, taste the blood that rested inches from the tip of his fangs, he was pulled away.

"Well what have we here?" a strange voice said from overhead. He could not see who it was even as he lay on his back: all he saw was black.

"Looks like a Vampire," another voice said, this one younger than the last. "Why's it snarling like that?"

He had not even known the loud snarls had left his lips as he'd bent over her, but now he could hear it, feel his lips curl: he needed to feed, desperately.

"Aye, it be a Vampire," the other said, "but it isn't Xavier."

"How do you know?"

"Look—no sword. That Vampire keeps his bloody sword close all the time, doesn't he?"

"Hell if I know—I've never seen him."

"Yeah, well, we gotta kill 'em, don't we?"

"Aye," the other said as Christian felt the hunger overcome him at last, "we do. Can't leave anyone that isn't with the Queen alive, can we?"

And he barely felt the hand on his arm when the other said suddenly, "Wait—what if we turned 'em—y'know. Into one o' us?"

The hand lifted from his arm. "You're talking far above your grade, boy. We don't have the power to turn 'em. And this woman... she don't look too good—she wouldn't survive the Vampire transformation. It'd be a waste of perfectly good blood."

He strained as best he could to listen to their words, but even that was fading fast: he knew somewhere in his mind that he was dying.

A warm light claimed him, and without opening his eyes, he surrendered to it, all else fading away completely.

✳

Christopher Black walked through the trees, feeling the eyes of the many Creatures upon him, annoyance growing as he moved.

He had first wondered what on Earth would possess a Vampire to allow so many wild Creatures into his woods. But then he understood Darien Nicodemeus to be a most strange Vampire. He gathered that much from random conversations overheard upon his journey to the Vampire's large home.

He walked past two Goblins, their thin arms long and overhanging, their long hands sweeping the dirt ground. Their dulled black eyes trained on him as he moved, and it was with a grimace that he sped up, pushing back thoughts that he had supposedly been born to this world of Creatures, but he had never truly seen it.

Kept, always, under lock and key, a miserable journey away in a high stone tower. Dracula all he had known until the night he had broken the lock, exhausted with his captivity, desiring to see what lay beyond his black stone walls, cracked wood floors.

The large stone bridge lay out before him as he stepped past the last tree, staring at the expansive stone castle, turrets cutting the dark air.

He took a simple step onto the stone of the bridge when the fire lit the air behind the high stone wall, and he took several steps back onto hard ground.

"*Bloody hell,*" he whispered, panic filling him. *Was that—was that a Dragon?*

He could barely ask the night any more frantic questions when the two large doors opened across the bridge and a hooded Vampire appeared in-between them.

"Who," the Vampire called, "are you?"

The more Christopher stared, the more he saw the dark Vampire carried a sword at his hip: the red traveling cloak flared open as he moved, waving a gloved hand through the air, closing the two doors behind him.

Which one was this?

"Christopher Black," he said, squaring his shoulders, removing the hood from his own head, planting his boots into the hard ground as the dark Vampire drew closer.

"Never heard of you," the Vampire said, hand on the sword. "What brings you to my home?"

He stared at him, eyes narrowing. *Which one?* "I am here for you...Darien Nicodemeus," he decided at last, squaring his shoulders, ready for the truth to reach him.

"Darien?" the dark Vampire said, and Christopher heard the hint of humor in the deep voice. "You've come at the wrong hour, Vampire. I am not my brother, nor would I ever desire to be." And he stopped moving, the hand on the handle of the sword tensing as he pulled it from its sheath.

The long sword gleamed in the night, a brisk wind blowing past, and Christopher took a step back. He watched in confusion as the Vampire pointed the sword towards him. "Whatever would you want with my brother, Vampire?" he asked.

"You are Damion Nicodemeus?" he clarified, regaining himself.

"The one and only."

He let a snarl escape his throat, staring upon the dark Vampire in budding anger. He had watched her...had he harmed her, touched her? "Where is Lillith Crane?" he said loudly.

His brown eyes widened in slight surprise, the sword dropping in his hand. It was a long moment before he replaced it back in its leather home with a flourish. "Lillith Elizabeth Crane," the dark-skinned Vampire said, moving towards him, "has no human family remaining. Her home was burned down by Lycans. Any Vampire who has lived on the surface knows that, Mister Black. So I will ask again: who are you?"

He stared, unable to speak. *Burned down by Lycans? How—why would Dracula let that happen? And to be sent here, watched over by these strange Vampires...*

"Where is she now?"

"She is with Darien and the Caddenhalls, Mister Black," the Vampire said. He had almost reached Christopher but had stopped just before the end of the bridge, his red traveling cloak cutting an impressive figure through the night. "But if you leave now, I daresay you can catch them in about four days."

"Four—what do you mean?"

"They left on their journey to aid Xavier Delacroix in those Yielding Fields or something," he said, clearly uninterested, his brown eyes examining the night sky above them. "Ah," he breathed needlessly, "Dammath rests at last. Well, if you'll excuse me, Mister Black, I've my own Vampire to gather. He should have been back by now."

Christopher said nothing as the Vampire stepped past him with an ease he could only admire, giving him a curt nod, and walked into the Creature-filled wood, turning his thoughts to this Yielding Field, and just where on Earth that could be.

❋

"One more push," Ewer Caddenhall commanded, and the Creatures pressed against the door again, a faint creak leaving the hinges.

"We've been at this for hours, Caddenhall," Peroneous complained, releasing himself from the door, shaking out his arms. "The damned door isn't budging."

Lillith Crane watched as the tall Vampire waved another hand through the dark. A burst of wind pressed against the wood where Peroneous had left it, a much more pronounced creak leaving the hinges.

As the Vampire continued to wave his hands, Dragor and Aleister pressed against the door, and she looked towards Xavier Delacroix, the two Creatures most near him.

His eyes were closed as he stood against a tree, chin tilted upwards, and he seemed to be breathing in the cold night air, though she could not be sure. The Creatures on either side of him stared around, as though they expected trouble at any moment, and Darien Nicodemeus sat against a nearby tree, his gaze upon the back of Ewer.

The more she looked, however, the more she saw his eyes appeared glazed, as though he weren't seeing Ewer at all.

"Darien?" she called.

He did not eye her.

Something like unease filled her throat as she coughed out the name "Ewer," never tearing her gaze from the dark Vampire. "Ewer something's wrong with Darien."

She heard the old Vampire's hands swish in the wind and what sounded like a grunt, quickly followed by a snarl, and she knew he looked at the Vampire's unmoving gaze just as she did.

"Oh no," she heard the whisper before he moved past, his wind blowing up her blonde hair. And even as it settled back on her shoulders, she could not tear her gaze from the sight:

Darien Nicodemeus rested against the tree through no will of his own: his arms lay slack at his sides, palms up, fingers curled slightly, his legs sprawled out before him. And the sight of it was so incredibly jarring, so remarkably impossible that she had to look away. Her gaze fell upon the Creature most near her, the hardened Vampire Dragor Descant. He had been pressing against the double doors of Cinderhall Manor with the others but with Ewer's movement, he had stopped and turned to watch what transpired with, Lillith saw, bemused eyes.

"Ewer," Dragor said, cutting across the strange silence that had filled the clearing.

All eyes moved to the gruff Vampire as he took several steps towards the tall Vampire that had kneeled beside Darien and began shaking him feverishly.

"Ewer," the Vampire repeated when Ewer did not still in his attempt to rouse the dark Vampire.

"What?" Ewer Caddenhall whispered, looking up from Darien. Lillith thought him to cry it was so heavy with grief he looked.

Dragor took another few steps forward, and Lillith saw his hand was on his sword.

"That Vampire is dead," he said.

Ewer looked as though he were to laugh, but he let out a sound much like a strangled sob and looked towards Xavier Delacroix near his tall tree. "You have that special blood," he said to the king, "you can know for sure if he—if he is—"

All eyes moved to Xavier, and he greeted them in equal skepticism. "I—Ewer—I don't know," and he watched Darien's blank stare, a shadow crossing his eyes. "I cannot smell his blood," he added after a terse moment of silence.

And Lillith gasped, for she knew she could not smell his blood either. No trace of it would reach her nose, but the pull that she had felt once awoken in a small inn in London still remained, the call to be near him, to heed his every word still filled her changed blood, for she knew he had given her his blood. She had been told what had transpired once James had leapt from her and moved for Darien, and she had spent the better part of the day fighting alongside the Vampires to reach Xavier Delacroix. So what was this?

"But he cannot be—he cannot be dead!" Ewer almost shouted, an old hand on Darien's shoulder.

She was pulled from her reverie when Dragor released the sword. "Do you not see, you damned Vampire," he said to Ewer who looked quite affronted amidst his grief, "your Master is dead—which means you damned Caddenhalls need not exist anymore." And he stepped forward, the sword aloft, gleaming strongly in his hand, Ewer's blue eyes held on it apprehensively.

"Dragor," a scarred Vampire Lillith had never seen before said, sending her gaze to him. He looked scared despite his scarred visage: his green eyes were wide, his mouth curling into a frown, "put away the sword."

"Why? The damned Vampire has more power than any of us combined, he is born from an Ancient after all," Dragor said, his gaze never leaving Ewer's.

At this Xavier stepped forward. "What?"

"The Vampire's mother was an Ancient—he's a direct line," Dragor went on, all eyes held on him, "I pardoned the Caddenhall family because they were useful to the first Dracula, but now that he is dead and Darien as well—"

"But he's not."

And their gazes found her.

"He's not dead," she said, the blood running cold in her veins against their stares. *What do I know of what's happening?* But still she found her tongue moving within her mouth: "He's not dead—I took his blood earlier today and I can f-feel it," and she felt Xavier Delacroix's glare upon her the most, "and as we are aware V-Vampires turn to ash when they are permanently dead, do they not?"

No one said a word until Xavier left his tree and stepped up to her, his gaze unreadable against the night. She felt a shiver claim her as he stood just before her, his energy—his blood, quite formidable: it easily overtook all her senses.

She was wondering how it were possible when he touched her shoulder, the hand gentle, yet heavy.

"You took his blood, Miss Crane?" he asked, and for the first time in a very long time she saw the hint of concern in his stare.

"I...he deemed it necessary to save my life," she said. "After James Addison attacked him—"

"James?" And the astonishment on his voice could not be ignored.

She nodded.

"What? How could my servant attack you?"

"He was...bitten by Lore, your Grace."

Xavier's green eyes darkened and she half-thought him to scream it was so murderous he looked, but instead he said, "Tell me, Miss Crane, have you felt different since you took Darien's blood?"

She eyed the Vampire that still sat against the tree, limp and unseeing, Ewer still at his side looking upon him in disbelief.

"I-I'm not sure. I do feel as though...he and I are tied. I was able to hear his thoughts once I awoke, my Lord."

"So it's a compulsion, then. It is akin to the one who turned you?"

"I do not know...who turned me, your Grace."

His downcast gaze said it all: *How terribly sad.*

For she had known all her life as a Vampire it was most... disgraceful to never know the one who turned you; that was where a Vampire could find a sense of great peace amidst the life that was the constant need for blood. She had only passed by these remarks, this cloud on her person for being "Princess of the Vampires," Dracula's special child...

And there it returned, the immense longing amidst the pull of Darien's hold...but it was not for Darien, it was for another...someone she could never see in her mind's eye...

She barely saw the startled look in Xavier's eyes as she stepped from him, not fully feeling her shoes press against the ground, the dark Vampire drawing nearer the more she knew her body to move.

All she saw was the calm figure of Dracula, beside him another Vampire shrouded in darkness, just there, but so very much out of reach.

She knelt at the Vampire's side, the gentle prodding of her blood propelling her forward, but she knew not where to focus, on the memory or the present, for it was so strong they both resounded within her...around her.

"What's she doing?" a woman asked somewhere outside of her mind.

"*You're a fool, Black,*" Dracula said to the shadowed figure, and all was gone now, nothing remained but the memory, and she could feel the hard wood of the chair beneath her as she sat in the large office, staring up at the tall Vampire, and the shadowed figure he spoke so vehemently to. "*A bloody fool. What the devil am I to do with a girl as young as this? What were you thinking?!*"

The dark shadow of a Vampire responded, the voice a wave of deepness, muffled by something keeping the fullness of his voice from being heard completely, "*I saw her in the fire...her parents were already gone—I could not leave her—*"

"That is not your decision to make!" Dracula interjected, his long white hair swaying behind him as he took a hard step towards the Vampire in darkness.

Beyond them the fire sparked high in its grate, and she eyed it in fear.

Yes, she'd been terrified, then, swept up in utter cold, removed from her family—and what was this about a fire? *Mother and Father, gone?*

"Lillith!" a new voice called, pulling her from long lost grief. She blinked, surprised to find her arm pressed up against Darien Nicodemeus's lips; she watched her blood as it dripped onto his front, the dark drops bleeding into the black of his traveling cloak.

She could not find the words, the vision of Dracula fading fast, the outline of the dancing fire behind him lining her vision the more she stared in horror at what she'd done.

Hands were on her shoulders in the next moment, pulling her up to stand, but she could not tear her gaze from Darien's bloody lips. *What the hell is going on?*

"Lillith," the voice whispered in her ear, and she turned her head, eyeing the shocked gaze of Xavier over her shoulder, "what just happened?"

"I," she began, not sure at all what to say against the impatience in his voice, "I don't know. I saw, I saw Dracula and then—"

He whirled her to face him in full, her blood rushing to her ears at his movement. She was in trouble, she knew it, for his dark gaze held her in place: she felt she could not move even if she desired to.

"And then what?" he asked, hands moving to her face, sure to keep her gaze just there. "What did you see?"

She opened her mouth to respond when a strangled sound issued from behind her.

Xavier's gaze left her, his hands sliding from her face, how she felt the cold of his hands still upon her skin. She watched as he stared at something behind her, mouth open in what seemed to be disbelief.

"Ewer," he cried, his voice a strangled sob, "what's happening to him?"

"I don't—" the old Vampire shouted behind her, but she could not turn to eye him, the gurgling sound growing louder, lasting longer. She stared at the lapel of Xavier Delacroix's shirt. No, she could not hear the continued frantic shouts of Ewer behind her, whatever was happening to Darien was her fault...for it didn't seem the Vampire was well...

"*Lillith...*" the strange voice sounded, pressing against her mind with ease, an absolutely horrid sensation filling her heart the more she remained. "*Lillith Elizabeth Crane.*"

It was a call. One she could not ignore despite the fear that filled her blood. Something was wrong, so very wrong, and that voice...it terrified her to her very core...

"*What the bloody hell?!*"

She turned, the gasp leaving her lips before anything else could: Darien Nicodemeus shook violently against the tree, a fountain of blood leaving his lips, drenching his front; his eyes were completely black, no white within them at all; his black hair clinging to his shoulders and back as it was caught in the blood.

But the voice still sounded within her mind, the horrible feeling growing in her blood the more she stared at the grim sight:

"*Lillith...you have freed me...*"

And she could not be sure from whence it came when Ewer, a most horrified expression dressing his old face, stepped quickly away from the shaking Vampire and exclaimed, "He's truly dying!"

No one else said a word, and she dared not tear her gaze from the black eyes that appeared so unseeing, yet held so wide within the handsome dark face, that was now darkening even further...

How was it possible? she thought amidst the rush of terrible dread that pressed around her, and from behind her she felt another force, saw the ground, the back of Ewer, and the side of Darien bathed in a red light.

No sooner had this red light touched Darien's shaking frame did his lips open wide, the blood rushing forth in a powerful stream, a terrible roar escaping his throat as well. His spine straightened as though he was pulled upright by invisible hands, and his arms swung out to the sides, straining against whatever filled him, his hands veined, fingers taut, bent oddly away from their palms.

She let out a cry of pain as the dread overtook her, bathing her in its heavy hold, but she could not tear her eyes from him, and it was as though she were forbidden the notion at all: she suddenly felt miraculously compelled to the retching Darien's side though she could not move.

A hideous sound left his lips in the next moment, and she heard Ewer's terror-filled shouts, the other Creatures' horror-filled screams, but she could only truly hear his, Darien's, terrible scream. And she thought, for a brief moment at least, that it sounded very much like a cry for desperate help.

And then the world caved.

Darien's hands, so strained in his pain, lengthened greatly, sharp black claws forming at the end of what was once his fingers. Great black webs connected each claw to the next, and his arms only grew bigger. His traveling cloak, so caked with blood ripped, unable to accompany the length of his arms and chest, now widening: she could hear his bones grow and crack, a horrified gasp leaving her lips.

He slumped forward, a groan leaving him, his legs growing and lengthening as well, his boots tearing from his ankles and feet as large black claws replaced them. And then his spine shifted, appearing to lengthen as well, and what she saw she could not believe:

His back broke, the skin spreading up and outwards in two slits along his back, but she blinked, focusing on it clearly: The long leathery skin held bones within it, she saw, and it was not skin at all, but as it stretched out, lengthening fully, the cry of pain still leaving Darien's lips, she realized they were wings. Bloody wings.

He lifted his head, staring upon the Creatures before him in animalistic hunger, but his face was no longer handsome.

His chin had lengthened considerably, a sharp point reaching the bottom of his longer neck, his ears long and sharp at their tips much like the Elves, and when he opened his mouth, she found nothing but fangs to show themselves along the night.

"Master Darien—" Ewer Caddenhall began to say softly before the Vampire was on his newly formed feet, his height that of the start of the branches of the tree.

He looked down at Ewer's usually tall frame, and Lillith thought he looked down upon someone he did not understand: his black eyes passed across Ewer's long frame in question, and he opened his many-fanged mouth, yet nothing left it but a miserable screech, not unlike the Satyrs' voices.

"Ewer," Xavier called somewhere behind her, "get away from him!"

But it was far too late.

Darien extended a long clawed hand, wrapping it around Ewer's face with a jagged grace Lillith could not fail in noticing. Before Ewer could let out a scream, Darien clenched his hand, Ewer's head collapsed into itself, his brains, bones, and eyeballs falling past Darien's long fingers, the blood spraying everywhere Lillith dared look.

Horrified screams rent the air, and Ewer fell to the ground, absolutely dead. The newly formed Darien Nicodemeus stared around at them all, faint scraps of his clothes clinging to his leathery skin, and with a horrific screech, he lifted into the air with two strong beats of his wings, and ascended into the dark sky, disappearing over the tops of trees.

The woman was still screaming, the Vampires were snarling, eyes red, the two Creatures beside the tree merely stared upon the dead Ewer Caddenhall in frozen shock, and the dark Enchanter was throwing up whatever he'd eaten.

And she, Lillith Crane, felt her knees give way before all went terribly black.

Chapter Fifteen

WINGDALE

Victor Vonderheide stared at the ruined buildings, the layer of black ash that coated the street, and he ran the bottom of his boot over the lump of dead Elite Creature, turning it over. The face was unrecognizable, the cloak no longer present on its body.

"This was magic," he said knowingly, turning an eye to the man at his side.

Joseph Gail nodded in consent. "Yes," he said, green eyes flashing in the dark, "strong, unyielding, magic. It's as if it hasn't been touched by this...waning of magic going about."

Victor frowned, staring at the other bodies not fully burned into ash. "So one of ours did this?"

"Hardly," the proud Vampire said, turning his sharp gaze to the rest of the burned town, "this was someone—something else."

Wondering how on Earth the Vampire could tell, Victor opened his mouth to speak when Joseph Gail said, "It's them, Victor. The Elf and the Vampire. This...stench in the air, it isn't Eleanor's."

And he focused on the air, indeed, it was nothing like Eleanor's dread, it was smooth, the trace of heady smoke filling his nostrils as he sniffed. Indeed, it was almost lyrical, that smell, why, he quite remembered the days Dracula would return from his week-long journeys with that smell covering his clothes and hair, as if he'd been bathed in it.

He was pulled from his reverie by the sudden whirl of the Vampire's dark red cloak: Joseph Gail had turned from the pile of bodies to eye the other end of the street, many trees lining the distance. "They went that way," he said, more to himself, it seemed. He lifted a gloved hand and pointed a finger to the horizon: Victor's eyes widened as a blue left it and began to move in a straight line several feet ahead of them. "C'mon, then, Vampire. They have a day's head start."

He said nothing, staring after the trail of blue light, the Vampire that followed it, finger still held aloft, not daring a glance back.

Magic, he thought dimly, *of course the Creature would know magic.*

Wondering which Enchanter taught the former King of Wingfield the Enchanting Arts, he stepped along in the Creature's wake, feeling all the more disheveled in this world and its many secrets.

※

Damion Nicodemeus was confused. Lucien Caddenhall had not returned, the skies were strangely dark even as the moon filled the sky, and he was growing immeasurably impatient to gather the sword.

What could have happened?

It was entirely unlike Lucien to move where bidden and not return in at least a day. He grimaced, replacing his hood atop his head.

He kept his eyes upon the black sky, unease canvassing him as he stepped through the trees. He had never been without Lucien before—at least he had never been unable to feel him, so why now? Did Eleanor reach him?

Impossible, he thought, stepping past a tall tree to eye the single cobblestoned road that lay between large mounds of black ash in-between destroyed buildings.

His brow furrowing, he stepped forward, leaving the hard ground to step upon the stone, the thick smell of that damned dread strong on the night.

He had barely made it three steps when he saw the familiar back retreating towards the line of trees opposite the ones he just left.

No, he thought, *couldn't be.*

But, indeed, the more he stared, the graceful gait pressing away from him, the more he could tell it was Victor.

"What's he doing here?"

He took a step, surprised when the ground appeared rough.

He looked down, his boot gracing a charred body.

With a cry of disgust, he stepped back, returning his gaze to the Vampire who had reached the end of Wingdale, proceeding to move through the many trees.

"What on Earth..." he muttered, stepping over the bodies, the dread filling the air, his mind. He moved for the Vampire, desiring to know what led him here, to Wingdale of all places, what caused such...death. For surely Victor couldn't have done this...

He followed in the Vampire's wake, moving for the trees as well, Lucien and the sword all but forgotten.

⁂

Xavier Delacroix walked numbly, mind blank as he stared at the girl on the ground, her large eyes covered by their pale lids, blond hair strewn every which way about her head. Once he reached her (it took quite a bit of time for his knees trembled vigorously, his right leg still burned), he knelt at her side, and without anything else to do, he placed a two fingers on her throat. "She needs blood," he said hoarsely, and with his words, he realized the chorus of "*My fault, my fault,*" echoed on in his mind beyond Dracula's words of encouragement. "She needs blood!" he said louder still, regaining his mind. His gaze traveled to the line of Creatures that cowered in fear near the doors.

Dragor Descant was the most visibly shaken of the group it seemed, for he still held his glowing blue sword in hand, but the more Xavier stared, the more he saw it shook wildly: he was quite surprised the sword did not fall to the ground. "What the bloody hell—what was that—what happened to him?!" the Vampire screamed, a free hand pointed to the spot the strange Creature had been just moments before, the brains of Ewer still upon the ground.

"I d-don't know," he stammered, not quite sure the Vampire was talking to him. He eyed Lillith again, unsure of what could come next. If he had not urged the girl to talk, to speak more on what had happened to her because of Darien, Damion, then perhaps she would not have moved...perhaps the faint trace of remembrance in her eye would have not propelled her feet. For he was sure whatever she regained, whatever she'd unlocked through way of the mind with his words was what had caused her to step to the dark Vampire, give him her blood.

"Damn," he whispered, lifting the unconscious Vampire into his arms. He rose to his feet, not surprised to find that his legs still shook, his body as well, for he was not at all sure of what he'd seen, except for this: That had been his friend, his bloody best friend before Dracula's secrets were uncovered. He had been a Vampire before he'd...transformed. A Vampire! So what? What *was* that?

He turned his gaze from the mess of blood and death that was Ewer Caddenhall, to eye the large doors of Cinderhall Manor. "Those doors—we must get them open," he said to the line of Creatures that looked gravely aware something dangerous had entered their world, now flew about freely. "Hurry!" *Now. Before it comes back.*

At this word, all Creatures started, although Peroneous was slowest to move towards the doors, Xavier noticed, his dark face covered in sweat, his eyes watering with what seemed to be tears.

Aurora, Aleister, Dragor, Amentias, and Aciel began to work on the doors despite their shaken appearances, using all manner of spell or physical strength to press against the wood, when Peroneous coughed, what looked like yellow liquid leaving his lips. He was bent double again, his retching loud amidst the bang of light and fists against the doors.

"Peroneous," Xavier called, the Vampire in his arms not stirring at his voice, "Peroneous, are you all right?"

The dark Enchanter shook his head sending droplets of stomach acid every which way, one of which caught on the hem of Aurora's red robe, sending her to cease her spell, mid-incantation, a look of great disgust upon her face.

"Blow it that way!" she shouted in exasperation although her voice noticeably shook.

"Sorry," he said through short breaths, wiping his mouth on the back of his sleeve as he stood.

His scared gaze roved the night until it fell upon him, and Xavier met it, moving for him, a still-harried Aurora wiping at the hem of her robes, muttering curses, though her fingers trembled as she grasped the thick fabric.

"Peroneous," Xavier said, feeling Aurora's gaze upon him in curiosity, her swiping lessening though he pretended not to notice, "I would like a word."

The dark Enchanter cleared his throat, straightening his robes and traveling cloak nervously. "Of cou-course, your Grace," he whispered, though his gaze met the ground.

"Aurora," he said, gesturing with his head for the Enchanter to hold Lillith, "if you would?"

She dropped the bottom of her robes, her brow furrowing. But before long, she complied, taking Lillith from him.

He tried his best to smile, but he felt it came off more as a grimace: she frowned as she turned from him and moved towards the other side of the doors. He did not turn to Peroneous until she passed the Creatures that were barreling their shoulders into the hard wood, their urgency tangible: he knew they feared Darien coming back just as he did.

"All right, Enchanter," he said, this thought turning him back to the bald man whose black eyes gleamed at him in the familiar fear, "tell me what it is you know about Darien—what happened to him."

He eyed the three Creatures still pressing against the doors before motioning with his head towards a tree. Xavier followed as the Enchanter moved towards it, not saying a word until his back pressed against it.

"What Darien Nicodemeus became," he said, taking a deep breath, swallowing before he went on, "is what...Dracula—the old Dracula was when I first saw him."

He blinked, not sure he'd heard the Enchanter right.

"Yes, your Grace," he whispered, a hand shaking as he wiped at his mouth again, "Dracula was that...monster that appeared. Now you see why I moved to do just as it asked." And he chuckled, though his voice cracked, a small tear leaving an eye. He wiped it away.

Xavier stared at him. "And how," he began, not sure how to proceed, "how did Darien become that thing?"

Peroneous smiled, though it did not reach his sad eyes. "Why do you think the old Dracula forbid you Vampires to drink from one another?"

He frowned, not having thought on this at all. He merely figured it was something Dracula desired to be done, not that it would have any serious ramifications, least of all anything like what he'd just witnessed...

"If we drink the blood of other Vampires we become *that*?" he asked after a long moment of grunts and creaks left the four Creatures at the doors.

"Apparently," he said. "As I gather it the more you Vampires drink the blood of humans, the more you are able to keep the form you hold now. The original Dracula left the womb with the bloodlust, your Grace, the...Potion I crafted for him made it possible to exist solely off this blood. I did not think about it before, but it does make sense that the Vampires can live off other kinds of blood...it stands to reason, however, that the more blood the Vampires drink of their own kind...the more it would turn them back into the thing the original Dracula desired to escape."

"That...monster," Xavier finished, great unease spreading through him.

No wonder Dracula moved so hastily to accomplish his many plans, he thought with renewed understanding, *no wonder the Vampire wanted me to reach the Goblet, drink from it...*

Pressed with the thought, he asked, "This Goblet of Existence I must drink from to bring peace to the Dark World..."

"What of it?"

"Is it made from the same...stuff you gave Dracula to help him keep the form we Vampires hold?"

At this the Enchanter closed his eyes, the wry smile upon his lips. Xavier watched as he leaned against the dark bark of the tree, fear clearly gripping his every sense, anger as well, and Xavier finally understood his desire to not speak on what he'd divulged back at Carvaca's castle.

"No," he said, "that is the work of the Phoenixes. All the Artifacts that exist," and he opened his eyes to watch him, "do so because they are *of* the Phoenixes. We small Creatures don't have their power."

He opened his mouth to speak when Peroneous eyed him in sudden question.

"Why are you asking me all of this, your Grace? Didn't the original Dracula divulge all his secrets to you in the book?"

And he could no sooner open his mouth to retort when the sword at his waist began to glow its red light strongly. Its heat intense: Xavier released the sword from its home along his thigh with a flourish, feeling the hot wind blow from the steel and press against his face: the unease fading slightly.

He and Peroneous could only stare at it before Peroneous let out a cry of surprise, removing his medallion from beneath his robes. It too blared hotly in the dark, shining a brilliant red light against the other Creatures; who had all removed their medallions from their chests and eyed each other in utter bewilderment, droves of heat pressing against them all.

Xavier could barely shout his confusion over the continuous roar of *"Protect the Dragon!"* that repeated in his mind, when a greater red light appeared behind the doors, beaming underneath the wood, and Xavier watched the Creatures step away from them, for the heat rose, yes Xavier could feel it, so warm, it reminded him wholly of his time in *The Immortal's Guide,* the sun pressing gloriously against his human skin—

A loud crash issued from the doors as they blew open in the next moment, a great gust of heat passing them all, sending their arms to cover their eyes, the blare of red light making it hard to see.

"Lord Delacroix?" the sweet voice sounded, piercing his ears with assured ease, sending his arm to drop, his eyes to narrow as he focused on the figure that stood in the middle of the doorway: the red light fading, allowing the large, marble hall to be seen behind her.

The large gold hall sparkled in the light of various torches placed high upon the walls; the golden bar set towards the back of the hall was just as he remembered it: its assortment of red, blue, and purple liquid-filled jars numerous upon the high shelves.

He sheathed the sword, its heat still blaring through the leather, but he paid it no mind: the woman stared around at them in unfeigned relief, her heart-shaped face marred with shadow, though her lips pulled up into a smile as she focused on him.

He stepped past them all, ignoring their alarmed whispers of "a human?" and "Alexandria?" to reach the woman who stood shivering, nothing but a long, thin chemise covering her slender frame. He undid his cloak without a word, caked in the dried blood of slain Elite Creatures as it was, and wrapped it around her shoulders, locking the clasp in place at her throat, which was, he was dismayed to find, splattered with dried blood.

"Are you all right?" he asked.

Closer to her, it became apparent that her brown-green eyes were beginning to water, her shock apparently leaving her. He said nothing as her chapped lips trembled, and then she inhaled a great gust of cold night air.

"I...I'm not sure," she said, her voice throaty with apparent lack of use, brown-green eyes wide. "That woman...she stabbed me... desired to know what power I held..."

"What?"

"The woman," she repeated, her gaze appearing to darken as she met his eyes, "Eleanor Black—she captured us—"

"Us?" Aleister asked.

She eyed him in alarm, only just realizing others remained in the clearing with them: she blinked upon the other Creatures in stifled surprise. "Y-yes," she said to the scarred Vampire, lifting a blood-covered arm to point behind her, deeper into the hall, "Christian is there."

Xavier followed her steady finger to eye the mass of black cloak that remained on the pristine gold floor, a puddle of black hair pooling around the Vampire's head, and even from where he stood, he knew the Vampire's eyes were not open.

The heat grew as he stared at his brother upon the floor, but he could not summon the strength to move when Aleister let out a strange sound, a much more coherent, "Christian!" leaving his throat soon after, and he moved past them to head past the doors and into the hall.

"*You alone must do it,*" Dracula repeated somewhere in the recesses of his tired mind.

He closed his eyes against the voice, the roar of many voices still screaming, "*Protect the Dragon!*" amidst the concerned shouts of Aleister who had reached his son and was now calling for the others to join him.

When he opened them, he was not surprised to find that the others surrounded the unmoving Christian, the scarred Vampire waving his hands through the air, gesturing for the Creatures to gather this and that.

He watched them step from him, Aurora Borealis the only one not moving to do as the Vampire bid: she had laid Lillith Crane atop a long marble table and set about waving her hands expertly over the Vampire's slender frame.

"Your Grace," a voice said from behind him, pulling him from the faint yellow light that was beginning to leave Aurora's slender fingers.

He turned to eye the two former Elite Creatures, eyes red, and he noticed they both held pale skin, the cold of death settling around them...

"What's wrong, Amentias, Aciel?" he asked, turning his back to the glow of the many torches, the strange darkness seeming to thicken in the night sky.

Amentias took a small step forward, short black hair blowing gently in a small breeze the movement conjured. "I haven't been able to hold the Vampire form since I touched the Ares," he said, his voice shaking with euphoria.

"And I," Aciel joined, "have not been able to turn from it, but now—now, it seems I can."

He narrowed his eyes. "You were in Vampire form, Amentias, when you came for me a day ago."

He nodded, and his red eyes appeared to darken with his reflection. "That was only because I had taken the blood of my fellow Creatures while they held the Vampire form. Now...it seems I can hold it without doing so."

The Ascalon pulsed at his side the more he stared at them. *Her Creatures.* Was it wise, indeed, to have them at his side? Had he been too hasty in agreeing to help them? To keep them safe?

But they had killed their own kind, yes, he had seen it with his own eyes, and they had taken their blood shortly after, why else would they move to do this if they were not truly out of her hand?

But to suddenly hold the Vampire form...what could have caused it?

The gasp left him as the realization reached his frazzled mind. "Darien," he said, watching their furrowing brows, knowing he had felt greatly changed, himself, as though what he was was fluid, elusive, something to be broken in the next moment the more he'd stared upon the thing the dark Vampire had become. "My friend, when he...changed...you were able to hold the Vampire form, weren't you?"

They nodded, though their brows were still creased, confusion filling their gazes.

"Tell me," he said, stepping up to them, moving away from the open doors, the myriad conversations ensuing within, "would Eleanor have anything to do with this?"

They shared brief bemused glances, before Aciel turned back to him and said, "How deep her influence goes is not debatable, your

Grace...but the power we witnessed was something we'd never seen before."

The smile was short, but it was there as he worked what way he could get them to understand his question. At last when it came to him, he took another step up to them, sure to keep his voice low. "That Vampire journeyed through *The Immortal's Guide* far before she did, my new friends. With this knowledge at your disposal, is it not possible that she could hold this same form as well? Render you, her Creatures, Vampire where Dracula's sword took the ability from you?"

They said nothing for a long time, and it was only when Aleister shouted, "Xavier, get in here!" that anyone said anything at all, and it was Aciel to do so:

"We must talk elsewhere, your Grace," and he cast furtive glances into the hall as he spoke, "Eleanor's...gifts are a mystery, even to me, but there are few things I have been able to discern in my time at her side."

He cast a gaze over his shoulder, seeing his father eyeing him impatiently, jar of what could only be blood pressed against Christian's lips.

He turned back to the thin-lipped Creature.

"Lead the way," he said, Aleister's shouts of disbelief following close behind as he stepped behind them, Aciel and Amentias's backs getting lost in the darkness of the trees as they moved.

Chapter Sixteen

CINDERHALL MANOR

The glass crashed against the floor, the remaining blood splattering against the marble in sickening splats.

"What's wrong? Why won't he take it?" Aurora asked from behind him.

Aleister cursed, pressing the Vampire's shoulders against the hard wood of the table to keep him subdued. It hardly worked: Christian thrashed, red eyes wide as he snarled viciously—

"What's wrong—what's wrong with him?!" Alexandria Stone cried.

Aleister eyed her; she stood opposite him, at Christian's feet, her brown-green eyes wide with her confusion. "I don't know—he won't take the *Anima*! And where is Xavier?!" he shouted in anger, turning his gaze to the open doors far behind her.

Peroneous and Dragor stood in the doorway as he'd requested, their gazes, he knew, searching for the Vampire that had walked off with Amentias and Aciel just minutes before.

What on Earth would possess him to walk off with them? Why would he just leave Christian here?

"Let me go, Vampire!" Christian screamed.

"You're out of control—you need to relax—" he retorted.

"I need blood!" he spat.

He felt his eyes darken. "We just gave you a whole jar of the best blood in the world!"

"It's not enough!"

He blinked despite the Vampire straining underneath his grip. "Not enough?" he repeated.

In his momentary surprise, he'd slackened his grip, and Christian moved, rising from the table, his bloody boots upon the floor in the next moment. And before Aleister could do a thing to stop him, he had appeared just before Alexandria, staring down upon her in a cruel hunger he knew all too well... But he could not have her blood—no one could...

"Christian!" he called, scarred hand outstretched to still the Vampire.

He did not turn: he remained staring upon her, watching her as though she were a small animal he desired to devour. "This blood—it is...so sweet," he whispered, his voice harsh, distorted in his need.

Blood? "You can't smell her blood, Christian," he said, although his voice shook with his doubt. How strongly he gazed upon her, how ravenously. "No one can..." But all the same he turned to Lillith Crane, who had just finished draining her own jar of blood, and now sat upon her table, watching what happened with bemused eyes. "Can you, Miss Crane?"

"No, not at all," she responded, eyeing the Enchanter at her side.

Aurora returned the gaze in confusion.

"I can," Christian said, bringing all gazes back to him, "I can, and I need it." He placed a pale hand on her neck, a slight gasp leaving her throat, her eyes heavy, almost closing in her euphoria.

What the bloody hell is wrong with them? "Christian," he said again, stepping closer to the Vampire, the woman who held his rapt attention, "you can't—whatever you smell—it *cannot* be her blood."

He turned to him at last, the red eyes narrowing in sheer contempt. "What are you prattling on about?" he said. The hand slid off her face as he turned to eye him fully, Aleister staring in alarm at his movements: they were crazed, directionless. But it made no bloody sense! Her blood could not be smelled, not at all, so how, why could he smell it? What on Earth caused this? "You truly can't smell that scent?"

He shook his head. "No," he said, regaining his voice, "and neither should you. She has yet to die, be changed into one of us— you shouldn't be smelling anything from her."

"You don't know what her blood does, do you?"

"What?"

His eyes closed and he sighed, the harsh chuckle leaving his throat. "Alexandria revealed a bit of her true power while we were trapped at Eleanor's. She..." and he seemed to think about the word best to use, "is the blood-stiller. She can stop the beasts—we Vampires. She can even stop Eleanor Black in her bloody tracks. And her blood," he went on, eyeing her again, "called to me. She chose me to have it."

"What on Earth are you talking about?" Aurora asked. Aleister turned to eye her, surprised to find she had moved to his side some time before: he had not been able to smell her blood, so strong was the desire of Christian. How it consumed all.

He opened his mouth again when a burst of brilliant light appeared through the open doors. Aleister could hear Peroneous and Nicholai scream, could barely see their arms lift to shield their eyes, when a severe voice sounded within the light:

"They're here, the lot of them."

✳

Aciel stopped beside a tall, mangled tree, the dark of the night slowly but surely giving way to morning: its dark hues were beginning to lighten, even as a low wind settled against them, blowing their cloaks up from their bodies.

"She kept her thoughts locked," he began, eyeing the anxious Vampire who stood just before him, interest clearly piqued, "I couldn't get close enough to her to warrant her release of her innermost desires, but there was a moment, brief however it was, when she held me as I turned into a Vampire where I could hear her mind.

"At first I thought it odd that she spoke to me so easily, having only known me for a week, then. But the more I stared into her eyes, the more I realized she couldn't control her thoughts—she was feeding me all of it, her innermost desires, the truth to her plans... It was the only way I could decipher her truth about you—the Vampire she desired above all else." He paused for a moment. "Whatever connection you two share, my king, is what propels her even now. I, as a Lycan, moved so quickly to end you where I could, but then, as her Creature, I saw you in a different light. You were no longer my enemy: you had become someone I desired to bow to, kneel to, just as I did for her. It was as if," and he chanced a glance to Amentias who shared it knowingly, "you were the one who turned us as well, shared in the blood that courses through our veins even now."

Xavier Delacroix said nothing, but listened, and Aciel nodded, knowing what it was the Vampire wished to hear.

"Whatever blood, magic, curses she used to force this transformation from beast to mortal to Vampire and back, holds tinges, scents, wisps of your blood. The allure of your blood is wrapped up in whatever we are, even more so in what she is. There were moments, in the beginning, that I smelled your scent so heavily around her, smelled your blood so thickly in her veins. Of course, she learned to control it, this lingering...hint of you that moved about her caves, but even before she sent me to the dungeons, I smelled it, knew it. And it is the reason, I believe, the other Elite Creatures so easily bend to her will to possess you, someone they had been only eager to destroy but hours before their own transformations: it is in your blood, her blood. You are connected by whatever she possessed to hold the transformations.

"You are, quite possibly, the link to transformations—it is why Amentias and I moved as we did to reach you. Scared though we were of what you might do given what we did to you...you were the only thing pulling our blood, giving us reason to exist where we no longer had in Eleanor's dread."

All was painfully silent when his lips closed, but he dared not think the Vampire had believed him. Aciel knew it was a long shot to even suggest so fantastic a tale as this, but he had had no choice. The Vampire desired to know of her secrets, this was the one thing he had clung to while his grace with her was fading: Xavier Delacroix, he would know, be the one to end her madness even as it clung so thickly to his skull, Amentias's.

But now as he stared at the Vampire, who looked quite sick, prepared to release whatever blood he'd taken some days before, he found the sliver of doubt to reach his dead heart. Perhaps, he thought, eyeing Xavier taking an unsteady step backwards, he was not the right Creature at all.

"All of her Creatures feel this way towards me?" he asked at last, looking upon them as though he'd never seen two Vampires properly. Aciel noticed his green eyes were darker than normal, marred by terrible guilt, no doubt.

"That we know of," he said, "it is common knowledge that you are one that must be acquired—it is her desire, so it is all of our desire. Those who remain at her side do not, cannot, question her word. It is law."

Xavier stared at him wildly, and Aciel thought he were going to choke him. Bracing himself, he lifted his hands, when all the Vampire said was, "How could we possibly be connected so strongly? My blood can't be anywhere near her...what she's become...I haven't..." His voice trailed, eyes widening as he remembered something long forgotten.

Amentias, who had been staring at the many trees around them, turned from his surveillance, and stared at Xavier. "What's wrong?" he asked.

Xavier did not meet his gaze, he merely stared at the ground.

"I...I," he began, running a shaking hand over his mouth, blinking hard as if willing away a painful memory, "I gave her m-my blood before she—before she turned into a Lycan. Oh God, I helped her, didn't I? I helped her become," and he waved a hand towards them, gaze haunted. "The blood of a Vampire...of course—of bloody *course*—I triggered the transformation—whatever missing piece she needed. And she'd told me—she damn well told me she'd uncovered Dracula's secrets. *Bloody hell.*"

Amentias cleared his throat. "What's he on about?"

But Aciel nodded, finally understanding just why she desired him so, regardless of whatever remaining feelings settled in the woman's corrupted heart. Here was the catalyst to great, terrible change, and Dracula had all but ensured he'd remained on his side, unable to be corrupted by what he had helped cause.

But they had gotten into the Xavier's mind, hadn't they? They had easily destroyed his senses, made him live an eternity by Eleanor's side, only to have it ripped away by the red light. Always the red light. Enchanted swords, cursed medallions, bloody red light.

"He," Aciel said, feeling the faint heat of the sun begin to burn his back as it rose between the trees, "is the one that helped Eleanor become an Elite Creature. And we are the ones that will help him destroy her."

"And if we destroy ourselves in the process?" Amentias breathed, releasing the pale form as well.

"We're already dying, Amentias," he said, feeling himself weaken as the blood returned to his veins. "We've nothing to lose, at least not from where I'm standing."

Xavier released the Ascalon, sending them both to take hasty steps back, its red light brilliant against the rising sun. "Something's wrong," Xavier said, turning from the sun to eye the tall white manor, just able to be seen through the thin trees.

"What do you—" Aciel began when the loud screams could be heard.

Without another word, they moved, Aciel wondering just how much of her influence still filled Xavier's mind.

※

Thomas Montague stared past the Enchanters to eye into the large manor, the many thoughts of her still filling his mind, although vaguely, since then, but they still remained. He strained his eyes, waiting for the light to die, waiting for their confused gazes to find him once more.

The Enchanters lowered their hands, their spell now done, and Thomas smiled.

Alexandria Stone was the first one he saw, her disheveled brown hair falling messily down her shoulders, her legs still bare, a large traveling cloak draped about her shoulders, and there beside her was a most ravenous-looking Vampire.

He observed this Creature for a few seconds, eyeing the red eyes, the lips turned up in a perpetual snarl, the fangs showing themselves, hair quite black, flowing freely down his back...

Xavier? he thought, motioning with a hand for the Enchanters to step forward.

They did as they were told, practically jumping over the bodies of the gruff Vampire and dark Enchanter at their feet, moving swiftly into the large hall, the Creatures within tensing at their movement.

Thomas followed in their steps, stepping over the frozen Creatures, their shocked gazes wide as they trailed his boots. Extending a silent thanks to Eleanor for the use of her two best Enchanters, he waved another hand and the coldness of death graced his skin, and at the cold wind that blew from his movement, the Enchanters stepped forward, the plain-looking woman in robes beside the scarred Vampire waving her own hands before they could do very much.

A blue translucent wall appeared, blocking the beams of light that left the Enchanters' hands. It was with sickening crashing sounds that the Enchanters got to work, using whatever spells they knew to break the wall where a young Vampire, blonde hair strewn wildly atop her pretty head, sat atop a table, her blue eyes wide as she eyed him through the wall.

Lillith Crane, he thought, remembering the night he'd destroyed her house with his men—the night Eleanor had sent her men to him, had stolen Mara...

He turned from the young Vampire to eye the tense Vampire at Alexandria's side again, the scarred Vampire waving his own hand to send strange sparks towards the other Enchanters.

Thomas stepped forward, moving towards the woman, the rousing chorus of *"Protect the Dragon! Protect the Dragon!"* surrounding his mind the more he stepped for her—

The ravenous Vampire appeared before him in the next second, much to his dismay, a cold smile gracing his pained face. "Not one more step," he said.

What happened to his ring? "Or what?" he said, glancing at the Vampire's hands: no ring upon any finger. *Indeed.*

"Protect the Dragon!"

Christian snarled, the scent of his cold blood reaching Thomas's nose; he merely raised a pale hand, waving it away. "What are you doing here?" the Vampire continued.

"The Queen desires your...amusing woman," he said, chancing a glance over the shoulder of the seething Vampire, seeing the cold gaze she planted upon him. *"I need you to—Protect the Dragon!"* He shook away the incessant thoughts. "Her...performance at the cave has...amazed us all."

"You don't get her," Christian snarled, "you Creatures cannot handle her power—"

"And you can?" he countered. "What? Sniveling and snarling as you are? You can't even control yourself near her—what is it? No ring? Is that why you're completely unguarded?"

His brow furrowed, and he looked as though he'd been slapped. "Her blood cannot be touched, except by those she deems necessary—able to touch it," he said, as though explaining something to a child, "you, Creature, will never be able to."

"I need you, Thomas, you alone can—Protect the Dragon!" He found his mind drifting to Eleanor's sudden transition to a human a day before—

A burst of light broke through the wall with a shattering crash, bringing all gazes to the wisps of translucent glass that were beginning to disappear in small puffs of smoke as they touched the spotless floor.

"Quickly, Aleister!" the woman Enchanter shouted, brandishing her hands in florid motions, as though she were wiping a long window. Thomas stared, as the hands met together in a loud clap just before herself, a burst of orange light moving from them to meet the Enchanters who had begun to step closer...

They were blown back the moment the orange light touched them, the scarred Vampire named Aleister rising from the floor, waving a thickly scarred hand through the air as well. But before he could see what the Vampire would do, he felt the cold blade enter his back, a startled groan escaping his lips.

The strong hand was on his shoulder as the blade was dug deeper, the cry growing as the pain filled his back, his abdomen, and he looked down, able to see the long sword sticking out of his front, a haze of red light barely covering it.

"What—" he coughed, blood leaving his lips.

As a strange rumbling packed the hall, the hand on his shoulder keeping him upright, he smelled the familiar blood, unable to quell the snarl that left his lips. *Xavier.*

"Thomas," Xavier said, driving the sword into him to the hilt, causing him to cough up blood that splattered against the floor at Christian's feet, "what brings you here?"

He opened his mouth to speak, but found he could not, and it was only when the sword's red light grew brighter, the rumbling reaching an unbearable high that he managed to sputter, "Lillian, Isaac, let us go!"

There came no response, and at first he thought them to have misheard, so gargled was his voice with his blood, but soon he managed to turn his head, and saw the bodies of the Enchanters on the floor, their eyes closed.

Damn, those were her best, he thought, crying out again as the pain spread through him further: The Vampire at his back had twisted the sword. More blood left his lips, and he closed his eyes, allowing the pain to reach him in full as he disappeared on her dread, the words of strangers trailing in his mind as he moved:

"Protect the Dragon!"

Chapter Seventeen

LOSS OF CONTROL

Victor stared at the splatters of blood that littered the grass at their boots, and clucked his tongue. "Someone's been injured."

Joseph Gail nodded in silence, his green eyes focused on the blood as he walked ahead. "Smells like Vampire. So Nicholai Noble is injured, eh? Never thought I'd live to see the day. Of course, with Dracula dead there isn't a soul, living or dead, to protect him— protect the ones who followed so closely in his stead."

He took his stare from the blood, to eye the red traveling cloak that swayed as the Elite Creature walked. Victor had known Joseph Gail was not an admired King of a Vampire City when Dracula still lived, indeed, Dracula had gone out of his way on numerous occasions to forget to send the King of Winfield an invitation to any event or meeting that would take place in the King of all Creatures' home.

It was a sting the King of Winfield had obviously felt for decades.

He stepped up, keeping in time with Joseph Gail's steps, wondering when, indeed, Joseph Gail lent his hand to Eleanor Black's adventurous causes. "And you're happy, are you," he asked slowly, eyeing the Creature as he kept his sharp gaze on the ground, "to be at her side?"

He blinked and looked up quickly, confusion filling his eyes. "What?" he asked, continuing their stride over the stained grass.

"Are you pleased," he said again, "to be at Eleanor's side?"

A wild gaze of desire filled his eyes at Eleanor's name. "Of course I am," he said, "aren't you?"

The words would not rise to his lips, the sudden question jarring him where he stood. "I...of course, I am," he said, regaining himself, walking beside the Elite Creature, the curious glare thick on his green eyes.

Victor felt her dread rise against his skin, felt it come from Joseph Gail, indeed. He knew her voice, so seductive, filled the Elite Creature's mind now, for it was so faint it danced through his own.

"You must become what is best, Victor," her voice whispered. *"You must do it now—before it is too late."*

I can't, he answered, feeling the surreptitious glances the Elite Creature at his side stole every now and again as they walked.

The voice continued but he did his best to tune it out, her dread filling his every sense, making it close to impossible...

He had just given up hope that he would be able to be rid of her voice, her damning presence, when Joseph Gail lifted a hand and pointed to something in the distance. "Victor," he said.

Victor eyed him before following his finger, an automatic nod bending his head. *Of course,* he thought, thankful that the voice had gone with a new focus to placate him, *of course they would run* here.

The high mountains canvassed the horizon, atop them the dark specks moving along their white, snow-covered bodies.

Victor watched the Dragons for a few moments when he felt Joseph Gail turn and begin walking in the other direction.

He eyed his long black hair as it swayed along his back. "Gail?" he asked, turning to face him as well.

"We will not do battle there—it is a compromised location," the Elite said, walking back across the long field of grass, the blades crunching under his boots.

"But they're there, aren't they? You can sense them through magic, can't you? If they're there I don't see why we can't—"

"Cedar Village is off-limits to us now, Vampire!" he snarled, turning so fast Victor felt the breeze before he smelled the dread. "Ever since those imbeciles delivered that Dragon to her door she has made it clear it would not be wise to return to the place! Those Dragons," and he pointed the same hand to the line of mountains far in the distance again, "know about us. They get one whiff of my scent and we're done for."

"Then send me," he said before the thought could plant itself within his mind. "I'm not one of you—those Dragons surely won't abject to a Vampire desiring a leisurely stroll through the village."

He scoffed, his gaze delirious. "You don't understand, Victor. Vampire though you may be, you have dwelled in her cave, you reek of her scent just as any of us. And your mind holds her thoughts. You are no better to take this 'leisurely stroll' than I. We will find another way—perhaps we can cut through Scylla, pass Pinnett, and get to them before they reach their destination."

He blinked, not understanding. Weren't the Elf and Vampire going to stay in Cedar Village? Regain themselves before moving on? Wasn't this the best time to capture them?

"What do you mean 'their destination?'"

Joseph snarled in frustration, a world weary sigh leaving his lips, and Victor could not help but feel he was holding up what was sure to be a long journey to gather these two Dark Creatures. "They're going to Xavier Delacroix, you idiot. The Elf's desperation, his bloody trail of red light—the Vampire's blood," he waved a hand to the grass, "they're going to the one Creature in this world that will grant them their protection. And as we know, thanks to Eleanor's brilliant mind on the matter, those medallions are beacons—they are tools that grow stronger when all Creatures who wear them are together! If we don't not reach them now, what the Queen is trying to do will be for nothing!"

"Granting the Dark World unseemly power through way of mixing the blood," he said without realizing it, "has proven dangerous despite its many advantages."

His green eyes narrowed. *"What?"* And he stepped closer to him, close enough, Victor realized, to smell her scent on the air.

"I," he began, knowing it would not do to have the Elite Creature at odds with him; he had spoken thoughtlessly, but he could not deny the seed of uncertainty in the back of his mind had started to grow its stem. Her energy was madness, her desires were undoubtedly madness, and here now, standing across from one of her Creatures, one that used to hold such high esteem in the Dark World, he was not sure he could continue to survive her dread, her words, the overwhelming, damning presence of *her*. He had traded one cruel desire for another, and it was not Eleanor he desired, but what she offered: protection, so that he could gather his mind on what next to do. But now that he was faced with the ever-looming transformation that would have to take place eventually, he found he could not go further. Not with her man at his back, bending his will, twisting his mind.

He opened his mouth to say just this, tired of her endless dread, the errant thoughts that filled his mind, no better than when Dracula had died, he at the helm of that other world. He closed it before long, convinced he could say nothing to this sycophant, nothing to one of hers.

It was with a gasp that he realized he was right back where he started, indeed, trapped in darkness, at the beck and call of Creatures far better than he, unable, he shuddered, to be free, truly not sure what that *was*. Not anymore.

"Victor?" Joseph whispered, pulling him from his mind, "Victor, what's wrong?"

He blinked at the voice, drilling the unease that arose in his gut down into the recesses of control. Control he hadn't had in quite a long time, but control nonetheless.

"Nothing, Gail," he said, a warming smile tearing at his lips, "come, I follow your lead. We are to go to Scylla, yes?" And before the confused Elite could say a thing, he had stepped past him, back in the direction they had come, mind most gone on what he had done, moving so quick to stand at her side, grief, jealousy marring his mind, then. And what had changed, indeed?

He felt the Elite's confused smile at his back, and he heard Eleanor's voice again: "*Join me, Victor. Together, we could do great things.*"

Great things, he scoffed, remembering Dracula to have said the same upon guiding him from the floor, *great things, indeed.*

He felt the wind blow against him, knew not its coldness or warmth, but he smelled the dread, the cruel air of the world, and he laughed.

※

Damion ran, the Creatures at his back laughing against the light of the sun. "C'mon, we can't let 'im get away!"

He did not slow, mind lost on where it was Victor could have gone—one moment the two Creatures were just in front of him, never stopping to sleep, the next they had dispersed in a brazen wind, a laugh that could not have been Victor's trailing on the air.

What the Devil is going on! he thought, running through the trees, feeling the dread claw at his back, reaching for his cloak, and the damned Caddenhall wasn't here—where was he?!

"Yaddley! Minerva!" he cried, running around a large tree, the ring atop his finger glinting in the sun's light. "Lucien!" He could not feel them, could not smell their blood, could feel nothing from the magic embedded in his blood... No, something was terribly wrong, something, he knew, had everything to do with *her*.

A harrowing laugh filled the air, and he looked up, skidding to a stop as the heavily cloaked Elite rounded the sky to hover just before him, the long face no longer hidden underneath the large hood. Damion saw the perilous grin on his face, the eyes so black with malice, greed, the sheer pleasure of having trapped one not like him...

He released his sword at last, pulling his gaze from the Creature when the rustling of leaves and grass sounded all around him. He whirled, the many Elite Creatures surrounding him grinning happily, greedily.

Lucien, Lucien, he reached, dismayed to find nothing but a terribly loud silence where the Vampire's response should have been. He waved the sword in hand. "All right," he said, though his dead heart pulsed with fear, "you want to fight? Let us fight!"

The ring strained within his skin, a wincing pain sending a sharp cry of surprise to leave his throat. He eyed his hand, holding it in the other, not understanding what he saw: the ring was cracked, broken in two, an unclean split, and even as he watched it, he felt the clamps release themselves from within his finger, watched in horror as the broken pieces of gold fell from his finger, clanking dully against the blade of the sword, and fell to the grass.

He stared at it for moments until the piercing heat of the sun graced his face. He cried out and hastily stumbled back into the recesses of the many trees, smelling their blood strongly now. It reeked of Eleanor, her damning lilac and blood, the dread that filled the world wherever he'd dared turn.

A burst of wind pressed against his back and he stepped away, dancing to the right, where another Elite stood, an arm outstretched to grasp his neck, but he ducked, turning to eye the other Elite who had attempted to stab him with a dagger of black smoke.

He stared at the strange blade, quite aware he'd never seen magic like it before, but he was quickly pulled from his bemusement by several other Elite Creatures, their cloudy daggers all swiping at his frame, the smoky casings appearing wispy, but quite solid when it graced his skin.

Slicing the sword across their chests, he watched them fall away, jumping back against trees or onto the blood-splattered grass, regaining themselves, despite the cuts beginning to bleed down their fronts.

He waved the sword, remaining up against the bark of a tree to keep himself out of the sun, smelling their blood on the blade, thoughts still stuck on how in the world his ring could have broken. It never had before...but then, Xavier Delacroix had never issued out more rings to those on the surface. *Of course.*

He regained himself, eyeing the many Creatures as they stepped towards him again, smoky daggers held high—

He barely saw one fly past his head until it planted itself into the bark next to his ear, and his eyes widened as he stared at it up close: its frame was black smoke, yes, nothing solid remained there, but the handle was a hard silver, tainted, it seemed, with a sticky-looking black liquid all along its body.

"My Lord!" a shrill voice cried, and he looked up, relief spreading through him as the blonde hair, the black cloaks blew amidst the green of the leaves above.

"Minerva! Yaddley!" he shouted in relief, watching as they slid through the tops of the trees, a fresh burst of cold wind reaching him as they landed atop two Elite Creatures most near tall, thin trees.

Minerva wrapped her long-nailed hands around the Elite's head as her boots pinned him to the ground, and turned, the snap resonating through his ears the more he stared. Yaddley worked next, planting a hard boot into the head of the Elite he stood upon, sending the skull to crack, blood spilling out from it, staining the grass beneath them.

She stepped off him, moving easily to the next Creature, dodging his swipe, placing her hand straight through his chest. He screamed desperately, her hand dropping his heart at the back of his boots, and with that, she pulled out her arm, the man remaining standing there for but a moment before he fell back against a tree, his dark eyes unseeing in the morning light.

Removing themselves from their stunned visages, the remaining Elite Creatures started for her, but Yaddley was upon two in the next second, the others stopping dead in their tracks. Damion watched in amusement as the Vampire lifted two of them by their throats into the air, squeezed tight, gasps and gurgles leaving their lips. He squeezed until they strained no more, and dropped them at his feet, a cold, although weak smile upon his face.

Something was wrong with him, Damion observed, beginning to move away from the tree, eager to see what ailed the strong Vampire so. He had made it but a step before the leaves blew in a wind Minerva had caused, her high-pitched scream at the remaining Elite Creatures disorienting them further, and the sun's light pressed itself against his face.

He cried out with the unbearable pain, felt the burning heat, smelled his flesh sizzle, and he slunk back into the shade, whatever it could afford him, watching as she leapt on an Elite, blue eyes wide in her utter glee, her brother disarming a few of them, smacking their smoky blades out of their hands.

When the Elites were all dispatched, Damion sheathed his sword, surprised to find his un-ringed hand shook, and then he realized it: he had been horribly afraid, yes, he'd thought he was going to die at the hands of her Creatures...

"My Lord," Minerva said, wiping the blood off her arms with the cloak of a very dead Elite upon the ground, "we've been looking for you. Where is Master Darien? We cannot smell him, nor can I—we locate Lucien."

She had removed herself from the Elite as she spoke, stepping towards him, her haunted beauty illuminated further by the light of the sun that shined freely upon her blood-splattered hair and clothes. Yaddley remained near a tree far from them, his expression thoughtful as he crossed his solid arms against his chest and waited.

Damion turned his attention from him, for he knew the Caddenhall had never liked him much, and truthfully, he could not say he didn't feel the same. He eyed Minerva again, watching her waiting countenance. She was calm, yes, she was, calmer than most should be after facing several Elite Creatures, never mind if there had been help. *She was far too calm*, he thought. It unsettled him, and he did not take his gaze from her dark blue eyes as he said, "I had hoped they were with you. I cannot smell them—feel them either."

Yaddley shifted his footing, bringing Damion's eyes to him. His equally blue eyes were serious as he said, "When she came for me, we moved for Master Darien's curse immediately—we were blown off course by many," he eyed the ground where the dead Elite Creatures lay, bleeding, "of that woman's Creatures. It was only last night that we realized we could not smell Master Darien's blood at all."

"How strange," he whispered, despite himself, never moving from the tree's rough skin: the sun was higher in the sky now, much more sunlight passing through open space in-between leaves. "How did you find me?"

"We caught wind," Minerva began, staring towards a sunny field before them, the same field where Damion knew Victor had disappeared just hours ago, "of a smell much like Master Darien's—it led us to you, Lord Damion. But it is strange, the smell—now that we are here—is definitely not yours."

"What do you mean?" he asked, staring at her, the pain of his finger still pulsing despite the lack of ring.

"It's very much...a new smell," Yaddley offered from his tree.

"Yes, new...but very much the same," Minerva finished.

His brow furrowed. "I fail to see what you're getting at." He felt incredibly uneasy under their gazes now, the sun the only thing keeping him in place. If it weren't there, if it was hidden behind a cloud, or if a sudden night fell, he could leave, he could be free...

"Something has happened to Master Darien," she said at last. "He is changed."

He tore himself from the dismal thoughts with her words. "Changed?" *What was she on about?*

Yaddley stepped forward, right across the backs and fronts of the slain Elite Creatures, not stopping until he stood just beside his sister, her height stunted by how high he reached. "He is nearby," he said, "Minerva can smell his blood...far more than she ever could that human woman. If something has happened to him, you do understand, Lord Damion, the plan put in place would be changed— that you would have to take his place in helping Xavier Delacroix, protecting him from this illness that plagues the world."

"I will not!" he shouted, stepping from the tree, the light gracing his skin, sending him to snarl in pain, pressing against it again. "What do you mean Darien is nearby—I can't smell anythi—"

But he could. The moment he tuned into the various scents around him, he was able to locate the smell most curious... It was utterly strange, how it mixed with the fear he had felt whilst being attacked by her Creatures, but now he could smell its nature, how free it was, dread all the same, but freer than Eleanor's stifling dread...

And then a great shadow loomed over the tops of the trees, blocking out the sun. He stared at it, unable to see the full extent of whatever it was, a stunning silence sweeping over the land.

No one said a word, or rather, no one could: he was very aware he could not speak against what it was, and as it swerved in the air, a huge gust of wind blowing up the leaves, their cloaks from their bodies, branches parted while some snapped, falling to the ground, allowing the sun to shine freely against the trunks of the trees.

He felt the burning heat again, the sheer pain of it gluing him against the tree, and he cried out, eyeing Minerva in his desperation.

Why, a smile rested on her lips, small, but it was there.

"What—what do you know? What is that—that thing?"

He eyed the leaves above, the large shadow no longer seen between the leaves, but the fear still remained...

Minerva stepped to him, the smile gone, and said, "Lord Damion, where is Lucien?"

He blinked, the heat still searing his skin. "I don't know! Please—get me out of the damned sun!"

She eyed her brother before turning back to him. "Things have changed, Lord Damion," she said, the light of the sun glowing upon her back, blocking the heat from reaching him at last. He breathed a needless sigh of relief, although his face still remained burned: he would need vast amounts of blood to heal, indeed. "You must lead us—you must fulfill Master Darien's duty."

He could barely focus on her darkening blue eyes as the large shadow returned, this time flying closer to the ground. It swooped low as if turning in a wide circle, and he was able to see what looked like a large bat-like wing spread wide, scrape along the bloodied grass, and then disappear within the branches of trees.

He blinked.

It was as if it had never been there.

But he had seen it...he had—

"Lord Damion?" Minerva repeated, her expression confused. He eyed her, not understanding how she could not feel that wind, for it blew across his face strongly, how she could not hear the rustle of the trees as the thing surfaced from the sea of green at last...

"I," he breathed, not understanding what was happening, what he had seen—and where was Victor? "I will take his place—I'll do it—just get me—get me out of the bloody heat!"

And without another word she grabbed his arm, and he felt himself be dragged along a cool darkness as the scorching heat of the sun disappeared for good.

Chapter Eighteen

DRIVEN BY DESIRE

Christian Delacroix paced the floor, the sight of her blood replaying over and over in his mind.

It wasn't bloody well fair!

Not that she do this to him, not again—it wasn't right! To reduce him to a snarling, sniveling Creature...

He snarled in irritation as he reached the wall and turned, resuming his previous steps across the bedroom floor. He paid little attention to the Vampire that sat, brow furrowed hard in contemplation, upon the edge of the large unused bed, following his movements with the saddest of stares.

He knew his father wanted to get to the bottom of his most "obscene" behavior, but he was quite sure nothing was wrong with him. At least, nothing he couldn't cure.

His eyes widened as the thought reached him for the millionth time since they were all bidden to separate rooms to sleep. *If only I could taste her blood...just a drop...* And then he would laugh to himself, knowing damn well a drop would do nothing to save him—of course, it would only make things worse...he would only want more...

"You claim," the scarred Vampire said at last, having never spoken since he'd entered the room just two hours before, "she chose you to have her blood."

He did not cease in his pacing, his thoughts, he merely said, "She let me smell it, see it—she wanted me to have it—whatever she is, she can control her light—her blood..."

"Yes, yes," he said, "but what *is* she? If she can still Eleanor Black's blood as you've said—her importance goes far beyond keeping safe—her powers, whatever they are, must be honed. Just think of the ease with which this can all be done with if she were at her full potential."

He did not miss a beat. "She already has a brilliant grasp on them, whatever happened at Eleanor's cave only stunned me with her control."

"Yes, well, let us see what your brother says about all of this, shall we? As I understand it she is not aware of what happened at Eleanor's, and even you cannot give us a full account. Xavier will surely want to keep her close now—especially if Thomas Montague is still knocking down our doors to gather her."

He felt his blood boil. Thomas Montague. Of course the Creature still searched, still hunted... Of course he could not know when to give up—and what a strange time to arrive at their door mere hours after they'd escaped her grip. One would think the Elite Creature would learn to cool his paws, indeed, he'd been greatly confused, scarred by Alexandria's actions last Christian could recall...

So why even bother showing up? Why still think he could stand in the presence of the woman that controlled all Creatures, and with a terrifying ease?

He took a deep breath, knowing it would not do to follow that train of thought. For wasn't he currently riding on an inescapable high from her blood so freely available to him but for a moment?

Wasn't he quite satiated thanks to numerous jars of *Anima* after Thomas had gone on a dread-filled wind?

But still he could not shake the desire that clawed through his veins, to grab her, to bite her, to taste her...

The snarl was quick as it ripped through his throat and Aleister was on his feet in the next second.

"Perhaps you should lie down," he said gently.

"I cannot rest," he said, "nor do I want to. She consumes my every waking moment, my every thought. To sleep would only drive me mad with my desire to—to have her."

A look quite knowing graced the Vampire's scarred face, and Christian could not help but look away. He knew what he sounded like, but he did not care—she was powerful, far too much, it seemed, and he was merely at her bloody mercy, unable to do anything more than let his desires cloud his mind... And yet she was the light that called through the madness, she was the sweetness in this world so bitter, so cold, and where he had been close to true death, far too close, she had saved him.

Denied him what he so desperately needed, yes, but she had saved him where it counted.

"Christian," Aleister said quietly, the tone of his voice making it quite impossible for Christian to turn to eye him, "you have spent the most time around the woman than any of us. Indeed, your... feelings for her have every right to be stronger than what any of us would feel for her. But you must understand that her truth has begun to show itself, and when it does in full, she may not honor, nay, remember whatever it is you two...share."

"Then why let me crave her blood? Why let me get so miserably close—I was inches from ripping through her skin and having it for my own? And when in that haze...in that red light she called me her 'chosen' one. Why, if she would not honor our connection would she call me that?"

He merely stared, his thoughts unreadable, eyes clear, and then at last he said, "Perhaps...it is just the tool of Dracula that remains in her blood...to call you—you were meant, as I am aware, to receive Dracula's sword upon your arrival back from the cabin with Xavier."

"I was what?" he breathed, all thought of the maddening woman, his hunger dispersing with the words.

"To hold the Ares, Christian," he continued, "you were the one Dracula desired to hold the sword if Evert is to be believed."

The door opened and in stepped Xavier Delacroix, the Ascalon still tight in his grip, green eyes murderous. "Everyone is still sleeping," he said, moving into the room, throwing the Ascalon atop the bed. "Which is excellent, because you and I, dear brother, have to have a little talk."

The gentle wind rose as the door was closed, and Christian shared a skeptical glance with Aleister. "What's happened?" he asked as the formidable Vampire returned to eye him.

"You tell me," Xavier said, and Christian could hear the anger on his voice. "What happened with Alexandria—and you! Why were you spouting all of that nonsense about how she *wants* you to take her bloody blood?!"

He thought of her blood, the sight of her heart pumping the liquid through her veins. "Because she does, Xavier."

"No," he snarled, "you will be straight with me! What happened at Eleanor's? Why were you on the cusp of death?"

"Victor tricked us, she sensed what it was before he arrived and did what she thought would be enough to still him, but he saw through the ruse—got his men to drag us off to Eleanor. Covered our eyes with some thick smoke so we would not see where we were being led, only removed when we were deep in her dirt halls. Thomas Montague was there, he saw her and nearly died from relief? I don't know—he wanted her, for some maddening reason. Asked me if I had my ring—I did not, it'd cracked whilst waiting in the

Dragon's Cavern for Victor to arrive. Eleanor showed up soon after, went to touch Alexandria, I—she could *not* touch her—I knew it even then. She rounded on me before she could get very far and touched *me*. I was under her...command? I'm not sure—it felt like a dream, surrounded in her dread...except it was no longer such...it was heady, alluring, I...dare I say it, I *enjoyed* being under her hand...until it was removed with a hard punch to my gut," and he eyed his brother as the memory returned. "I was in some other chamber; Alexandria was nowhere to be found. I endured their taunts, their strikes—they wanted to know where you were—I would not give you up, would I? One even turned into a Lycan," he shuddered, "before Thomas Montague turned up, did away with them as though possessed, undid my chains, and led me to her."

He paused, the memory striking him hardest: the sight of her strong gaze never wavering as they met his...Eleanor Black seemingly without her power...

"What happened, Christian?" Xavier asked, his lips parted, eyes wide with a need Christian knew all too well, but it was not to hear of Alexandria's abilities, of this he was certain.

With a slight frown, he said, "She was...beautiful. More so than she has ever been as we have been with her. She seemed to control... something...well, I suppose it was the power within her blood, she seemed to have perfect control of it. She looked at me, but it was as though she was seeing through me, and the command with which she bade Eleanor with mere words...

"She is truly a force to be reckoned with when she is turned, brother. At any rate, Eleanor leapt for the sword, now able to hold it as she was a normal human woman, and Alexandria expressed her discomfort at this predicament—she said she had hoped Eleanor would not be able to hold it, would not think to do so. But nevertheless, she told Eleanor that it mattered not that she would hold the sword, for when she left the endless tunnels, Eleanor would be rendered incapable to grasp it again.

"She then bade me to follow, and I did at once, entranced as I was by her effortless nature in all things.

"We left on a strange, soothing wind, and arrived in some woods, I believe it was just outside of Eleanor's cave, I'm not sure. She was unconscious, I was weak for want of blood. I heard more Creatures off in the distance, grabbed her, and ran as far as I could.

"I could move no more after a time, fell to my knees, and then it happened: Her blood... I saw nothing but the lines of her veins, the beating of her beautiful heart, and it was as though nothing else mattered, and indeed nothing did, for I was in desperate need as I later learned upon my waking here."

He sighed shortly before continuing on, "It felt much like it did a few days ago, before we traveled to the Dragon's Cavern—I had been a mess, two weeks without blood as I was—"

"Two weeks?" both Vampires interjected.

He stared at them. "This is what I meant by her control—she, while in her sleep-like state since we'd returned back to London on the back of the Dragon, rendered me incapable of feeding."

"What?!" Xavier cried while Aleister's eyes narrowed as though he couldn't believe the words. "You should have said something! Sent word in a letter! Or better yet shown your face in the Vampire City at all!"

"What would that have done?" he countered, amazed that he was being berated now of all times, mad for her as he was. "I would not dare leave her side, not after Lore showed up at our Manor door, bit your servant! And the journey to the Vampire City is what? Two days on horseback? I hadn't the blood to fly, let alone think—there was no way I would be able to transport there."

"You wouldn't be able to," Xavier said, eyes brimming with unchecked anger, "there is a magic barrier several miles out from the place. It is made so no one can just appear at the gates at will. But all the same, you *should* have sent word. If the woman was showing such alarming—she could very well be dead tomorrow! Her body can't take what she must become, it is a wonder she was able to survive this long!"

"And what must she become?" he asked, staring at his brother in grave curiousness. "You must know, right?"

"She is the key to stilling the Lycans...their blood—"

"See!" he said, waving a hand to Aleister. "But she does more than that, Xavier. She stills my blood—*Eleanor's* blood—she rendered the bloody woman human, Xavier! Eleanor couldn't transform, couldn't call forth her...power...hell she could even hold Dracula's sword. Alexandria's...blood is the key to ending all of this. And if she is to die...I—I must be the one to secure her transition."

A sweeping silence passed through the room with the two Vampires across from him sharing unbelieving glances. And after a few harrowing moments of this, one of them broke the silence, Xavier doing so with a jarring laugh.

"You have proven yourself incapable of this control you speak so highly of, Christian," he said once his fit was done. "And regardless of whatever you believe calls you to her, you cannot be the one to change her...your blood is not the one that can."

"And yours is?"

"Yes."

"*He called me the blood-stiller.*" Alexandria. Her presence alone could meet the insatiable need that filled his blood, and if Xavier would not understand, Aleister, then he would be with the one person that would...for he was sure she felt it too...was sure she did it on purpose...needed him to taste her blood, turn her as well.

He turned from both Vampires, stepping for the door when Xavier appeared just before it, brow furrowed. "You're not thinking of going to her, are you?"

He said nothing, his anger welding his mouth shut.

"Oh, no no no, Christian," he said placing a hand on his shoulder, guiding him to the bed. Christian sat much against his will, watching in seething rage as his brother took a seat beside him. "I think it would be best if you...were not alone with the woman from here on out."

He opened his mouth to speak, alarmed when the words would not rise to his lips, and then he saw it in his brother's eyes: how dark the green appeared, a thick black smoke appearing to swim within them.

"From what Aleister tells me you were more than ravenous when you awoke—he had to hold you down to keep you subdued. You were seconds away from tearing off Alexandria's head. It would be best, naturally, if you were to travel with me to gather the sword Dracula has left for you."

He could not believe what he was hearing. To mock him, whatever emotions had spurred within the week he'd been around the woman, and now this, forbidding him from being around her when it was what he needed most?

He attempted to stand, but was quite surprised when he found he could not: it was as though his legs would not move.

He eyed his brother again, alarmed when the black smoke within those eyes appeared to thicken. *What was wrong with him?*

He turned to Aleister to see if the scarred Vampire had seen this sudden change, but Aleister was not looking at them, he had taken to staring out a large window, the red light of the medallion at his chest glaring through his shirt, traveling cloak long removed.

Was it possible Xavier was under her control again?

He turned back to his brother, watching the eyes so full of the smoke never release themselves from him, and then Xavier said, "We will move once everyone is well rested. Last night's events rattled all of us."

"What events?" he found himself saying at last.

"The...corruption of Darien Nicodemeus," Aleister said from the window sending both brothers to turn. "He...turned into a horrible... monster, Christian. Killed Ewer Caddenhall then flew off in a whirl of...I can only akin it to Eleanor's dread, though it is...so much more."

"What?"

"Darien Nicodemeus is...an original Vampire," Xavier said, bringing his gaze back to him. "Peroneous told me it was a form very similar to what Dracula shared before bequeathed immortality."

"When did this happen?" Aleister asked, clearly intrigued.

"Right after Darien turned," Xavier said, rising from the bed, straightening his shirt. And without another word, he left the room, the door closing behind him as he moved. The Ascalon all but forgotten atop the bed beside Christian.

He stared at it, the unease and questions churning in his mind. What would cause that strange smoke? Darien Nicodemeus...an original Vampire? What on Earth did that mean? To travel with Xavier to gather this sword...what was happening?

He rose from his seat just as his brother had done, moving around the bed to eye the disgruntled Vampire who had stared at Xavier in bewilderment just as he had done.

"Aleister—something is wrong with Xavier," he started, not wanting to believe it. But what other option was there? To leave the sword behind...Xavier never did that, ever.

"Don't I know it," he said, much to Christian's surprise. "Yes, there is something wrong with him. He didn't even come to see if you were all right after you and Alexandria had appeared within the manor walls."

His eyes widened. "What? Why wouldn't he do that?"

He shrugged, his face belying the discomfort he felt with the topic at hand. It was possible he had not desired to have a conversation on Xavier's mind once again. Christian could understand: neither did he. "I called after him as wildly as one does when their son is near death and their other refuses to come when called. He went off with Aciel and Amentias into the woods. Returned only when Thomas arrived." He waved a scarred hand. "We know the rest."

He was quiet as this news reached him, and then, "What? S-son?"

A look of surprise, and then realization passed across his face. "Ah. I never got the chance..." And Christian watched as he waved a scarred hand through the air, his green eyes appeared to glow, and then it was as though a veil had been lifted over Christian's head, a cloud suddenly dispersed by a blinding sun's rays.

He stared upon Aleister in new light, seeing the exact way his scarred face held great traces of Xavier's countenance, of his own... "How can this be—"

"It is a long story—what is best now is that you know. I did what I could for you, for Xavier, and I am bound to Dracula's hand because of it."

He blinked in the light of the sun, and turned to stare at the sword upon the bed again. "Xavier...knows, doesn't he?"

"Of course," Aleister said. "Dracula let slip whilst he traversed *The Immortal's Guide*," and he stepped closer, placing a hand on the Vampire's shoulder, "now let us focus—you were worried for your brother's wellbeing?"

He blinked, recalling when he would cease to feel Eleanor's dread when Aleister would bid him not to focus on it, how compelled he felt to do as the Vampire said even beneath Alexandria's blood. He stammered, and with a flash of Aleister's eyes, he spoke, knowing he was being commanded by the one who turned him. He could recall the Vampire's gaze as he stared upon him when he, Christian, was but a human man. But that was not what was important now. "Those are Elite Creatures—why are they with Xavier?"

A satisfied look passed across his face. "They seem to have fallen out of Eleanor's graces. They are with us to give Xavier information on her plans, her power. Though I am not sure how much of this has come to be shared..."

His voice trailed as the door was opened again, Aurora Borealis appearing there.

Christian watched his father step to her as though bidden, a scarred hand upon her face in a gesture most tender. He turned from the expression, feeling quite rude in their presence. He was only called back when Aurora said, "Am I the first awake? I can't find anyone else's rooms—this place is a maze. I just passed Xavier in the hall, he looked disturbed. Is there something else we must be concerned about, Aleister?"

"When it rains it pours," he answered, removing his hand from her face, a trail of her black hair following the end of a finger as he did so. "Xavier does not deem it wise for Christian to remain around Alexandria Stone any longer."

Shock graced her face. "Whatever for?"

"Apparently he is incapable of controlling himself around the woman, something Xavier has feared since she was first found."

Christian stepped forward, bringing her gaze to him. "And what do you think...father?" For how strongly it was returning to him, now. The man's charming smile whilst human, his mangled face whilst on the floor of their old home, bleeding to death.

"I think," he said, "that your...obsession on her blood is... troubling, but that you will not harm her if you can help it. The control you possessed earlier this day when just before her was admirable... but one cannot be sure how long you can sustain that control. It is a careful dance we must play, Christian. And if she must be bitten, and soon...I cannot say who would be the better to give her their blood.

"Xavier is...displaying worrying signs once free from the Vampire City, and I'm not sure how clear his blood is having been under Eleanor's control for that week as he was. And now to have Elite Creatures at his side...

"And you, Christian," he said, his expression softer in the light of the sun, "if she calls you to her, then nothing any of us can do will be able to stop that pull. If Dracula's blood flows through her veins, then we can be assured that whatever she desires, she will soon possess."

He smiled, hearing the Vampire's ease at his situation, whatever words laced this contentment. *At least,* he thought staring upon the scarred Vampire who had taken to speaking with Aurora in serious tones, *there was someone on my side.*

※

Xavier stepped down the many flights of marble stairs, remembering when the large hall had been filled, corner to corner with Vampires.

A time long past, he thought, reaching the last step, moving across the long hall where splatters of Thomas Montague's blood remained. It was not enough that the Creature had arrived here, but that he had moved, once again, to take the curious woman.

His thoughts returned to Christian's words whilst in the room. *"She stills my blood—Eleanor's blood—she rendered the bloody woman human, Xavier!"* Of course he could not be trusted, not after what he, Xavier, had seen from him. He was truly unhinged, returning his fury to Alexandria only after Thomas had disappeared in a burst of dread.

It had taken all of them to pry the Vampire from her—and though he hadn't gotten what he desired—her blood, Xavier was sure what he had come close to attaining only fueled his passions more.

To still Eleanor Black, he thought, wondering just how they were to move to secure the sword from the elusive woman's grip.

To be near her again...he had to admit the thought had been pressing on his mind since told he had helped her create these Elite Creatures. And wouldn't that be right?

That he move to stand at her side, for weren't her Creatures not worthy of such a right? Weren't they only fodder for her true purpose? To acquire him.

Wouldn't he make it easier for her, considerably, if he merely showed up at her door, heart in hand, eager to right the many wrongs that had stunned him and the world since Dracula's death?

He blinked, the thoughts passing through his mind ones he did not recognize. Fear quickly replaced the confusion as he settled back into reason. The blood on the floor shined in the light of the torches placed about the great hall, and he remembered Thomas Montague's need for the woman. Was it what he, himself desired for Eleanor Black? Was it, indeed, no different at all? The desire for these women?

He stared at the stairs, guilt passing through him as he remembered how he had berated Christian for feeling as though Alexandria's blood was calling to him.

He suddenly felt very much that Eleanor's dread was doing the same for him.

I can't lose myself to her again.

But wasn't it already happening?

He was broken from these unbecoming thoughts by a horrible roar sounding from outside the manor doors.

He tensed, frowning when he realized the Ascalon was not at his side.

"What do you mean that monster is Darien?!" a very familiar voice said from outside the high walls

His brow furrowed. "Damion?" he called, stepping towards them.

"Bloody hell! Yaddley get those bloody doors open, will you? I will not burn to my death out here in this godforsaken sun!" Damion was yelling.

Curious more than anything, Xavier reached the white doors and pulled down on a golden handle.

The sun's light blinded him momentarily, the scene before him unbelievable.

There kneeled Damion, badly burned on his face and hands, crouching up against a tree, shaking terribly, a most angry, yet bewildered Minerva raising her slender hands to do battle with the newly-formed Creature from last night:

The darkness had not done it justice, Xavier thought, staring upon it now. It was large, at least nine feet tall, his wings folded into its long, large back as it raised its own large claws-for-hands, mimicking Minerva's stance. Its eyes were large in its long skull, cruel as it eyed her in what appeared to be anger, the many fangs glistening in the light of the sun.

If he had not seen Darien turn into the thing several hours ago, he would not have believed it could have once been a Vampire.

"Xavier Delacroix?" a new voice sounded from several yards away.

Xavier tore his gaze from the monster to eye Yaddley Caddenhall, who had stopped walking towards the doors when they opened. The Vampire looked just as formidable as had been described in *The Caddenhall Curse*, but he could not believe the size of the Vampire: he met his height, with a muscular frame that was to be envied. Xavier remembered reading that this particular Caddenhall had been endowed with brilliant physical skill, but staring at him now he wondered how much of it was magic.

"Xavier?" Damion called in surprise from his tree, looking up from badly burned hands to glimpse him. "Why is Xavier here?"

The monster let out a roar in his direction at Damion's words, pushing Minerva Caddenhall off itself with what seemed to be annoyance, extended its large wings, and with a ferocious flap, was off the ground, flying through the air with the same jagged grace Xavier had witnessed when the sky was not bathed in light.

He stilled the shiver that threatened to rise. That thing was what Dracula had been...swarmed in this new dread. He imagined the sky filled with thousands of the monsters, an unsettling tinge of new fear to fill him.

"You are, quite possibly, the link to transformations..."

He shook away the dread that filled his dead heart, wishing the Ascalon was at his side. He felt naked without it, even more so with the knowledge that such a being was loose in the world...but what could be done to stop it?

"Darien!" a new voice sounded, sending him to whirl in alarm, the sight of a frantic Lillith Crane running straight towards him causing his brow to furrow. He moved out of the way as she bounded past him, her dark blue eyes on the sky as she reached the dirt ground at last.

She wore white breeches, on her feet were white boots, golden buckles clasping around her calves. Her ruffled blouse danced in the slight breeze that passed, and Xavier marveled at the sight of her, quite clean, her blonde hair whirling behind her head.

"Where—where is he?!" she cried. "He was here! I felt him!" And she eyed him, her dark blue eyes wide with a neediness Xavier had seen in his brother just moments before. "Xavier—he was here, wasn't he?"

He knew not what to say, unsure if he should tell her the truth or disappoint her with a lie. She looked ready to fly away herself after the monster—and without knowing what more Darien would do, he could not allow it to happen.

"Lillith," he began, his words slow, "you must calm down—"

"Her?" Minerva said, rising to her feet from the bloody ground, kicking aside the rotting corpse of Ewer Caddenhall she had landed next to. "What's she doing here?"

"Minerva?" Lillith breathed in astonishment, eyeing the rest of the clearing. Her blue eyes narrowed on the badly burned Damion still cowering against his tree, the stoic Yaddley standing close by. She turned back to him, confusion replacing her anxious air. "Xavier what are they doing here?"

"Excellent question," Aciel said, and they all watched as he appeared from behind a tree most near Damion, Amentias close at his heels. Their mouths held traces of blood, the wafting smell of Elite Creature drifting off them in droves. "We watched them do battle with the Creature, your Grace. It was the strangest battle." His eyes gleamed with a knowing Xavier understood. Something more had happened during the battle he could not relay here.

Clearing his throat, he gestured with a hand for all Creatures to enter the manor. "We will get to the bottom of this if you would all enter Cinderhall Manor. It is safe, enchanted by various Enchanters—I promise you, no Creature will be able to enter it."

With begrudging stares, all Dark Creatures began to move towards the doors after seeing there was nothing else that could be done, all save Damion who still cowered against the tree, ring not upon a burned finger, Xavier noticed.

He caught Aciel's eye and the Creature obliged: he waved a careful hand over Damion's head, a shroud of black smoke immediately removing the heat of the sun from his head. The burning flesh still smoked, and Xavier stared at him, realizing he had never seen the Creature so damaged before.

He watched Aciel lift the burned Vampire to his feet, and begin to guide him towards the manor doors, until several footsteps sounded from the stairs.

He turned to eye them, Peroneous and Dragor taking the lead, behind them an alarmed Aleister, Christian, and Aurora.

"We've some company," he said to the lot before they could question what had happened.

"Is that Damion?" Dragor asked as the burned Vampire was passed right before him.

They all watched as Aciel led Damion to a golden bench beside the doors, the smoke still issuing off him.

"I've never seen a Vampire burned in the sun before," Aurora said absently as Lilith stepped from them, ringing her hands.

Xavier did not falter in noticing the tenseness in her shoulders. As the others stepped down from the stairs, moving for various parts of the large hall to gather things for Damion, Xavier moved for Lillith, glad the burn on his leg had subsided with a good helping of *Anima* some hours before.

"Miss Crane," he said, watching her long hair shake as she turned to eye him, "how did you know Darien returned?"

"Know?" she repeated. "I could feel it in my blood. He...calls for me, he needs...needs—"

"Needs you?" he finished, beginning to find it tiresome how all that surrounded him felt some attraction to another in some way.

"Well, yes," she said, folding her arms, "I know how it sounds but I do feel responsible for...making him...whatever he is."

He bit down the urge to say he knew how she felt, and instead said, "What does he want...when he calls you?"

"He wants to be free," she said, brow furrowing, "I think he means death, but there are other times when he seems confused... convinced he must aid you... 'Protect Xavier,' he kept saying last night before I could sleep."

"Protect me?" He stared at her. It was a while before he said, "Did Dracula enlist Darien's help to protect—protect the king?"

She nodded. "It was why we came to these woods. Darien insisted we move as soon as we could. He and his brother were arguing about arriving here at all, I believe, before we left their home."

He turned to eye the still-shaking Vampire whose hair had gone in the fire. *He was almost as bald as his brother,* he thought wryly, *twins no matter what their faces, hm, Damion?*

He shifted his footing as the new thought reached him: the image of Swile pointing to the green curtain against the wall. Did Damion truly lead the Elves through some secret tunnel to infiltrate the Vampire City?

All matters of the Dark Creatures around him fell away as the thought grew stronger. Could the dark Vampire know some secret truth that he did not?

And Dracula...why would he make this damned Vampire a member of the Vampire Order right after he'd staged a bloody war?

"Serves him right," Dragor said suddenly from his side, "a day in the sun. Those Caddenhalls should have let him burn."

"I take it your hatred for him extends past him gaining a place in the Order before you."

He chuckled, a large hand waved through the air. "He's troubling, sneaky, a liar. Even when he was a soldier in the Armies, he never showed me the respect I'd deserved. And where he should be moving to aid you, he's gone off doing the Phoenixes know what with his bloody servants."

He could only agree. It did not help matters that Damion did not move, as his brother had tried to do, to aid him on his journey. After all, isn't that why Dracula had inducted him? Because he had the Caddenhalls at his disposal?

And what had he been doing with them? Clearly they knew their former master was no longer fit to rule them. He recalled the night he had overheard Ewer Caddenhall telling them that if one Invader was not present long enough in the lives of the Invaded, then the next Invader had full control. *So if that was true,* he thought, leaving Dragor, to step for the dark Vampire, *Damion Nicodemeus had full control of Minerva and Yaddley.*

"How'd you let this happen, Damion?" he asked, sending the now-healing Vampire to look up at him in bemusement.

Once his skin returned to its healthy death-glow, his long black hair growing atop his head, he flexed his jaw, and said, "I got lost." His words hoarse as though his vocal chords had been reduced to ash.

As he cleared his throat, Xavier eyed the stoic Yaddley, silently bidding him to move so that he could take a seat beside his former 1st Seat.

It was a while before he did, moving away with Minerva to go gather another jar, and Xavier sat along the hard bench, staring ahead at Dragor and Lillith who were deep in conversation.

"Lost," he began, "on your way to Eleanor's side, or lost in the more figurative sense?"

He felt the affronted glare the Vampire bade him, but he did not turn to eye it. Too much was happening, had happened, and now the very Vampire he had desired to question on those matters three years before had appeared at his door. He would not doubt the forces at work, not anymore.

Christian mad, Lillith corrupted, Alexandria...whatever she was... It was all screaming back to Dracula. Dracula, the one who created this human, Dracula the one who desired to give Christian his very sword, Dracula, the one that forbid them to drink the blood of a Vampire.

"What," Damion coughed, "makes you think I wanted to join... her?"

He eyed him at last, the black hair fully regrown. He stared at him for a long moment, remembering when he trained with the Vampire, guided him, helped him, dodged his sword, watched him embrace Eleanor Black time and time again—

"It is where all Dark Creatures are going now," he said, feeling her dread fill his heart. "Since I haven't seen you in quite a time, I figured you'd...switched sides."

"I am not Victor," he said, wiping his mouth with a shaking, ring-less hand.

An eyebrow rose. "You've seen him?"

"He's the reason I..." he said, waving the same hand across his singed cloak. "I was on my way...to look for Lucien Caddenhall when I came across Victor. He was with another Creature...no, I did not catch who it was."

"Where?"

"Wingdale...what remains of it. It's been burned to the ground... as well as a few of her Creatures."

"They burned Wingdale to the ground? Whatever for?"

"They searched for something...Victor and this other Creature. I followed them all night 'till they disappeared a day's journey from the Mountains of Cedar."

He was silent as this news reached him, and then, "And you? What would happen for you to get caught in the sun, sans ring?"

"Her Creatures caught up with me, and I defended myself," he said simply.

"Is that so?"

"Quite, now if you'll excuse me," and he rose to his newly-healed legs, "I have to find Lucien."

"I still can't smell him, Master Damion," Minerva said, approaching them again, a full jar of blood in her hands. Yaddley walked close behind her.

"You haven't reached your Age," he said dismissively, all eyes on him as he straightened his badly singed cloak, replacing it over the burned pant-leg of his breeches. "Thank you for your...delicious blood, but I really must be on my way." And without another word, he moved for the closed doors, Aurora and Aleister standing most near them. They eyed Xavier as he approached, and Xavier nodded, watching as they moved to stand just before the doors, blocking the Vampire from going further.

"Really, now," Damion said in annoyance, turning back to him, "this isn't necessary. I merely wish to gather my Vampire—"

Xavier stood at last. "You don't seem scared of your brother, Damion, or have you forgotten what he's become?"

His face fell, and Xavier knew he had not thought of the winged Creature at all since he'd healed. "I knew whatever Dracula got him tied up with would catch up to him eventually, but I never thought..."

"Yes," Dragor said, stepping forward to meet him, "you never thought he'd become the being he is because you've been too preoccupied doing who knows what to pay attention to what surrounds you. You were always off doing your own bloody thing—making deals with Elves, ruining our world!"

His eyes widened. "What happened, then, was for the greater good—"

"For *your* greater good!" Dragor shouted. "I was awake when you kidnapped me, Damion, I heard your plans, how strongly you desired the Ares!"

"*What?*" Xavier said, striding forward. His glare caught Christian, and he held it, a look of confusion gracing both their faces.

"He wants Dracula's sword, Xavier," Dragor went on, glaring upon the dark Vampire who looked most despondent. "He knows of its power—wants it for his own. He thinks if he can hold it he'll be the rightful king."

"But the power of the sword is merely a tool," Aleister offered from behind Damion, "just as these medallions. It doesn't hold any real power save the gem in the guard of the sword."

"But I saw it!" Damion shouted, rounding on them all. "I saw it and I felt it—that power. I've never felt anything like it. That is the true power of Dracula's reign over this world—the sword. Even Eleanor saw it, she was there with me, she touched the gem, said she never felt anything like it."

Dragor snarled, raising the sword at his waist out of its sheath. "Enough of this madness! You won't see sense even though it stares you clear in the face. Even now!" Xavier looked at the steady blue glow that centered on the long blade, wondering what magic enabled it do so.

Aleister stepped between Damion and Dragor, his scarred expression fierce. "Dragor, stand down."

"I will do no such thing," he snapped, "we let him go and he gets in the way, ruining what must be done so that he can get his grubby hands on a sword not meant for him?" A cold smile lifted his lips. "He only wants to get to Eleanor Black, only wants to rekindle what was there before her death."

"Enough!" Aleister shouted, pushing Dragor away from himself. *"Xavier..."*

Dragor laughed, swinging the sword in hand. "I'm a defender of the bloody throne, Aleister," and he raised the blue sword higher so all could eye it, "it is my *duty* to defend the king, to do any and all things to ensure all who are made to help us reach our goals, do."

"And I am the protector," Aleister countered, as if it mattered, "but that doesn't excuse your actions. You cannot cut down a Vampire just because he desires something he cannot attain!"

"Hey!" Damion shouted.

"Xavier, kill him, end his life before he ends yours..."

"Everyone needs to calm down!" Peroneous Doe yelled over the din that had arisen as the Dark Creatures began to argue heavily amongst themselves. All eyes roved to him, his black eyes angry as he remained on the stairs. "Let us regain our minds, shall we? Her dread floats through us all, let us not forget. It corrupts us, even in the smallest of ways. We cannot let it win."

"Xavier...do it. Kill Damion before he ever reaches me...touches me...kisses me—"

"No!" he cried, moving in a blink to grasp the sword in Dragor's hand. He turned with it just as swiftly, pressing the blade against Damion's throat.

The Vampire froze, as did everyone else, and somewhere far away, Xavier could just make out Christian's voice: "His eyes!"

"Xavier?" Damion breathed, alarm dressing his dark face. "What—release the sword! It's *me*, Damion. Your eyes. They're the same black smoke that covers the Elite Creatures' blades..."

Nonsense, he thought, the sword beginning to glow its thick blue, shaking with a tremendous power. But still her dread would rise, and he felt his hand shake, fighting the dread within him, the spell on the sword.

"Xavier, stand down! Please!" Aleister cried where other faint voices were shouting the very same, but he could only hear hers... only feel her wind surround him, call him, pull him...

And then he was standing several feet away from her, her long black hair unbound behind her head, on her body a beautiful black dress, the bodice silver as it clinched perfectly around her midsection. She whirled and danced in a large, empty hall, one he vaguely recognized against the dark, but that did not matter. All that mattered was that she was there, and he was here, back where he belonged.

He stepped down the old, crumbling stone steps, the tails of his suit jacket flying out behind him as he stepped to her, an arm sliding around her waist, her red eyes staring lovingly upon him.

As they danced around the old hall where the bodies lay unmoving, the music a tune only they could hear, she said through red lips, "You've come back to me."

"I'm sorry I kept you waiting," he replied, moving carefully over the back of his father as he lifted her into the air, "they seem to think they know what is best for me."

"Who?" she breathed, landing gently on her heels.

"The others," he said, afraid he'd come back too late.

"Oh," she said simply, "they don't matter anymore. We killed them, don't you remember?" And she spun away from him, the darkness around them parting to reveal the floor in full:

He recognized the back of Aleister, the bloody prints of his shoes appearing on the scarred Vampire's shirt as he stared, the covered back of the Vampire beside him reaching him next.

Christian.

He lay unmoving beside his father, hand intertwined with another Vampire, one he did not recognize at first. He stared at her, the tendrils of her long brown hair falling around her pale face in serene beauty, and he knew at last what Christian had seen in the woman.

As he looked around the rest of the floor, he caught the familiar heads of Peroneous, Dragor, Lillith, Aurora and others, a river of blood flowing between them all.

"We killed them?" he whispered, an emotion he knew he should have been feeling not rising to his dead heart.

She wrapped her arms around his abdomen, her face pressing into his back. "Mmm, yes, wonderfully so."

"But why?"

Something was not right, it was something he could not place, but he felt it all the same: they should not all be dead.

He turned to her, forcing her to release her hold on him. She stepped back in bemusement.

"Eleanor, why did we kill everyone?"

"Because," she said, a look most familiar gracing her face, and he was wholly reminded when she looked like this before, just before she'd burst into a Lycan Creature, "they could not take what we truly are."

The unease grew. "And what is that?"

"Before the Vampires, there were the select few who held the blood of pure. The Elite. I have recreated them, Xavier. In you, in me."

"What have you done?"

272

"No," she said, a strange smile on her face, "the question is what have *we* done."

And then it happened: she screamed as her nails grew longer, darker, the skin on her hands tighter, grayer. He watched in complete horror as she bent double, a wretched gasp leaving her throat as her spine lengthened and grew, the bones from her shoulder blades pressing outward towards the sky.

Her bodice fell away as blood drenched it, the large wings spreading up and outward as they flexed in the dark air.

He could not move as her head lifted, no longer holding her long hair, but longer now, her completely black eyes peering into his soul, or so he felt.

He could not move as he watched her...it...this beast survey him back with a frenzied intensity.

And then it opened its mouth and revealed its many rows of sharp fangs. "*Join me,*" it said, though its mouth never moved to form the words.

"I," he whispered, the fear returning in full.

Its head titled to the side in question.

"I can't," he mouthed at last, the smell of death and decay reaching his nose in a sudden burst of wind.

"*Too late.*"

And he raised an arm, horrified to see it lengthen and grow just as hers had done, but before the claws could fully form, he swiped at it, a defiant roar leaving his lips.

"Xavier!" several voices cried, sending him to blink, greatly confused when the monster was gone, the most frightened expressions of the others gluing themselves to the sword he held in a tight, shaking grip.

He stared at it, felt it glow with its cold light, and then he saw the blood at the tip of the blade, and his brow furrowed.

Damion Nicodemeus held his throat, a river of blood spilling forth from behind his hands, brown eyes wide, held upon him in sheer disbelief.

"No," he said dully, a fresh horror surrounding him. Dropping the sword where it clanked to the floor, splattering against Damion's blood, he went on, not hearing himself, "I didn't mean to—I—"

"The jar!" Aleister shouted to a horrified, spellbound Minerva, who would not release the jar of *Anima* from her vice-like grip. It took Aleister several seconds to pry her fingers off it, and move to Damion where he undid the top. He pressed it to Damion's lips, forcing him to drink.

Xavier barely watched as the special blood spilled fruitlessly down Damion's chin, the blood still spilling from his throat. "I didn't mean," he whispered absently, as Aleister stepped away, the jar of Anima empty now, a hopeless look on his scarred face.

"We need Unicorn Blood," he said as Damion fell to his knees.

"There's no time," Aurora said, her eyes wide on Damion's head, "he needs blood. Any kind."

But no one stepped forward to aid the dark Vampire, who was trying to speak, but failing miserably in the wake of his vocal chords severed.

When at last it seemed they were all to watch Damion suffer terribly for several moments more, new footsteps could be heard approaching the stairs.

Xavier looked up first, quite surprised to find Alexandria Stone still alive, looking quite rested as it were. The blood had been washed off her skin, his traveling cloak gone from around her shoulders, instead a ruffled blouse much like the one Lillith wore covered her torso, a pair of brown breeches resting on her long legs. At her feet, he saw as she stepped down the stairs past a bewildered Christian and Peroneous, were black riding boots.

No one said a word as she stepped past them, moving carefully to kneel just before the bleeding Vampire.

"No, Alexandria," Christian said from the stairs, panic and something more on his voice, "don't!"

But she swung back her hair to reveal her neck, a sweet, unrelenting scent drifting to his nose as she did so, and Xavier knew what that was.

How could her blood smell so enticing? he thought, the dread returning. He watched in startled silence as Damion lunged for her, biting into her neck with a great, horrible need.

※

Thomas Montague clutched the golden ring even as his fist shook tremulously, the blood making it hard to keep it in his grip.

He had returned as quickly as he could, a strange wind carrying him, not to her cave, but to another wood, one he was not familiar with. It had taken him several tries to get to her home, even as he bled from the wound Xavier had given him the night before.

Damned Vampire, he thought in anger. To finally see him, reach him—and to be driven to his knees by the Vampire's bloody glowing sword... He shook his head releasing the embarrassment the memory served, and focused on the present.

He was still injured, still bleeding, but he had not been able to find Eleanor—she was gone somewhere he could not know doing who knew what and he needed to speak to her!

The woman was there! As was Christian, Xavier! And how deliriously the younger Delacroix spoke of her—her power. He eyed the ring once more, wondering why the Vampire did not have his ring upon a finger. Why, he called himself her chosen, the one she wanted...

But she had shown herself to he, Thomas in his dreams for the better part of three weeks, she had promised him such gifts, the woman he could not live without—

But it had been lies, he thought, rising to stand from the modest-sized bed he'd laid on since his return. He eyed the small room he'd been given upon his word that he would gather Alexandria Stone for Eleanor Black, and figured he'd have to work his way back up into her good graces.

That was all well and good, he shrugged, wincing as the wound still bled, hurt, stung, he was not entirely sure he desired to be at her side for much longer.

But with what the Vampire said, he could not deny he was very intrigued as to what the woman could *truly* do. And if Christian Delacroix knew her power, could be so unguarded without the ring on his finger, he was dangerous, terribly so.

He had desired to tell Eleanor this, burned with it, but found himself confined to his room, instead.

There was no one around that would want to hear this besides her, and he wouldn't dare let a thing slip to Victor Vonderheide, Vampire he still was, nor would he tell her new favorite, Joseph Gail. There was no telling what that sycophant of a Creature would do, bending over backwards to complete her will. And what then? *He* would be tasked with the gathering of the human?

Not on his life, of this, Thomas was certain.

He'd remained in Vampire form since he was not able to turn, the injury as bad as it was. He had requested a human that had yet to be transformed be sent to his room, but that had been a few hours ago.

Now he grew ravenous, only made worse by his anger at being ignored, being without blood, made to bleed at all by Xavier Delacroix.

The door opened and the man stood there, head down, shaggy brown hair unkempt atop it, the Elite at his back pushed him into the room, nodded at Thomas, and departed swiftly.

Once the door closed, Thomas stepped up to this man, chains tying his hands together behind his back, and lifted the stubbly chin, sending the tired, brown eyes to gaze into his weak, hungry ones.

"Did not want to turn?" he asked, smelling the man's fear, his blood.

The need grew.

"I—I'm not sure what's going on," the man said weakly, and Thomas noticed he shook at his touch.

"You don't know why you are here?" he asked. *Weren't they told what would happen once they stepped through the barrier?* "You followed one of her Creatures here, surely—made the oath to become one of us?"

"One of—" the man began, looking up into Thomas's eyes for the first time. He saw the utter fear that existed there, the palpable unease that filled the man, smelled it next on the man's blood, the brown eyes widening as they found his, red in all of their hungry glory. "My God!"

"Yes," he said, the smell of the blood propelling him forward; he grasped his neck and bent his head, the need ripping through his body, sending his mind to blank, "your God." He broke the skin, his fangs pressing into the large vein that rested there, and his mind, screaming with the stark need, thought on how strange it was the man had not known what he was there for.

The man's scream left his lips, Thomas unable to stop it as his attention was placed on the blood pooling past his own, the scream in his mind dulling to a whisper at last.

He did not stop until the gash Xavier's sword made closed entirely, the pulse of the words in his mind an echoing call.

The man fell from his grip and landed on the stone floor with a dull thud, and Thomas stepped over him, moving for the door, quite sure he would not be reduced to waiting for any woman to call, not anymore.

※

Christopher Black stepped behind the tree, the large...whatever it was soaring over the clearing ahead.

The manor stood resolute against the afternoon air, and no one stepped from it, nor could he hear anything within it, yet he was sure Damion Nicodemeus was there. He'd thought on the Forest of Yielding after all, and this was where it'd led him—right into a small army of those dread-covered Creatures.

They'd fell upon him in a uniformly strategic manner, blades of smoke drawn, slicing and stabbing him wherever they could. He had just made it out with his life, firing the white arrows he had stolen from a dead Elite once able to do so, sending them all to freeze, unable to move.

And now he stared at the tall white building, not daring to move forward until that...thing that flew above it was removed. It was large, dipping in its movement, brushing the tip of a large wing against the flat top of the manor, a screech of what seemed to be impatience leaving its long throat.

"Bloody hell," he whispered, eyeing it as it rose in the dark blue sky, heading towards him, dipping again once it reached the top of trees.

What the Devil is that thing? he thought, as its massive body passed overhead, a rush of wind and a strange smell sweeping past him with its movement. He covered his nose, unable to stand it: it was a sickly sweet smell, the smell of death, the smell of stark decay.

The leaves fell to the ground around him, the trail of the branches and more leaves flittering to the grass where it flew over the tops of trees towards the large black lake. He followed the large shadow as best he could, until it disappeared in the water. Even from the distance he was able to make out the floating corpse of the ashen, once yellow Dragon. It floated along the water's surface.

The thing now gone, he turned his mind to the Vampire he had chased, the woman he would lead him to...

He turned to eye the manor once again, the image of the large Creature having shaken him, (for what on Earth could it have been?) and stepped for the large white doors, stepping over the corpse of a beheaded Vampire as he moved.

The smell of death was thickest here, a rush of anticipation returning as he thought of being returned to her, reunited in truth...

A trembling hand reached for the white bow settled on his back, and he released it from its black strap, a cold breath steadying him as he reached out another hand for a bloody arrow in its casing along his back as well.

He stood just before the large white doors, a strange chill seeping through his dead heart. Something was odd about this place, its largeness holding within it, something dark, foreboding, he felt.

He hesitated for moments more, pulling back on the arrow, aiming the head straight for the white doors, and then he heard it:

"Alexandria...what—why did you do that?"

"Because he needed it."

Quick footsteps drew nearer to the doors. "Alexandria you shouldn't have—Alexandria?"

There was the sound of a body hitting the floor, a hungry snarl, and then the sweet smell of blood, but it was not normal, a human's yes, but immensely alluring, and still he drew back harder on the arrow, his grip steady as he waited.

It was not long before the doors opened against the afternoon air and the dark Vampire emerged from the darkness, the heavy scent of blood, all manner of it following close behind. He snarled in surprise, letting the arrow fly, the dull thunk it made as it sunk into Damion's chest echoing on in his ears even as the many voices sounded urgently behind the shocked dark Vampire who had fallen to his knees, the shade of the manor keeping him safe from the light of the sun.

His red eyes widened in his surprise as he grasped at the arrow, but all at once his fingers grew slack, his snarls faded to whimpers, and he fell to the ground, the "crack" of the arrow breaking beneath him getting lost in the weary shouts of the many Creatures now appearing in the doorway.

Christopher lowered the bow at last, feeling the medallion burn with a searing heat at his chest, his black eyes widening as he eyed the silent Creatures, their mouths closing as their gazes moved to the red light blaring through his cloak.

"Lillith...Crane," he whispered, eyeing the blonde Vampire next to a serious-looking black-haired Vampire with piercing green eyes.

Whatever this Vampire said, he could not know, the sight of her blue eyes mesmerizing him, sending his heart to race, his blood to boil—

"Lillith," he said, louder still, "it's me."

He was not aware all other voices had died, only that she'd bade him the gift of her voice after many horrible, lonely years:

"I'm sorry," and her brilliant gaze seemed to harden in the dark of the building, "who are you?"

He bit back the disbelief in his throat that would have shown itself as a snarl of frustration, and merely said, "Christopher Black, Miss Crane."

Before she could say anything more, a scarred Vampire said, "Well then, Mister Black, you should get inside. You've saved us a lot of grief showing up here as you did." And he stepped aside, a few other medallion-bearing Creatures doing the same, allowing him entry into the manor.

He glanced at her as he stepped around the unmoving Damion Nicodemeus, but she would not reach his gaze. The pit of despair he had not allowed to flourish over the years flared in his heart, for here it was: she didn't know him.

Thinking only of Dracula, how the Vampire placed some sort of magic on her to keep her memories subdued, he stepped past her, smelling her sweet scent, how wonderful it was—

A new scent reached him and he stopped dead in his tracks, the scarred Vampire moving further into the grand hall to kneel beside an unmoving mass upon the floor.

He eyed the brown waves of hair that spilled out around the head of the woman, her eyes closed, but even in this there was a power to her frame...or perhaps it was the faintness of the red light that covered her entire body.

He stared upon her for moments more, the scarred Vampire whispering words over her, when the serious-looking Vampire said from his back, "You're Christopher Black?"

He turned to eye him, an eyebrow raising as he stared at this Vampire. His hair was long and black, straight as though pressed, a ruffled blouse covering his chest, flecks of dark blood decorating it, dark breeches adorning his legs, back riding boots on his feet. He wore no medallion, but Christopher felt such...a presence in this Vampire. Why, he almost felt he should kneel.

"Who are you?"

This Vampire shared brief glances with the others at his side, and then he said, "I am Xavier Delacroix."

He stared at this Vampire, eyeing closely the others who bore medallions. They all looked scared, if not battle-worn, and indeed, their medallions still bathed the air in red.

He pulled the memory to his mind, the strange man slipping the heavy golden necklace around his neck as he slept, and once he'd awoken, he found he could not remove it, could not make the strong man undo what he'd done.

He had thought it Dracula's desire, the bloody medallion resting on his chest forever, but now that he stared upon the others, he was not so sure Dracula had placed it around his neck, or indeed, even a Creature of this Earth.

"Xavier," he said at last, fighting the ever growing urge to kneel, "I'm afraid I can't place who you are."

He stepped forward, his movement fluid, cold, and Christopher knew there was something in this Vampire's dead heart that could never be touched.

"I am your king, Christopher Black," he said as though it should have been known, "and you...are my knight."

Chapter Nineteen

AN ENCHANTER'S CONVICTION

Nathanial Vivery had done away with her Creatures a few hours before, and now continued his trek away from the Vampire City, thoughts hardened on his particular task. He'd tasked Westley Rivers with overseeing the Vampire City in his absence; he would tell Xavier his reasoning for leaving when the time came for it. He could not dawdle, he had owed it to himself to move, and swiftly.

A cold shudder overtook him as he pressed forward within her dread, the book at his side swaying in the black satchel, the magic within unable to spill out unless he desired it.

※

Victor stepped along the ash-filled streets of Scylla, the serious Creature at his heels whispering words Victor could not recognize. He daren't disturb the Vampire from his spell, knowing it unwise to do so, especially when that very Vampire was at her beck and call.

Ignoring the mumbles that filled the air, he focused on the vague scent of bleeding Vampire that was not her dread. The blood was not as strong now, and he figured whatever wounds Nicholai had gathered, he had healed from them just as quickly. *Tainted medallion*, he thought, mind rapt on what Eleanor had discovered of the necklaces. That they were tools made to help Xavier, that they bore the same red light as the other Artifacts, but unlike them, the medallions were unguarded, unshielded from her energy.

Once she'd had the foresight to use her ever-growing energy to her gain, she'd used it without fail. But she had been scared, he remembered, hesitant to even think of mixing her energy, her magic with what Dracula had forged. He had thought it strange, her resistance at first to do what she had only spoken of so vehemently as what was needed, "to completely eradicate any trace of Dracula from the Dark World."

But he had watched her falter, he had watched her sit in a strange fear, one she would never voice, of course, but it had been there. So when one of her men returned to her one night with news that he had felt some of his power go into a medallion when facing the skilled warrior of a Vampire, she had seemed to gain her courage.

And then, Victor recalled, she had tasked her Creatures with the watching of Carvaca's castle, she had placed he, Victor there just in case Xavier returned to speak with that Ancient Creature, that try as they might, they could not reach to destroy.

More of this magic, he thought, eyeing the road ahead, seeing not a soul, nothing, indeed, but more charred buildings.

He felt a dismal lethargy wash over him as the voice of Joseph Gail continued on at his back, more mutterings of strange tongue yielding nothing but confusion in his mind. He thought again on Arminius the Elf, Nicholai Noble, their importance, and most troublingly of all, what they would do if they got back to Xavier.

What *he* would do if he saw the damned Vampire.

Being in Christian's presence had been testing enough, just the sight of the face so similar to the one that had gotten all the bloody praise had been enough to send him reeling. And as they marched towards these Creatures, he knew a new sense of unease to trickle down his spine, slip into his dead heart: *What could I do against him?*

He knew, as strong as he was, as skilled with sword as he was, that he would be able to level with Xavier, after all, he had many a time whilst training the very Vampire, but now...

He remembered the sight of the green eyes when the Vampire had returned to tell him Dracula was dead.

Something else was in him, he thought, something revealing, how curious part of him was to see it again, uncover what truth lay beneath those green eyes, but part of him felt he already knew.

It had been in his strong desire to kneel at the Vampire's feet when Xavier had stepped through the doors, and it had been in his voice, how it rang on in the air with the presence of more. With power only one other Vampire had held in his life.

He shuddered, not desiring to think any more on matters most upsetting, for if it came to that—seeing Xavier again—he would deal with it as was best, with cold, calculating precision.

As it was, nothing good would ever come from allowing ones fears to reign free in one's heart.

He had seen it enough in Eleanor and himself to know this truth.

"...*Marach, marach, enrut alp toil,*" Joseph whispered at his side, snapping him from his thoughts.

He turned to eye the Creature, the once green eyes now a glowing blue, the same blue that trailed from his fingertip. The more Victor stared, the more he was aware the Elite Creature had spotted something up ahead that was not yet visible: His brow furrowed as though trying to figure out something troubling.

"What is it, Gail?" he asked, following the finger where the blue light was fading fast.

"An Enchanter," he said, never tearing his gaze from the glowing sun ahead, as though this Enchanter was right before them.

He sniffed the air, the cold smell of death and blood reaching his nose with unsettling ease. "I smell Vampire," Victor said in confusion. "Are you sure there aren't two of them?"

The blue gaze darkened until it was black, and Victor could see the dread swimming within them, so thick, he was amazed the Creature could see anything at all. He rethought this the moment it passed across his mind.

"There's only one—it's an Enchanter." And he stepped from him, moving further up the street, a tall gate made from the bones of what seemed to be humans creaking in a strong wind that blew up as he moved.

Victor stared after him for a moment before stepping at his back, a hand on the sword at his waist.

The smell of Vampire grew stronger as they moved on the wind Joseph Gail conjured, and before Victor knew it, his boots had left the charred street and he glided forward, the cloak of Joseph Gail billowing wildly in front of him.

They moved on this smooth air for several minutes before rounding what used to be a corner, and then Joseph charged forward, the air becoming a terrible sweep of dread as it carried him like an arrow towards a Vampire clad in red—

Victor's eyes widened as he watched Joseph's smoky daggers miss the Vampire's red head on the wind by inches, this mistake sending the Vampire to turn in alarm.

He gasped.

The golden eyes widened in their own astonishment as he raised his arms, a blue wall appearing from the depths of nowhere, a soft wind blowing past Victor as Joseph met it with a crash.

Victor did not step forward as the Elite Creature got to his feet, smoky daggers all but thrown at the blue wall in agitation, none of them breaking through.

No, Victor remained where he stood, quite a distance from the two Creatures, knowing all too well what that Vampire was capable of.

Nathanial goddamn Vivery.

He watched in slight annoyance as Joseph let out an angry scream, his clothes beginning to rip from his body...

Bloody hell, he thought, knowing it a most inopportune time for the damned Creature to change form.

He sheathed his sword, watching with cold interest as the fully grown Lycan charged repeatedly into the wall, large cracks appearing along its transparent surface. But the Enchanter-Vampire was prepared, Victor saw.

He pulled out a golden book from a leather satchel at his waist and as it glowed, the blue wall fell, and the raging Lycan started forward, a large paw sweeping for the Enchanter's red head, Nathanial said some unintelligible words, and the Lycan froze in mid-air.

He stared at it for moments more, Victor able to see Joseph quivering in his sheer anger, unable to move, to perform the task most desired by all Lycan Creatures...

But of course, Victor thought with a wry smile, waving two fingers to Nathanial who had just seen him, *true Lycans had not been seen since the destruction of London.*

Nathanial stared at him, then moved his glowing golden eyes back to Joseph Gail, seemed to consider something, and then he was gone in a burst of bright green fire.

Victor did not step forward as the sparks from the flames caught the Lycan's fur, sending him to whine horribly, fall out the sky, and roll along the ash-covered ground. He merely stared, a twitch playing at the corner of his lips.

Funny, he thought as a naked, human Joseph Gail rose to his feet, anger clear on his haughty features, *how* his *Creatures still possessed the use of magic to perfection.*

The smile was full as Joseph Gail walked back to him, sweat pouring from his skin that glistened in the sunlight. As he gestured towards the bone gates behind him, he had a strong feeling that they would not be reaching the Elf or Vampire any time soon, if ever.

It was as if, he thought, following behind the bitter man who trekked gingerly up the dark stone path to the tall double doors of the dark manor, *Dracula did not desire it.* And if there was one thing he knew about Dracula, it was that his will could not be countered, if only a speck of it still lived.

And as he thought back to Nathanial Vivery's mastery of magic just moments ago, the destruction of Wingdale at the hands of Arminius, he knew Dracula's will was still being exercised. It would take the permanent death of the Vampire who housed that will to destroy it completely. And that, he knew, was the reason Eleanor would fail.

※

She stared out the window, eyeing the many Enchanters within the immeasurably large hall, their excited chatter reaching an all-time high as the hour drew near.

She eyed the red hoods throughout the crowd below, the faint spark of the Enchantment placed upon their robes shimmering in the sunlight.

Any word? she thought with a breath, directing a whiff of the sliver light towards the five Enchanters.

The hoods moved from side to side as the sliver light reached them, the remaining Elves, Enchanters, and their protected Fae staring upon the single marble podium to the back of the large, open hall.

Sunlight beamed upon their heads, causing their thick fabric to shine or their hair to glisten in the light, and she turned from them, the large white room she stood in spotted with black singe marks upon the walls.

His words filling her mind the more she stared at them, *"I have given the Vampire too much power."*

And now you wish to see it all undone, she thought, stepping to a wall most near her, running a gloved hand over the black smudge that was her spell from days before.

The monster that later became the Vampire Creature had warranted such an act, and if the Phoenixes had intervened, she thought with trepidation, then who were they to say otherwise? It had seemed the best option, indeed, she remembered the day Equis met with the Phoenixes at last to give the polished Dracula, not only a bit of his magical gifts, but all of them, all spells, all potions, everything.

The Head Phoenix, Equis had said, had given him a short speech on how much the Vampire would need it, that the journey he was to go on to right the wrongs of his birth warranted the extensive knowledge of the arcane.

However, when Equis finally did bequeath the Vampire with the knowledge, it was said the Head Phoenix had waved a hand and something else had been given to Dracula, much to Equis's dismay:

All of his magic, complete control of it.

She remembered when Equis returned to the mountain, his stricken gaze alarming her further the more he would not speak, and then he'd said the only words he would for days: *"He gave him all."*

And then he'd slept. For years and years, only waking every few months to hear on the state of the Enchanters in the Dark World. And she noticed his power was never what it was, not after that trip to the Nest. He was changed, destroyed, and with the Elite Creatures now wreaking havoc on the world, he had grown restless, eager to regain what was lost...and by any means.

Philistia blinked, the wisp of sliver light appearing at her nose, and then, *"Madame, they grow weary."*

She heard it, not bothering to step to the window and peel back the blue curtain. The raucous cries issued vehemently through the solid walls, a low rumble of the foundation beginning to sound. *Restless*, she thought, squaring her shoulders, preparing herself to address them at last, their anger at being used by the Vampires, haunted by the Elites a horrid illness that had spread throughout all magic-able Creatures.

It was time to end it, she thought, not at all sure Equis's larger plan would be received as easily as the words that burned in her throat.

Chapter Twenty

DELIVERANCE

Eleanor stepped from the woman, placing a hand atop hers. "Such a dear," she said, releasing the woman's hand to grasp her head. With a quick turn, the woman was dead, fallen back against her wooden chair in a limp heap.

"The Enchanters think they can get away with this?" she asked the quaint cottage at large, Javier Theron at her side staring upon the woman with blankness.

"What would you have us do next, your Grace?" he asked, bringing her gaze to him.

She folded her hands before herself, the thick cloak she wore swaying along her body as she moved. "This Summit needs to be shut down. The Enchanters already with us are loyal to our cause, even if they cannot take either form. Whatever these Enchanters think they will accomplish by...gathering together on Equis's door will not stand."

He shifted his footing, his black cloak swaying around his boots. "You wish to send some men to infiltrate it," he guessed.

An eyebrow rose at his words, the quaint fire most near the wooden chair burning at her back. The young Elite was bathed in the orange glow. "Send men?" she thought aloud. "No, I will pay these Creatures a visit myself."

His dark eyes widened. "But what of Victor? Xavier?"

She stared at the dead Enchanter in the chair, then around at the various statues, trinkets, and brightly-colored liquids in their clear jars along old shelves. *Such sad magic,* she thought, *it's needless, these various odds and ends to accomplish ones goals.*

She smiled at the power she'd gained with Xavier's blood, the whispers of magic that had poured into her mind whilst she traversed the fire of the damned book.

Yes, she had more power than she'd bothered to share, once. Now, however, with the news that these Enchanters were joining together to fight, no doubt, she found comfort in the fact: her power was being recognized. Feared.

The sudden thought of the woman's words reached her next, in the haze of her contemplation, a condescending answer to the brilliance that was her power, *"This light does not hold him back...it propels him forward. It is your dread that stills him."*

"Your Grace?" Javier called.

Blinking, she stared at him, the righteous hum of Alexandria Stone's words repeating their annoying vibration through her skull. "Victor," she began, clearing her throat, "is doing his duty. He moves for the tainted Vampire to still him from reaching Xavier. As for Xavier...he must know I acquired his brother, that woman. I imagine he is most upset with me. Last my men received, he and his merry band of men were off killing all who stood in their way—that is to be expected. He will hide from me yet... I shall journey for Equis's home, Javier. You must go back to the caves, you must wait."

"Wait?"

"For my word. Once the Enchanters are put in their place we can refocus our goals."

He said nothing as she stepped from the dead Enchanter and moved for the old wooden door, able to hear his footsteps moving after her as she pushed down on the old handle and swung the door wide.

The modest Town of Pinnett was alive this afternoon, various Enchanters and Elves strode the dirt paths in-between the rows of wooden and stone cottages, their hoods down as they conversed jovially with one another.

The world burns and no one cares, she thought with a smile, stepping down the small three steps to the Enchanter's home. She replaced her hood atop her head, beginning to step along the path with the others, when a terribly loud explosion cut through the scattered din of the Creatures' voices.

Several cottages down, the rather large building sprang into flame, its glass exterior melting quickly in the fire, a colorful smoke issuing from the open ceiling at the top of the building.

"It's the Apothecary!" an Elf most near her shouted.

She watched with Javier as all Elves and Enchanters moved hurriedly towards the burning building, neither of them taking another step. "Could it be your men?" he asked, as more shouts filled the air and doors flew open against the low sun.

"No," she breathed, "no one has been assigned to Pinnett."

He said nothing but stared, her thoughts clamoring to who it could be. She could smell no trace of Vampire or Elite in the air, only more Elf. Indeed, this seemed to be nothing more than a mere unfortunate occurrence.

She eyed Javier, turning her thoughts from matters that did not concern her to this Summit the Enchanters had conjured, remembering the words Alexandria Stone had told her with remarkable confidence, *"Enjoy your ability to hold which evades you, you will not be able to hold it for long."*

✳

Damion Nicodemeus coughed up blood, a steady hand pressing into the dirt beneath him as he moved to stand. *Bugger,* he thought, a fresh pain pounding in his skull. Blackness met his memory as he tried to recall what happened, where he was.

A cry of fright left his lips as he eyed the sun, surprise greeting him when he realized he was not burning, indeed.

What the devil?

He stretched out a hand, curious more than anything as the light graced it. He could not feel the heat. *How?*

The high-pitched screech rang against his ears, sending him to cover them, the sound piercing his already aching skull. "What—"

There it was, the large, winged Creature, soaring swiftly overhead—and then it was gone, lost behind the large, white building he had not seen until now.

Now what was this? he thought, staring at the building. Why, it seemed so terribly familiar—

The sharp pain clawed at his chest, then, sending him to look down in alarm: blood poured from his chest, the small hole just over his heart. He stepped forward in apprehension, feeling something sharp digging into it. He could barely question when he was hit—and with what—when the screech returned, the large Creature swooping low over the roof of the building, its leathery wings spread wide.

The wind it conjured blew his hair and frayed cloak from his body, the gasp leaving his lips needlessly as he watched it swerve in the blood-ridden clearing and land several feet from where he stood.

Its black eyes were small within its long, dark head, the many sharp fangs within its mouth glistening with its saliva, beads of it dripping down its pointed chin.

He could not move under that gaze, however animal it was: there was something captivating there, as though it desired to command attention in any way, shape, or form.

"What are you?" he asked, his voice quiet in the afternoon sun against the Creature's deep, jagged breaths.

It extended a large claw, the long, sharp nails curling to reach what should have been its palm, and then it pressed its claws against its chest, the long, curving scar there embedded deep in the black, leathery skin.

Damion narrowed his eyes, staring upon this scar, a vague sense of knowing covering him...

It extended its claw again, repeating the action, bringing it to his chest next.

He shook his head, not understanding what it wanted in the least. *That scar...*

It roared, extending its large wings, blowing back the multitude of trees behind it, and then it started forward on a burst of fresh air, heading straight for him.

The tremendous beating of his dead heart resounded in his chest, sending his blood to boil with what should have been fear, instead he felt invigorated, relieved. *If I'm to die for good*, he thought, able to smell the Creature's strange scent, old life and anger, *let it be quick*. He spread his arms wide, prepared for the Creature to pierce his pained heart with the terribly large claw stretched out...

A great wind was knocked out of him as the Creature barreled into him with the force of a raging Lycan, throwing him back against the tall doors, but before he could cause any serious damage to the wood, the Creature moved upwards, dragging him along, its large wings beating vigorously as it worked tirelessly, rising into the multi-colored sky, the dusk settling around the line of the world.

Yes, up here, against the air, the sun he could not feel, Damion felt free, quite sure the Creature was carrying him, if not to his death, then something that would help him, indeed. He felt, as he looked up at the terribly sharp chin, the beady black eyes, he *knew* this Creature. And then the words returned to his vision, sending a sharp line of pain to cut through his skull, *"You don't seem scared of your brother, Damion, or have you forgotten what he's become?"*

What he's become?

The scar.

He eyed it as the Creature moved with its wings, rising and lowering in the sky as they flew over mountains, various shades of green...

Darien, he thought in surprise.

The Creature screeched once, keeping its animalistic gaze on the horizon.

The peace fled with the Creature's answer, a dryness filling his mouth despite the fresh blood that dressed his tongue. And all at once he knew the Creature was not taking him to his death, no, he was quite sure his brother, regardless of the form held, was moving to do Dracula's will, and just as Minerva and Yaddley had done, was forcing him to be a part of it.

✳

The bang against the doors froze him in mid-speech and he turned to eye them, as did everyone else.

"What the hell was that?" Aleister Delacroix asked, exasperated that he'd been interrupted yet again.

"My savior," Xavier responded, rising from his chair.

"Don't you move, Xavier!" Aleister shouted, turning on him again. "You're not right—we will not move until we get her out of your mind."

He snarled his anger but Aleister did not flinch.

"If I could be so kind as to inquire," the newest Vampire to have joined them said from a quiet corner, "just what is going on?

I thought you Creatures were moving to protect the Dark World or some such nonsense."

Aleister did not turn to eye him, he kept his gaze on Xavier, watching the green eyes for any sign of black, any sign of thick smoke, indeed. He saw none.

"My brother, although he is king," Christian answered from a bench, "is most troubled by Eleanor Black."

"I can see that," Christopher Black said, and Aleister could hear him rising from his own chair, "I meant why hasn't anything been done to remedy it?"

At this he turned, watching the bedraggled Vampire step closer to the middle of the hall where he stood before a furious Xavier. "Things *were* done," he countered, "they just didn't...stick."

"Nothing is wrong with me," Xavier said, but Aleister waved a hand, silencing him, his attention still placed on the tired-looking Vampire whose long black hair fell in slight waves around his hardened face. His eyes were black, blacker than Aleister had ever known a Vampire's to be, his brow furrowed into a perpetual crease of unease, concentration. *He was a Vampire,* Aleister noted, *unaware of what to do with his newfound freedom.*

He turned to fully eye this Vampire, the snarl Xavier gave to his back not concerning him in the least. "Tell us, Christopher," bidding the Vampire's dark eyes to find him, "how *did* you resist the medallion for this long?" Knowing it had taken all his strength and indeed, all his will to resist the insatiable heat he could feel...

His dark eyes appeared to shine in the light of the torches around the long hall, and Aleister saw his gaze move to a most removed Lillith, who sat far away on a cushioned bench, her blue gaze on the elaborately designed ceiling. "I would not be persuaded to move for a mere bauble," he said at last, his gaze moving back to Aleister's, "the only reason I arrived here was for Lillith Elizabeth Crane."

He could not speak, and it was not until someone said, "I don't understand," that Christopher Black said anything at all, "We have a special connection—the smell of her blood pulled me here—that you Creatures happened to be here as well is merely coincidence."

"So you're saying," Xavier interjected, stepping around Aleister with little to no care to stand before Christopher, "that you weren't even going to show up—that you were trailing Lillith's scent instead of moving to fight?"

"I am," he answered, glaring down Xavier with equal indifference, "and I'm not ashamed to say it. She has been kept from me for far too long. It ruined me not being beside her, unable to protect what I had created...what I'd caused."

Aleister stepped forward as all eyes watched, his brow furrowed as he was quite unsure he heard what he did. "What *are* you?"

"I am a defender," he answered back, ignoring the snarl that left Xavier's lips, "as I was told by Dracula. If you are asking me what I am outside of this little...group, I am a Vampire, turned by Dracula, and as I am told, Eleanor Black's brother."

"What do you mean *as you are told*?'" Xavier asked before Aleister could have the chance. "Surely you've met her...she knows of you?"

He stared at him, seeing the coldness, the anticipation in his eyes. *He doesn't care about stopping her,* Aleister thought in renewed alarm, *he only wants to know more about her! Bloody hell—Aurora, Peroneous, Dragor!*

They appeared at his side in the next moment, emerging from nothingness, medallions blaring red in the light of the torches around the great hall. "What's wrong Aleister?" Aurora asked, her dark eyes shining red in the glare of their medallions.

"Xavier's lost to her," he said, before the Vampire could retort, "we must move for the Ares without him. We've let this gone on far too long—"

"Let what go where?" Xavier said, his anger rising: his eyes were now red as he glared at them, though Aleister knew it was not from their medallions. "You would dare move for my brother's sword without me? I am your king! What's this talk of me being under her hold? I'm bloody well fine!"

"If you were fine you would not have attacked Damion Nicodemeus with Dragor's sword!" he countered, sending a solid silence to fall over the hall. He felt all eyes on his back as he stared at his son, the green eyes cloudless, yes, but a new power had begun to form within them, something he could not recognize... "You were on fire in the Vampire City," he went on before anyone else could, "you were wonderful to move us out of our minds, our slumps—to make us venture out into the Dark World and do what must be done. But the moment you stepped foot outside of that City, Xavier, her energy was able to reach you. And I'm quite certain it was the only reason those Elite Creatures are with us now—because your influence has been corrupted by her."

The silence spread as his words echoed against the tall walls, and he would not dare stare at anything—anyone else: Xavier looked murderous, and for the first time since they were reunited, Aleister felt the Vampire capable of killing him in cold blood, not looking back.

"Is this how you all feel, then?" Xavier asked next, his voice quiet, a stark contrast to the rage in his eyes.

Aleister did not turn to eye the others but felt the incoherent mingle of courage and shame spread throughout the room.

Xavier scoffed. "I see." And he released the sword he'd retrieved from Christian's room an hour ago, its red glow bathing his face in the light: He looked downright frightening.

Aleister released his own sword as the Vampire pointed the blade of the Ascalon straight at him.

"Aleister, don't," Aurora said, the remaining Members of the Order issuing similar warnings.

He was not sure he *could* strike the Vampire, the red light shielding them from true attack, but he held the sword aloft all the same.

"Xavier," Christian said, leaving his bench where he'd sat with Alexandria, "what are you doing?"

The whiff of special blood hit his nose and Aleister knew the woman was allowing them to smell it just as Christian had said: She'd walked right beside him to reach them in the middle of the hall.

"No, Christian," Xavier said with a smirk, the tip of the Ascalon twitching still pointed towards Aleister's chest, "father is right. I have been unable to stop thinking about her, unable to keep her presence out of my mind. And if what Aciel said is true, it will help put at ease the fears that plague me."

He almost lowered the sword as he said, "Aciel? What's he told you?"

Xavier smile wavered, as though unsure he should say anymore, and then he bared his fangs, sending them all to take a step back, disbelief fueling them more than anything else they felt.

Aleister knew grief to hit his dead heart, so fresh, so clear. *We're losing him*, he thought, staring at the Vampire before him, and in a strange trick of light he thought he saw Dracula standing there, staring upon him in just as much defiance, just as much anger, fangs glistening in the red light. But he blinked and it was Xavier, the Ascalon tight in a well-trained hand.

"They filled your mind with lies, haven't they?" he asked, unwilling to relinquish his grip on his sword despite the continued shouts of concerns from all around them. All except Aciel and Amentias, Aleister noted. They had gone to procure their blood, had yet to return. "Haven't they?!"

"Not lies," he said, his black hair beginning to lift from his shoulders, causing Aleister to gasp in shock. "They spoke truth: I am just as responsible for the Elite Creatures as Eleanor."

"*What?!*" he spat, Christian making a sound much like a strangled Lycan.

He never lowered the Ascalon as he began to step backwards for the slightly broken doors, his green eyes moving to each of them as though daring them to move. "I gave her my blood before she turned into a Lycan Creature in that cabin, my blood the catalyst to a great change in whatever she'd discovered from the book."

He sheathed the sword as his back pressed against the doors, his wind rising in its ferocity, sending the torches to blow out, casting them in a faint darkness: pink light still peeled through small windows high above their heads.

His cloak billowed up around him, his eyes still red, though Aleister thought they held a look of sadness more than anything else, and then the Ascalon's red light dispersed as the doors opened, Amentias and Aciel appearing in the growing dark, their mouths dripping with fresh blood.

They were barely able to say a word before Xavier turned to them, grasping their shoulders, pulling them forward as he lifted off the ground, gone before the dust could fill the doorway.

Chapter Twenty-One

DEPTHS

"We have to go after him!" Aurora shouted as the faint night air drifted through the doors, her eyes wide with fear, tears spilling from them. "Aleister!"

Alexandria stared at the scarred Vampire who remained staring upon the empty doorway as though transfixed, the sword falling out of his hand to land upon the blood-stained floor.

He did not move, he merely stared as the sun set behind the thick row of trees in the distance and said, "Why?"

"Why?" Aurora repeated in exasperation. "Because he's our king! Your son! He can't be off with those two—you know this better than I!"

"I don't know anything," he spat, his bluntness jarring her although he never tore his gaze from the darkness outside, "and neither do you. Do not pretend Dracula gave any of us anything we would *truly* need to face madness like—like *this*." The last word leaving his trembling mouth in a hiss.

No one said a word, their gazes turning from the scarred Vampire stuck in his grief, his emotion palpable through the thick smell of blood, of death that filled the room.

And then Aleister went on, his words sharp on the cold air, "We were told something different from what he experienced in that book, you remember, Aurora?" He turned to eye her, the other Creatures that stood there finding his troubled gaze in alarm. "He didn't know what we were talking about when we mentioned *The Immortal's Guide* before the lake, we had no idea he was *human* while he traversed the book. Why would that be? Why would Evert lie to us?"

"Perhaps he did not lie," Aurora offered, "it was Tremor who helped the original Dracula make the book—perhaps he did not tell Evert, his power has been in serious decline for centuries."

"You're not understanding, Aurora," Aleister said, a wave of his cold air passing across Alexandria next. "The Vampire had a different experience in the book than what we were *told*. We're not being given in the full story. Think! What would Dracula have to gain by not telling us the same things as his successor for the throne?"

Peroneous stepped forward, the medallion's glare from his chest sending his bald head to gleam in the red light. "A secret he is keen to keep."

Aurora stared at him, her confusion mirroring what Alexandria felt. Why wouldn't the Vampire give them the full truth? After all, he had been nothing but helpful in her dreams, lending a hand where possible, speaking to her more and more...telling her things...things she could actually remember when awake...

"What secret?" Dragor Descant asked, a hand on the sword Xavier used to spill Damion's blood hours before. "Granted we've all done things we are more than ashamed of, I'm sure, to stand here today with these glowing necklaces at our chests, and I was not under the impression by any means that the Vampire had told us each the full truth, but what else did he keep from the one Vampire meant to take his bloody place?"

They stared at each other in silence, this question lingering on in their ears, and then the harrowing-looking Vampire with slight waves of hair, a dirt-stained blouse, said, "He could control magic."

Alexandria heard Christian snort at her side, saw Aleister, Aurora, Peroneous, and Dragor let out equally incredulous sounds.

"Come again, Christopher?" It was Dragor, his serious eyes on the newcomer with disbelief.

He stepped forward, brushing past her, the smell of old water, blood, and death pressed against his clothes. She watched him as he moved, stepping to Lillith Crane who had remained atop her bench, lost in pressing thought. "He could control magic," he repeated, Lillith's eyes moving to him when he spoke, "could control it with an ease I could only admire."

"That's bollocks," Peroneous shouted.

"No," he said, extending a hand for the young Vampire to take, "it's the truth."

"And how do you know?" the dark Enchanter called.

A strange smile lifted a corner of his lips as she took his hand at last and rose from her seat. He turned back to eye them, sure to say, "Because he kept her from me using it—the length of the Curse, the amount of magic needed to keep it constant around my prison...only a Creature who possessed absolute control over the art could do such a thing."

Much to her surprise Aurora and Aleister said together, *"Permanence."*

"Permanence?" Christian asked, a slight snarl escaping his throat. Alexandria eyed him seeing the frustration in his black eyes: he was having a hard time following the conversation just like her.

Christopher stared at him, a grand sense of indifference emanating off him as he grasped Lillith's hand. *She was all that mattered*, Alexandria thought.

"It is a Curse...bidding one to stay where the caster desires," Aurora offered, still staring upon Christopher as if she didn't believe he existed, "for the length of time the caster remains...alive. Nothing can undo it, besides the caster, of course. But it wanes every few years or so...has to be replaced."

"One such moment came," Christopher went on, a distracted Lillith staring out the open doorway as though someone were going to appear there any moment, "and I took my opportunity to escape. I was not unhappy...I was just...restless. I wandered around until I came across a burning home." And his disturbed gaze found Lillith's frame once more, Alexandria able to see the longing within it...

No one said a word, the implication upon the Vampire's words a sudden poison it seemed no one dared touch. *He turned her?* Alexandria thought, seeing the distasteful gazes the remaining Vampires bade the pair with this realization.

Her brow furrowing, she caught Christian's gaze. His grimace deepened, the thought coming through her mind as though it were her own, *"It is unbecoming to turn anyone without Dracula's express permission."*

"Oh," she breathed, watching the haunted gaze in Lillith's catching blue eyes. The few times she had seen the young Vampire she had been too scared to look directly into her eyes, but now she did, quite able to see the seething anger within, the desperation forming them. *She'd been turned against her will...*

"So yes," Christopher said to the pressing silence, the slight wind that blew into the dark hall, "I turned her—saved her—"

"And Dracula placed her in the Vampire Order," Dragor finished, his expression astounded in the glare of red. "Bloody hell, I always knew she was a strange one—never seen Dracula keep one so young so close, but this—his bloody secret turning a forbidden—I take back what I said. There is too much Dracula did not bother to share."

Aleister waved a hand, begging silence. When he had it, he said, "So you were born human to turn into a Vampire?"

Christopher released her hand, the movement sending Lillith to eye him in confusion at last: she had not known she held his hand at all. "I was born human, yes," and when met with their bemused gazes, he went on, "by the time I was born, the Phoenixes had managed to take what I believe that Enchanter had made," he said with a nod to Peroneous, "in order to make it so that those born after Dracula, Eleanor, the few others created, could come out human instead of..." And then his expression darkened.

"What?" they all asked in unison.

He stared out the wide doorway, his eyes on the darkness there as though something would come through it within seconds. "Dracula...he was here," he said, "before I came here he flew around this place—"

"That beast was not Dracula," Peroneous said shortly, heading him off. "It was Darien Nicodemeus."

At the name Alexandria saw Lillith's attention return to the conversation at hand: her piercing eyes were upon Peroneous as though he offered her a gallon of blood.

"Darien who?" Christopher asked, when a familiar smell drifted through the doors.

Alexandria covered her nose, all Vampires snarling, their eyes on the open doorway, the medallions dimming casting them all into thick darkness.

The figure appeared in the doorway, Alexandria able to feel all others tense around her, Christian moving to shield her: she could feel his back brush against her face.

"Who's there?" Aleister shouted, stepping past them all to stand before the doorway.

The thick smell of Lycan drifted past the doors making her cough: she felt her eyes water, the sting of grand distaste of that blood, the stench it carried making her utterly nauseous. The Vampires snarled.

And then the figure stepped forward, his voice deep in the darkness. "Master Christian?" he called. "Is that you?"

"James?" Christian breathed, the slight snarl escaping his lips along with his astonishment.

※

Arminius slapped the Vampire across his face again. "Snap out of it!" he shouted.

"But Eleanor moves for us," Nicholai whispered. He cowered along the hard wooden floor, his arms rising to cover his face from any more attacks, anymore phantoms Arminius could not see.

He had been that way since they'd arrived in Cedar Village the night before, lost in visions of horrible monsters, to which he could only utter, "No, no—I will not fail you—not again."

It had driven Arminius mad. He knew the Vampire and Elite Creature were on their trail, the wound Nicholai had sustained from a rogue Enchanter's spell a nasty one: it'd split his side open, causing a nasty gash, his blood to spill along his leg and boots, drenching the ground in his blood.

It had been all he could do to hobble with the now-injured Vampire at his back, the Vampire screaming and ducking from things only he could see.

And now they remained in a cottage an Enchanter had been kind enough to vacate: One look at he and the Vampire and she had dispersed without another word, hopefully to get more help, Arminius had thought.

But that had been yesterday. Now...now he knew he was on his own.

He stared down at the still whimpering Vampire who cowered up against an old, cobwebbed corner, gash all but healed with a quick spell he could conjure once safe.

Quite on his own.

"Damn it all," he muttered, pressing back the thin, gray curtain to see what more went on outside.

The balls of fire still lit up the dark sky, the rush of the river several cottages down cutting through the silence when the Dragons' fire would cease for a moment.

He returned the curtain, turning back to the dark cottage, ignoring the cowering Vampire. He moved to the dark book atop the low table with an unsteady hobble, and picked it up, staring at the pages in the dark.

No matter how much he read them, nothing he needed would enter his vision, nothing at all. And how often the words changed when he tore back the hard cover.

Childish magic, he thought with disdain, throwing the book down on the table where it crashed against a glass of river water.

Nicholai let out a scream as the glass shattered, the shards flying to the old floor.

He ignored him, unable to do anything more for the Vampire— no magic would leave his fingers, his throat—he was sapped.

Thinking back to how easily he had done away with the multitude of Elite Creature back in Wingdale, he eyed the dim medallion at his chest. It had surely helped him, then, giving him the power he needed to cast the most auspicious spell, *Sacrade Elipsum.* He had not even known it would do away with the Elites the way it had: his mouth had moved on its own, his hand working the spell as though it had always known it, though he had never cast it before.

Stranger magic still resides in this world, he thought, turning back to the window, a restless energy riding just underneath his skin.

The Dragons still did battle with the Enchanters out there, he saw, the spurts of large fire dancing past the robed men and women whose eyes were black in the night, their spells fresh, bright with a life Arminius could only dream of.

And when one would try and blast the door, Nicholai would scream in his panic, and the medallion would flare, as though keeping them at bay.

He stared at it again, wondering if it were guided by beings still very much alive, for it seemed to have a mind of its own the way it flared and died.

Another raucous bang on the old wooden door pulled his attention from the medallion, and surely enough it sparked to life, casting a steady glow over the door, the Creature beyond it getting blown back against the dark air: Arminius could hear the Creature's curses beyond it.

He only smiled as the Elite tried again, settling himself in the large chair that faced the door, knowing it would be a long night, indeed.

Chapter Twenty-Two

HELP

Xavier pushed the Creatures away from himself as he landed on the hard ground. His thoughts had pulled him away, far away from where the damned manor sat, the Creatures within it looking upon him in clear discomfort.

"Bloody hell," Amentias whispered, staggering on his landing. He teetered on a boot before catching himself, steadying, rising to stand. "What the devil was that, your Grace? What happened?"

Aciel, who had landed easily along the hard ground stared at him, his thin lips curled into a frown. "Something's changed," he said, waving a hand forward for Xavier to explain himself.

He did not wait to say, "Aleister knows I've been...lost to her... again."

"Ah," Aciel gasped, his red eyes bright in the night. "I wondered if her influence had truly waned from you."

He opened his mouth to respond when the smell of thick dread reached his nose. "This way," he whispered to them, pressing himself between two buildings as they followed his lead.

He waited in silence, the dread growing until the line of Creatures marched past at last, low hoods upon their heads, features lost to the night.

He caught the surreptitious gazes Aciel and Amentias shared in the light of the vague moon, annoyance tugging at his mind. He waited until the line of Elite Creatures were well down the street, before he said, "Something you care to share?"

The thin-lipped Creature stared after the Elites, his eyes unreadable in the darkness. "We need to move now, if those Creatures are roaming the Dark World at their leisure, she has truly stopped caring about maintaining secrecy."

He observed the dread thick in the air, always thick, always there. "It was secrecy she was trying to maintain?" he said dryly. "I thought she was trying to capture me."

"Always," Aciel said, staring at him in the dark of the alleyway, "but I gather since you have evaded her time and time again, she no longer cares as much about gathering you. It is possible her attentions are placed elsewhere."

The slither of jealousy flared in his dead heart, surprising him. Feeling it linger in a pitiful lump of disdain, he said, "So we make it easier for her." When their stares betrayed the confusion they felt, he went on, "We give her what she wants: Me."

At their hesitant, fearful silence, he found his voice, "I harmed Damion Nicodemeus, not only because he's a sorry cod, but because I was lost to a vision of her, yes, Aciel, I was lost to my mind again. She was there...we danced...over the bodies of my friends, my family... And then she became the thing Darien became. The thing Dracula once was."

"That monster?" Amentias clarified.

"Yes. I did as well," he said to their confusion, "became the monster. At least my arm," and he stared at his right arm, remembering as it grew and lengthened, the panic tightening in his throat, his dead heart, his gut. "I cannot...allow myself to harm anyone else. It is obviously safer away from them where I can do no harm."

"But what about their medallions, the things Dracula set in place?"

"They can no sooner still her influence than I can still my need for blood. She is everywhere, and when anyone mentions her, her dread," he eyed them, "her Creatures, her voice pierces through all. I cannot escape her any more than I can lead this damned world."

They stared at each other again, something seemingly missing from their understanding of his words.

When at last he grew tired of their silence, Amentias asked, "So what will you now do? And why take us with you?"

"Because you have been the most honest Creatures I've encountered since I left the Vampire City," he said, running a hand over the handle of the Ascalon, unable to feel heat from it at all, "and I know what you say is the truth because I have seen it with my own eyes...felt it." He eyed the empty street, smelling the air for anymore Creatures, Elite or not, and when satisfied all was clear, he stepped out of the alleyway, the former Elite Creatures following his back.

He began to step in the direction the line of Elite Creatures had walked, when Aciel said, "You're not truly going to her," and he saw the great fear that filled the Creature's strange eyes.

"I am," he said, thinking of the haughty Christopher Black. *Her bloody brother*. "Don't worry, Aciel, Amentias," he continued, seeing their heavy trepidation, a hand on the Ascalon, "she won't harm you. After all, you're with me."

※

Scores of Enchanters filled the grand hall, Philistia staring down at them from the podium with feigned confidence. The dark of the night did not touch this place, for it was always day here, her hands trembling as they waited for her to continue, to share what was necessary, what was just. And yet...she gripped the edges of the podium for support.

Equis still slept, his proclivity for unconsciousness most maddening to her, but she knew she could not wake him, even when his Enchanters were at his door. Had been here for days. Waiting... waiting—

She caught the gaze of the red-robed Enchanters throughout the impatient crowd, saw their unease at the state of their peers, and she cleared her throat, knowing, Equis be damned, she had to still them somehow.

When the multitude of voices died, she began, her voice stretching to the tall walls of the hall, even reaching the ears of the Enchanters and Elves who stood many miles away at its entrance:

"These rules have been put in place as just and necessary as any of our laws for the protection and preservation of our kind.

"But we have noticed, Equis and I, just what has been corrupted by the continued use of these very laws: The Vampires' power."

At this, a plume of concerned whispers spread across the crowd, and then one Enchanter shouted, "Yes, what *of* the Vampires? Is it true that they are the reason for the lack of magic?! And our Fae—" he gestured towards a beautiful blonde right beside him, clean and clad in a flowing white dress, "they can no longer see very far into the future!"

Philistia stared at them, hesitating even more: it was not her place to do this, to say these things, but the more Equis slept—

"The matter of the Fae have been recorded, and his Greatness and I are working diligently to—"

"To ensure the Fae have their gifts of Sight returned, you Enchanters have your magic ultimately restored."

The various gasps that passed through the crowd told her all she needed to know: Equis had awoken, his smooth voice cutting across hers even without standing at the magically enchanted podium.

She turned along the marble stage, his long black hair unbound, flowing behind his head, the long blue cloak he wore flowing swiftly around his boots, and as he walked to her, she could see the shimmer of protective air cast around him, and she saw the sadness in his eyes: The ability to remain around Enchanters was dwindling.

"Equis!" several Enchanters shouted.

"His Greatness!"

"Help us! *Please!*"

"What must be done?!"

He lifted a gloved hand high above his head, waving it slowly in an arc as though he waved goodbye, and all fell silent. With a soft glare around at the many Enchanters, Elves, Fae, he opened his mouth, a tired breath escaping him, and said, "As Madame Philistia has already imparted—the power the Vampires hold over us is nearing its end—we must be diligent in working against them, these Elite Creatures as well. We cannot afford to waste any more time resting, waiting. We must strike back against these fiends, retake, not the Dark World, but the world for ours. We owe every Creature that has been here before these beasts and abominations that simple right."

A raucous explosion of cheers split the earth at the words so calmly uttered. Philistia stared at him, her expression blank. *He had their full support,* she thought in disbelief, yes, not one Enchanter or Elf looked at all upset with what he had said. Indeed, they *were* tired of being used. *How much easier this would make things, indeed.*

He turned to her while the Creatures were talking excitedly amongst themselves, and said low so only she could hear, "Eleanor Black moves for us at this very moment."

And before she could say a word, he had turned back to his Creatures, sure to say, "There are many ways we can fight, my Enchanters, my Elves...we must open our minds to the possibilities—"

She turned away, unable to hear anymore. *She was coming here? That woman? Here?*

Tales of the Elite Creatures' reign of terror passed through her mind as she stared at the open doorway leading into the castle where she did her work. Lane, destroyed. Quiddle, overtaken. Cedar Village, attacked. London...she closed her eyes at the memory of the mess that was London. She, herself had gone to oversee the painstaking process of ensuring the city was restored to its former glory, the death, the bodies all around a most horrible scene.

And now the woman responsible for all the death, the destruction, was coming here, to Merriwall?! She eyed him as he spoke, wondering what more would plague them before they could find peace.

She heard nothing of his speech, mind lost on just what they were to now do if she really was coming here—and for what? *And how*, she thought staring upon the long black hair of the Ancient Creature just before her, *did he know?*

It was not until he turned to her, a great smile upon his face, feigned for them she knew, a placeholder to hide the terror he felt, and pressed a hand along her back, beginning to step towards the castle's many sitting rooms that she realized he was trembling.

✳

"Oi!" the Elite called to the others, "he's over there!"

Nathanial ducked seven fire-laden arrows as they whizzed overhead, his golden eyes on the tall black stone wall to his left, the wall that was said to lead one to Merriwall—the place Equis lay his head.

"Blights fall upon your head!" a female Elite shouted, and he turned his head despite himself to see the swirl of madness that pressed against her face, lit up by the balls of fire in her hands.

He ran faster, turning his gaze to the high stone wall, the whisper of a spell pressing against his throat. How it would not rise past his lips...but he needed it...needed magic, more than ever—

More balls of fire spread across the jagged rocks he ran across, his boots not slipping as he ran. He knew the proper spell to counteract their incessant following, knew it, but he would need the book...so long had he gone without his Fyre.

"Try this, Vampire!" another Elite shouted, this one sending lightning bolts to cut the dark air, sending it to light up momentarily, its sparks fizzling with loud swooshes as it touched the black rock at his feet.

Still he ran, able to see the high mountain several yards ahead, the same jagged rock as the land he traversed, how he had moved endlessly to reach here, to reach Merriwall Mountain—

The lightning struck the hem of his cloak, sending it to spark with blue flame. He dropped to the jagged stone at his feet, feeling the pain of the flame strike his skin. *Pain?*

Before he could ponder further how in the world he could *feel* the flame sear his side, he reached for the satchel, the power within it sending the leather to shake with the intensity of it...

Stifling a scream, he did his best to ignore the rising fire at his other side, knowing the spell he needed was in the book—

A ball of fire smashed into it in the next second, sending the black leather to burn, and with a cry he removed his hands from it, watching in panic as the flame graced the golden book.

"*Repolate!*" he heard overhead, shouts of joy rocking the air, getting lost in the bubble of his clothes, flesh, and flame.

A rush of wind pressed against him next, the book partly burned as the fire dispersed from its body, but not his clothes.

He summoned the spell from memory, not sure he could cast it now, on fire and pained as he was, and he was just prepared to grab the book when the large red Dragon appeared from over the wall, its large wings blowing the Elite Creatures from the sky.

He reached for the book, his fingers gracing the cover as the Dragon landed, its silver talons digging in the hard stone, breaking it here and there as it settled itself atop the expanse.

The Elites had flown off beyond the wall, Nathanial sure they traversed the water beyond it, their shouts of terror fading as they flew.

The gust of wind the Dragon had created with its landing had sent Nathanial's fire to rise, moving quickly to consume the rest of his clothes, his skin...

The Dragon placed two red eyes upon him, nodded towards the book as if to say, "Use it."

Without a word, Nathanial peeled back the pages, glad when the words shone in gold ink from the aged pages:

Vanishing/Banishing Fire and Other Tools of Nature

There, wedged between a spell for erasing snow from one's yard and a curse to send fire to ruin another's crops (or whatever you planned to do), was the spell he sought.

"*Incend, Icsend, Stolle,*" he chanted several times, quite aware the fire had destroyed a good part of his robes, his skin. The pain was insurmountable, made all the better when the fire was finally extinguished, and with careful movements he rose to stand atop the black rock, closing the book as his gaze met the Dragon's.

"Ragnarok," he said simply, the Dragon's long head nodding kindly.

"Hello, again, special Vampire," he said, a rush of thick black smoke leaving his large nostrils, "I see you've gotten yourself into some trouble. From Cedar Mountain I saw you traveling between the houses, figured you could use help...wherever it is you travel." His red eyes stared thoughtfully on the mountains in the distance, another plume of black smoke leaving his long snout.

"Yes, I could," he said, his gaze moving to the wall, the mountains a few days away, "what happened in Cedar Village?"

"Eleanor Black's strange Creatures threatened the town. Worca is setting them to fire as we speak."

"And she was fine with you leaving to follow me?" He thought of the larger Dragon's disdain for any Creature that was not a Dragon.

"She hardly knows I am here," he said, taking short steps towards him, cracking the jagged rock. "Let us go then. Hop on."

Nathanial stared as the Dragon dipped his large head low to the ground, waiting for him to climb aboard his back.

He soon obliged, stepping carefully over the Dragon's eyes, pressing what was left of a boot against the top of his head. He scaled the long back, settling himself in-between the wing blades, and as Ragnarok righted, he tore off the sleeve of his cloak and wrapped it around the book, taking the extra fabric to fashion over his badly burned shoulder. He winced and shook as the knot he'd formed pressed against his shoulder blade, but he held tight to the book in its man-made sling as it was, digging his heels into the Dragon's back, signaling he was quite prepared to leave.

As Ragnarok rose into the air, the cold wind of the night pressed against him, the large wings flapping strongly on either side, and he stared back over the jagged path he had ran, barely able to see the line of mountains in the distance, the tiny sparks of orange light filling the sky before going dark once more.

Chapter Twenty-Three

HUNGER

Victor did not believe Joseph Gail was any closer to locating Arminius than he was getting to Xavier. They'd sat in the strange manor for hours, not leaving once Joseph Gail had found a change of clothes.

It was the scattered way the Elite Creature perused every inch of the strange, black-splattered manor as though bidden, his sense for magic apparently ruined: he could not locate the way the Elf had journeyed, his constant griping on something being 'in the way,' causing Victor to go mad.

He pressed his boot against the high black doors ago, anger surging through him, and still from somewhere far within the maze that was this damned manor, Victor was able to hear Joseph Gail shouting, "No—this isn't the way out either!"

A snarl ripped through his throat as he banged a fist against the doors. They had opened to let them in, so what was this? *Why can't we leave?!*

He sunk to the bloodied floor before the doors, smelling the dread stick against the walls, the halls so very ripe with stale death.

He thought back to the corpse of the white Lycan upstairs, how strange it had been to stumble upon that, the massive crater in the ceiling. *What had happened to Scylla?* The question falling to reason as he rethought it. Of course. Eleanor happened to Scylla. Eleanor's men, more likely, no doubt.

He kicked a smattering of debris away from him, letting a low, needless sigh lower his chest. *My worst nightmare,* he thought, hearing the words, "There has to be a way out, my magic isn't gone!" rung on throughout the many hallways to reach him, *being stuck here with that.*

And why? *Why* on Earth were they trapped here?

He'd gone over the number of reasons this could be once the initial panic had faded: he'd accidentally locked the door behind him as he'd closed it once Joseph had stepped over the threshold, they'd stumbled into some strange curse, already placed here by previous occupants, or the most outlandish, even in his mind, they were trapped there because...well, they simply were.

But he couldn't accept that answer, no, there had to be a *reason*.

It was why he rose to his feet, turning towards the doors, prepared to barge against them again, when the glint of orange light caught his eye.

He stilled mid-barrel, turning completely to see this thing. It hovered beyond a window to the right of the hall. He had half a mind to call Joseph down, but thought better of it once the thing started to press up against the window's glass.

He stared at it, not understanding what he was seeing, when the few torches around the entrance hall dispersed, the light of the ball, he saw, the only thing shedding light.

It slid through the glass as though it were water, and despite being pure fire, it did not melt the glass. He watched this ball glide gently across the hall to where he stood just before the high doors, silence pressing his lips shut.

This, he thought, staring upon the medium-sized flame in wonder, *is what Dracula kept from me.* He was sure of it, a certainty burning in his dead heart the more he stared upon it, no amount of Eleanor's influence, Dracula's lies, or Xavier's knowledge cutting through this belief. *I have found his secret.*

The more he stood there, staring upon it, he could hear whispers, various multiplied whispers, all coming from the ball of fire. Its flames leapt and sparked from its body, embers dancing off the miniature sun as though eager to be free, and still the whispers grew louder...

"*Protect...*" he heard before the ball exploded, Victor barely able to hear the faint cry of a bird over the splinter and fire of the doors: They'd been blown away in the explosion, the dark of the night, the cold wind blowing into the doors, beckoning to him.

He stared at the stone path available to him with wide eyes, wondering what on Earth it was that had helped him, when Joseph Gail could be heard, regrettably, drawing nearer to the long staircase, "Victor, what was that? Are you all right?"

"Yes," he called back, eyeing the spot where the ball of fire had hovered: on the ground lay a ball of hard, black stone. Without thinking, he picked it up, smoke leaving it where his hand touched its hard body, the certainty growing the more he stared at it. "I'm fine. I've broken the door down—we can finally leave this godforsaken manor."

He heard Joseph Gail descend the stairs behind him, and slipping the stone into a pocket of his cloak, he wondered what being had given him this gift, and what indeed, it wanted to protect.

※

Christian Delacroix stood behind the tall doors, listening with rapt attention to what it was the Vampire told her, the thoughts of

Alexandria Stone's blood interrupting the conversation every so often, but still he listened:

"...and you're saying," Lillith Crane whispered, and he could almost see the confusion in her beautiful blue eyes, "you truly turned me—that you were the one?"

"Yes," Christopher Black answered, Christian able to hear the impatient footsteps along the fine ground as the Vampire waited for something Christian could not know. "Like I said, Dracula kept me from you—forbid me from seeing you—"

"Why?"

"Because he was scared, scared anyone would trace the curious young girl he had placed in his stead back to me—"

"No," she interrupted, and Christian could hear the edge to her voice, "I mean why bother turning me? Why not let me die?"

Stunned silence pressed on beyond the door, Christian preparing to leave when Christopher said, "You were alive, your parents were dead—I did what I felt was best—"

"You did what my blood compelled you to do," she retorted.

With this, Christian took his leave, quite sure the Vampire wouldn't spill whatever great truth it was believed he housed. He stepped through the unlit hall where the many Dark Creatures had mingled, shouted, where Xavier had slashed Damion's neck, disappeared through the white doors...

"Well?" Aleister asked once he passed Minerva and Yaddley Caddenhall asleep on two benches, ascended the many stairs to return to the finely decorated room he'd slept in the night before.

"They only quarreled," he said, Alexandria rising from a chair at a desk, her gaze interested but tired: dark circles had reappeared beneath her eyes, "on her nature—his...guilt. I don't believe that Vampire knows—or cares—about anything more than her." And she moved to stand beside Aleister, the smell of her blood free to his nose... He wondered how Aleister could not smell it, could stand beside her and not rip into her neck—

"Damn," he whispered, green eyes distracted as he moved around Alexandria to stand before the burning fire Aurora had lit before turning in. "Dracula's...deception has really surpassed all imagination. No," he said suddenly, turning to eye them, "that Vampire knows more than he must be letting on—Dracula controlling all of magic, it's ludicrous."

"But Nathanial Vivery," Alexandria said, bringing all eyes to her, "he knows magic—didn't you train him, Aleister?"

He nodded, silence gluing his lips together. When at last he opened his mouth it was to say, "I know he lied to the other Vampires about learning magic, but now that I think on it, he did command the spells and such that he passed to the Vampires chosen with far too great a fluidity.

"I left just before the project could be complete," he said, an unsteady hand waving through the air as he turned to eye them, "what he did with the other Vampires in the project is Victor's knowledge."

Silence passed across the room as they all thought on these words, and then Christian said, "So Victor Vonderheide knows of Dracula's mastery over magic—he could have told Eleanor."

Aleister shook his head. "We are losing this war," he said, "losing to a woman who still holds Xavier's heart—and the bloody Vampire—*Dracula*," he snarled, "couldn't tell us the damned truth. I saw it in his eyes," and he stared at them wildly, "I saw the madness in his eyes—knew he couldn't be trusted. It was why I left after he made me turn you, Christian. I couldn't take being tied to him anymore."

Christian's heart pulsed once, the thought overtaking all reason before he could call it back, "Xavier, could he not have gone to confront Victor?"

Their gazes met each other in the orange light of the room, and then Aleister said, "We need Aurora, Peroneous. We need to move. We cannot sit here...if we won't get anything from Christopher, as lost as he is on Lillith, we must search for the truth ourselves."

He watched as the scarred Vampire stepped around them as he talked, moving for the door. "How do you propose we do that?" he called before the Vampire could round the doorway. "Without Xavier aren't we stumbling around in the dark?"

Christian watched his green eyes, so vivid in the fire's glare, darken, and he knew Xavier's departure had blackened the Vampire's dead heart further.

"With Xavier we were stumbling even more in the dark—that Vampire couldn't still what would happen any more than any of us could have held him down to still it. If what he said was true, that his blood helped create this dread, those Creatures..." But he fled from the door as his words were lost to him, venturing down the hallway towards, Christian knew, the other Knights' rooms.

He took a step towards the door, but the hand that grasped his arm sent a surge of desire to pour through him, and what little had held him from her since he'd awoken to *Anima* being poured down his throat fled completely.

"Alexandria," he began, staring at the open doorway, hearing the footsteps of his father's boots fading, "he needs me—they need me. I can't—"

"Can't what?" she asked, her voice sweet, innocent, even, the calling scent of her blood reaching his nose in the next second, sending a snarl to escape his throat, all thought on his father, Xavier gone with little to call it back. The scent clawed at his brain, his mouth watering, the need for blood destroying all else. The snarl ripped through his throat, but still the hand would not leave his arm. *What*, he thought, *what could she want? Why let me smell it so freely?*

"I can't—your blood," he answered, staring upon the door, unable to move as the grip on his arm tightened, "rid me of it—please."

The grip slackened ever the slightest, and he turned to eye her in his surprise. Her brown hair fell in slight waves around her head, her brown-green eyes appearing to darken in the light of the fire to her right. She slowly crossed both arms, a slight shiver claiming her body. "I'm not allowing you to smell it," she said in confusion.

He narrowed his eyes. *Is she playing with me?* How it filled the air, wiping all other blood, all other scent from the Earth!

"I want to talk to you about something that has been bothering me," she went on, tearing his thoughts from her blood, if only slightly. He nodded after a while, unable to say anything more, quite aware that if he opened his mouth he would move right for her throat. "Yes, well," she began, staring into the fire, her long hair swung over a shoulder, revealing her neck, the blood that swam within the veins, "when Lord Nicodemeus was...suffering at Xavier's...cruelty, it was the strangest thing but I...I smelled his blood...as easily, I suppose, as easily as it is you Vampires do."

And she turned to watch him, her gaze slightly hidden, as though she were embarrassed at her words, finally spilling them from hesitant lips.

Despite it all, he was impressed: She had kept this to herself for most of the day when he was sure, if he were human, he would be quick to spill it. She had moved to give the ailing Vampire her blood, not caring that his blood stained her knees, she had moved to do it, because, as she had told Xavier, *"He needed it."*

He thought to speak, but could say nothing against that stare, how brightened it was in the light of the fire, and that blood...

He took a simple step towards her, and he felt as though he glided on air...

"I have come to terms," she said snapping him from his mindless movement. He ceased moving forward, teetering on the ball of a foot, able to reach out and grasp her neck if he desired, but she kept talking, his hand remaining at his side. "I have come to terms with my...death. And I know all that is happening to me is the result of this death coming. The red light...my grandfather's...blood, it keeps me together...keeps the other Dark Creatures together. I know it," and she looked up to eye him at last, "I feel it in them, in those medallions... but I don't, Christian, feel it in your brother. Xavier, though he may hold the title of king, appears confused, greatly distracted by her. He won't be able to help us figure out what 'blood-stiller' means, I'm afraid." And she hugged her arms as though terribly cold, the weakness in her eyes growing stronger, the light of the flames she stood just before dancing in her eyes.

"Alexandria," he started, when they closed, her eyes, closed as though bidden, as though something else called her, far, far away from where he stood, desiring to taste her blood, a Vampire without a ring upon a finger, most unguarded, most hungry...

She fell back, her brown hair gliding through her air as she sank, her blood splashing through the air in thick waves as she fell, landing against the hard floor without a sound.

He stared at her, her eyes closed against the light of fire, and how beautiful she looked...

He was not aware of himself moving closer to her along the floor, brushing back her hair from a shoulder, a quaint view of her neck apparent, and although he could not see her blood in its veins, although he could not see her beating heart, he felt it as he pressed a finger against the thick vein that pulsed in her neck, smelled it, why, he practically tasted it—

"Christian!" the alarmed voice shouted from behind him, and then he smelled it, the magical blood of Aurora and Peroneous, the cold blood of Dragor, of Aleister, and most upsettingly, the horrid blood of James Addison.

He did not turn to eye them, but remained staring down at her. Her eyes closed, cradled in the wonderful world of unfettered sleep. *You will be the death of me*, he thought as the many hands grabbed at his shirt, pulling him up and away from her. He kept his gaze on her even as he heard his father shout, "You didn't!"

"I didn't," he repeated vaguely, still staring upon her, seeing her chest rise and fall steadily. *Unconscious*, he thought with slight relief, *not dead*.

The hard hand slapped his face as the others that held him upright dug their nails into his shirt. The pain was slight, but it was still pain, and he tore his gaze from her to eye the Creatures on either side of him, Peroneous and Dragor, their glares fearful, worried. "I didn't," he repeated, louder this time.

Aleister stepped just before him, blocking his view of her, much to his dismay. He had to keep his gaze on her, had to—

"What happened?" Aleister asked. "What did you do?"

"I—nothing," he snarled, anger tearing at his dead heart. She was unconscious, her blood everywhere, and still they would blame him! "I did nothing! She—she was talking—mentioned how Xavier is in no place to help us—"

"Help you what?" Dragor asked.

"Help us figure out her dream. She had a dream before we ventured to *The Dragon's Cavern* due to Victor's letter," he explained to their exasperated gazes, "in the dream she told me a Vampire was there—we believe it to be Dracula—he told her she was 'the blood-stiller.'"

"The blood-stiller?" a new voice asked. It was Aurora.

He nodded, not caring if she could see it or not: she remained near the door with James. He kept his gaze on his father, silently threatening him to see the truth, that all he'd spoken was truth, yes, marred with his ever-growing desire for her in more ways than he could count, but still it was truth! "That's all she said," he continued, "before she fainted. But something is different this time."

And he watched as Aleister turned along sweet air to watch her as well, his gaze concerned. "What is different this time, Christian?" he asked, never looking back at him.

He pressed against their hands, quite surprised when they held him in place: A snarl of frustration left him. "She won't rise from this...encumbrance! Something happened as she closed her eyes," he said, not wanting to say what he feared.

"What?" Aleister, Dragor, and Peroneous asked.

The disgusting scent of Lycan, of dirt and blood, rushed into his nose with the Creatures' words, causing him to snarl involuntarily. "I don't know—it was as though she were possessed...called to something."

The heavily scarred Vampire stared at her, eyes widening upon Alexandria along the floor. And before Christian could ask what he thought, he tore past him, his footsteps thundering out of the room.

They faded before long, Christian unable to spare special attention to their whereabouts, for the woman held his gaze, and all at once he found himself unable to look away. *She was beautiful*, he thought as the orange light bathed her frame in its glow, illuminating her blood-stained breeches, the blood-stained blouse she wore, its ruffles flattened at the collar along her collarbones, her chest. She looked ethereal in that glow, and although she did not move, he could not help but feel she was calling to him again, her blood wrapping itself around his every sense.

"Christian?" he barely heard someone ask, as he felt the hands at his arms and shoulders peel away, undesired, unneeded...

He was before her in the next moment, kneeling at her side, an absent hand pressing against the line of her hair, holding her head in place.

He could think of nothing, indeed, only feel her blood pull him closer, and the hand moved around her hair, cradling the back of her head to lift her up to his chest, his head lowering as his gaze found her neck.

So free, so inviting, the vein just there... How it had alluded all but now...yes, now...

"Christian!" a myriad symphony of voices danced through the air, pounding against his eardrums in the next moment, and he pulled himself away from her, the scent of her blood peeling away from his nose, still beckoning, disappointment covering that scent.

He turned his head, a most alarmed Christopher Black, Lillith Crane, Minerva, and Yaddley Caddenhall standing behind Aurora and James, their eyes wide, fear-filled.

He merely stared at them, meeting their confusion and marred disappointment with rushing embarrassment: he felt her head in his hand, felt the line of the vein he had been moments from breaking under a thumb, and a low sigh left him.

"That's it," Aleister said, marching past the Creatures that lined the doorway, "we are leaving Cinderhall Manor—we are going to gather Arminius and Nicholai, and we are going to get to the bottom of Dracula's mess, his secrets, even if it kills us." He waved a scarred hand, Christian's hands flying from her, sending her head to fall back against the ground. Another scarred hand was waved through the air and Christian found himself on his back before the fire, the glare of the green eyes over him holding his gaze.

"No more, Christian," Aleister said, "no more. I have lost one son; I will not lose another." And he left him, giving him his back as he began to lift Alexandria from the floor, cradling her in his arms as he rose to stand.

He sat up, staring at his father, the Vampire who turned him, as he left the room with the woman in his arms, Aurora, Peroneous, Dragor, Minerva, and Yaddley shortly following suit. He heard their many footsteps press down the hallway before reaching the long staircase to reach the grand hall.

A quiet curse left his lips for he felt it, then, the invisible wall of order that kept him from desiring her blood—the blood that called to him—that *needed* him. A louder curse left him as he rose to stand, turning to face the door, stopping short as he eyed the man that stood there, brown eyes steady upon him.

"James?" he whispered, unable to say anything more as the woman's blood fled him, James's blood resting on his nose the more he stood there.

"Master...Christian," he said as though it pained him.

Christian eyed him seriously since he first laid eyes on him the few hours before. The man, for he was no longer a boy, this Christian was well aware, filled out the shirt he wore well: the defined shape of his arms, his abdomen, and chest strained against the fabric. His dark brown hair, which had grown considerably since he was last seen, a bloody mess, was darker, to the point of being black it seemed, and when he opened his mouth again, Christian could not help but focus on the modest amount of dark brown hair that had formed along his chin, around and over his mouth.

"Is there," he began, "something wrong, Addison?"

For he had known the man had been stuck with Lore, had only just escaped him to find them by following their scents along the air; he'd shared that much.

The head cocked to the side as though in mockery, and then he said, "No, my Lord, nothing, I just worry...for Miss Stone's...health. Is there anything wrong with her? Is she sick?"

He saw the way James's hands were curled at his sides as though he were tense, quite prepared to fight. His gaze narrowed upon his brother's former servant. "She is dying," he said, desiring to reach the others, the desire to taste her blood all but almost gone... Almost.

"Dying?" he repeated, shock grazing the face so hardened by worldliness, it made Christian uneasy. "Why?"

He began to step forward, pressing past the man, knowing he needn't explain himself, explain what would take days to relate. As he reached him, pressing past him in the doorway, he felt the flare of anger rise from James, and he snarled, the low growl leaving James's lips next sending his eyes to narrow.

"Where *is* Lore, James?" he asked.

"I don't know," he answered quietly, "I'd left him, Master Christian."

"I thought you said you'd escaped from him."

He said nothing, his dark brown gaze only darkening the more he held the gaze, the light of the fire swimming in them, keeping his secrets... For Christian was sure the Lycan held something in that cold gaze, no longer the dutiful servant, at his Masters' beck and call.

"Christian! Lycan!" Aleister's voice sounded from the end of the hallway. He peered around the doorway, able to see the scarred Vampire before the stairs, green eyes angry. He said nothing more to the Lycan Creature, stepping around him to reach his father, very aware he could feel the proud glare piercing daggers at his back.

Chapter Twenty-Four

THE GOBLET

"**D**ragon tail, wolf's bane, hemlock, Elf's ear..." the Elite Creature whispered to herself as she walked idly past the tree he had been unceremoniously thrown beside a few moments ago.

Darien had flown off some moments before, his large wings breaking the thin branches of trees that grew in abundance here. Wherever here, was. He had been greatly lost as to where the Creature had placed him, merely remaining against the tree in case the Creature returned, but now he moved with the woman's voice just feet from where he stood:

He peered around the tree, able to see her in the dark: She wore a shimmering silver robe that danced against the dark.

"Hmm," she whispered with a frown, the large hood down along her back exposing her face clearly, her hair which fell in red tendrils just above her shoulders, "I'd have to substitute the rose thorn for something else...something with a bit more bite..."

She was lost to the trees the more he stared after her, and after chancing one last glance at the dark green leaves, the sky above his head, he pressed against the hard dirt, determined to keep her in his sights. *Whatever my brother had become,* he thought, *why ever he took me here—left me—I must find out on my own.* And the more he kept his gaze on the silver robes several miles ahead of him, he smelled the dread in the air thicken.

She couldn't be an Elite Creature, he thought, unable to smell any hint of Vampire or Lycan blood however warped it might have been...

The more he followed, barely hearing her continued whispers to herself against the night, he was struck with an odd sensation: he felt as though he'd been here before. But that was impossible, he didn't recognize anything he saw, indeed, these woods were none he'd ever traversed.

The woman stood before a tall tree now, not moving forward, and he stilled in his movement, pressing behind a tree of his own, hearing the squelching sound of his boot against ground. He looked down, quite surprised to see blood, not yet completely dried, staining the ground.

And then he smelled it, quite familiar, mixed in with a fainter, yet stronger scent.

Christian Delacroix and Alexandria Stone have been here, he thought with wonder, staring at the dark puddles atop the dirt, when a fresh scent pressed against his nose.

Elite. Many. Far too many.

Fear pressed against his chest as he chanced one last glance down to his boots, and then pressed on, moving for the silver trail ahead. It danced between trees, and he almost thought the woman to disappear, it was so far away she appeared, when she stopped, a vague light shining against her hair to her left.

He stilled despite being quite a distance from her, very prepared for something to emerge from the mouth of the cave and swallow her whole.

Nothing did, and he was amazed when several more Creatures, cloaked now, emerged from the cave, ascending what looked like stone steps.

He watched the woman exchange greetings with these Creatures unable to see if they were men or women: low hoods hid their features.

The woman appeared to smile, and then she stepped past them, a long-fingered hand waving vaguely through the air as she descended the stone steps into the cave.

The Creatures remained, and the more he stared at them, the more he was able to see the thick smoke that seemed to center around them, lingering on the dark air as though stuck to their cloaks.

That smoke, he thought, another sharp pain slicing through his skull as the memory returned:

Surrounded by that smoke, the knife at his head formed in that smoke. *Elite Creatures,* he thought, *and that smoke.*

Lucien! he remembered with a jarring pain to his mind once more. *Of course! I was traveling to get to Lucien—and the damned sword.*

A cold fury rose in his chest, replacing what little fear had lingered upon seeing the Creatures, and he snarled, the memories returning in a flood of blood, pain, and desire.

Lucien never returned. Never came back. He always comes back!

He stared at them, none of them moving along the night, remaining before the entrance and he knew they would never leave.

As he pondered how on Earth he was to get inside the cave, a great gust of wind blew against his back, causing him to turn in alarm.

There he was, hovering in the air, large black wings sending the trees to bend away...Darien. *He'd returned, but where had he gone in the first place?*

He watched the large Vampire hover there for moments more, an aged scroll held in a claw. He released it, Damion watching as it flew through the air, far over his head, the Vampire pressing forward with a powerful flap of his large wings.

He followed Darien as he flew through the air, moving above the trees, a great shadow spreading even more darkness on the ground below.

Damion watched in awe as Darien let out a loud roar, sweeping straight towards the line of Elite Creatures, the flames at their back shining strongly, sending shadows to hide their fronts in darkness. He watched in wonder as Darien grasped one, flying off into the air, the Elite screaming fearfully through the night. Indeed, the others brandished their swords and moved after Darien, his large, winged figure cutting an impressive shape through the darkness.

Excellent, he thought, seeing the cave's entrance bare, and he rushed forward towards it, thoughts on Lucien's whereabouts, the sword filling his mind—

It rolled in front of him as though pushed, bumping against a tree's bark, causing him to still, eyeing it warily.

That Darien desired him to undo the dirtied ribbon around the scroll, read the words etched into the parchment, he did not doubt, but he would not, nay *could not* allow himself to be deterred from his goal. *The sword. Lucien. The sword.*

He stared at it despite these thoughts, a curse leaving his lips as he stepped for it, scooping it up as he reached it. The ribbon frayed as his thumb passed across it, thoughts running to just what it was the Vampire who had changed wanted for him to know...

A low curse leaving his lips, he ripped the ribbon with a nail, opened it, and by the vague light of the cave's entrance read:

> *Darien,*
> *The Goblet*
> *-Evert*

He stared at the word for another moment, not understanding it in the least. *A goblet?* he thought, wondering what use he would have with this pointless letter. It made no sense, nothing sparking to mind the more he stared at it.

With a disdainful "tsk," he threw the parchment at his feet, stepping over it as he moved forward towards the mouth of the cave, his eyes widening as he left the woods at last and stood just before it.

Several torches were lit along a long tunnel, the dark steps just before him leading down into the cave, indeed. He wondered what had kept Lucien, smelling the dread thickest here, a hand rising to cover his nose with a sleeve of his cloak, he was dismayed that he could not merely release the smell with the thought: it stuck.

"Bloody hell," he whispered, stepping down the stairs, wishing greatly that he'd brought Minerva and Yaddley along, a great unease spreading throughout him the more he stepped along the stone.

Lucien, he thought, guiding the word towards the Vampire, the chilling silence pressing against his ears, his aching skull.

"...If we were to move forward..." he heard from nearby, the sound seeming to emanate from a coming corner. He froze as the voice continued, "And if she's there who cares? If you ask me, Victor's the better option to get what we desire..."

His gaze narrowed as he thought on these words, not understanding any of it. Slowly, carefully, he pressed forward, turning his attention to keeping quiet: his boots made not a sound against the hard ground, his wind not blowing out the torches lit every few steps as he moved.

Where the tunnel ended, the hallway split, hesitation keeping him from moving further. *The sword,* he thought, feeling the boy's curse, as faint as it was pull him along to the right. *Lucien?!* he thought in amazement, stepping quickly now, no Creatures emerging from the darker reaches of the many tunnels to cut him down.

Indeed, all was far too quiet, but such was his luck, he hardly cared. On he went, thanking the monster of a Vampire for dropping him where it seemed Lucien remained prisoner. The curse grew stronger with every step he took past the many stone doors, Lucien's gift for remaining in the dark spurring him on. *Perhaps he wasn't a prisoner...perhaps he merely got lost—trapped by an unrelenting Creature...*

New voices sounded far away at the end of another tunnel, but he pressed on, the hopes of reaching the sword a fire at his boots. The crunch of his heels echoed loudly in his ears, and he was sure, the ears of Eleanor's Creatures that filled these many tunnels, but still he moved—

He'd just rounded a tight corner, Lucien's blood strongest in the air here, when the blade was at his throat. The strangled snarl left him as the blade was pressed up against him, and he heard the harsh whisper in his ear, "What's a Vampire like you doing in a place like this? More importantly how did you get past the barrier?"

The overwhelming scent of her dread pressed against his nose, the blood he'd taken from the curious human still fresh on his tongue, and how it seemed to rise in his veins, doing its best to keep Eleanor's dread from sinking further into his dead heart... But how impossible that was.

The Creature pressed the blade against his throat, and he felt the cold of his blood slide down his skin, bleeding into the collar of his already destroyed cloak.

Damn. "Barrier?" he choked, the Creature's nails digging into his shoulder, keeping him in perfectly pained place. "What bloody barrier?"

A harsh laugh filled his ear, the hand thrust into his back, pushing him against the blade. A cry of pain rang through the dark stone tunnel as he stumbled forward, free of the Creature's grip, a hand at his throat.

He landed on a knee, the rough ground scraping at his breeches, but he hardly cared. The cut was no longer bleeding. *Healed completely? Impossible...I haven't had blood in—*

The taste of the woman's blood still lingered on his tongue, his blood burning cold in his veins, his dead heart. He felt invigorated as he rose to stand, the sword at his side heavy in its sheath.

He pulled it out just as several more Elite Creatures rounded a corner, their gazes angry as they eyed him, all manner of smoke-infused weaponry raised high in their hands.

"Capture him!" the Elite who still held the knife tight shouted, sending the others to run forward, a haze of their thick smoke filling the tunnel.

What the devil? he thought, moving forward, the dread unavoidable as it passed through to his nostrils, his blood burning hot now, as though a shield against the dread.

Silver blades sliced through the smoke quite near his head and arms, but he felt the change in the air before they could reach him. He slipped out of the way here and there as the Elites moved along their smoke, a furious thought rising to his mind the more he dodged their attacks. *Eleanor. What if she was here? Here amongst these Creatures?*

This thought distracted him for the second it took a sword to plunge through his sleeve, slicing through his arm, a snarl of disbelief and anger leaving his lips. He cursed himself as soon as he did, the other blades convening on his location: all manner of blade now pointed towards him. The sword in his own hand trembled, the thought of Eleanor being here, living here reaching him in a cloud of humiliation, but he swung it all the same, the brief thought of Lucien being here, trapped here shining in his mind. *The sword! The power! Perhaps he had it—perhaps he needed my help in gathering it...*

He heard the cries and snarls through the haze, smelled the dread-filled blood fill the air, and satisfied, he moved forward, doing his best to turn his thoughts, his senses from her. She wouldn't help him, he knew, she would merely get in his way if her Creatures were any indication of her stance on his importance.

Dead heart beating quickly, he tore his arm off the sword and left the cloud of smoke to move down another long tunnel, this one venturing downward at a slight angle, the smell of Lucien's scent, his curse quite immense here.

He did not slow as he heard the Creatures speaking loudly amongst themselves, arguing over where he could have gone, and once again he wrapped himself in a steady silence, his boots not making a sound against the rubble and dirt beneath him.

He was halfway down the tunnel when he saw the piles of ash just underneath a torch against the wall, the orange light brightening the ash as if expanding upon its importance.

He slowed, though he did not know why, Lucien's scent everywhere he dared tune his senses.

And then he smelled it, the rancid smell of somewhat fresh death, just ahead, yes, he looked up from the ash to eye the stone door housed in slight darkness as the torches were not lit most near it.

Such death, he thought, stepping over the piles of ash to reach the door, *what could have caused it?* He almost thought it was where Eleanor left the bodies of those that would not—could not become whatever she now was...

A vague thought of the spell the Enchanter had placed upon him, Darien returned as he stared at the black stone, nondescript in all its normalcy, and he half-thought, somewhere deep in the recesses of his frazzled, scared mind that Darien knew where he was, what he aimed for, and wanted him to gather...well, something else.

"Where could he have gone? Check all the corridors!" a loud voice sounded from far behind him.

Without another thought, he sheathed his sword and pressed his hand in a slight groove in the stone and pulled, a slight groan escaping him as he strained, the cut in his arm completely healed.

He paused once the door was open, sure someone had heard the hard stone scraping against the dirt, but no, the voices beyond this tunnel were moving further away.

How curious.

Without another thought, blood boiling in his veins, he moved into the resolute darkness that greeted him, a damp scent of water, blood, and death all that remained here.

Turning off his sense of smell, he proceeded, quite alarmed when he found he could not.

The more he stepped into the darkness, the light of the corridor beyond the stone door fading behind him, he more he was aware he had no choice but to smell the horrid scents all around him—

And then he felt it, his boot brushing up against something soft, whatever remained underneath it hard, solid as though stone.

Confusion gripped him anew as he pondered whatever it could be at his boots, and why couldn't he see it? A Vampire's sight was well enough to see in the darkest of nights. *So why*, he thought in renewed fear, *can I not see* anything?

Indeed, he tore his gaze from where his boots remained to eye the rest of where he stood, but he could not tell if it were a room, another tunnel, or something else: all was lost to him.

A strong feeling of being pressed into something he could not understand clawed at his mind but he shook it off, determined to get the sword, whatever this strange darkness was be damned. *More of her tricks*, he scoffed although uncertainty gripped his heart.

Regaining himself as best he could, he took a step forward, alarmed when he pressed against what felt like a back. The back of a person.

"Fantastic," he whispered, stepping forward, his every step into darkness taut with surprise, more backs of the dead available for him to navigate.

He stepped across the numerous sea of backs and some torsos for what he deemed a solid hour before he reached anything new at all. It came with a hard smack to his head.

Tearing back, he rubbed his forehead until the pain subsided, eyes narrowing as he released his hand and touched at the solid wall before him. *Great.*

Continuing to press against the stone for any entrance, or anything, indeed, he chanced a look back, surprised to see how far away the stone doorway appeared; it was the size of his thumb.

Turning back to the wall, the sword he was sure remained somewhere beyond it, he continued to press against it, feeling for any abnormality, any strange space, any groove similar to the door he'd passed through to get here.

After several minutes of searching, he found it: a slight groove just above his head, fashioned in such a way that he could slip his fingers inside, turned towards him. He pulled.

The wall immediately swung open, sending him to step hastily backwards over the bodies of the dead. Elite Creatures now that he focused on their scent, and when the whole stone of the wall had lifted to touch the ceiling, a brightness pressed against his eyes making it quite hard to see.

When at last his eyes adjusted, he stared at the large room before him, dark stone like the one he remained in, but different for two reasons:

A glowing gold necklace lay on a dark stand in the center of the room, the red gem in the center casting its red light, and just beside it, atop its own stone stand stood a golden goblet.

He stepped forward, not sure why. The sword was not here, and indeed there was no exit from the room. He had wasted his time, but still...he could not stop himself from stepping up to the medallion, staring down at it, whatever anger should have been burning in him, whatever anxiousness he felt to reach the sword no longer having a point.

"Darien," he said aloud, very aware now that his brother had done this, moved him to come here, placed him here, not to find Lucien or the sword, but gather the bloody cup.

Yes, he felt it now as he lifted the goblet from the stand, surprised when he felt something slosh around inside it. He peered inside.

Blood.

Mere blood.

The anger he knew should have already risen threatened to burst through his chest, but it was subdued as soon as it had spurred.

Blood.

That woman's blood.

He smacked his lips, tasting it on his tongue, within his mouth, feeling it pulse, boil in his veins.

What has she done to me? he thought, recalling that he could now walk in the sun sans ring, that he could stand, no, thrive in Eleanor's dread, that he could move, not for the damned sword, but for what his brother, a Vampire most tied to Dracula's mad plans, desired.

"The Goblet," he said aloud, almost laughing as he realized he had been tricked, indeed. Forced to move for Xavier and his madness despite knowing it would not lead to anything substantial.

Yet here he was, holding a cup his monster of a brother had been tasked to acquire before he'd spouted wings. *What power could this cup of blood possibly hold?* he thought, considering it. It was quite normal, no etchings or markings upon its body. It was merely a damned cup.

Damion laughed again, only stopping when the shimmering light appeared in the air before the stands.

He watched it in bewilderment, its shimmering growing, a solid blue light appearing next, taking the shape of a man.

"What—" he began, the Vampire coming into view the more the blue light grew, bathing the walls, necklace, and goblet in its radiance.

A tired smile graced the Vampire's familiar face. *"Damion Nicodemeus,"* he said, his words bouncing off the hard stone in waves that rattled on in Damion's ears long after he'd finished, *"welcome to better plans."*

He opened his mouth, unable to know if he saw things clearly. *Dracula?* "No," he managed to breathe after a time. *Dracula is dead.*

"Give the Goblet to Xavier," Dracula said, keeping his brown eyes upon him, shimmering in the red light of the medallion, *"give the Goblet to the king."*

And before he could say a word, turn to eye the new voices that had sounded most near the first stone door before the sea of death, the Goblet shook in his hand and Dracula disappeared in a flash of blue light that blinded him.

The voices were just as his back now, but he could barely drop his arm and turn to them when the medallion atop the stand glowed brilliantly, shedding its red light throughout the small room.

He could barely stare upon it alarm, marveling at how in the world it was Dracula had appeared to him, when the hands were at his back and shoulders pushing him down to his knees. A cry of fright left his lips, and even as they held up his arms, his gaze on the dark stone of the stands before him, he was aware his right hand would not open, the Goblet's cold metal would not leave his hand despite their attempts to pry it.

"You're lucky the Queen isn't here to see this, Vampire," an Elite Creature said from behind him. "She'd kill you on the spot for trespassing like you have."

Damion snarled, pressing against their hands, dismayed to find he could not shrug them off. *A bloody cup.* He could not find the words to respond as they lifted him to his feet, the Goblet unable to fall from his grip, the liquid within never slipping over its brim, and when they turned him towards the door, pushing him forward into the black of the room, he realized Ewer's words had been littered with truth.

"The sword you seek is in a place you won't want to venture, Lord Damion."

A place I won't want to venture, indeed, he thought as he was pushed deeper into the tunnels, deeper into Eleanor Black's dread.

Chapter Twenty-Five

NATHANIAL'S BLOOD

He stood over the bodies of the Elite, Aciel and Amentias taking the blood of the corpses, no longer caring that they did not turn to ash. *Something in their blood...my blood, that caused it, surely,* he thought.

"Are you done?" he asked them after a time as he scanned the road for any sign of human or Dark Creature. He saw none, though he was quite sure it'd change soon; the Creatures behind him were not going about their business quietly, next it would be the smell to send the humans to rise from their beds, candle holders in their hands, terror in their eyes...

A particularly loud slurp made him turn around to see Amentias rising from his chosen Elite Creature whose neck was now a shiny gash of red. He wiped his mouth with the back of a sleeve. "Now I am," he said with a content smile, though Xavier understood the Creatures no longer needed to feed from their brothers; they did so just to be sure.

"As am I," Aciel said rising from his meal as well.

"Excellent," he said with badly suppressed impatience, eager to move, to reach her. "Now, do you know where Pinnett is?"

Amentias's eyes shined red in the dark, uncertainty darkening their ethereal glow. "Supposedly just past Scylla," he said.

"Something wrong, Amentias?" he asked, not liking the Creature's clear unease.

He stared at a point past him. "You still have not told us what you plan to do once you reach Eleanor, your Grace."

Ah. He turned to them both, seeing their fear, if only magnified by their blood-lusting gazes. He placed a handle on the Ascalon which had not glowed since he'd left the others, and said, "I feel nothing can be quelled by evading her...if she enters my thoughts like she does...I plan to approach her."

"And?" they asked together.

"And," he said, lingering on the word, knowing he had not thought that far. He'd just desired to get away from Aleister's incessant ruling. *The Vampire had only moved to scold me once he saw I was under her hold—and what did that mean? Being under her hold? Was I truly lost to her again?* He stared at the two Creatures before him, unable to smell her dread from them at all. *No,* he decided then, *not lost to her. This connection we share...there must be a way to sever it.*

He turned from them, moving from the dark of the hallway to step into the vague light of the street. "Come," he said, feeling their bewildered glares at his back, "we shall get my horses from my home and journey to Pinnett."

He heard the Creature move to reach him, smelled the wafting scent of Elite Creature blood, a sickly mixture of Vampire and Lycan air. "Will you kill her?" Amentias asked, and he chanced a glance at the Elite as they walked down the street, seeing the utter desperation in his eyes.

Trapped, he thought knowingly, *they were trapped in her madness.* He closed his eyes as the thought returned, vivid and complete, but not trapped no. Free. He had held her with pride as they watched their Creatures, yes, their Creatures destroy a whole town, the many Vampires, Lycans rampaging over all...

"Xavier? Your Grace?" Aciel's voice sounded through the memory, causing him to blink upon the narrow eyes of the Elite.

He looked around, surprised to see they had stopped just before a very different *The Dragon's Cavern*. The door was black, misplaced within the doorway as though hastily pressed up against it, the wood peeling where it touched the edges. On the black wood were the painted words, *The Dragon's Cavern* in red.

He did not need to press his nose against the wood to know it was blood. He remembered what Christian had said, that Victor had called he and Alexandria here to capture them—

"*Xavier,*" her voice whispered on a cold wind, "*come to me.*"

"Eleanor?" he breathed, ignoring the confused glares of Aciel and Amentias against the streetlamp's glare.

"*Xavier, hurry!*"

"Eleanor!"

"Your Grace, what—"

He grabbed the hand that graced his shoulder, breaking the bones within his grip, but he found little time to care, she was calling him, needed him desperately!

"Xavier, please!"

"Your Grace!"

He released the hand of the strange Creature before him, not entirely seeing either of them, she was calling him, needed him—

"Xavier!"

He blinked, confusion quickly replacing the all-consuming desire to reach her. He stared upon a most alarmed Aciel, a terribly pained and angry Amentias who held his fingers in a hand close to his chest.

"She's gotten into your mind," Aciel said with dark knowing. "You're not free of her at all."

He could not speak, his mind still numb on her fading words, how fast the pull of her voice had called him, blinding all—

"Screw this, Aciel," Amentias said through bared fangs, bringing all eyes to him, still gripping his fingers as they cracked and healed, "I'm not hanging around with a Vampire that clearly wants to go back to her—and not to kill her! She'll end us the moment she lays eyes on us!"

A silent truth seemed to dance in Aciel's red eyes as Xavier stared at him, then he moved, stepping past he and Amentias who was still bent double, clutching his fingers. "Be that as it may," he said, his words sharp as they filled the night air, "we've no choice. Xavier, we follow your lead—wherever it may take us."

※

He clung fast to the back of the Dragon as he soared over the jagged rocks, only grown larger as they neared the black mountain atop which sat the City in perpetual sun.

The false sun shone high above the mountain's peak, pressing against the now real rising sun that blanketed the horizon. "Almost there, Vampire," Ragnarok roared, his large wings dipping slightly as they passed through clouds.

He bent low against the hard scales, the wind tearing at his eyes, remembering when he rode atop the Dragon to reach Cedar Village, Xavier atop another Dragon... The memory faded as the city neared, the large white stone building gleaming in the light of the white sun just above the building's round roof.

He could hear the many voices below as the Dragon slowed to a hover, and he could see the shimmering cloaks of the Enchanters, Elves, and Fae along the many roads within the city.

"Do you think you can make the jump, Vampire?" Ragnarok asked as gasps and curious shouts reached them in the air.

Although low, it was still quite a distance, and the wind that blew his hair wildly as he rose atop Ragnarok's scales made him hesitate. He had come all this way, indeed, eager to see what Equis had come up with to keep magic in the Dark World, but now, staring down at the many confused Creatures, he rethought the severity of keeping so many magically-abled Dark Creatures in one place.

With Eleanor Black about the world it was reckless indeed, the many bouts he'd faced to get here with her Creatures showing him that enough. And Victor...

He returned his thoughts to the present with a particularly loud snort from the Dragon, black smoke filling the air, passing across his face as the wind blew wildly up here. "Vampire," Ragnarok warned.

He patted the Dragon's back in thanks, gripping tight his book in its man-made sling, and slid off the Dragon's back, a rush of wind blowing up all around him as he eyed the white stone of the street below where the Dark Creatures moved out of the way to give him space to land.

As he reached the ground, he was aware a new gust of wind blew far overhead, and he looked up once his boots hit the hard stone to see Ragnarok's tail swishing in the sky as he headed back to Cedar Mountain.

At once Enchanters and Elves surrounded him pulling at his cloak and sling. "Is it true?" he heard, his gaze on the tall stone building several miles ahead through the rowdy crowd. "Is it true the Vampires' reign is nearing its end, that we will have our powers back?!"

"Sorry," he said, pushing through them to reach the round building further up the street, "I don't know—no, please—I must see Madame Mastcourt—"

"Nathanial Vivery!" the divine voice echoed through the streets, cutting his words in two. All other Enchanters and Elves let out cheers, their eyes placed on something higher than street-level.

He looked up past the high buildings on either side of the street, and there, several buildings down stood Madame Mastcourt atop a high set of stairs.

Enchanters, Elves, and Fae most near these stairs stepped away from them, heads bowed in reverence as the dark woman, hair coiled in short black hair, stepped down the stairs, commanding all who stood around her with her presence.

She held her beautiful face high, her cheekbones lined with a severity he could only admire, whatever intimidation she exuded suddenly blanketed by obvious fear as she neared. Her robes, long and black only emphasized this power she held, her long-fingered hands gloved in black leather.

"Nathanial," she said kindly once within speaking distance, an arm extended as though to wrap him in a one-armed hug. She did not. She merely placed her hand along his back, guiding him forward through the line of light stone the other Creatures revealed for them, leading up to the staircase, the high double doors set within the tall building open, inviting them in.

As they walked down the street, she leaned towards his ear. "We've waited far too long for you, Mister Vivery."

"I've wondered what for," he said, feeling his book glow with magical energy at his side; he'd removed it from its sling and held it bare in a hand now.

She smiled kindly, although her brown eyes were wide with the same fear. "In due time," she said, her voice steady.

They said nothing more as they walked along, her waving a gloved hand in greeting at the anxious Enchanters and Elves, the Fae whose eyes appeared darkened. As he wondered how it were possible, they reached the steps and climbed, the tails of her robes' skirts trailing along the stairs behind them.

"Do not look back," she whispered as they proceeded through the double doors, two women moving to close them once they passed. They stood in a grand hall, various doors placed around the three walls before them, several Enchanters reclining in high-backed chairs, holding glowing books close to their noses as balls of light swirled around the large room, sending the room to sparkle in light, creating various shadows to dance upon the wall and floor.

"Now," Madame Mastcourt said, removing her hand from his back, stepping from him to reach a door nearby. She waved two hands across the door, and it opened, a very large room he was not sure was supposed to be there (he had not seen enough size for this room outside of the building) coming into view.

The white room was modestly furnished, a high white couch in the center of the room immediately capturing his attention: the man who sat within it quite large, the back of the chair reaching his lower back.

She stepped into the room with hurried movements, wringing her gloved hands before herself.

The more she moved, the more he saw on the opposite side of the room, two doors remained open, a dizzying sound of what had to be voices sounding beyond it. He was torn from this sound when the man stood after sharing low words with the Enchanter, his frame impossibly tall.

His long black hair was unbound against his back, the long robes he wore glittering in the light of the false and real suns that shone into the many windows around the room.

"This is Nathanial?" he asked, his voice penetrating, reminding him wholly of Evert's voice, his presence, indeed.

"Yes, Equis, this is the Vampire," she said, stepping back as the tall man stepped around the couch and moved towards him.

He bowed, without knowing what else to do. "Your Greatness," he said, rising to stand, "it is an honor to meet you, I only wish it were under better circumstances."

"As do we all," he sighed deeply, a kind smile upon his face.

He was confused, quite sure the man should have been Ancient, frail, if not unable to move, then reclined to a bed as was Evert, only rising every so often to tell a few Creatures what must be done. This confusion must have passed across his face, for Equis said, "What troubles you?"

"I merely wonder," he said, staring towards Philistia who did not meet his gaze, "why I was called here, received such...a welcome."

"Oh," Equis said jovially, moving away from him along the couch, only stopping every so often to eye Philistia with a needy, knowing glare. "Yes, let's get to the bottom of the matter. You, Nathanial Igorian Vivery are a most...curious creation."

He said nothing, letting the Ancient Creature continue.

"You are a Vampire who was given the...gift, hah, of Enchanting by Dracula, a Vampire most...empowered in the Arts. You were one Vampire who mastered it without any help, though it was found you needed, not only your book of Enchanting Arts, but the Fyre of the Phoenixes's Nest.

"This is fantastic," Equis went on before Nathanial could understand what more to say, "a Vampire able to learn, to grasp the Enchanting Arts and not die under the weight of it all." He turned to eye him in full, Nathanial seeing the strange look in his eyes. "You are a most...fantastic Creature."

"This," he began, unsure of how to say it, "is all very well and good but you still haven't explained why I was given such attention and the others weren't."

"They weren't the ones that traveled with Dracula throughout the world, searching for imbued Artifacts crafted by my brothers,

Mister Vivery. You were. It is why you stand before me today... It is why you will save the Enchanters where I cannot."

His book burned in his grip, but still he held it tight. "What do you mean where you cannot? You are Equis the Ancient Elder, you have power we mere book-holders cannot even dream—"

"I have no power!" he shouted, pushing his words into the recesses of the strained silence, only broken by the raucous cheers of the Enchanters outside the doors. "I have no bloody power, do not placate me with fanciful terms, endow me with false power I do not, nor have I ever held. Your bloody creator, that Vampire, has all the power, over magic, over—over the mere importance of blood."

His eyes widened as Equis's anger filled the room, the collected image of the Ancient Creature shattered in the rage that filled the broad shoulders, the indignant glare.

"What do you mean you have no power?" he asked, despite the pit of unease that rose in his stomach as he watched the angry Creature, the silent Enchanter beside the couch. He had always known Dracula held control over magic, but he had assumed Equis, at least, held the true power of it. *What was this?*

"I mean I have no power, Dracula's death destroying what magic remained in this world."

"And what—why am I here?" he asked for the third time, biting back the feeling that he would like the answer, indeed.

Equis stared at him as though the answer should have been clear, and then a low sigh whistled through his pursed lips. "Your blood, Vampire," he said at last, Philistia shifting her footing uncomfortably in the large room, "you are here to give me your blood."

He opened his mouth to say he did not understand, but Equis waved a hand, begging his silence, and removed a glove, the hand that shined in the light of the suns covered in a strong blue light. "It is faint," Equis said, seemingly to himself, "but it is enough."

And before he knew it, the blue light left the large hand and pressed forward in the room, reaching him in a flurry which spread against his chest. "Wha—"

The light stung as it touched him, and even through the cloak, the robes underneath, he felt the pain against his skin, as though something was threatening to leave it, to claw at his rib cage until it would burst. *My blood.* His knees hit the floor as all manner of spell, of counter curse fled his mind, his eyes on the dark Enchanter beside the couch, begging for her help: his mouth would not open, his tongue not finding lease within his mouth.

"Equis," Philistia whispered, tearing her gaze from his to watch the Ancient Elder in sheer discomfort, "Equis, this isn't right! There has to be a better way."

"Silence, Philistia," he hissed, the blue light growing brighter the more Nathanial felt his blood gather at the front of his body, "gather the cup."

She did as she was told, Nathanial saw through blood-drenched eyes, moving for a cup atop a glass table before the couch. He watched in strained silence, blood pouring from his eyes and ears, as she walked to Equis and gave him the cup.

He took it with his gloved hand, placing it just beneath his blue one, and Nathanial watched in confusion, great pain, as the blood traveled in a line across the room, leaving his cheeks, his ears and filled the cup to the brim.

Equis formed a fist with the blue light of the hand focusing the spell, and the light died at once, Nathanial slumping forward against the hard floor, very aware he could not move; he felt weak, like he was dying, permanently this time, the feeling in his arms and legs all but gone.

I can't move, he thought, what should have been panic dulling to a dim anxiousness.

He heard the Ancient Creature called Equis swallow, heard the slight gasp that left Philistia's lips, and felt, as it rumbled along the ground, the waiting shouts of the many Enchanters outside the open doors...

"Well," Philistia breathed, Nathanial very aware the sun's light one he was able to feel. It began to burn along his exposed skin, the heat unbearable. *It shouldn't be possible.* "Did it work? Do you feel anything?"

The cup clanked to the floor, a grunt following it, and then silence.

It was a long time before anyone spoke, and it was Equis to do so:

"I feel it, Madame Mastcourt." And Nathanial was vaguely aware of the heat, the different-colored light that doused the room in its multicolored glow far over his head.

He closed his eyes as the heat of the sun pressed against his skin, becoming more than an annoyance, something dragging him away, indeed, leaving him to coast on a fitful sleep of misery and pain, the flames engulfing him in full.

Chapter Twenty-Six

PROTECT THE DRAGON

The skies lightened as the sun rose against the mountains of Cedar, Arminius all but fed up with the Vampire's cowardice: He whined and groaned as though someone or something poked sticks at his sides.

"Nicholai," he breathed, bending over the Vampire for a third time, eager to see him rise, to see the black smoke of the medallion fade, for the damned Creature to regain his sense, "focus on my voice!"

He repeated the assurances until the Vampire tore his gaze from the wall to eye him wildly. "Arminius?" he breathed, his voice very low, lower than he'd ever heard the Vampire ever use it before. He watched in hesitant relief as the Vampire sat up upon the old wood, staring around at the small cottage they remained in. "Where are we?"

"Cedar Village," he said, extending a hand for the Vampire to take. He placed his weight on his cane as he helped pull the Vampire up to stand.

"Cedar Village," Nicholai repeated, staring around at the wooden home, "I take it we were chased here."

He ignored the sentence, brushing past the Vampire to reach the window where he pulled back the curtain, eyeing the few remaining Elites that slashed and clawed at the Dragon on the ground. *She still fought valiantly*, he thought, replacing the thin cloth. Turning back to face the Vampire that had strode the length of the small house to observe the number of books resting along an old wooden shelf, he saw the many stains and tears in the Vampire's cloak and shirt.

"You must need blood," he said, his cane clicking against the old wood as yet another blast of fire lit up the field several cottages down.

He made a face, turning to eye the fireplace. A low fire still burned. "You need to explain what happened to me," he said, giving him his full glare, "I'm sure I wasn't the best companion to drag around the Dark World."

He pressed on the cane as he moved for the armchair just before the fire. Groaning slightly, he sank into it, waving a long-fingered hand for the Vampire to take a seat just beside him. Once he was seated, rocking back and forth in the wooden rocking chair, Arminius began, "You...were lost to Eleanor Black's madness when her dread touched your medallion."

"I remember that much," he said, blue eyes dark with thought. "I remember waking up in a badly destroyed town..."

"Wingdale," he said, staring into the orange flames, hearing more shouts from the Elite Creatures, the Enchanters outside the wooden walls. "It was destroyed by her Creatures. We escaped, but I must admit," and he let a low, tired sigh leave his lips as he sank back in the chair, "I feared you would leave me for her."

"I would never," Nicholai said at once, sitting forward in the rocking chair; it creaked loudly as he did so. Arminius thought it would break. "Her...dread was everywhere in my mind but it was not her I feared."

"What do you mean?"

The tall Vampire seemed to shrink within the chair as he sank back, his shoulder-length silver hair waving around his neck as the chair rocked with his full weight upon it. A long-nailed hand gripped tight an armrest. "Dracula," he whispered as yet another large plume of fire lit up the coming dawn.

He shifted in his seat, the memory he'd seen whilst attempting to return the medallion to its former red glow sparking in his mind. Fear flared in his heart in full, his own medallion at his chest blaring to life with the notion. "Do go on," he said, knowing what he would hear.

His sharp gaze moved to the curtained window as yet another plume of fire brightened the sky, the terrible roar shaking the foundation of the small home. Once it was gone, he cleared his throat, and said, "He desired me to watch over a human woman he felt would listen to his every word. With the mixing of blood, he hoped this human would be able to harness immense power we Vampires otherwise would not be able to possess.

"He was partly right," he said, shifting in the chair. The creak it made was drowned in yet another earth-shattering roar. "The woman he'd...convinced to bear his child was able to hold this power...yet she did not want to. Once introduced to our world...the World of Vampires, of Lycans, Giants, Dragons, she fled.

"I was with him when he received word of her death...it was at a time he could not...keep his true face from being seen for longer periods of time. That only came later, but of course he was to die before he could truly master the curse he'd been given."

Arminius, who had been listening with rapt attention, coughed, bringing the Vampire's gaze to him. "His true face?" he asked.

"Dracula," Nicholai said after an unnatural silence pressed against the walls, only broken by a raucous laugh, punctured by short balls of fire, "is not the Creature you or I have had the...pleasure to witness whilst in his office, confined by four walls, a city that followed his every movement. He is...monstrous—a being quite capable of animalistic cruelty to the highest degree. And yet," he sighed, "he has kept his secret brilliantly."

He thought back to the terrible Winged-Creature he had seen in Nicholai's memory, the red light rising to quell the unease... "What is he?" he asked quietly, fearfully, quite sure he had been tricked to working for the monster before he truly knew what he'd done. "Truly?"

"He is what he was since birth," Nicholai said, "a monster driven by his bloodlust. The only thing separating we Vampires now from him is our human-like qualities. Though the bloodlust...we could not escape that."

There was silence for a long moment between them, the rough voice of a Dragon outside saying, "We've more of her Creatures!"

Arminius, interest far more than piqued now, would not rise from his chair until he heard all of what the Vampire kept. "The woman. Tell me about her."

"She conceived a daughter with Dracula before her death. The girl...she was human enough but he was convinced he would get it right with her."

"What did he do?"

"Spelled her," he said simply. "Visited her every few years or so. And when the time came...he tasked me with the procuring of her safe...appearance before him."

"That didn't go well I take it."

"I'm sure everyone knows she ended up at that damn Vampire's home," he said, the bite of anger pressing against his voice as he spoke, "of course, the spell I did to remove her from Dracula's hold misfired."

"You learned magic from Dracula, I take it?"

"He would not deny me the knowledge when I asked for it once I saw what he was capable of."

"Smart lad. I take it you saw Dracula as this...monster while encumbered?"

He merely nodded and said nothing more.

Arminius nodded as well, knowing the conversation was at its end. What more secrets the Vampire desired to keep would be fine, for now.

He rose to stand, leaning against his cane for support, and walked gingerly to the curtain once more, pulling it back to see a most curious sight:

Beyond the number of cabins and cottages before the rushing river, various Enchanters and Fae were leaving their homes, Garden Gnomes at the hem of their robes and dresses, following them as they waded through the river, moving to reach the large red Dragon in the center of the sprawling field before the sharp mountains of Cedar.

He did not turn as the Vampire peered over his shoulder to gaze out the window as well, only to draw back immediately with a cry of pain.

He turned at once, watching as Nicholai slunk back into the shadows where the light beyond the curtain could not reach. "What's wrong?"

"The sun," he said, his pained expression all Arminius needed to know. A gloveless hand covered his face where the light had touched him.

"It burns you?" he asked dimly, not understanding it. "I thought you were protected, took Dracula's blood—"

"I did," he said angrily, the confusion just there beneath his words. "I bloody well did. As did the rest of the Vampires in the Order—I should be able to walk in the sun!"

He turned back to the window, pulling back the curtain despite the Vampire's snarls at his back, for he'd felt the spark in the air, but it could not be possible.

But it was.

There, just beyond the rushing river, the magically rebuilt homes, were the number of Enchanters and Fae. They circled the Dragon, their faces gazing somewhere off in the distance, their hands high in the air, their faces cruel and angry in the morning light, yet somehow relieved...

And then it happened. One by one streams of brilliantly colored light left their hands, not dimming, never dimming, strong and resolute, a cry of fright off in the distance filling the air.

He turned back to the Vampire who had slumped into the rocking chair, cradling his face, angry snarls leaving his lips. "Nicholai," he said, joy finding his throat despite all he'd just heard, the fading thoughts of the winged Dracula almost completely gone, "Nicholai—magic! It's back!"

The Vampire glared up at him with one blue eye, a pitiful sight against the bright flames shining against his haunted frame. "How are you so sure?" he asked, his eye red now as the flames jumped within it.

He pressed the cane to the floor, his intent sure. And not soon after did the medallion glow a brilliant red, filling the room, the Vampire swallowing the blood that appeared in his mouth in grateful surprise.

Once he'd swallowed his fill, he rose from his chair, his burns healing as he did. "Dracula's blood," he whispered. "But it's impossible."

He waved a hand through the air, a bright yellow light leaving his fingertips, gliding swiftly through the air to press against the door, which opened against the sun. Nicholai took a tentative step away as the light reached his boots, but Arminius knew with fresh blood on his tongue, the door thrown wide, the Vampire would be able to hear the swirls of energy tearing the sky, reaching their targets with beautiful precision and ease.

"I thought magic was fading," Nicholai said dimly.

"Listening, were you?" he responded smugly, the smile wide upon his face despite himself. However it happened, it was a true blessing, he knew. "We've a leg up in this war after all!" And without another word he stepped from the cottage, glad to be free of it at last, yet he had made it only two steps down the stone path leading to the small home when he turned back, dismayed to find the Vampire still in shadow. "Nicholai?"

His eyes were still red, bright in the dark, and they were trained on him in terrifying knowing: Arminius felt a bizarre fear ascend his spine though he did not know why until the Vampire said, "I can't follow you, Arminius."

He turned in full, his cane tapping impatiently against the stone. "Nonsense," he said, "you've just had Dracula's blood—come, we waste time—Victor may not stand a chance against our magic but I still would not like to be cornered by him again. We must get to others, the king."

"I can't walk in the sun," he repeated coldly, and he stepped backward near the small staircase as though bidden.

Irritation furrowed his brow, but truly the Vampire would not budge the more he stared at him, the sounds of the Enchanters' spells issuing powerfully against the sky sounding louder against his back.

"Truly Vampire," he said at last, "what's gotten into you? Only just risen from her madness—"

"It was Dracula," he said, not daring to step forward, "Dracula's madness everywhere I dared turn."

"What the devil are you talking about?"

"I told you, Elf," and he bared his fangs, much to Arminius's surprise, "Dracula is what I feared when that medallion went black. At first it was Eleanor, but her presence could not hold a candle to the real threat. It's what burns in my blood this very moment. Perhaps it is why I cannot walk in the sun any longer."

"You can't be serious," he said, not desiring to listen to this madness. He was a bloody Knight, tasked by the Phoenixes to do what must be done! So what was this talk of Dracula? The thought returned with greater clarity, the sight of the monstrous beast towering over a kneeling Nicholai, large head cocked to the side as though greatly curious to understand the Creature he stared upon... A cold shiver replaced the heat of the sun along his back, and he blinked, the fear rising in his chest, the medallion blaring once more.

"Fine," he said after a time, staring at the Vampire's medallion: it still remained black in the dark, "stay here. I shall get Xavier, the others."

He stepped up the few stairs to close the door, seeing the confusion he felt mirrored in the Vampire's red eyes. *Damn*, he thought as he began to step away from the Enchanter's spells, the Dragon's burst of flame, only hoping against great hope that Victor Vonderheide did not reach the Vampire greatly changed, locked in the damning dark.

※

James Addison pressed along the path alongside the Creatures, not understanding why they moved as slowly as they did, or why indeed the woman did not rise.

She lay strewn across the scarred Vampire's arms, eyes closed, hair down along the Vampire's side. It swayed as they moved, brushing past the handle of his sword, the guard's silver gleaming in the light of the sun.

He thought of her importance, her power the more they walked, Lore's words finding his mind with every step, *"Infiltrate their group, James. Gain their trust. End her life. It will be easiest, I imagine, when the woman is very near death."*

And how near death she seemed to be. He clenched his jaw against the work he knew he would have to do, to transform, to rip, to tear, to bite, the many Vampires around making this something of a task, indeed.

He snorted again, eager to release their disgusting blood from his nose. How it clung and stuck to his hair and clothes, never ceasing, never dying.

The world would be better off without them, he thought, focusing on their importance, their power. It was inherent in all of them, more steadily the woman now as time passed.

He was wasting time, he knew it. She would very nearly meet her end at any moment—

He stepped forward to grasp her hair in a fist when the cold hand tightened around his wrist, stilling him from moving further. The low growl left his throat as the fire rose against the cold of the hand pressing against his wrist, and in another moment the hand was removed.

He looked up into the red, tired eyes of Christian Delacroix, the Vampire who held no ring on any finger, shielded only by ceiling of shadow placed over his head, keeping the sun from reaching his skin.

"What are you doing, James?" Christian asked, the wind blowing up around them with his words.

"Miss Stone," he lied, tearing back his arm from the Vampire's icy grip, "her eyes fluttered, I thought she would awaken."

He watched in slight amusement as all Creatures stopped moving, their eyes on the woman in Aleister's arms. It was a long time before the Vampire turned to the circle, and placed her on the dirt path at their feet, his green eyes serious as he watched her. With a heavily scarred hand, he wiped a strand of brown hair away from her face. "She sleeps," he said after a time.

James watched as his gaze rose to greet him, the coldness, the contempt he had come to recognize as the trademark of the Vampire just there beneath that glare.

"Are you sure you saw her eyes flutter, James?"

"I am sure," he said coldly, never dropping his gaze.

At last the Vampire relented, looking back down upon her, moving his arms beneath her when a brazen wind blew their hair and clothes away from their bodies. James smelled it first, a whirlwind of dread and Lycan blood furling through the air. He stared ahead towards the simple dirt path that lined the horizon, the trees on either side of it, confusion dulling his senses, and then he saw him.

Small as he climbed the horizon, quickly growing as he drew near, his every step one held with power, a grace that could not be denied. With every step his formidable frame drew near, the long tattered cloak he wore over his unbuttoned shirt, breeches, and boots splattered with dried blood in places, ripped in few others.

It was not until this man was a few miles away that anyone did anything at all, and it was Dragor to do so. James watched as he raised his glowing blue sword high in the air, shouted something James could not catch, a large blue wall appearing just before them, transparent in the sun's light. The large Vampire lowered the sword after a moment, Christian sure to say, "Thomas?" his stare, James saw, on the figure beyond the rippling wall.

All Creatures tensed; Enchanters not holding important women raised their hands prepared to cast spells; Vampires snarled and lifted swords, daggers, or arrows from their backs, holding them aloft, prepared to strike; and he, the only Lycan among the party, stepped backwards, away from Alexandria, yes, but more importantly, away from the battle that was about to begin.

※

Thomas was tired, but not more than he was angry, for he was very, very angry. He had not been able to find her, to tell her the Vampire's plans, tell her how strongly it was the Vampire pined for her. No, he had not been able to locate Eleanor Black, because, he had decided, she did not wish to be found.

Now he stared at the group of Dark Creatures, the familiar blue wall that separated them from him, and he grimaced. The woman, wrapped in Aleister's arms, lay dormant, yet the blood he had smelled, the red light that had found him wherever he dared roam would not fill his mind. *How odd*, he thought, a blind step forward spurring his thoughts, *it appears she is just a normal human.*

But to give him great dreams of Mara, to beg for the thing he possessed—

The blast of red sparks hit his shoulder, sending him barreling back against the air, all former thought dispersed with his anger. He steadied himself, landing on a knee, but before he could move to prepare a strike, yet another blast of light hit his other shoulder. It felt as though his arms were numb, reduced to ash, but he lifted them all the same, rising to his feet with steadying breaths.

"Watch out!" the female Enchanter screamed beyond the rippling wall.

They tensed but they did not move as he rammed his damaged shoulder into the wall, slight cracks appearing in its surface. The pain was great, his anger, frustration stronger. *Where could she have gone? And when I have the woman in my sights again?*

As he pushed himself into the wall, the cracks growing larger, deeper, he heard the Vampires' snarls, but he could hardly care for them: his eyes were on the woman, her pretty face as he thought on all the ways he could kill her. Ruin her, just as she'd ruined him, humiliated him with her many lies—

"*Symbolia Menta!*" the scarred Vampire shouted, and all at once he found himself lifted several feet into the air, his numb arms unable to move at his sides, his fingers straining against his thigh to reach the sword at his hip. He stared down at them, their fear clear in their eyes, fear, yes, and something else he could not readily place—

He fell out of the sky to land with a hard thud along the ground, bewilderment causing him to rise as the spells focused on his shoulders faded, his arms returned to him, the sight beyond the now vanishing blue wall focusing his attention.

All Vampires were on fire, the strange black ceiling placed above Christian Delacroix gone, subjecting him to the light of the sun. His eyes were wide balls of fire, mouth wide through the flame that ripped at his skin. Thomas watched with great curiosity as the scarred, burning Vampire dropped the woman brusquely in his pain and moved with the others towards the line of trees off the path, the Enchanters waving their hands and shouting spells as they followed in their apprehension.

What on Earth? he thought, staring after the burned Vampires, their skin sizzling in the shade.

He could only stare at them for but a minute when the Lycan most near lunged for the woman at his feet.

"No!" he shouted, smelling the strong, familiar scent of Lore on the arm of the man as he had wrapped an arm around her waist, dragging her to his side as he moved to stand.

Father?

The man stared at him with black eyes, the heat of his transformation just there on the air, for he was quite prepared to turn, Thomas was sure, the growls leaving his throat only assured him of this most disturbing fact.

Lycans cannot turn in broad daylight, he thought, wondering if this man was a Lycan, or something more, but he could not be, he smelled nothing like an Elite Creature...

"Alexandria!" he heard one of the Vampires beneath the shade shout towards them: he could smell the cold blood cutting through the burgeoning Lycan's smell of blood and dirt.

Neither of them turned to eye the Creatures trapped in the shade, the Enchanters that would not leave them, confused, he was sure, of their sudden combustible nature. He merely stared on the man, smelling his father, knowing, somehow his father had moved again, moved to keep her from him.

"Unhand her, boy," he said, his form very much human, but how quickly that could change.

The man said not a word, the hair atop his head, along his chest, and arms growing rapidly, his nose lengthening and blackening against the sun as an inhuman howl left his throat. And as he grew, the woman remained under an arm, his black claws digging into her back sending her to bleed over them—

"Bloody hell," one of the Enchanters shouted, "Xavier's servant is a bloody Elite Creature?"

"No," a most pained voice responded, one he recognized as Christian's, "the man was bitten by Lore...somehow he holds the similar blood."

Impossible! Thomas thought, removing the Ares from his hip. The red gem gleamed in the light of the sun, an unsteady hand pointing it towards the snarling Lycan before him. "What the devil are you?" he asked, his voice pressing all others to absolute silence. *It was impossible—father wouldn't dare—*

"You must be blind, Creature," the Lycan responded proudly, its many fangs glistening against the light, "I am a Lycan." He growled, sending a great whiff of dirt and blood to cover Thomas's nose.

He retched, allowing the blood of a beast to claim his skin. The horrible scent before him swiftly became bearable as he stepped on hind paws, bigger perhaps than the ones he stared at now. He grasped the leather handle of the sword with his large claw before it could fall to the ground with his transformation, his black eyes trained on the woman in the beast's grip, her blood leaving her in droves to spill atop the dirt. She was very nearly dead, he knew. But she couldn't die, not yet, not now. *I have to be the one to kill her!*

Anger pulsed through his heart at he stared at the Lycan, hearing the miserable snarls of the Vampires beneath the trees, and then he smelled it again: coarse fire, heard the scream of overwhelming pain, the snarl of sincere frustration—

"Christian, you can't go out there! Not without your ring!" another Creature was saying.

"Ring?" another Vampire scoffed (he could smell the cold blood). "None of us have our bloody rings and we got burned all the same! Rings don't matter—and we've all taken Dracula's blood! This shouldn't be possible!"

What? he thought, turning for only a second to eye the line of miserable Creatures against the line of trees to his right. They were all huddled over, some kneeling along the bright green grass, others leaning up against trees, badly burned hands clinging to the bark as though dissolving into the tree would release the pain they felt, keep the sun from returning to set them ablaze once more. The Vampire he assumed to be Christian Delacroix had been pulled back by two Enchanters: he sat against the base of a tree, hair gone, skin terribly burned, clothes stuck to what was left of his skin, he was hardly recognizable.

Thomas was distracted from the sight of this strange spectacle when the ground shook before him and he turned in alarm, furious to see the Lycan's short tail waving at him as he ran on hind legs, the woman still pressed against his claws.

He started forward, quite sure he would not allow his bloody father the honor of killing the woman, no, she was his target, his to exact his revenge. Indeed, he thought on her absolute righteousness when she had told the bloody Vampire to 'claim his prize,' a prize that was his! That he held even now, and still she would not rise from the Lycan's damned nails to see that he held it, to see that he was the one bidden, able to do so?!

The gem in the guard glowed as he ran, and he was able to feel the startling heat lift from it, his paw rising through the air with the sword as he thundered on his hind legs after the beast, the blade pointed straight for the beast's back—

With another tremble, a loud, *"Protect the Dragon!"* it pulled from his claws, and he stopped in bewilderment, staring as the sword flew through the air to land with little resistance straight into the back of Lore's newest pet.

A strangled howl left the Lycan's long mouth as the blade pierced his fur, and he fell forward, a heavy thud echoing through the trees as he landed atop the dirt, a great cloud of it rising in a plume to cover the woman, the beast, and the sword.

When it faded at last, Thomas able to see the large mass of black fur, he released the Lycan form, allowing himself to regain a human one, his need to fight dead. He stepped up to the bleeding beast, the smell of its blood pressing through his nose with its harshness, but it was no longer stifling.

He turned his gaze from the beast to eye the woman who had been dislodged from the black claws with the fall. She lay on her side, back facing him, the five holes about her spine still bleeding, bathing her white blouse, the ground in its red hue.

Despite her blood so freely available to him, he could not smell it, not even the hint of human blood it should have been, for whatever mystical being she should have been, was supposed to have been, she was no longer, he knew.

With a scowl, a sound of anger leaving his throat, he made to pull the sword from the Lycan's back, alarmed when a burst of red light left its entire body, the red gem glowing strongly against the sun...

"What?" he breathed in alarm, very aware a strange sensation swept over him. He suddenly felt as though he were locked in a tight compartment, unable to breathe against the air that swam around him.

He could barely question what kept him glued to where he stood, unable to reach out for the sword, its red light extending several feet around it in all directions.

And he turned to eye the direction he had just run, seeing the two Enchanters leave the trees, the medallions glowing at their chests. They stepped along the path in quick movements towards him, each holding an arm aloft, a steady red light leaving their hands, and he narrowed his eyes.

Them? He could not move as they neared despite his strong desire to do so, feeling his mind go slack, but he could just see the woman's hand wrap around the black leather handle of the sword before he was unceremoniously lost in darkness.

※

"What do we do now?" Peroneous asked, holding his dark hand aloft, staring down at the naked man who had fallen, lost in an apparent sleep.

Aurora Borealis groaned, the red light fading as she squeezed the handle of the sword, pulling it out of the Lycan with great effort.

The beast's large back lurched with the movement, and she tensed, but that was all he did.

Turning to the woman, the sword limp in her hand, for she could not hold it high, she knelt at her side, observing the holes embedded in her back. She clucked her tongue, settling the sword against the ground at the woman's head, waving Peroneous over.

He dropped his hand, the red light dying from the medallion, the sword's gem, and stepped to her.

"I don't know what the bloody hell is going on," she said, waving a hand over the woman's back, focusing the spell, confused when the holes would not close, "damn," she whispered, "I thought we'd had our powers returned to us."

"We do," Peroneous said, kneeling at the woman's front, "and the Vampires have had theirs taken from them, do you not feel it, Aurora?"

And she focused within, feeling the power press against her heart. Yes, it had returned. She opened her eyes, staring down upon the woman. *But why won't it work against her?*

"We can worry about this later," Peroneous said, pulling her from her doubts. She looked up to see his dark face serious as he looked at something over her shoulder. "Right now, we need that Vampire."

She turned her head to follow his gaze, eyes widening as she saw Christian on hands and knees, badly burned, yes, but hungry, his eyes red through the dark the trees afforded him: they were only held on Alexandria.

"You're not seriously considering giving Alexandria to him?" she asked, turning back to him, but he had already lifted Alexandria in his arms, already stepped over the Lycan to reach the snarling, confused, pained Vampires.

"Wait, Peroneous!" she cried, words lost to deaf ears: he charged forward as though he had not heard her at all, and then she was able to hear it, against the snarls of the Vampires, the particularly vicious snarls of Christian, the thunder of Peroneous's boots against the ground.

"Protect the Dragon!"

Chapter Twenty-Seven

A NECESSARY EVIL

Christian could feel nothing but pain, as he clawed at the ground, the woman's blood rushing through his senses the more he remained. *Damned sun!* The snarl vicious as it left his lips. He had always heard it most troublesome to be caught in the sun sans ring, but he had never known the true pain, the depths to which the fire in the sky would rain down upon his very being with little remorse, indeed! What he felt was beyond pain, it encumbered one, hell, it had taken all his bloody strength to lift and rise to step into the sun only to get burned again when the damned Lycan had impaled her with his bloody claws. The sun the only thing keeping him from her, for it were night, if it were dark, her blood would be his...

Alexandria! Another snarl. Whatever budding feelings of affection he'd found for the woman overtaken by the sheer desire, need, compulsion for that beautiful, compelling *blood*.

"Peroneous, not yet!" he heard Aurora Borealis cry further down the path back the way they'd come.

He looked up from his rumination to see the dark Enchanter carrying the woman, yes that blood was nearing, indeed, it was nearing, *closer*—

"He was over here, my Lord!" a new voice sounded against the sun, sending his head, despite the blood that called him, towards the direction they had traveled upon arriving here two hours before.

He felt all trembling Vampires behind him turn and look along the horizon just as he did, the gruff gasps leaving their lips as he eyed them, several darkly cloaked Elite Creatures appearing along the dirt path, their eyes gleaming red in the light.

"Bloody hell," one shouted in disbelief, causing all of them to draw their weapons.

"Damn," he heard Aleister whisper behind him, but he could not turn to eye his father, see the pain he held: it hurt far too much to move more than he already had...and how he needed blood!

Peroneous, who had been drawing near with the woman, blood pouring down his arms, staining his already bloodied robes, stopped dead upon seeing the line of Elite. He was several feet from the line of trees, close enough for Christian to get his agonizing full of the woman's blood, but unable to truly taste.

"Aurora, use the sword against them!" he shouted, Christian watching as he kneeled, placing the woman along the road, her fingers arched towards him, their tips caught in the shade.

"It's bloody well heavy, Doe!" Aurora shouted angrily.

The dark Enchanter stood; leaving the woman, he ran for the line of Elites, sure to shout over his shoulder as he moved, "Aren't you an Enchanter, woman?!"

Christian no longer heard the sparks of magic that passed across the sky, he no longer saw the Enchanters, Aurora with the sword in a glowing red hand, charge for the Elites, dodging their arrows, their staffs, no, he could see nor hear nothing but the woman several feet from him.

A need he had felt once before when close to absolute death, attacked and destroyed by Eleanor's Creatures resurfaced, his sight black, thought gone, only able to see the lines of her blood, her beautiful, beating heart.

Without a thought, he began to crawl towards her. "Alexandria," he snarled, a seed of anger flaring in his heart as he thought on how she was able to keep his need for blood from him, how her blood was now only his to smell, "whatever you are..."

But his words failed him as he neared, just there, able to grasp her fingers, pull her into the shade, the blood leaving her back still trailing from the puddle created, staining the blades of grass.

She was cold, a cold he could feel in difference to his own, and now, just before him, in easy grasp, he was able to see the veins of her blood, all else lost to him besides the beating of her beautiful heart.

"What—no, you can't," he heard his father say weakly from his tree, pulling him from her blood for only a moment, able only to see the darkened veins of the badly injured Vampire, the dead heart which pulsed only once.

Her blood pulled him back to her, and there in the sight of the veins that pressed against the body he could not see, he saw the largest one at her neck.

With trembling hands, he pressed against her bleeding back, bringing her up to his chest, only able to see the largest vein within her throat, and with nothing else to hold him back, indeed, he pressed against her neck, breaking the vein, his fangs cutting the vein in two as the blood poured freely into his mouth.

Sweet and heady, the blood slid down his tongue, the taste what he'd smelled for weeks, and all at once he found himself healing: his skin shed its burns, the strength returning to his hands, arms, and legs, as he gripped her tighter, eager for more. The red light within him and around him only growing, he knew, the more he sucked.

He felt his hair grow and lengthen along his back, and heard the clear shouts of battle along the road, the particular birds chirping high within the trees, the incessant snarls of pain from the Vampires behind him...

Yet before he could enjoy his newfound strength, his power, the blood that poured down his throat suddenly burned, and he released her, grasping at his throat, turning from her, a startled gasp leaving his lips in a long, painful wheeze. The burning reached his dead heart, sending it to pulse just once, powerfully, painfully, before he was able to hear the Creatures along the road continue their battle. Without turning, he knew three Elite Creatures were dead, a fourth nearly there, and he turned to eye the road, eyes widening as he saw he was right:

Three tattered cloaks lay atop the path, an Elite Creature kneeling before Aurora who held the sword aloft with a red, glowing hand, and as he watched, she plunged the long blade into the Elite's open mouth, slicing through, he knew, his every unneeded organ, only for the tip of the blade to appear in-between the Creature's legs.

The fresh smell of Elite was different now, no longer dread-filled, dark in its suffocation, it was now lighter, somehow, easier to withstand, and as Peroneous sent a blast of blue light straight towards the few remaining Elites who had seen their own die by the Ares, he turned back to the woman along the grass just before him and saw her clearly for the first time in hours.

She was white, paler than he'd ever known a Vampire of European descent to be, her lips blue, dark circles under her eyes, no longer from a lack of sleep, but indeed, a greater form of it. Her hand was outstretched towards him, her blood staining the brown waves of her hair, and without another thought, he bit into his wrist, let the blood spill from it, and placed it over her cold lips.

And waited as the Enchanters continued to fight Eleanor's Creatures with the glowing, bloody, sword.

Chapter Twenty-Eight

THE BLOOD

Xavier smiled, having never made it to his home to retrieve the horses, the Elite Creatures that had found them soon after pushing them out of London, towards Scylla. They had fought these Creatures with ease, moving into Pinnett with the rising of the sun, but upon seeing that she was not there, they had pressed forward for Cedar Village.

Now they stood before the rushing river, the body of Joseph Gail at their feet. Victor, they had been told, had flown off towards another set of mountains far in the distance, once bombarded with the large red Dragon, the powerful Enchanters and Fae that had encircled her.

It was believed that he had given up the search for Nicholai Noble, and Arminius, the latter of which Xavier had not seen. The setting sun pressed along the tree-lined horizon, and many of the Enchanters and Fae that had bowed and kneeled at his arrival into Cedar Village, were now in their homes, reinforcing much-needed barriers and protections, helping Fae do the very same.

Nicholai, now free of the cottage, a hand on the black medallion at his chest, stared down at the corpse of Joseph, sure to say, "He fought to the end. I saw it when the sun wasn't pressing against the glass. Wouldn't budge with his own magic. Seems it's no match for what these Enchanters have, though."

Xavier stared at him, thinking only of Eleanor, the news that Victor had escaped doing nothing to warm his heart to the Vampire in the least. "And just how would they gain this magic? I heard from Aurora, Aleister, something was happening to it."

The large Vampire shrugged his shoulders. "I hardly know. All I know is earlier today I was talking to Arminius about Dracula, Alexandria Stone, and the sun didn't agree with me."

"I felt the same thing," he said, recalling the startling heat of the sun when pressed by the Elite Creatures. By the time he'd reached Cedar, the sun had already begun to set and he found he could move as he pleased. "I thought it most odd...but if the Enchanters have their power returned to them..."

"We seem to have ours taken from us," Nicholai finished, turning to go back towards the cottage. He only stopped when he saw Xavier was not following. "Coming, your Grace? There is much we must discuss. We must search for Arminus as well. He went off to gather you."

He stared at the closed eyes of Joseph Gail, the hole in his chest, and then eyed the two former Elites at his side, neither of which had been affected by the sun. He turned back to Nicholai. "No, Vampire, I will head on. There is someone I must speak to."

He turned in alarm along the steps. "What do you mean, your Grace?"

"Do not worry yourself," he said, motioning to Aciel, Amentias that he was ready. They had spent far too much time here indeed, waiting for the sun to set.

Before the Vampire could say another word, he, Aciel, and Amentias were in the air, flying towards the very mountains he could feel Eleanor journeyed towards.

✳

They had given the remaining Vampires their blood once it was agreed they could no longer huddle in the darkness of the trees. The darkness was all around them now as night had, gratefully fallen.

Now somewhat refreshed, they moved again, all except for Christian Delacroix.

He had stayed behind to watch her. To stare her in her eyes when they opened, for he was sure they would.

His blood still lingered on her lips, but they would not open, to drink, to taste, to yell, to scream. They would do nothing, and indeed, he felt he had been far too late in giving her his blood. For surely it would not take this long for the woman to rise.

He recalled his own transformation for the hundredth time since they'd killed the remaining Elites and he'd assured Aleister he would be fine, he had risen from the floor in only a matter of minutes, or so it had seemed.

Had it taken longer to turn into a Vampire?

He remembered the pain, the aching need for more in his bloodlust.

But truly, had it been so long?

He stared around at the dark of the night, unsure of where they were. This uncertainty had almost compelled him to rise and take Alexandria with him, moving along the path to follow the others where possible, but Aurora had told him if ever he were ready to follow, she would send a beacon for him to grasp.

He had had no idea what it meant at the time, so engrossed was he in the watching of the woman, but now he felt quite foolish in his relentless desire to stay.

Had I made a mistake? he thought again, feeling misplaced, kneeling along the grass before her, feeling as though he could take on twenty of Eleanor's Creatures, and in Lycan form, but unable to move, for he was unsure if—when, she would open her eyes.

Xavier would destroy me, he thought with a small smile, staring down at her blood-stained lips. *"You cannot be the one to change her...your blood is not the one that can."*

But despite the words, he found a peace within himself. Her blood had done more than rejuvenate him, allow him more life on the Earth, it had centered him, giving him some sort of meaning. Where before he had moved to watch her if only to please the damned mess of the Vampire, and where he was driven to near madness because of her blood, how it called to him, and only him, he was now content, no longer needing to push and prove his merits against the others.

For he saw how lost Xavier was, leaving them all to go to her. For he was sure that was where he traveled. He saw it in his eyes the more he would stare upon his brother. *He was trapped*, he thought, *in her, with her.*

What had Dracula thought, making him king? Why place so much responsibility upon the Vampire's shoulders if he (Dracula had to of known) the Vampire would not receive it well?

He eyed the sword the Aurora had placed at his side before traveling with the others, sure to say, "It is yours, rightfully," a twinkle of something sad in her eyes.

But he had never touched it. He was not sure how he could when he could not even turn the woman who held the power to still Lycans, Elite Creatures, and Vampires, into what she was destined to become.

He had failed, and miserably.

The red gem in the guard shined as though freshly polished and he could not help but stare upon it, wondering why Dracula desired him to hold the sword. Had he already agreed to make Xavier king at the time? Had he moved already to procure he, Christian, a place near the throne if ever Xavier would fail?

These thoughts darkening his mind, he exhaled a cold breath he did not need, and gripped the cool leather handle.

At once the energy surged up his arm, straight into his dead heart, and Alexandria, the sword, the dark of the night disappeared.

He stared upon a much younger Alexandria as she kneeled before an unlit fireplace, a different darkness spreading past the window most nearby, here. The room was quaintly furnished, the house modest, indeed, and as younger Alexandria lifted her dolls in her hands, the thing appeared outside the window.

Christian stared in disbelief, a great knowing filling him that it was Dracula, but it could not have been:

The thing's face was long, chin sharp and pointed just before its long chest. Its skin was leathery, gray as it stretched against its long body, the large wings beyond it stretching out as a loud roar left its many-fanged mouth.

For some reason the young Alexandria did not turn from her dolls, her dressing gown white as it fell around, spilling along the wooden floor. She was oblivious, Christian knew, to this thing that watched her. Had always watched her...

"The blood-stiller," a voice said, a voice he had never heard, but he knew it to be Dracula's all the same. *"Bind the blood, do what you will, repel it, remove it, accept it, destroy it. But never taint it."*

He opened his eyes, a blood-curdling scream filling his ears in the next moment, and he barely had time to recover before her back flew off the ground as though bidden, pale arms stretching around her waist as she sat forward along the bloodied ground, the scream never ceasing...

"Alexandria," he said, but she did not seem to hear, on and on she screamed as though something he could not see tormented her endlessly. "Alexandria! Please! I'm here! I'm here!" And he touched her with his free hand, a gentle graze along a shoulder, and at the touch she turned her head to him, mouth closing abruptly, her once brown-green eyes now a very familiar red, her face white against the night, but not from dying, she was already dead. No, her face shone in the dark with a reverence, such a wondrous beauty that he could not help but move his hand to her cheek, welcoming the cold he felt, pressing his lips to her bloodied ones without another thought, silencing the scream that threatened to rise in his throat.

※

Eleanor whirled along the jagged, black rocks, smelling the Vampire far before she saw him.

"Victor," she called, surprise reaching her where purpose presently fled.

She waited but a few moments more before the white dot through the night grew larger, and then he landed atop the rocks, his expression pained, winded, indeed, his normally perfectly, placed hair was disheveled along his back. He was no longer the controlled Vampire he had pretended to be.

"Eleanor, wait," he said, his violet eyes flashing in the night, "Joseph is dead, and we never found Arminius, that Vampire—the damned Dragon, those Enchanters—"

She raised a hand to silence him, a smile desiring to lift her lips, but she would not dare let it show. *Order must be maintained at all times*. "It's quite all right, Victor," she said much to his surprise. His eyes widened as though he'd been pardoned a permanent death.

"What? All right?" he repeated, alarmed. "What about the plan? How you teared into my mind ensuring the bloody medallion was reduced to nothing?"

"Your anger is most unbecoming," she said, "now, if what you tell me is true about those Enchanters at Cedar Village then my visit to the mountain behind me," and she waved a hand to the dark rock several miles away, "is moot."

Victor merely stared at her. "Eleanor, I beg your pardon, but you made me think capturing the Vampire was of highest priority, that I should leave my first duty to capture Xavier, *per your order*, and now I greet you only to find you *calm* amidst the chaos. What more do you keep?"

The smile broke through, despite herself, and in the cold wind that pressed past blowing her hair and cloak from her body, she said, "You misunderstand my desires, Victor. I only moved for the Enchanters once I heard they were here, another pawn in my scheme to be coerced, but if they have been moved to their own whims already," she shrugged, "there is nothing that can be done. We still hold great magic at our disposal—" She closed her mouth as the thought came to her.

When he stared at her with pained eyes, she went on, "You only need turn, Victor. It doesn't make you a...monster to be what I am. Just think, once you are like me you will be able to harness magic, walk in the sun should you chose, drink blood if it suits you—eat food if it moves you."

His eyes widened at the words, 'eat food,' and she knew he was seriously considering it for the first time since he'd agreed to work for her. The stretching silence pressing along the rocks, the wall to her right, and she smiled more, despite not wanting to influence his thoughts with her mind, no, it was important more than ever now that Victor make this decision, this step on his own.

"Eleanor," he began, his wrinkled brow creased even more as he thought, and hard, on her words, however, what words he would say, she would never know:

He turned along the rocks to eye the Creature that flew towards them along the night, and even from the distance his green eyes were serious, piercing through the dark.

"I don't understand," Victor breathed.

"It can't be," she joined, eyes widening as he neared, landing along the rocks just before Victor, and for the first time she noticed the two other Creatures with him:

They were pale, their Vampire forms quite apparent, one whose brown hair fell to his shoulders and back, the other whose black hair was short, swaying atop his head in the fierce wind that blew from their bodies.

They were with him the whole time? Impossible. For she was sure she would have heard, she would have known.

"Eleanor," Xavier Delacroix said, black hair blowing in a strong breeze, gaining her attention, stepping past Victor to stand just before her, "we must talk."

※

Darien Nicodemeus pawed at the ground with a large clawed foot, the silver talons digging into the dark Earth with great ease. How the whims of nature yielded to his desires now.

He cupped the dirt in his claws, sniffing it deeply with the two slits for nostrils that were embedded in his long, black face.

A shrill screech left his many fangs as the saliva slid down his pointed chin.

Behind him his wings folded into his back, settling against the desire there. The desire to fly, to search, to journey for the one thing he knew was the Great Vampire's wish.

For he was tied to him, now.

Even more than he'd been before.

And as he cradled the Earth in his claws, unable to remember the time when they resembled human hands, he let out a roar, searching for the golden thing his brother held.

About the Author

B esides being addicted to vampires, blood, and a good, steaming cup of tea, S.C. Parris attends University in New York City, and is the author of "A Night of Frivolity," a horror short story, published by Burning Willow Press. She is the author of *The Dark World* series published by Permuted Press, and enjoys thinking up new dark historical fantasies to put to page next. She lives on Long Island, New York with her family and can be found writing ridiculous articles for CLASH Media.

BOOK

14

Peter Clines

Padlocked doors. Strange light fixtures. Mutant cockroaches.

There are some odd things about Nate's new apartment. Every room in this old brownstone has a mystery. Mysteries that stretch back over a hundred years. Some of them are in plain sight. Some are behind locked doors. And all together these mysteries could mean the end of Nate and his friends.

Or the end of everything...

Michael Clary
THE GUARDIAN | THE REGULATORS | BROKEN

When the dead rise up and take over the city, the Government is forced to close off the borders and abandon the remaining survivors. Fortunately for them, a hero is about to be chosen...a Guardian that will rise up from the ashes to fight against the dead. The series continues with Book Four: *Scratch*.

Emily Goodwin
CONTAGIOUS | DEATHLY CONTAGIOUS

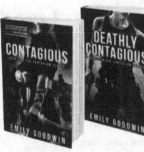

During the Second Great Depression, twenty-four-year-old Orissa Penwell is forced to drop out of college when she is no longer able to pay for classes. Down on her luck, Orissa doesn't think she can sink any lower. She couldn't be more wrong. A virus breaks out across the country, leaving those that are infected crazed, aggressive and very hungry. `

The saga continues in Book Three: *Contagious Chaos* and Book Four: *The Truth is Contagious*.

PERMUTED
PRESS

THE BREADWINNER | Stevie Kopas

The end of the world is not glamorous. In a matter of days the human race was reduced to nothing more than vicious, flesh hungry creatures. There are no heroes here. Only survivors. The trilogy continues with Book Two: *Haven* and Book Three: *All Good Things*.

THE BECOMING | Jessica Meigs

As society rapidly crumbles under the hordes of infected, three people—Ethan Bennett, a Memphis police officer; Cade Alton, his best friend and former IDF sharpshooter; and Brandt Evans, a lieutenant in the US Marines—band together against the oncoming crush of death and terror sweeping across the world. The story continues with Book Two: *Ground Zero*.

THE INFECTION WAR | Craig DiLouie

As the undead awake, a small group of survivors must accept a dangerous mission into the very heart of infection. This edition features two books: *The Infection* and *The Killing Floor*.

OBJECTS OF WRATH | Sean T. Smith

The border between good and evil has always been bloody... Is humanity doomed? After the bombs rain down, the entire world is an open wound; it is in those bleeding years that William Fox becomes a man. After The Fall, nothing is certain. *Objects of Wrath* is the first book in a saga spanning four generations.

PERMUTED
PRESS

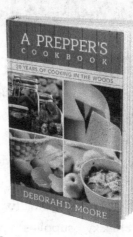